P9-DFJ-190

ONCE UPON TIME,
THERE WAS A WIZARD...

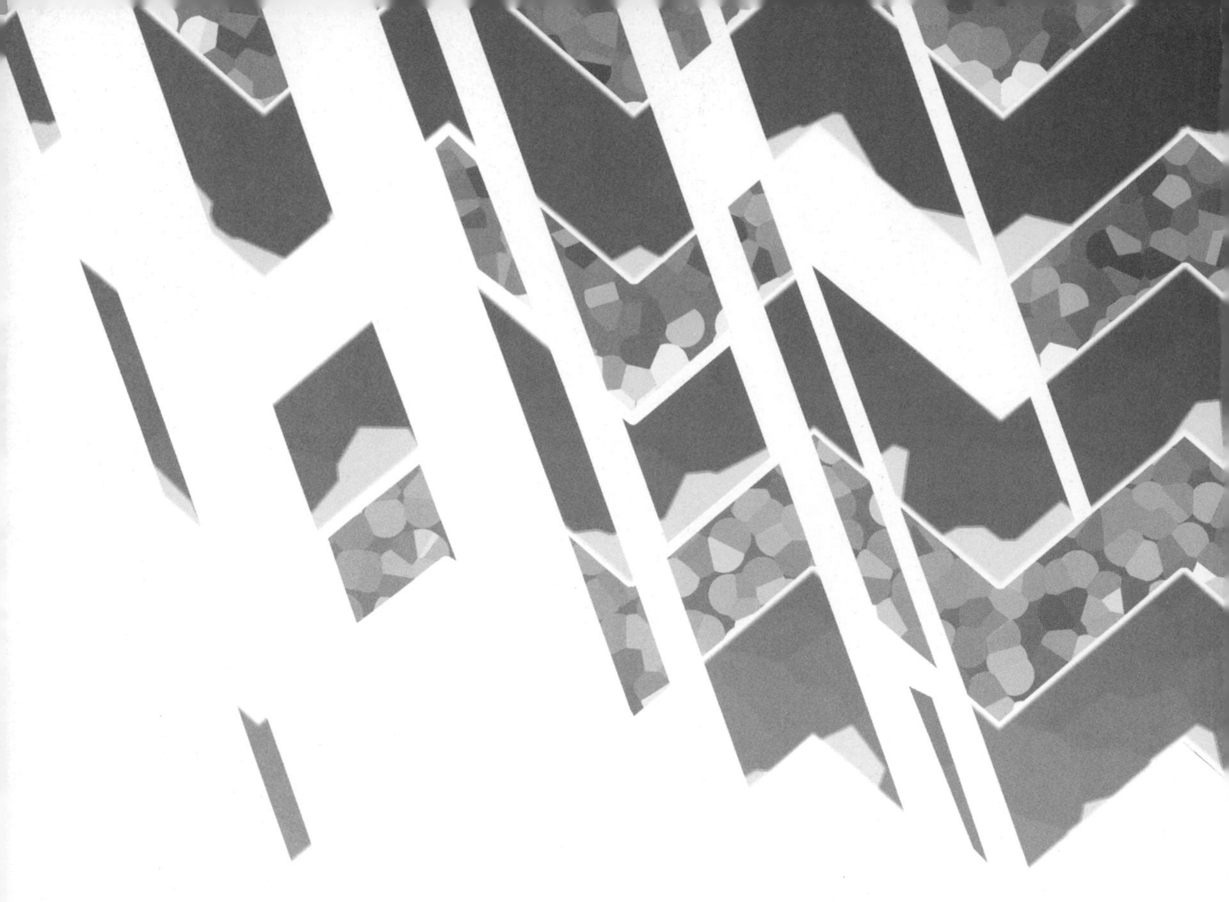

# THEN IT ALL WENT TO HELL.

## IMAGE COMICS, INC.

Robert Kirkman—Chief Operating Officer
Erik Larsen—Chief Financial Officer
Todd McFarlane—President
Marc Silvestri—Chief Executive Officer
Jim Valentino—Vice-President

Eric Stephenson—Publisher
Corey Murphy—Director of Sales
Jeff Boison—Director of Publishing Planning & Book Trade Sales
Chris Ross—Director of Digital Sales
Jeff Stang—Director of Specialty Sales
Kat Salazar—Director of PR & Marketing
Branwyn Bigglestone—Controller
Sue Korpela—Accounts Manager
Drew Gill—Art Director
Brett Warnock—Production Manager
Leigh Thomas—Traffic Manager
Tricia Ramos—Print Manager
Briah Skelly—Publicist
Aly Hoffman—Events & Conventions Coordinator
Sasha Head—Sales & Marketing Production Designer
David Brothers—Branding Manager
Melissa Gifford—Content Manager
Drew Fitzgerald—Publicity Assistant
Vincent Kukua—Production Artist
Erika Schnatz—Production Artist
Ryan Brewer—Production Artist
Shanna Matuszak—Production Artist
Carey Hall—Production Artist
Esther Kim—Direct Market Sales Representative
Emilio Bautista—Digital Sales Representative
Leanna Caunter—Accounting Assistant
Chloe Ramos-Peterson—Library Market Sales Representative
Maria Eizik—Administrative Assistant
IMAGECOMICS.COM

CURSE WORDS VOLUME #1: THE DEVIL'S DEVIL, FIRST PRINTING. JULY 2017. Copyright © 2017 SILENT E PRODUCTIONS, LLC. All rights reserved. Published by Image Comics, Inc. Office of publication: 2701 NW Vaughn St., Ste. 780, Portland, OR 97210. Contains material originally published in single magazine form as CURSE WORDS #1-5. "CURSE WORDS" its logos, and the likenesses of all characters herein are trademarks of SILENT E PRODUCTIONS, LLC, unless otherwise noted. "Image" and the Image Comics logos are registered trademarks of Image Comics, Inc. No part of this publication may be reproduced or transmitted, in any form or by any means (except for short excerpts for journalistic or review purposes), without the express written permission of SILENT E PRODUCTIONS, LLC or Image Comics, Inc. All names, characters, events, and locales in this publication are entirely fictional. Any resemblance to actual persons (living or dead), events, or places, without satiric intent, is coincidental. Printed in the USA. For information regarding the CPSIA on this printed material call: 203-595-3636 and provide reference #RICH–740053. For international rights, contact:foreignlicensing@imagecomics.com. Standard Cover ISBN: 978-1-5343-0221-1 Roadshow Edition HC ISBN: 978-1-5343-0456-7 Forbidden Planet/Big Bang Variant ISBN: 978-1-5343-0461-1 Jetpack Comics Variant ISBN: 978-1-5343-0462-8 Newbury Comics Variant ISBN: 978-1-5343-0464-2 DCBS Variant ISBN: 978-1-5343-0463-5

image

# CURSE WORDS

## VOLUME ONE: THE DEVIL'S DEVIL

CREATED BY

# CHARLES SOULE & RYAN BROWNE

COLORS BY
**RYAN BROWNE &
MICHAEL GARLAND**

LETTERS BY
**CHRIS CRANK**

COLOR FLATS BY
**MICHAEL PARKINSON**

LOGO BY
**SEAN DOVE**

BOOK DESIGN BY
**RYAN BROWNE**

# ONE

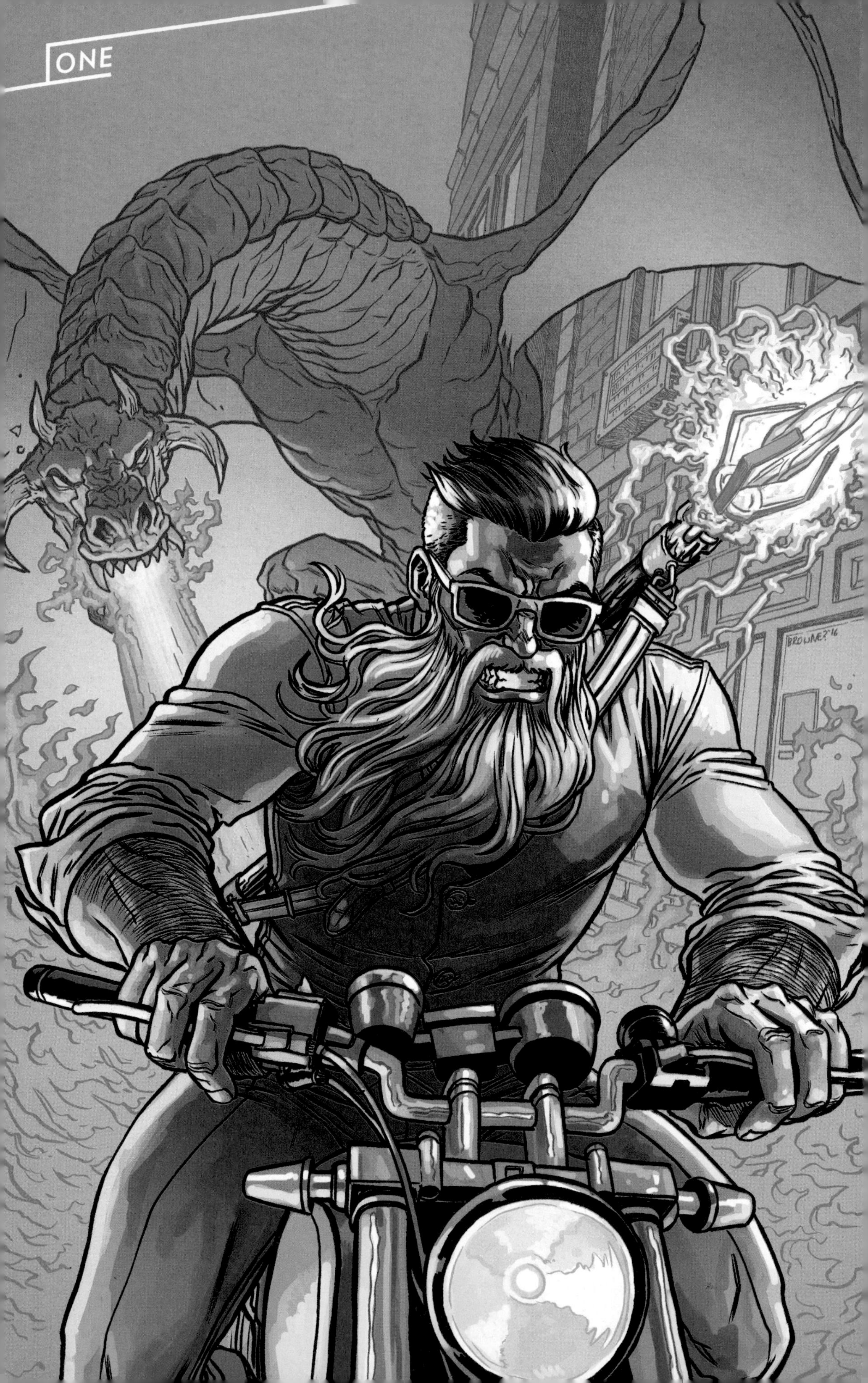

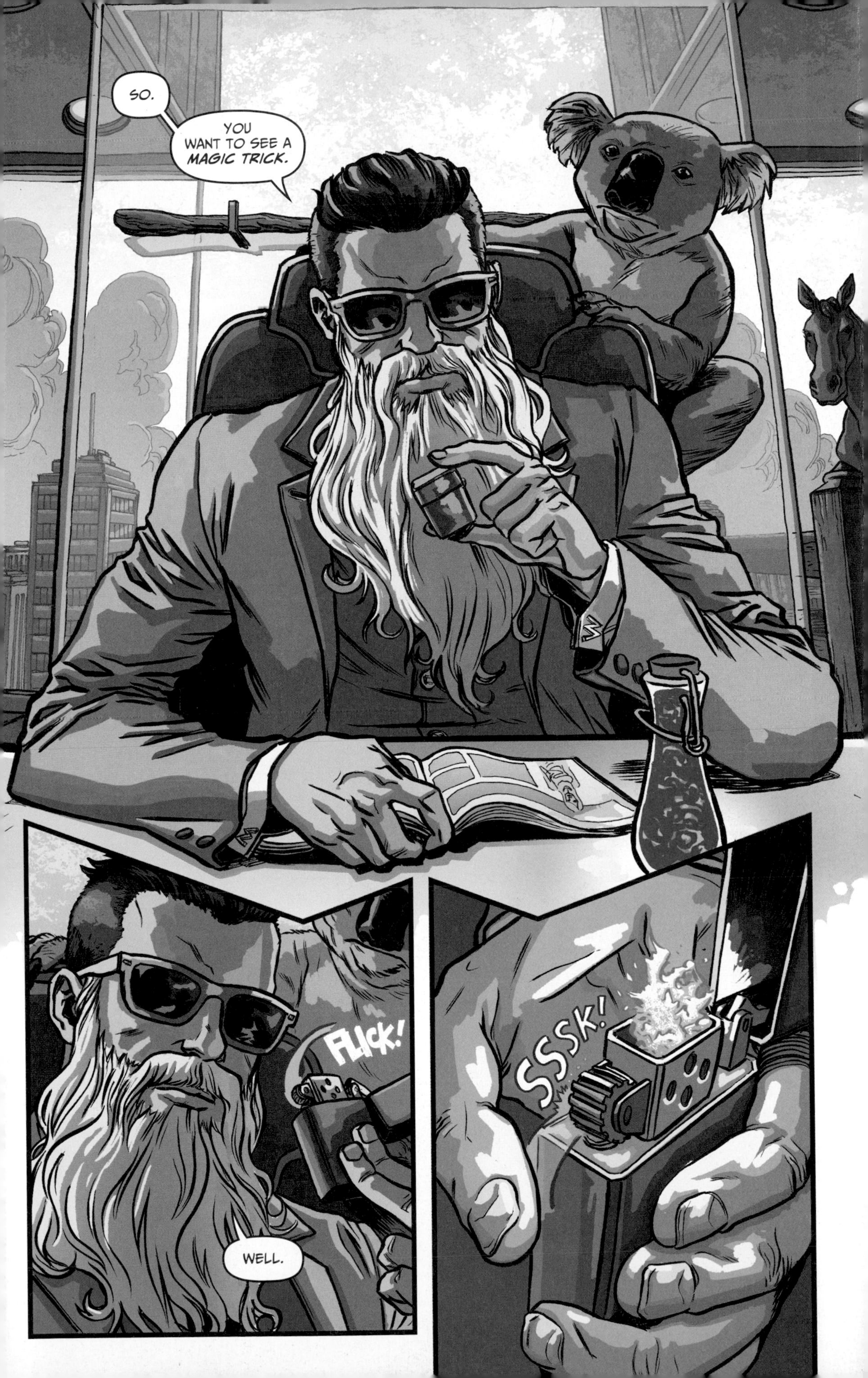
SO.
YOU WANT TO SEE A MAGIC TRICK.
FLICK!
WELL.
SSSK!

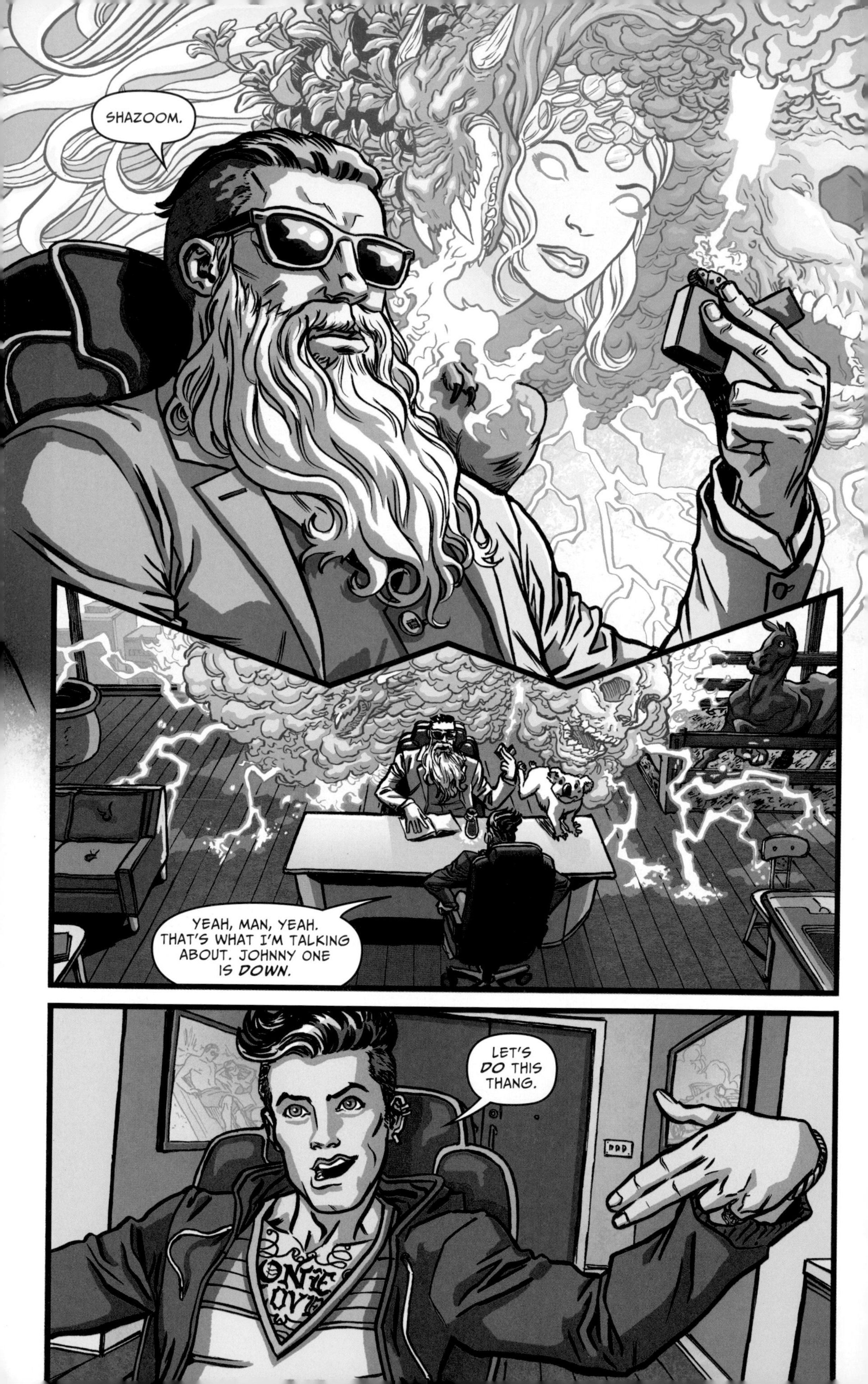
SHAZOOM.
YEAH, MAN, YEAH. THAT'S WHAT I'M TALKING ABOUT. JOHNNY ONE IS DOWN.
LET'S DO THIS THANG.

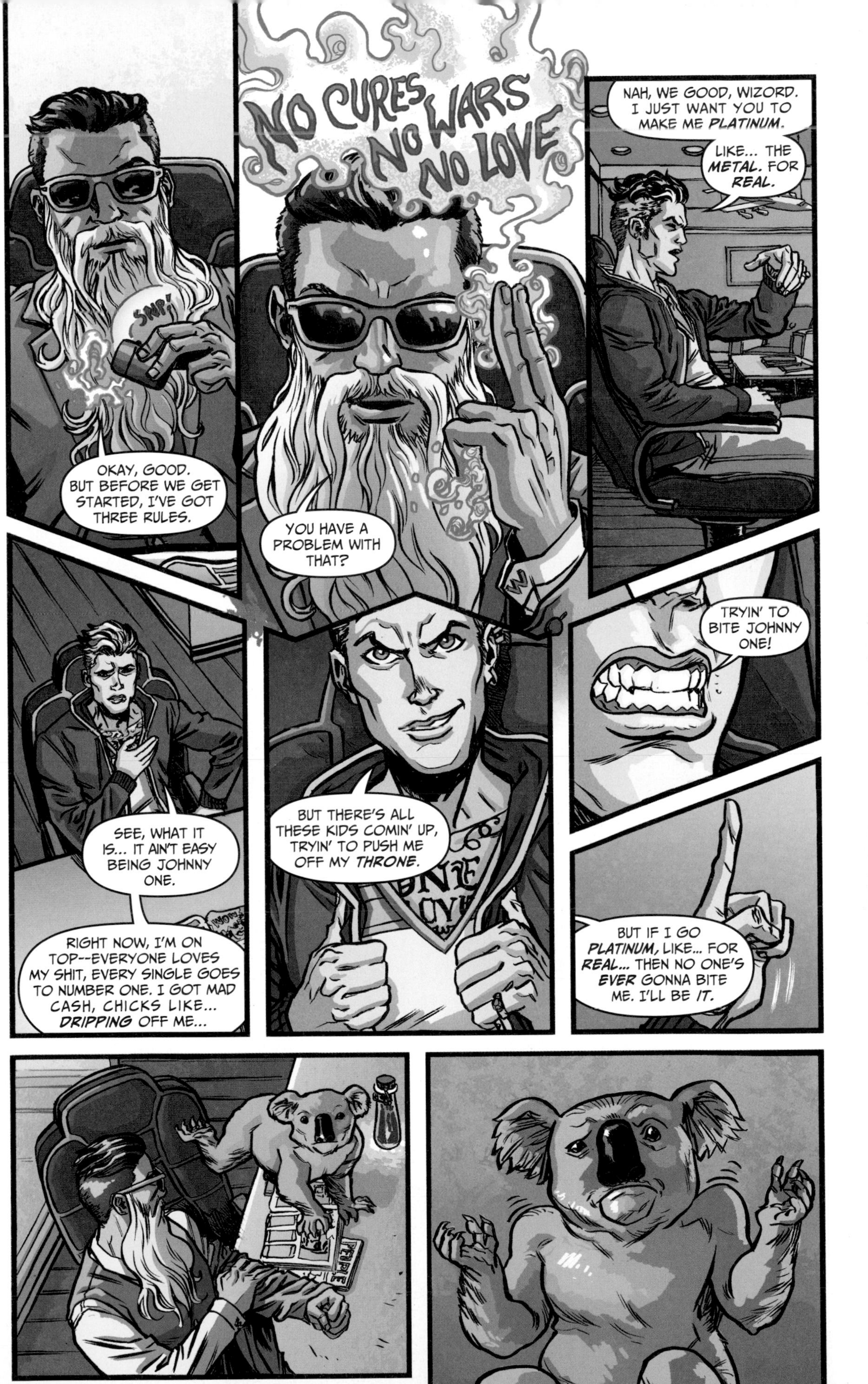
SNIP!
OKAY, GOOD. BUT BEFORE WE GET STARTED, I'VE GOT THREE RULES.
NO CURES NO WARS NO LOVE
YOU HAVE A PROBLEM WITH THAT?
NAH, WE GOOD, WIZORD. I JUST WANT YOU TO MAKE ME *PLATINUM*.
LIKE... THE *METAL*. FOR *REAL*.
SEE, WHAT IT IS... IT AIN'T EASY BEING JOHNNY ONE.
RIGHT NOW, I'M ON TOP--EVERYONE LOVES MY SHIT, EVERY SINGLE GOES TO NUMBER ONE. I GOT MAD CASH, CHICKS LIKE... *DRIPPING* OFF ME...
BUT THERE'S ALL THESE KIDS COMIN' UP, TRYIN' TO PUSH ME OFF MY *THRONE*.
TRYIN' TO BITE JOHNNY ONE!
BUT IF I GO *PLATINUM*, LIKE... FOR *REAL*... THEN NO ONE'S *EVER* GONNA BITE ME. I'LL BE *IT*.
PEOPLE

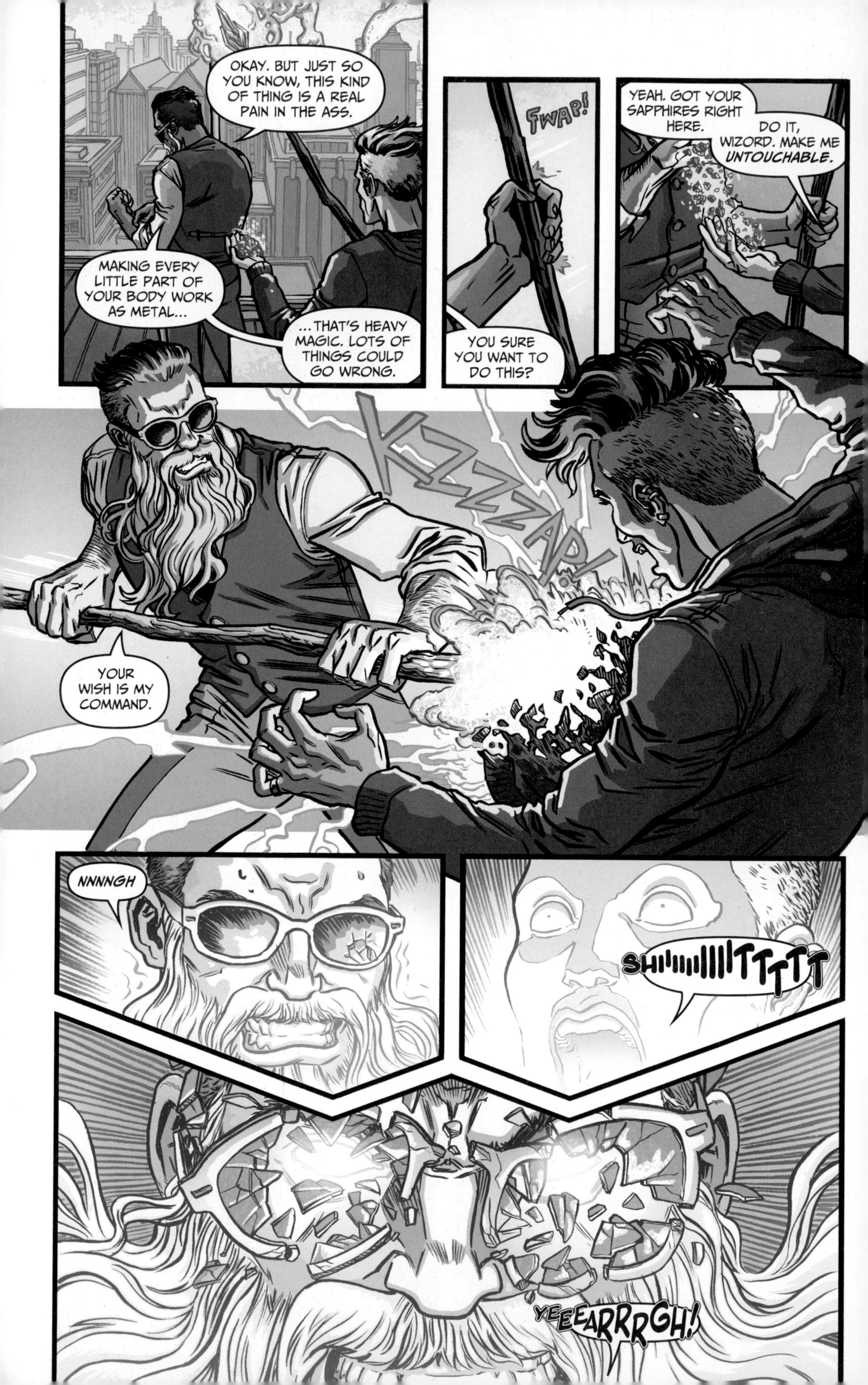
OKAY. BUT JUST SO YOU KNOW, THIS KIND OF THING IS A REAL PAIN IN THE ASS.
MAKING EVERY LITTLE PART OF YOUR BODY WORK AS METAL...
...THAT'S HEAVY MAGIC. LOTS OF THINGS COULD GO WRONG.
FWAP!
YOU SURE YOU WANT TO DO THIS?
YEAH. GOT YOUR SAPPHIRES RIGHT HERE.
DO IT, WIZORD. MAKE ME UNTOUCHABLE.
KZZZZAP!
YOUR WISH IS MY COMMAND.
NNNNGH
SHIIIIIIIIITTTTT
YEEEARRRGH!

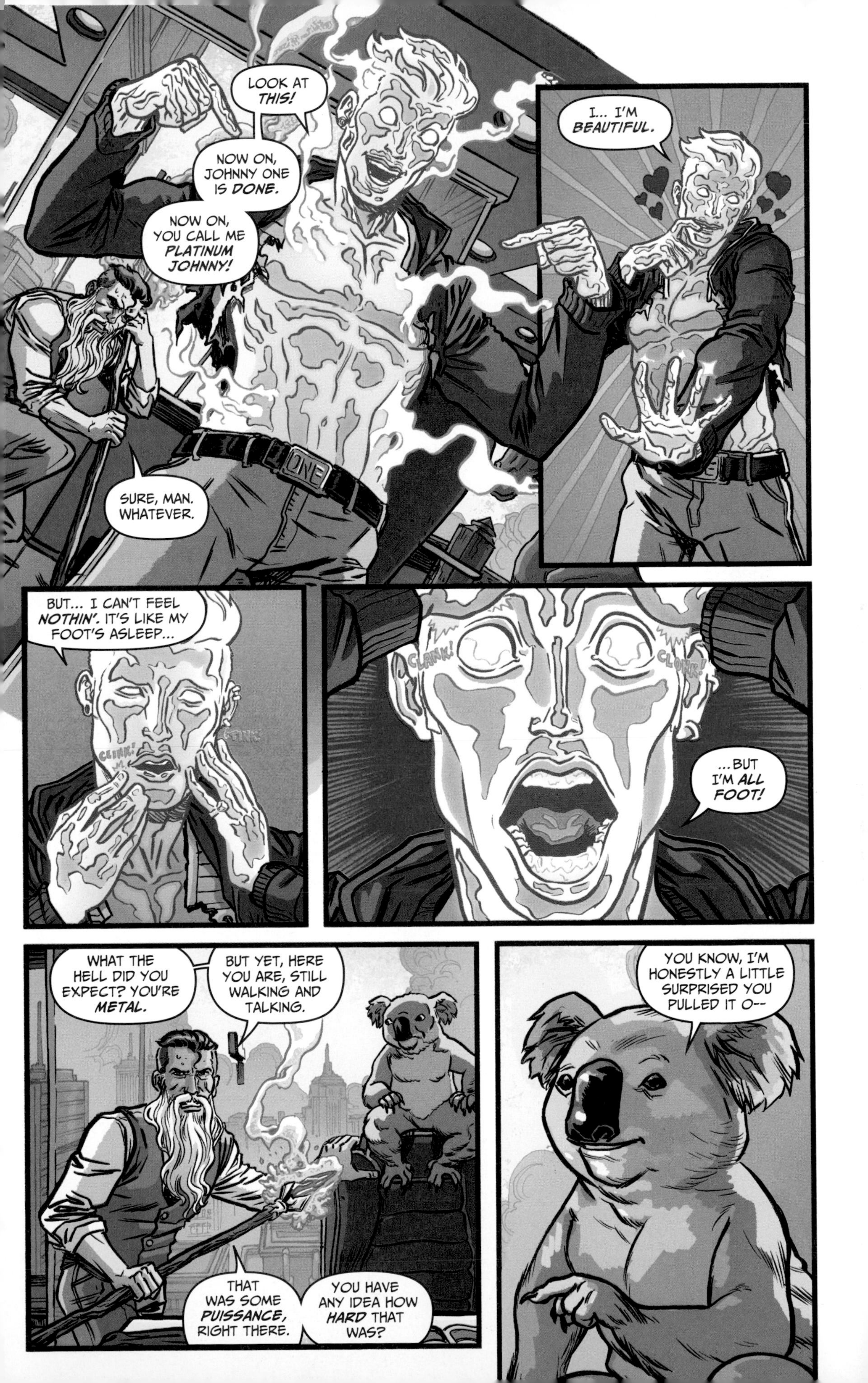
LOOK AT THIS!
NOW ON, JOHNNY ONE IS DONE.
NOW ON, YOU CALL ME PLATINUM JOHNNY!
SURE, MAN. WHATEVER.
ONE
I... I'M BEAUTIFUL.
BUT... I CAN'T FEEL NOTHIN'. IT'S LIKE MY FOOT'S ASLEEP...
CLINK!
CLINK!
CLANK!
CLONK!
...BUT I'M ALL FOOT!
WHAT THE HELL DID YOU EXPECT? YOU'RE METAL.
BUT YET, HERE YOU ARE, STILL WALKING AND TALKING.
THAT WAS SOME PUISSANCE, RIGHT THERE.
YOU HAVE ANY IDEA HOW HARD THAT WAS?
YOU KNOW, I'M HONESTLY A LITTLE SURPRISED YOU PULLED IT O--

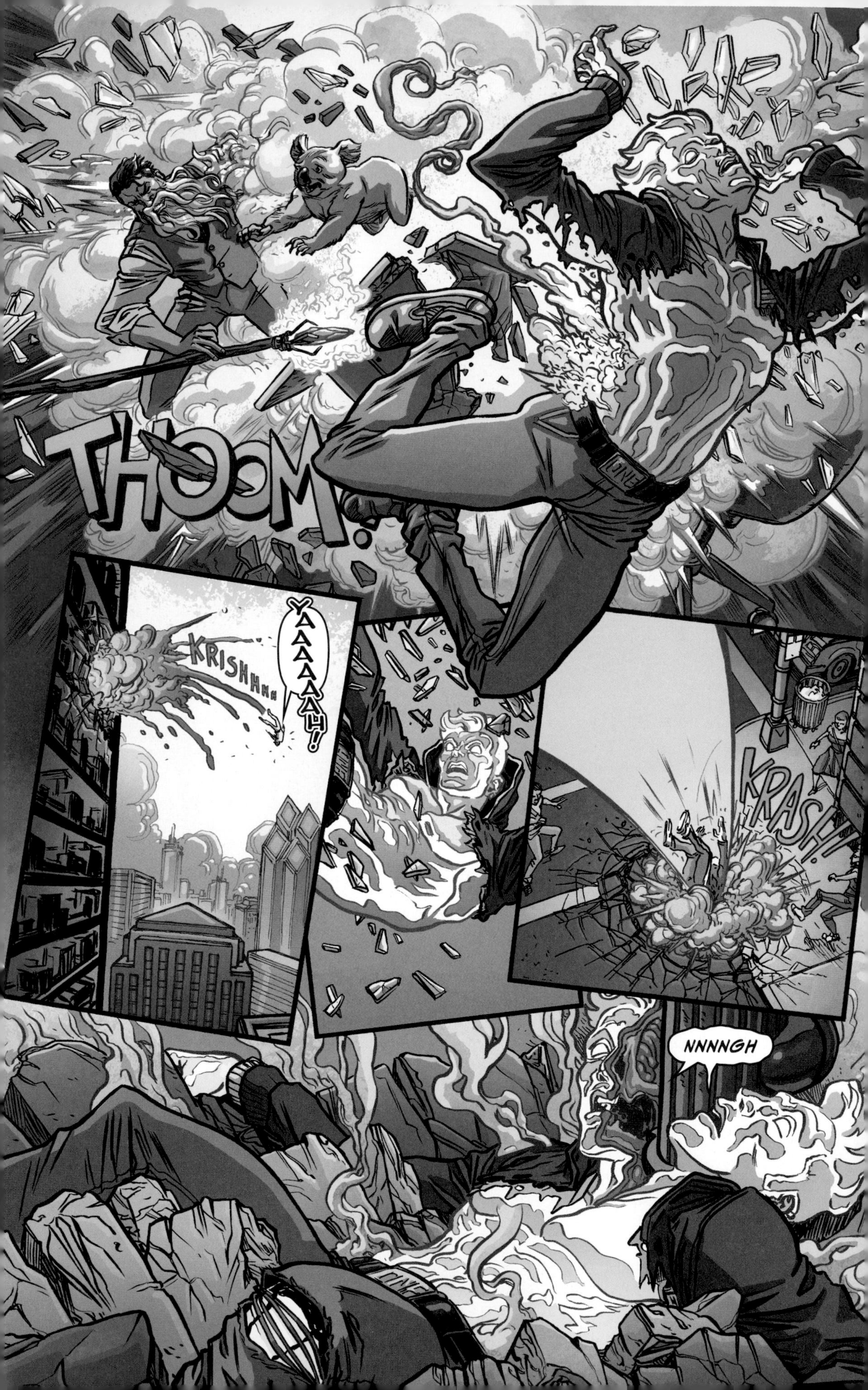
THOOM!
KRISHHHH
YAAAAAAH!
KRASH!
NNNNGH

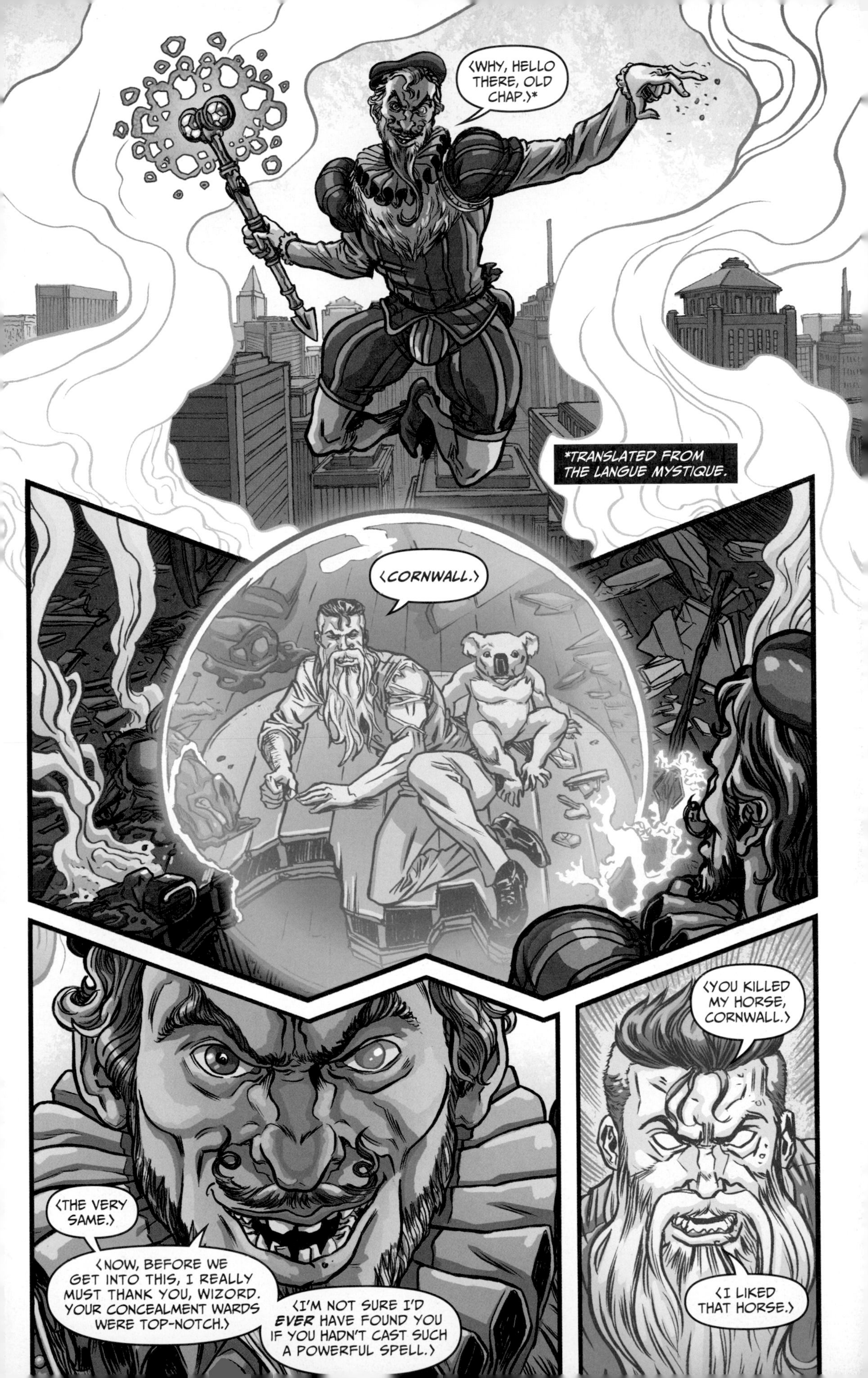

‹WHY, HELLO THERE, OLD CHAP.›*
*TRANSLATED FROM THE LANGUE MYSTIQUE.
‹CORNWALL.›
‹YOU KILLED MY HORSE, CORNWALL.›
‹THE VERY SAME.›
‹NOW, BEFORE WE GET INTO THIS, I REALLY MUST THANK YOU, WIZORD. YOUR CONCEALMENT WARDS WERE TOP-NOTCH.›
‹I'M NOT SURE I'D EVER HAVE FOUND YOU IF YOU HADN'T CAST SUCH A POWERFUL SPELL.›
‹I LIKED THAT HORSE.›

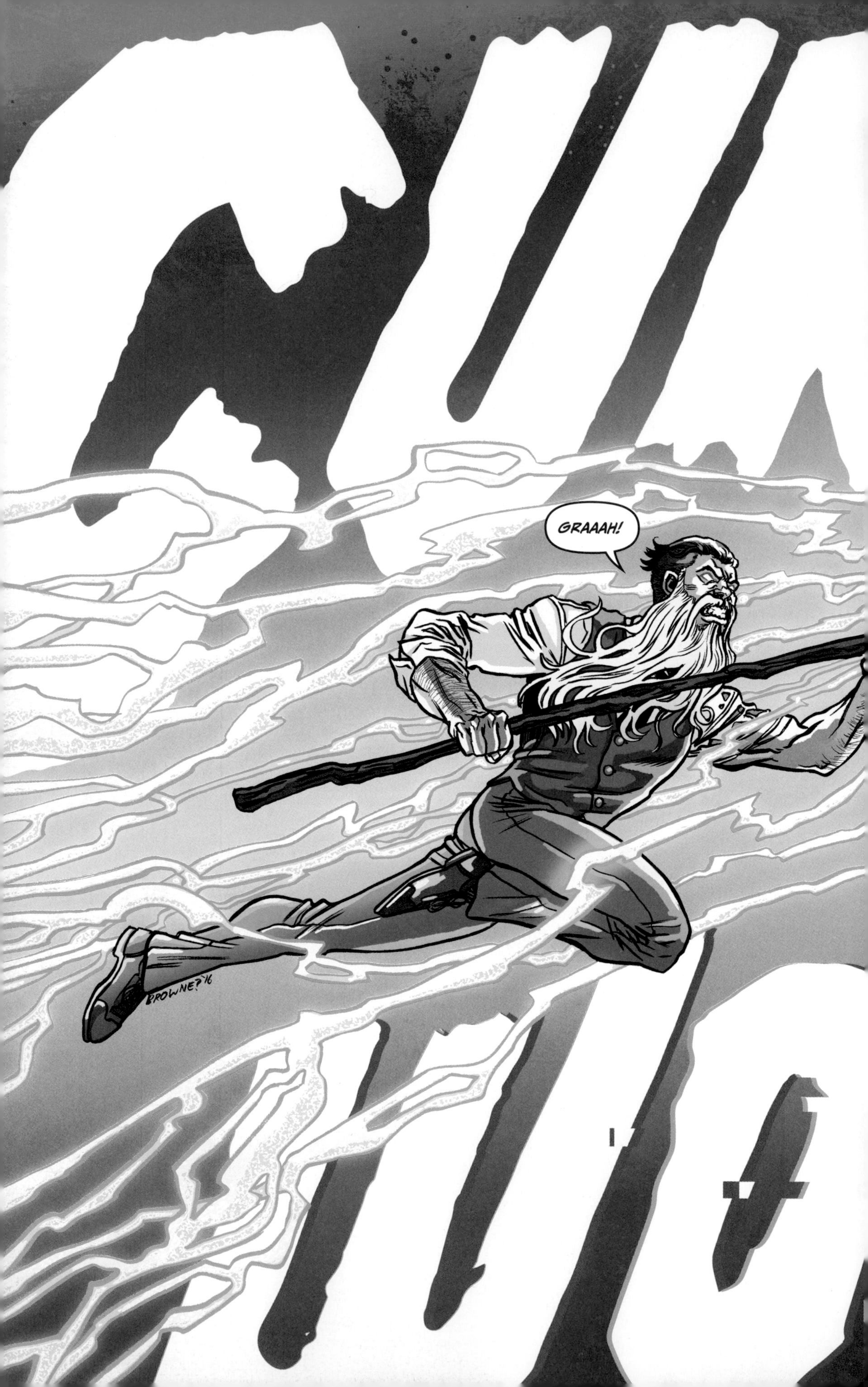
GRAAAH!
BROWNE '16

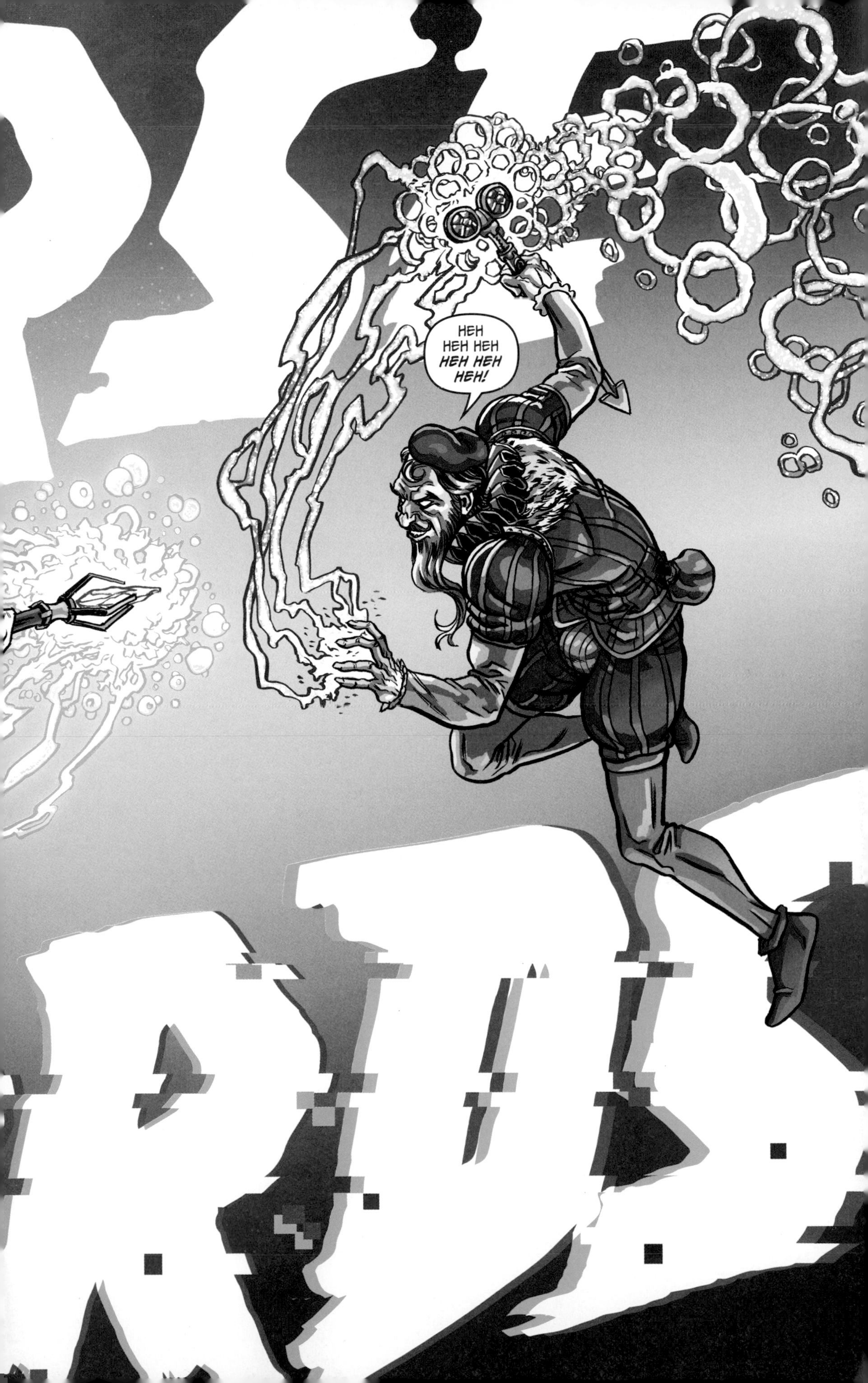
HEH HEH HEH HEH HEH HEH!

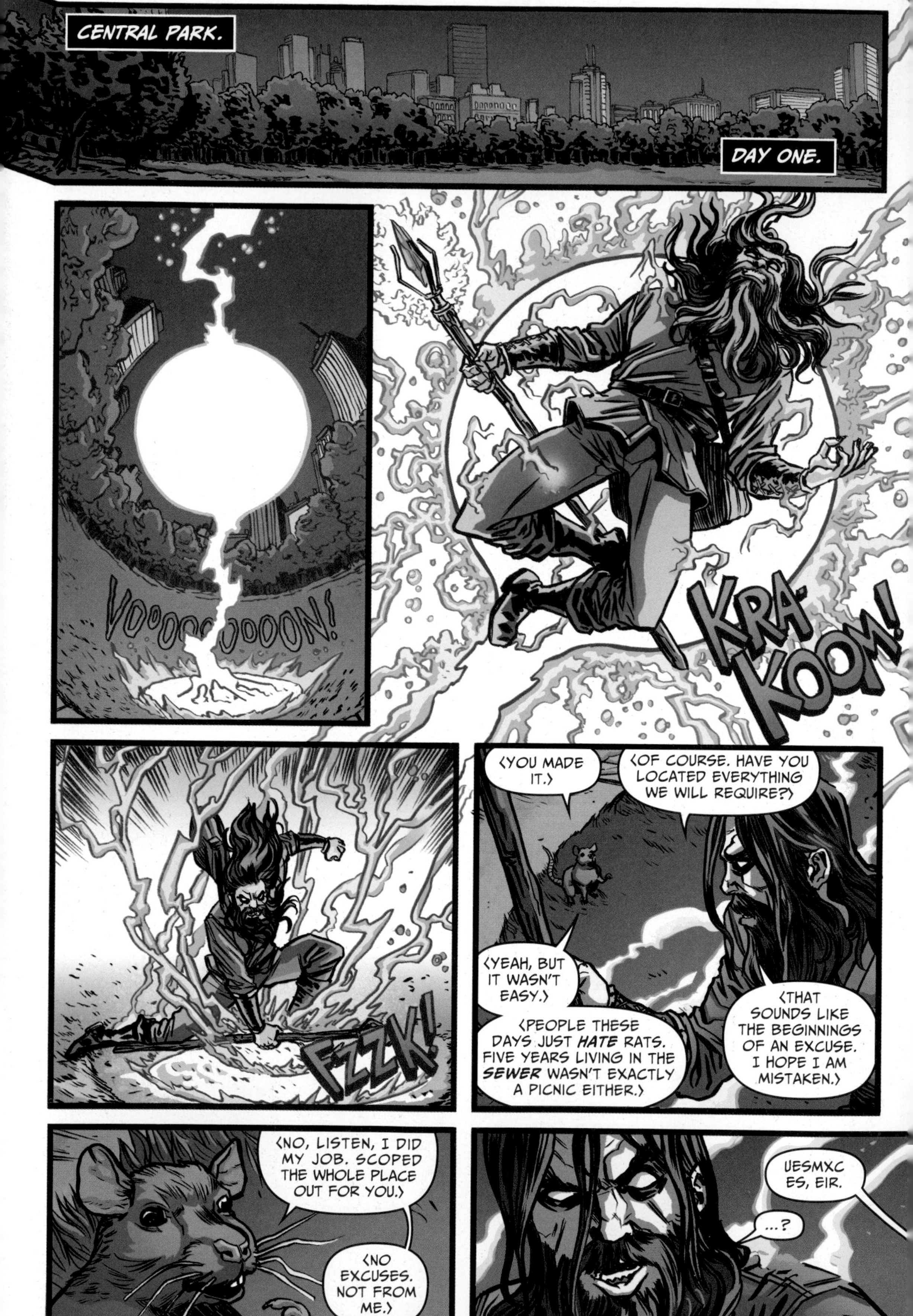
CENTRAL PARK.
DAY ONE.
VOOOOOOOOON!
KRA-KOOM!
FZZK!
〈YOU MADE IT.〉
〈OF COURSE. HAVE YOU LOCATED EVERYTHING WE WILL REQUIRE?〉
〈YEAH, BUT IT WASN'T EASY.〉
〈PEOPLE THESE DAYS JUST HATE RATS. FIVE YEARS LIVING IN THE SEWER WASN'T EXACTLY A PICNIC EITHER.〉
〈THAT SOUNDS LIKE THE BEGINNINGS OF AN EXCUSE. I HOPE I AM MISTAKEN.〉
〈NO, LISTEN, I DID MY JOB. SCOPED THE WHOLE PLACE OUT FOR YOU.〉
〈NO EXCUSES. NOT FROM ME.〉
UESMXC ES, EIR.
...?

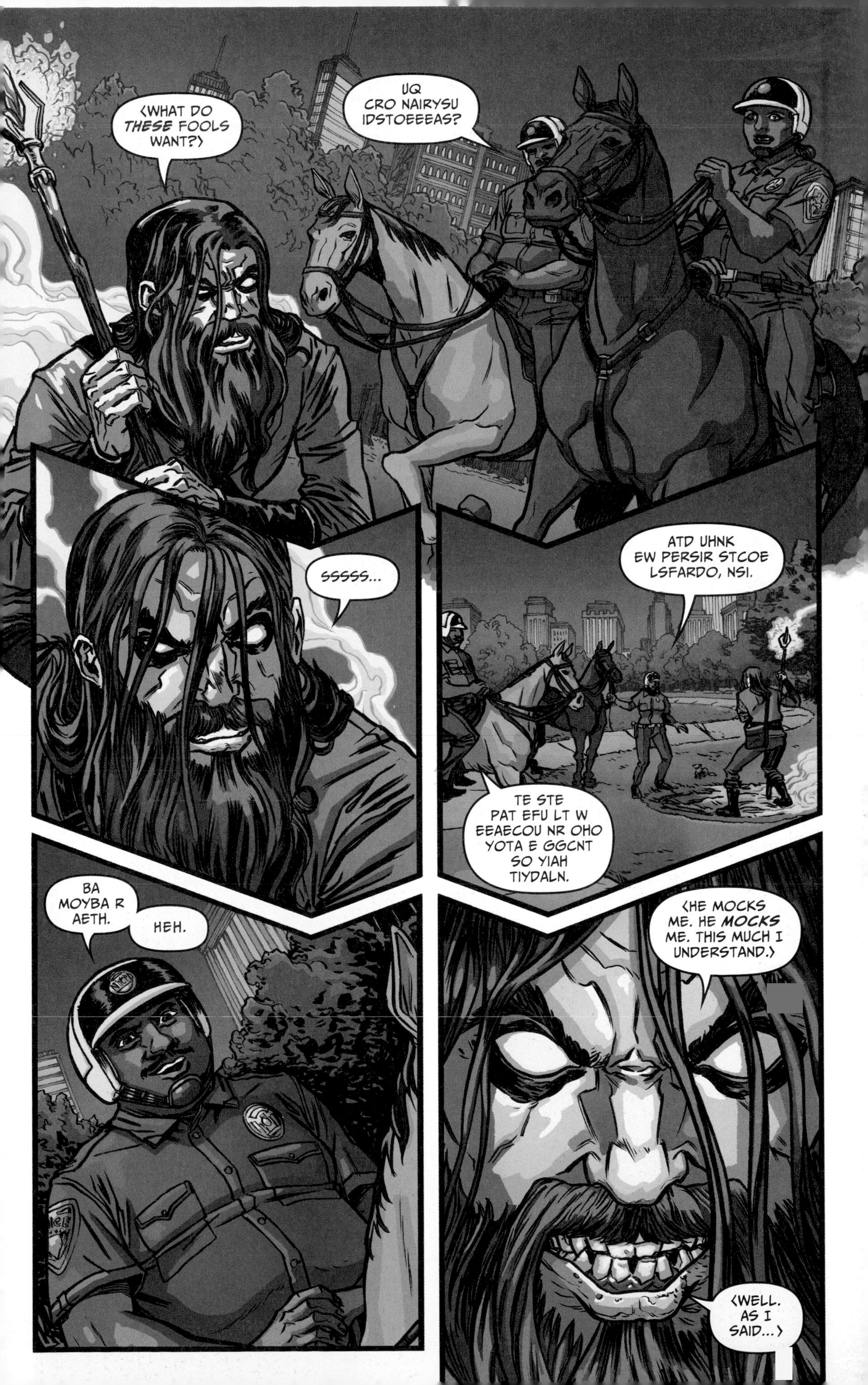

‹WHAT DO *THESE* FOOLS WANT?›
UQ CRO NAIRYSU IDSTOEEEAS?
SSSSS...
ATD UHNK EW PERSIR STCOE LSFARDO, NSI.
TE STE PAT EFU LT W EEAECOU NR OHO YOTA E GGCNT SO YIAH TIYDALN.
BA MOYBA R AETH.
HEH.
‹HE MOCKS ME. HE *MOCKS* ME. THIS MUCH I UNDERSTAND.›
‹WELL. AS I SAID...›

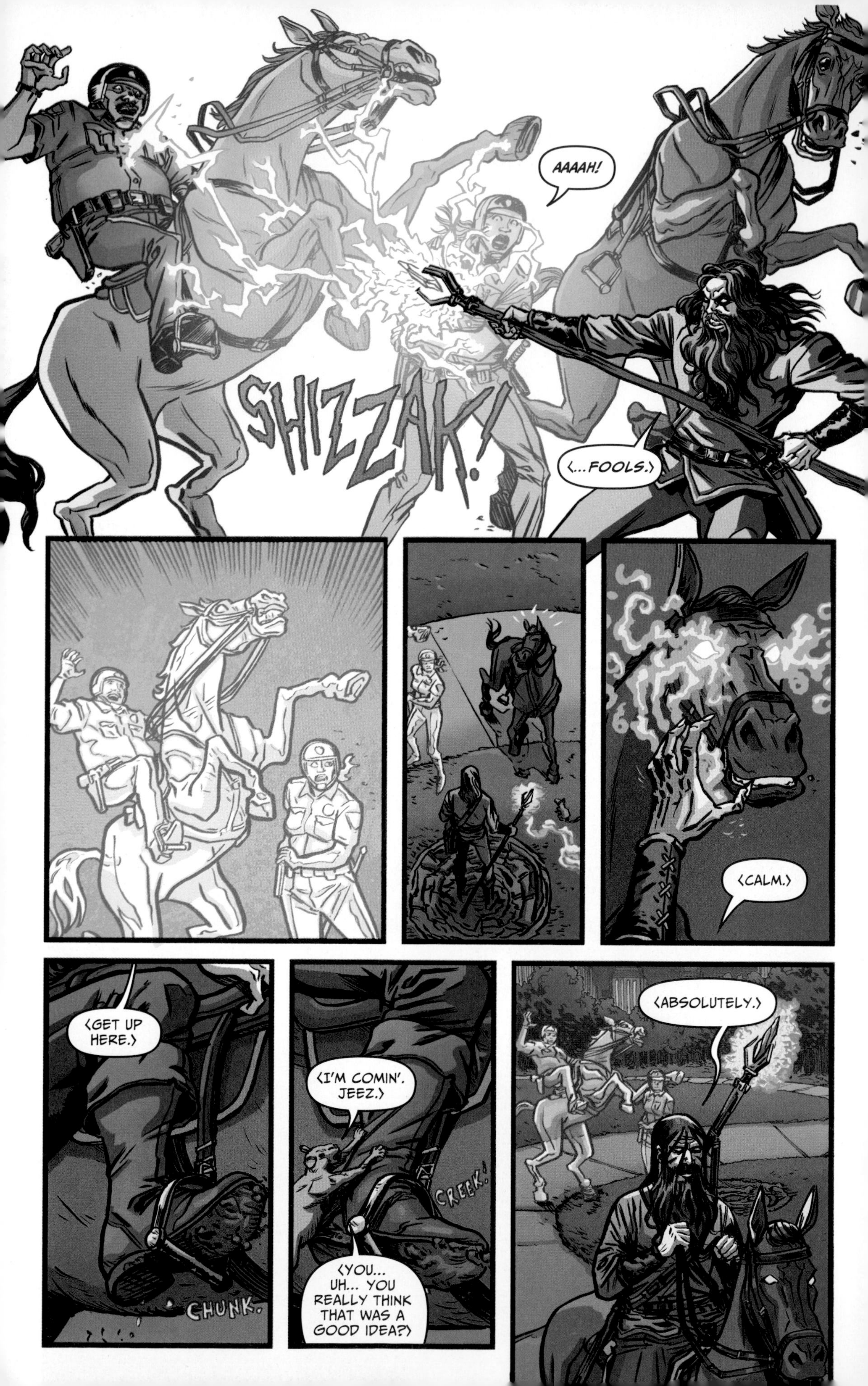
AAAAH!
SHIZZAK!
‹...FOOLS.›
‹CALM.›
‹GET UP HERE.›
CHUNK.
‹I'M COMIN'. JEEZ.›
CREEK!
‹YOU... UH... YOU REALLY THINK THAT WAS A GOOD IDEA?›
‹ABSOLUTELY.›

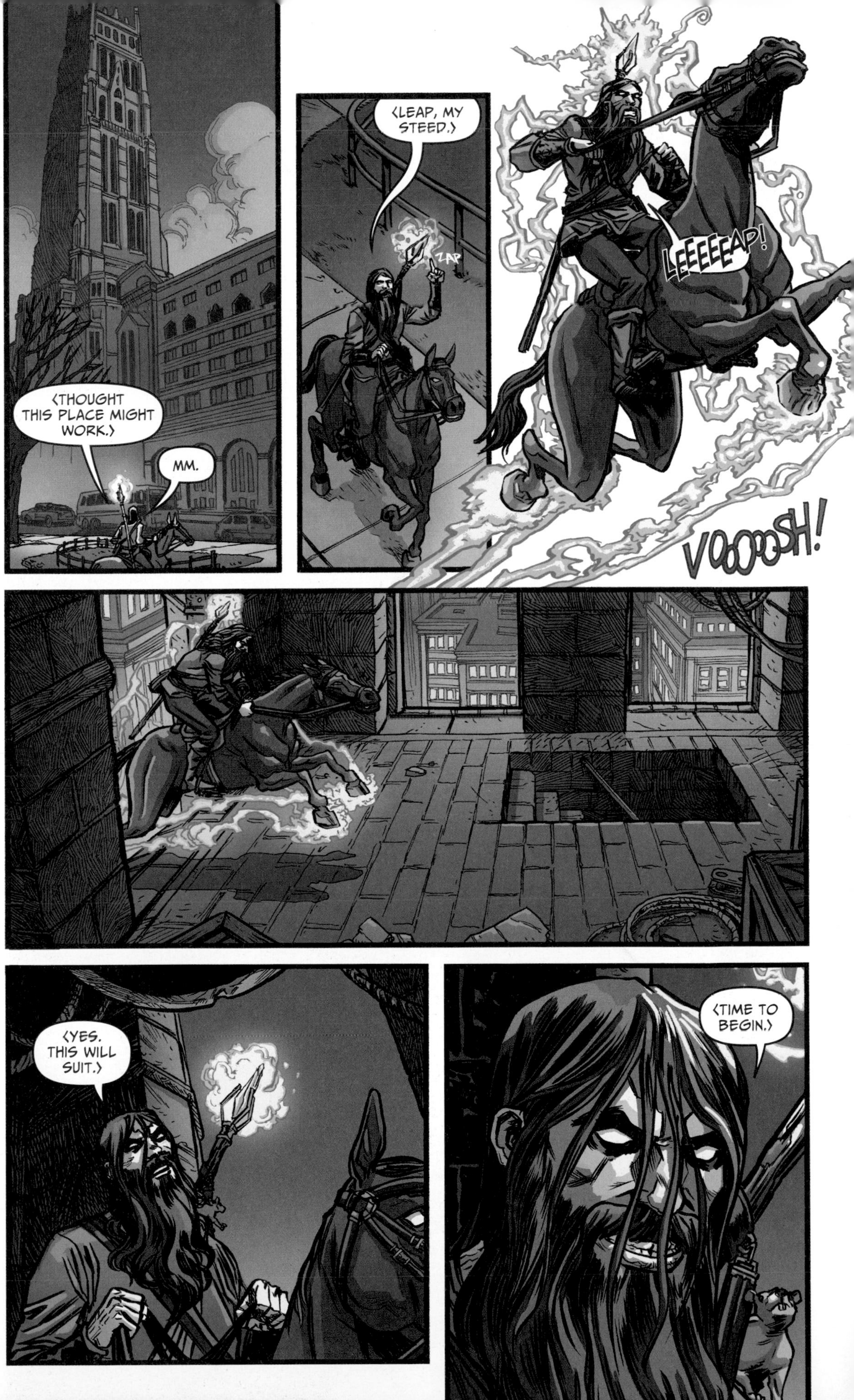

‹THOUGHT THIS PLACE MIGHT WORK.›
MM.
‹LEAP, MY STEED.›
ZAP
LEEEEEAP!
VOOOOOSH!
‹YES. THIS WILL SUIT.›
‹TIME TO BEGIN.›

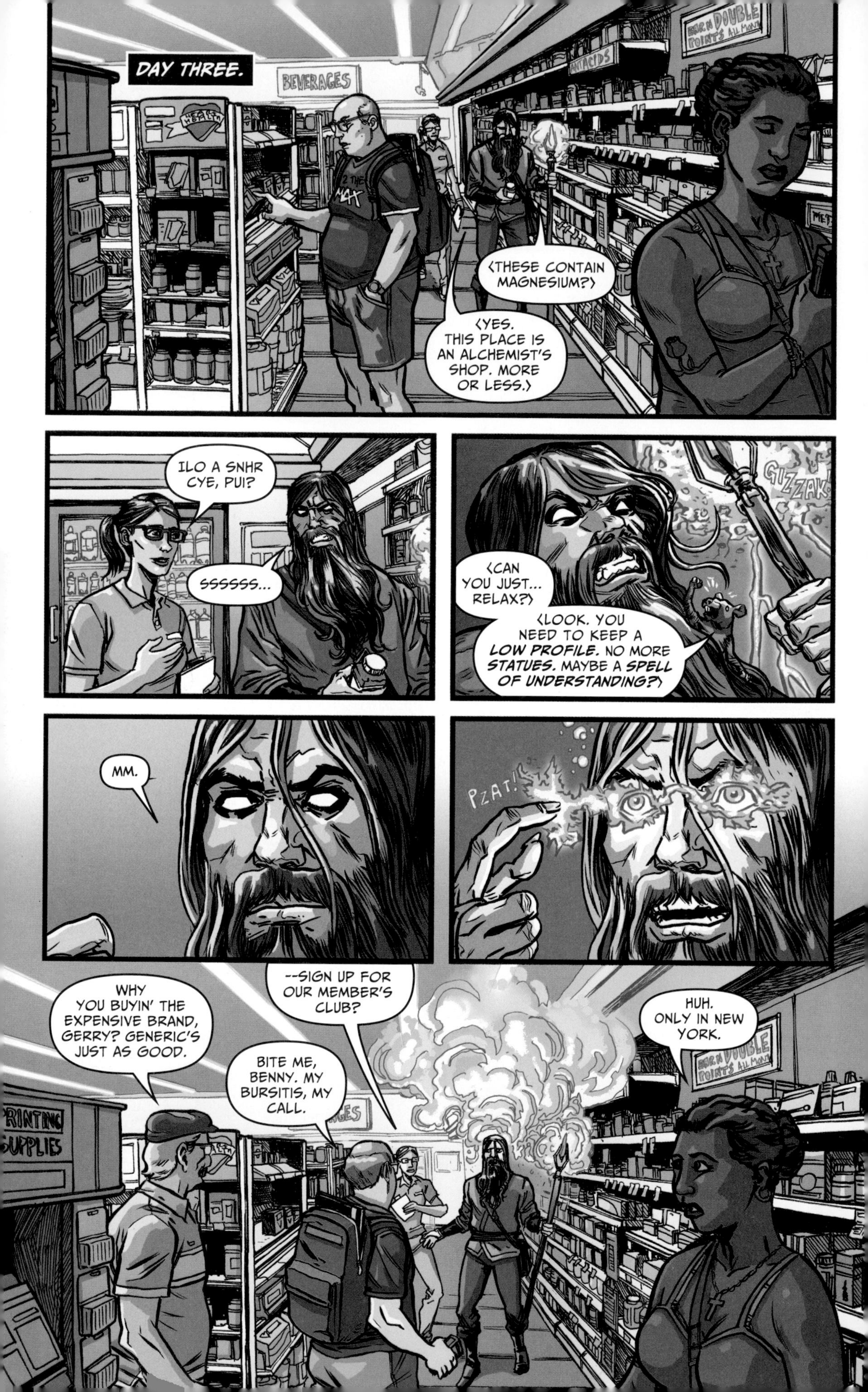
DAY THREE.
BEVERAGES
ANTACIDS
EARN DOUBLE POINTS ALL MONTH
2 THE MAX
‹THESE CONTAIN MAGNESIUM?›
‹YES. THIS PLACE IS AN ALCHEMIST'S SHOP. MORE OR LESS.›
ILO A SNHR CYE, PUI?
SSSSSS...
GIZZAK!
‹CAN YOU JUST... RELAX?›
‹LOOK. YOU NEED TO KEEP A **LOW PROFILE.** NO MORE **STATUES.** MAYBE A **SPELL OF UNDERSTANDING?**›
MM.
PZAT!
WHY YOU BUYIN' THE EXPENSIVE BRAND, GERRY? GENERIC'S JUST AS GOOD.
--SIGN UP FOR OUR MEMBER'S CLUB?
BITE ME, BENNY. MY BURSITIS, MY CALL.
HUH. ONLY IN NEW YORK.
PRINTING SUPPLIES
EARN DOUBLE POINTS ALL MONTH

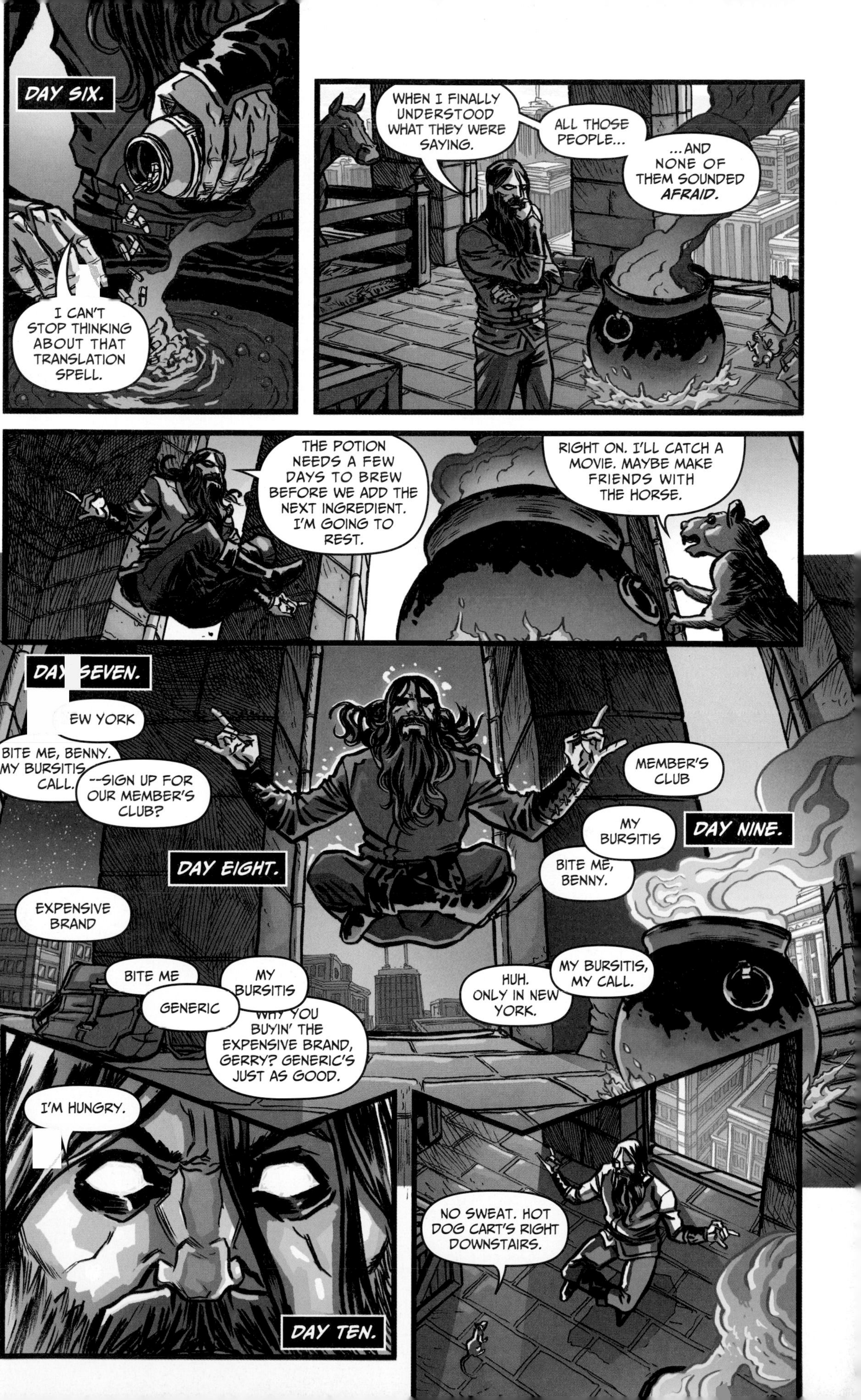
DAY SIX.
I CAN'T STOP THINKING ABOUT THAT TRANSLATION SPELL.
WHEN I FINALLY UNDERSTOOD WHAT THEY WERE SAYING.
ALL THOSE PEOPLE...
...AND NONE OF THEM SOUNDED AFRAID.
THE POTION NEEDS A FEW DAYS TO BREW BEFORE WE ADD THE NEXT INGREDIENT. I'M GOING TO REST.
RIGHT ON. I'LL CATCH A MOVIE. MAYBE MAKE FRIENDS WITH THE HORSE.
DAY SEVEN.
EW YORK
BITE ME, BENNY. MY BURSITIS, CALL.
--SIGN UP FOR OUR MEMBER'S CLUB?
MEMBER'S CLUB
MY BURSITIS
DAY NINE.
BITE ME, BENNY.
DAY EIGHT.
EXPENSIVE BRAND
BITE ME
MY BURSITIS
GENERIC
WHY YOU BUYIN' THE EXPENSIVE BRAND, GERRY? GENERIC'S JUST AS GOOD.
HUH. ONLY IN NEW YORK.
MY BURSITIS, MY CALL.
I'M HUNGRY.
NO SWEAT. HOT DOG CART'S RIGHT DOWNSTAIRS.
DAY TEN.

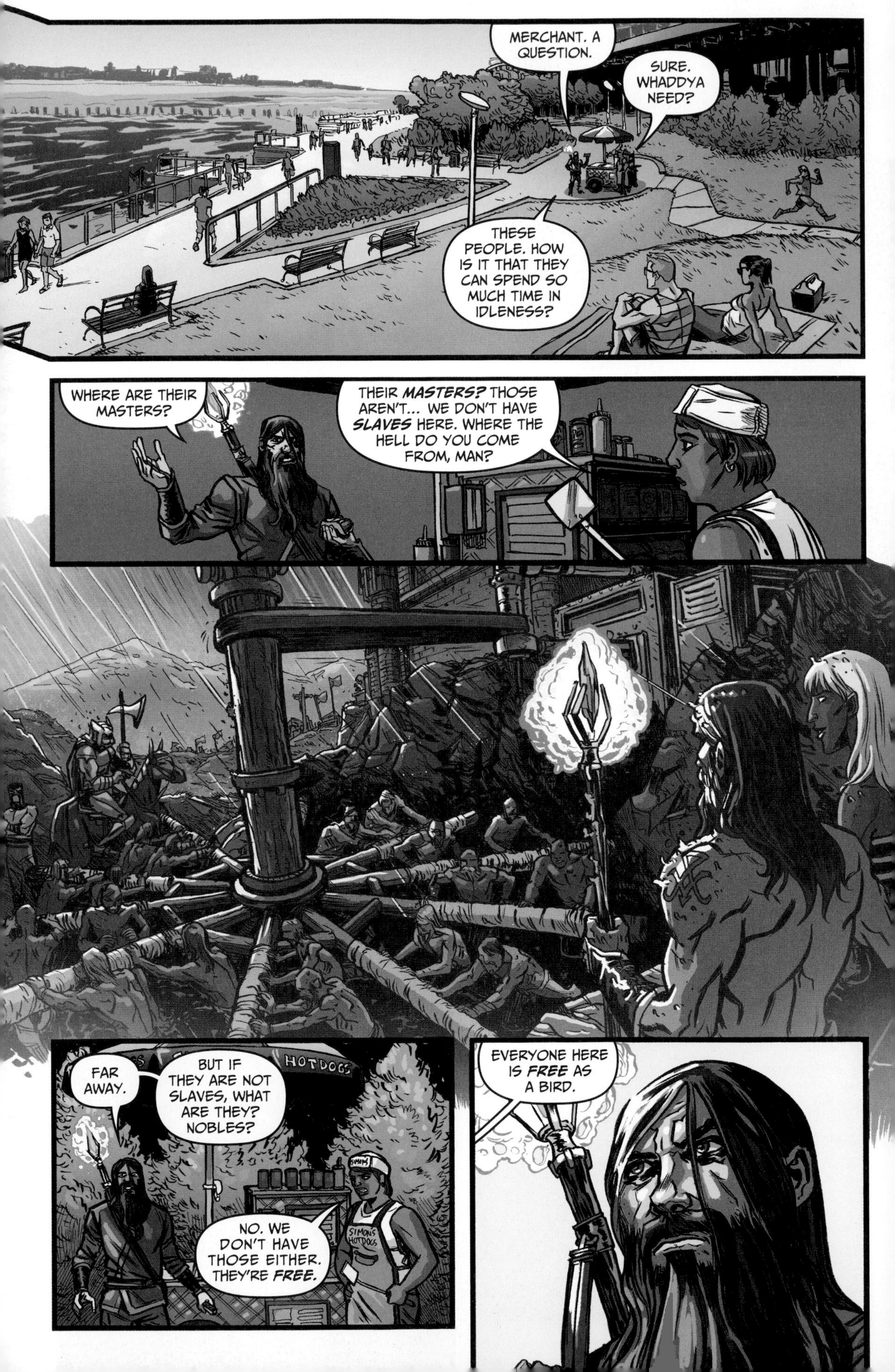

MERCHANT. A QUESTION.
SURE. WHADDYA NEED?
THESE PEOPLE. HOW IS IT THAT THEY CAN SPEND SO MUCH TIME IN IDLENESS?
WHERE ARE THEIR MASTERS?
THEIR *MASTERS?* THOSE AREN'T... WE DON'T HAVE *SLAVES* HERE. WHERE THE HELL DO YOU COME FROM, MAN?
FAR AWAY.
BUT IF THEY ARE NOT SLAVES, WHAT ARE THEY? NOBLES?
HOT DOGS
NO. WE DON'T HAVE THOSE EITHER. THEY'RE *FREE.*
SIMON'S HOT DOGS
EVERYONE HERE IS *FREE* AS A BIRD.

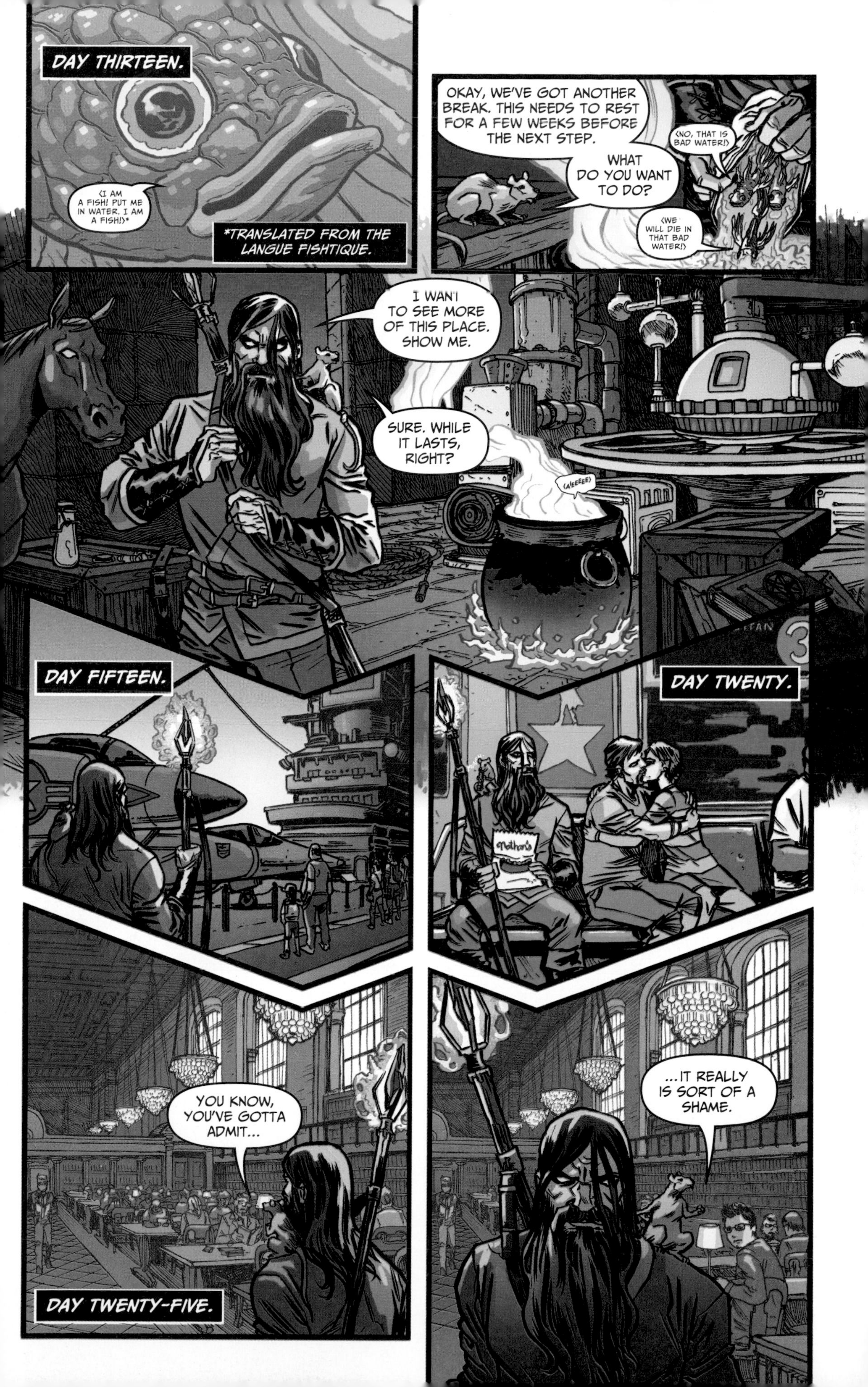
DAY THIRTEEN.
‹I AM A FISH! PUT ME IN WATER. I AM A FISH!›*
*TRANSLATED FROM THE LANGUE FISHTIQUE.
OKAY, WE'VE GOT ANOTHER BREAK. THIS NEEDS TO REST FOR A FEW WEEKS BEFORE THE NEXT STEP.
‹NO, THAT IS BAD WATER!›
WHAT DO YOU WANT TO DO?
‹WE WILL DIE IN THAT BAD WATER!›
I WANT TO SEE MORE OF THIS PLACE. SHOW ME.
SURE. WHILE IT LASTS, RIGHT?
‹AIEEEEE›
DAY FIFTEEN.
DAY TWENTY.
Nathan's
DAY TWENTY-FIVE.
YOU KNOW, YOU'VE GOTTA ADMIT...
...IT REALLY IS SORT OF A SHAME.

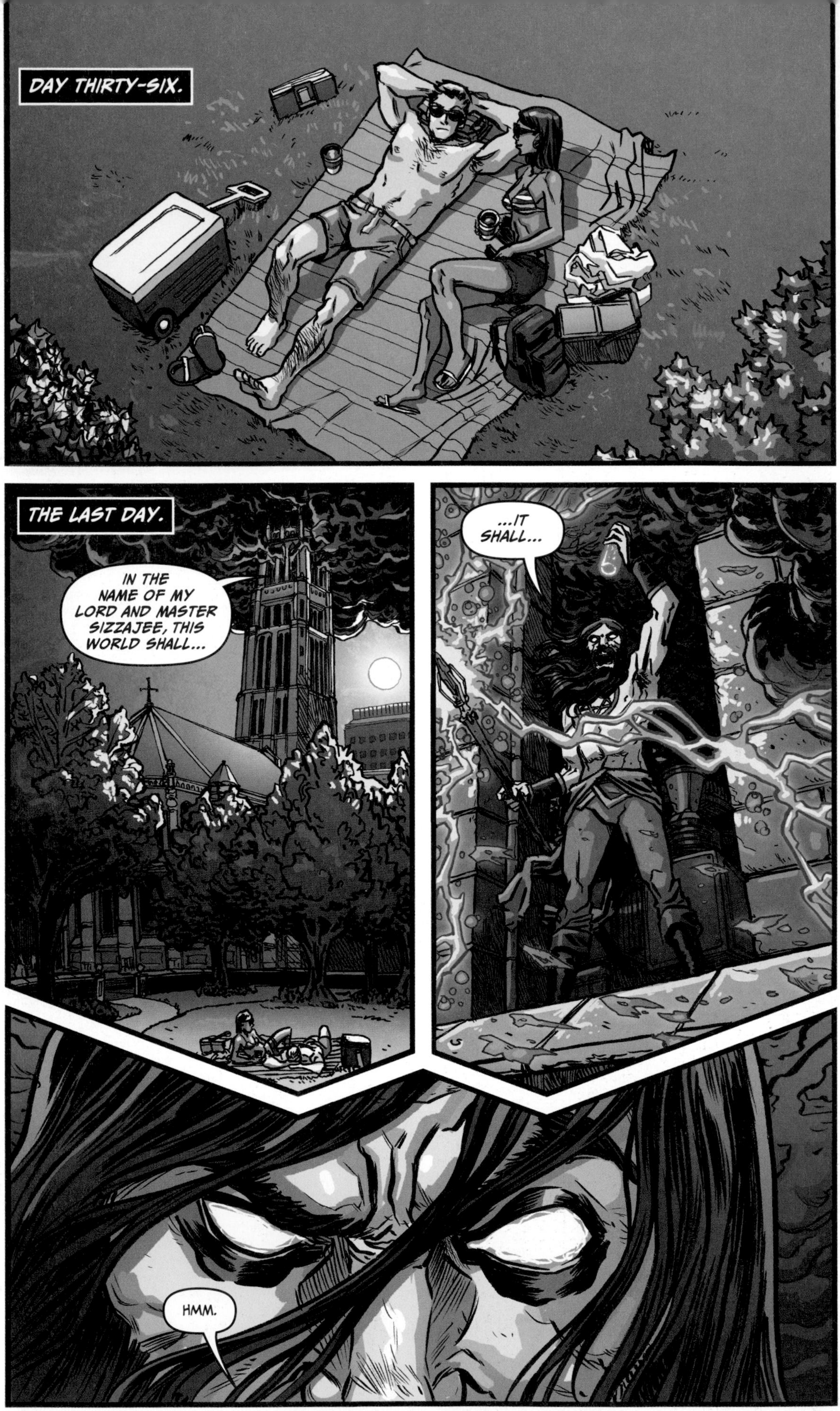
DAY THIRTY-SIX.
THE LAST DAY.
IN THE NAME OF MY LORD AND MASTER SIZZAJEE, THIS WORLD SHALL...
...IT SHALL...
HMM.

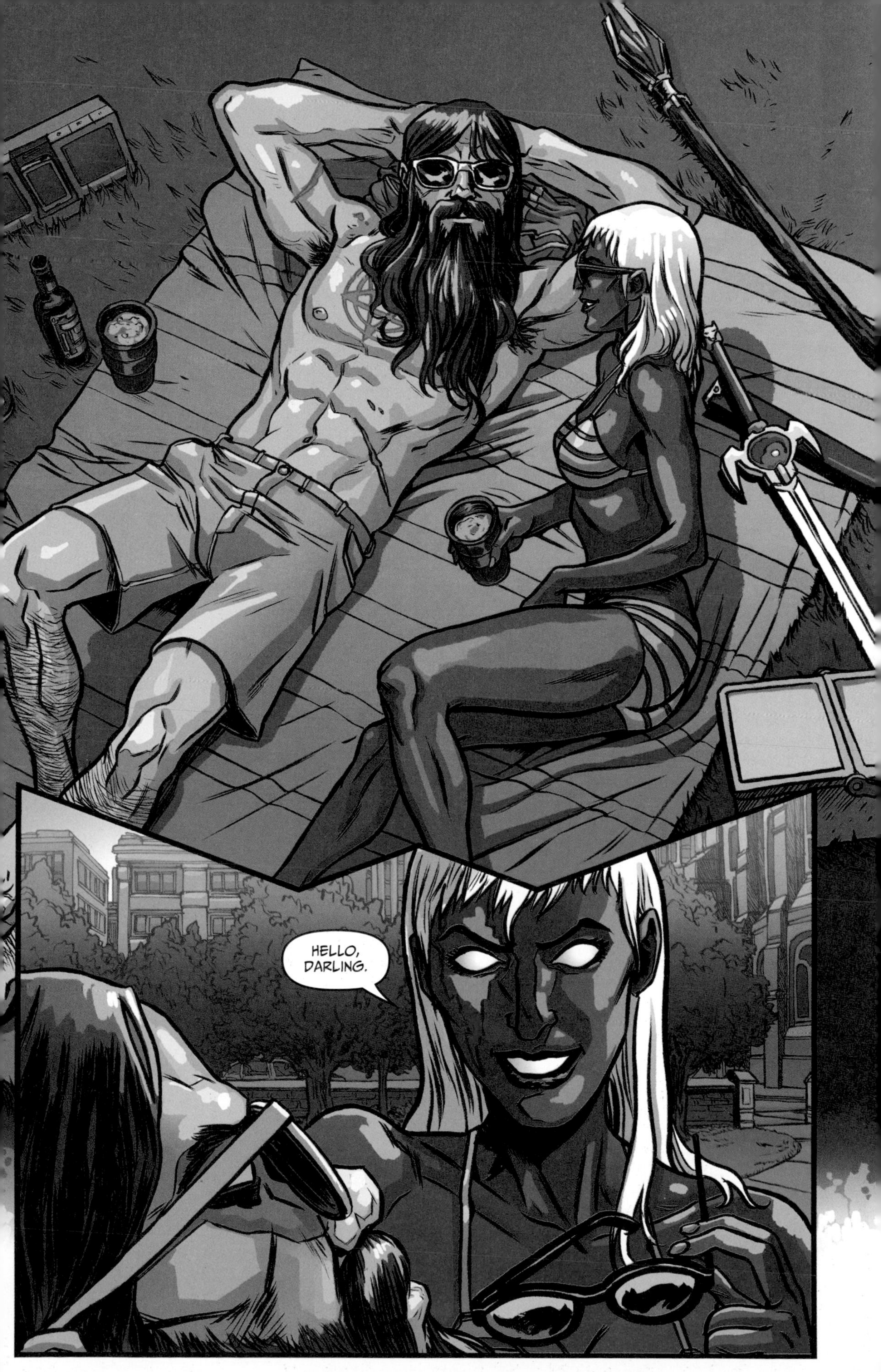
HELLO, DARLING.

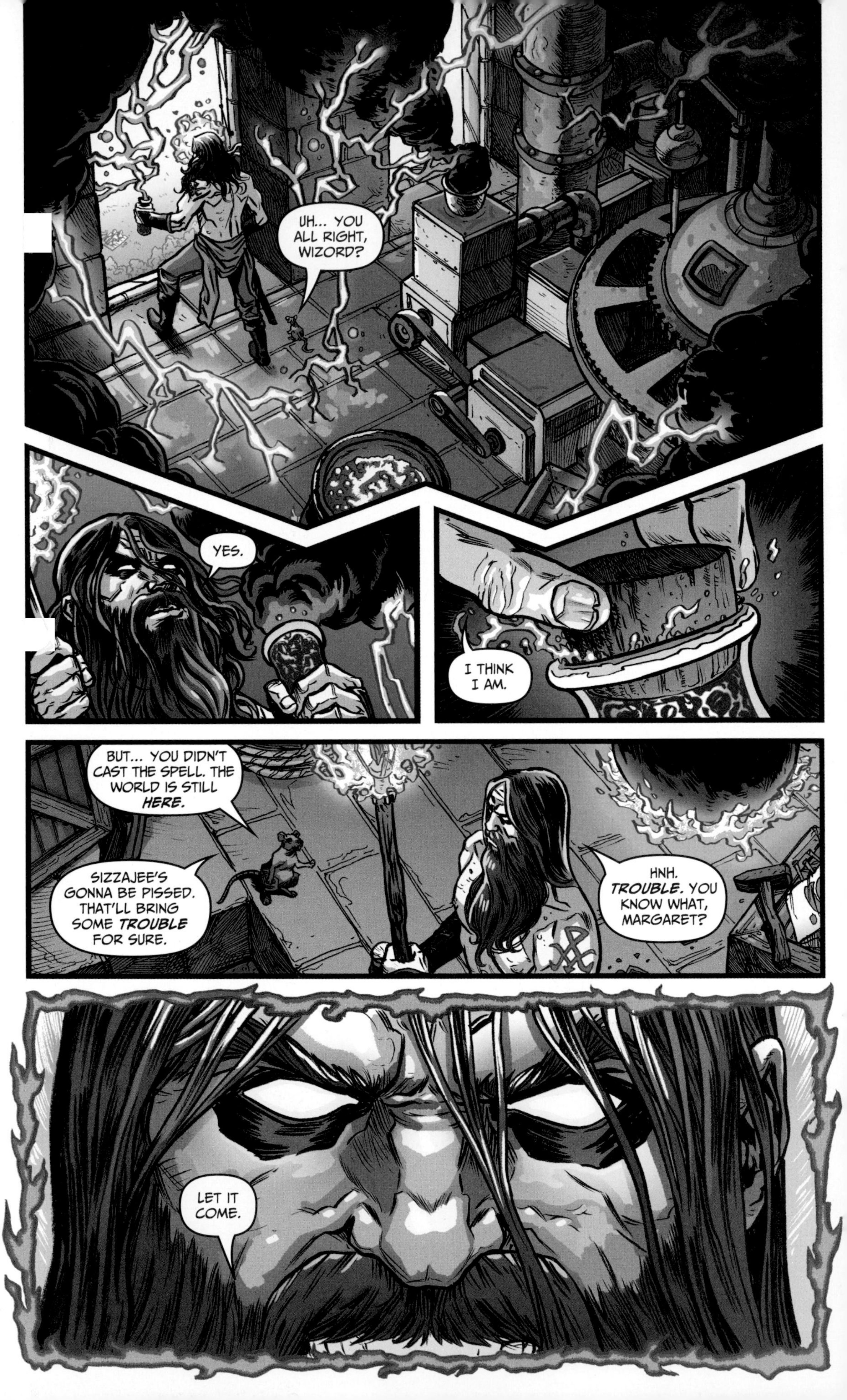
UH... YOU ALL RIGHT, WIZORD?
YES.
I THINK I AM.
BUT... YOU DIDN'T CAST THE SPELL. THE WORLD IS STILL *HERE.*
SIZZAJEE'S GONNA BE PISSED. THAT'LL BRING SOME *TROUBLE* FOR SURE.
HNH. *TROUBLE.* YOU KNOW WHAT, MARGARET?
LET IT COME.

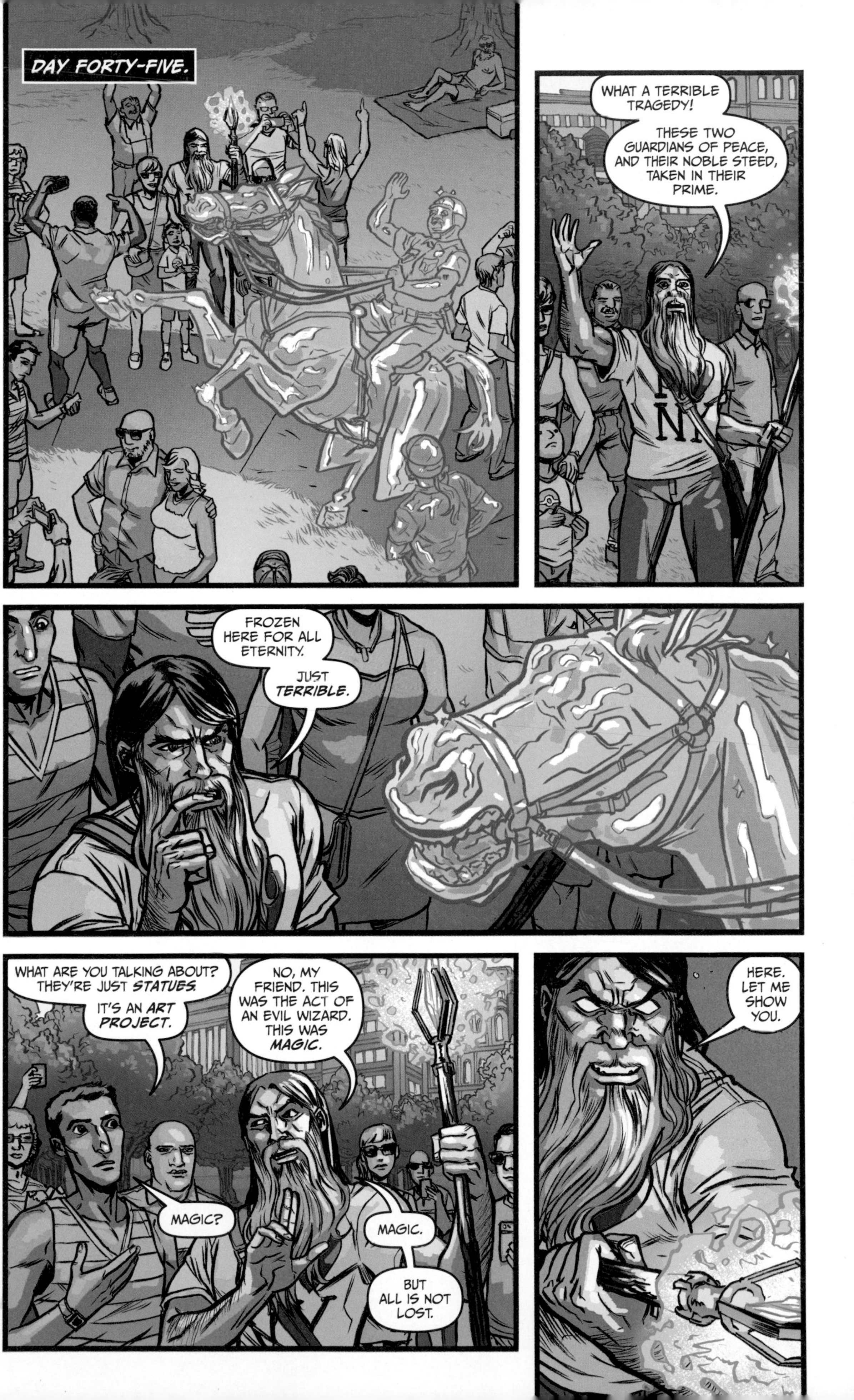
DAY FORTY-FIVE.
WHAT A TERRIBLE TRAGEDY!
THESE TWO GUARDIANS OF PEACE, AND THEIR NOBLE STEED, TAKEN IN THEIR PRIME.
FROZEN HERE FOR ALL ETERNITY.
JUST TERRIBLE.
WHAT ARE YOU TALKING ABOUT? THEY'RE JUST STATUES.
IT'S AN ART PROJECT.
NO, MY FRIEND. THIS WAS THE ACT OF AN EVIL WIZARD. THIS WAS MAGIC.
MAGIC?
MAGIC.
BUT ALL IS NOT LOST.
HERE. LET ME SHOW YOU.

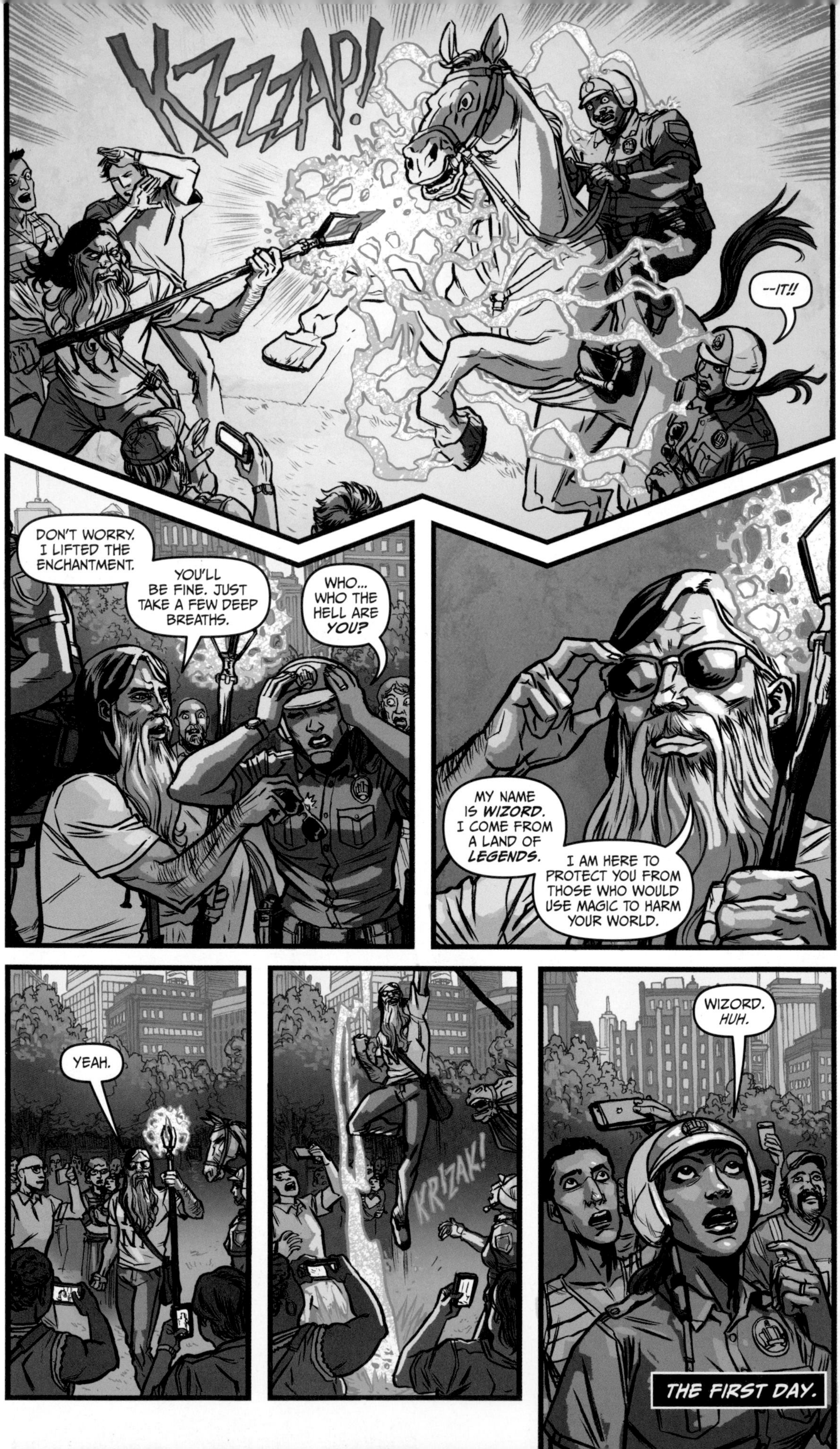
KZZZAP!
--IT!!
DON'T WORRY. I LIFTED THE ENCHANTMENT.
YOU'LL BE FINE. JUST TAKE A FEW DEEP BREATHS.
WHO... WHO THE HELL ARE YOU?
MY NAME IS WIZORD. I COME FROM A LAND OF LEGENDS.
I AM HERE TO PROTECT YOU FROM THOSE WHO WOULD USE MAGIC TO HARM YOUR WORLD.
YEAH.
KRIZAK!
WIZORD. HUH.
THE FIRST DAY.

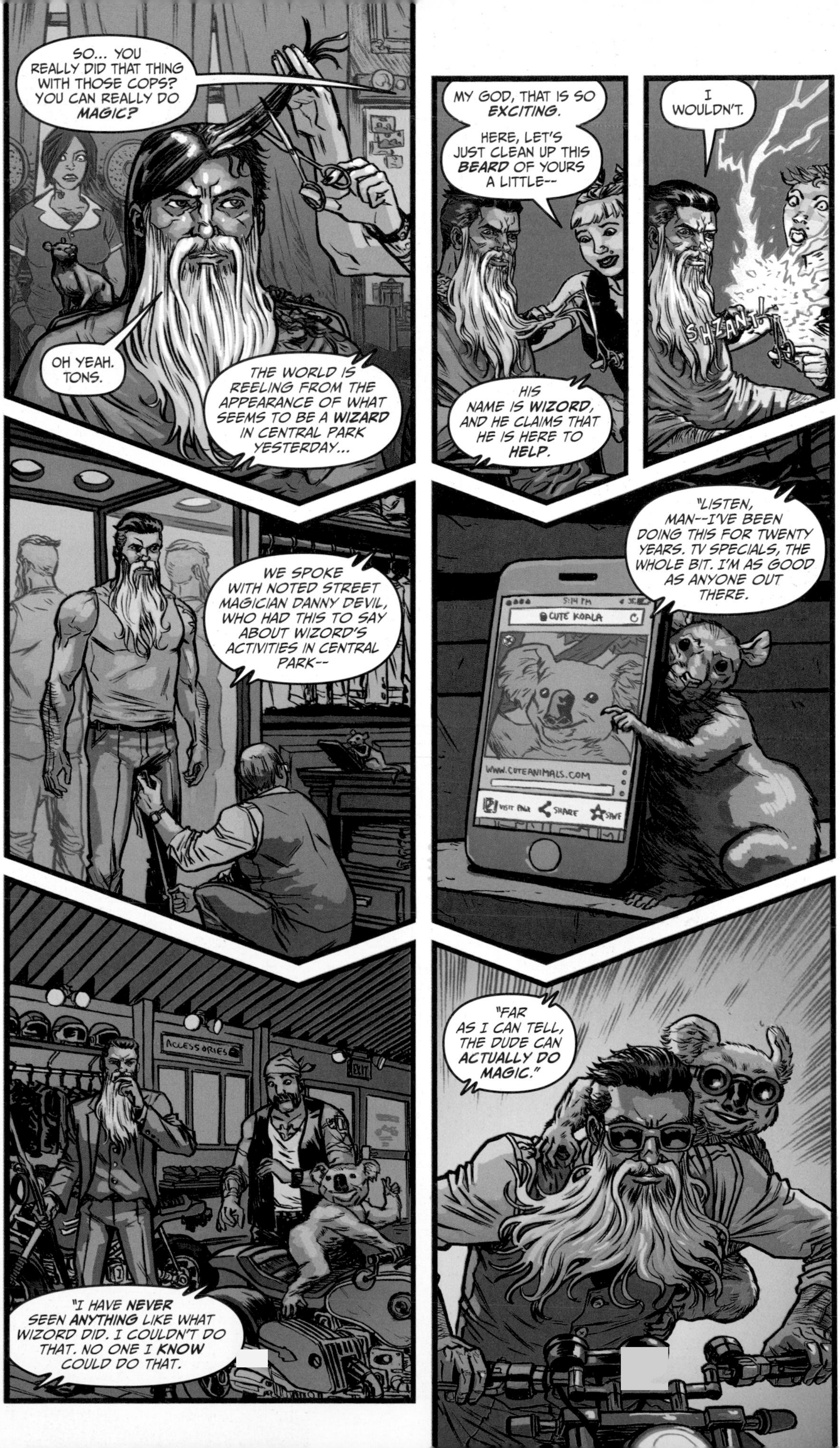
SO... YOU REALLY DID THAT THING WITH THOSE COPS? YOU CAN REALLY DO MAGIC?
OH YEAH. TONS.
THE WORLD IS REELING FROM THE APPEARANCE OF WHAT SEEMS TO BE A WIZARD IN CENTRAL PARK YESTERDAY...
MY GOD, THAT IS SO EXCITING.
HERE, LET'S JUST CLEAN UP THIS BEARD OF YOURS A LITTLE--
HIS NAME IS WIZORD, AND HE CLAIMS THAT HE IS HERE TO HELP.
I WOULDN'T.
SHZANT!
WE SPOKE WITH NOTED STREET MAGICIAN DANNY DEVIL, WHO HAD THIS TO SAY ABOUT WIZORD'S ACTIVITIES IN CENTRAL PARK--
"LISTEN, MAN--I'VE BEEN DOING THIS FOR TWENTY YEARS. TV SPECIALS, THE WHOLE BIT. I'M AS GOOD AS ANYONE OUT THERE.
5:14 PM
CUTE KOALA
WWW.CUTEANIMALS.COM
VISIT PAGE
SHARE
SAVE
ACCESSORIES
EXIT
"I HAVE NEVER SEEN ANYTHING LIKE WHAT WIZORD DID. I COULDN'T DO THAT. NO ONE I KNOW COULD DO THAT.
"FAR AS I CAN TELL, THE DUDE CAN ACTUALLY DO MAGIC."

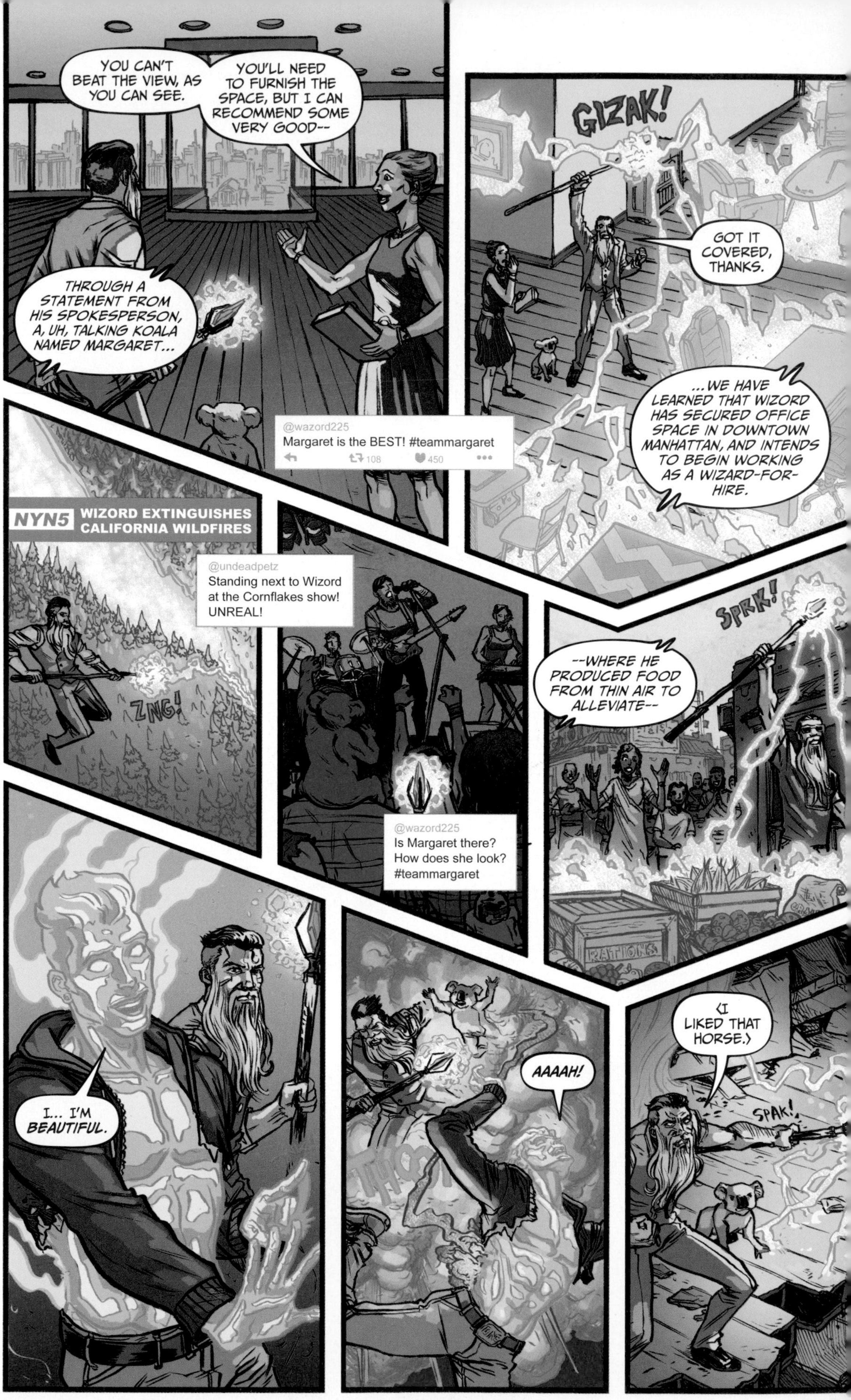
YOU CAN'T BEAT THE VIEW, AS YOU CAN SEE.
YOU'LL NEED TO FURNISH THE SPACE, BUT I CAN RECOMMEND SOME VERY GOOD--
THROUGH A STATEMENT FROM HIS SPOKESPERSON, A, UH, TALKING KOALA NAMED MARGARET...
GIZAK!
GOT IT COVERED, THANKS.
...WE HAVE LEARNED THAT WIZORD HAS SECURED OFFICE SPACE IN DOWNTOWN MANHATTAN, AND INTENDS TO BEGIN WORKING AS A WIZARD-FOR-HIRE.
@wazord225
Margaret is the BEST! #teammargaret
108 450
NYN5 WIZORD EXTINGUISHES CALIFORNIA WILDFIRES
ZNG!
@undeadpetz
Standing next to Wizord at the Cornflakes show! UNREAL!
@wazord225
Is Margaret there? How does she look? #teammargaret
SPRK!
--WHERE HE PRODUCED FOOD FROM THIN AIR TO ALLEVIATE--
RATIONS
I... I'M BEAUTIFUL.
AAAAH!
⟨I LIKED THAT HORSE.⟩
SPAK!

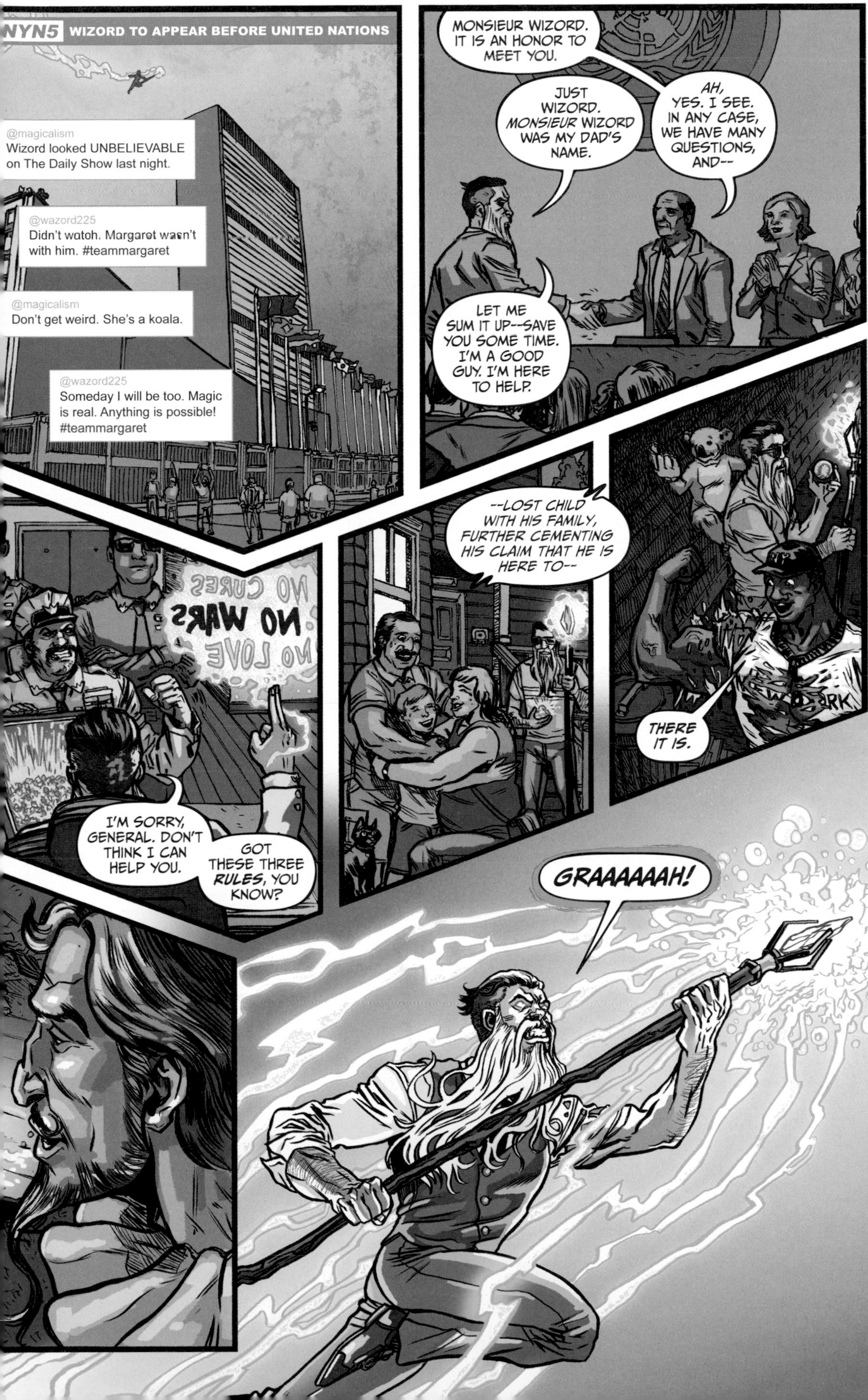
NYN5 WIZORD TO APPEAR BEFORE UNITED NATIONS
@magicalism Wizord looked UNBELIEVABLE on The Daily Show last night.
@wazord225 Didn't watch. Margaret wasn't with him. #teammargaret
@magicalism Don't get weird. She's a koala.
@wazord225 Someday I will be too. Magic is real. Anything is possible! #teammargaret
MONSIEUR WIZORD. IT IS AN HONOR TO MEET YOU.
JUST WIZORD. MONSIEUR WIZORD WAS MY DAD'S NAME.
AH, YES. I SEE. IN ANY CASE, WE HAVE MANY QUESTIONS, AND--
LET ME SUM IT UP--SAVE YOU SOME TIME. I'M A GOOD GUY. I'M HERE TO HELP.
NO CURES NO WARS NO LOVE
I'M SORRY, GENERAL. DON'T THINK I CAN HELP YOU.
GOT THESE THREE RULES, YOU KNOW?
--LOST CHILD WITH HIS FAMILY, FURTHER CEMENTING HIS CLAIM THAT HE IS HERE TO--
THERE IT IS.
GRAAAAAAH!

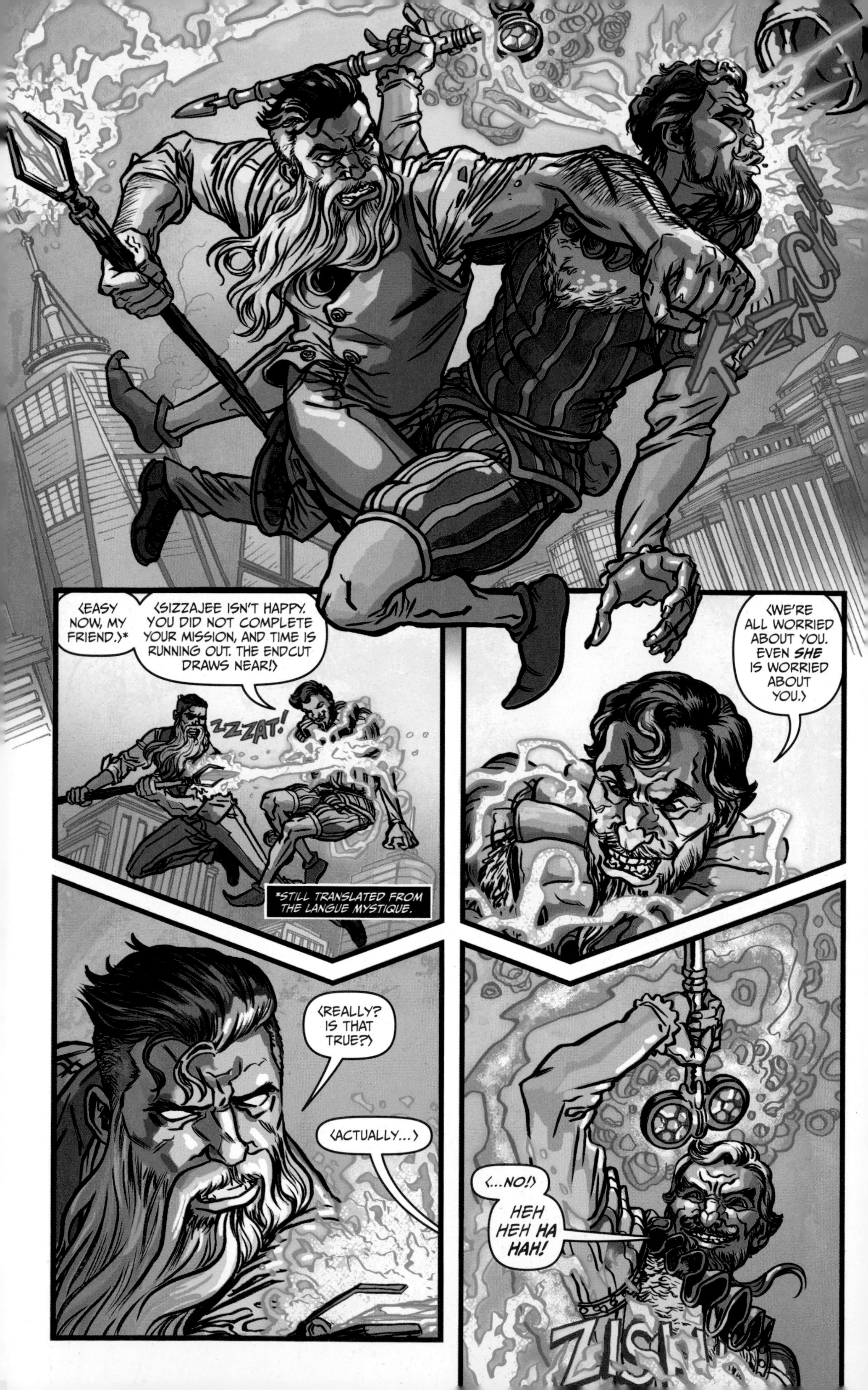
KZZACK!
⟨EASY NOW, MY FRIEND.⟩*
⟨SIZZAJEE ISN'T HAPPY. YOU DID NOT COMPLETE YOUR MISSION, AND TIME IS RUNNING OUT. THE ENDCUT DRAWS NEAR!⟩
ZZZAT!
*STILL TRANSLATED FROM THE LANGUE MYSTIQUE.
⟨WE'RE ALL WORRIED ABOUT YOU. EVEN SHE IS WORRIED ABOUT YOU.⟩
⟨REALLY? IS THAT TRUE?⟩
⟨ACTUALLY...⟩
⟨...NO!⟩
HEH HEH HA HAH!
ZISH!

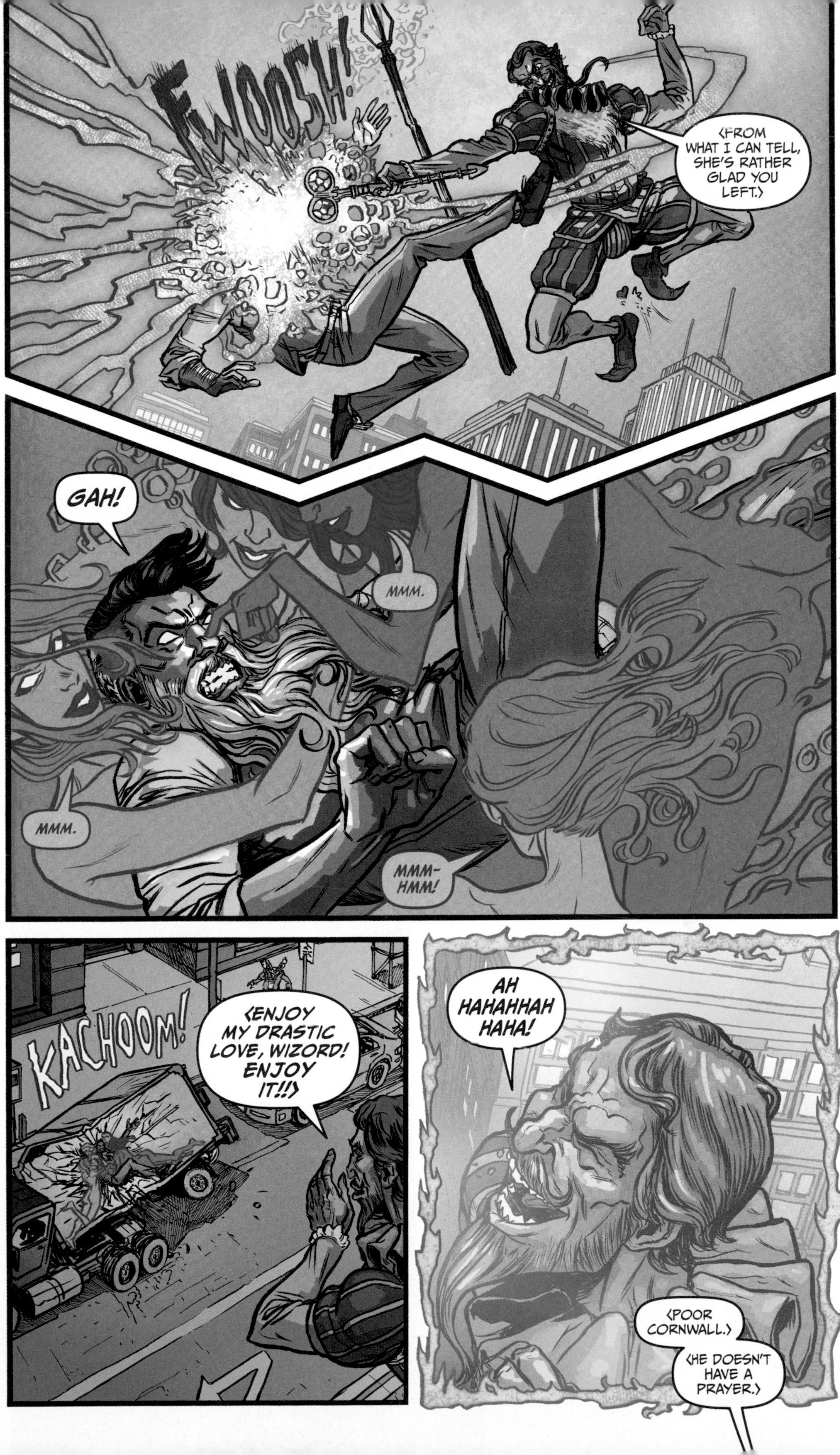
FWOOSH!
‹FROM WHAT I CAN TELL, SHE'S RATHER GLAD YOU LEFT.›
GAH!
MMM.
MMM.
MMM-HMM!
KACHOOM!
‹ENJOY MY DRASTIC LOVE, WIZORD! ENJOY IT!!›
AH HAHAHHAH HAHA!
‹POOR CORNWALL.›
‹HE DOESN'T HAVE A PRAYER.›

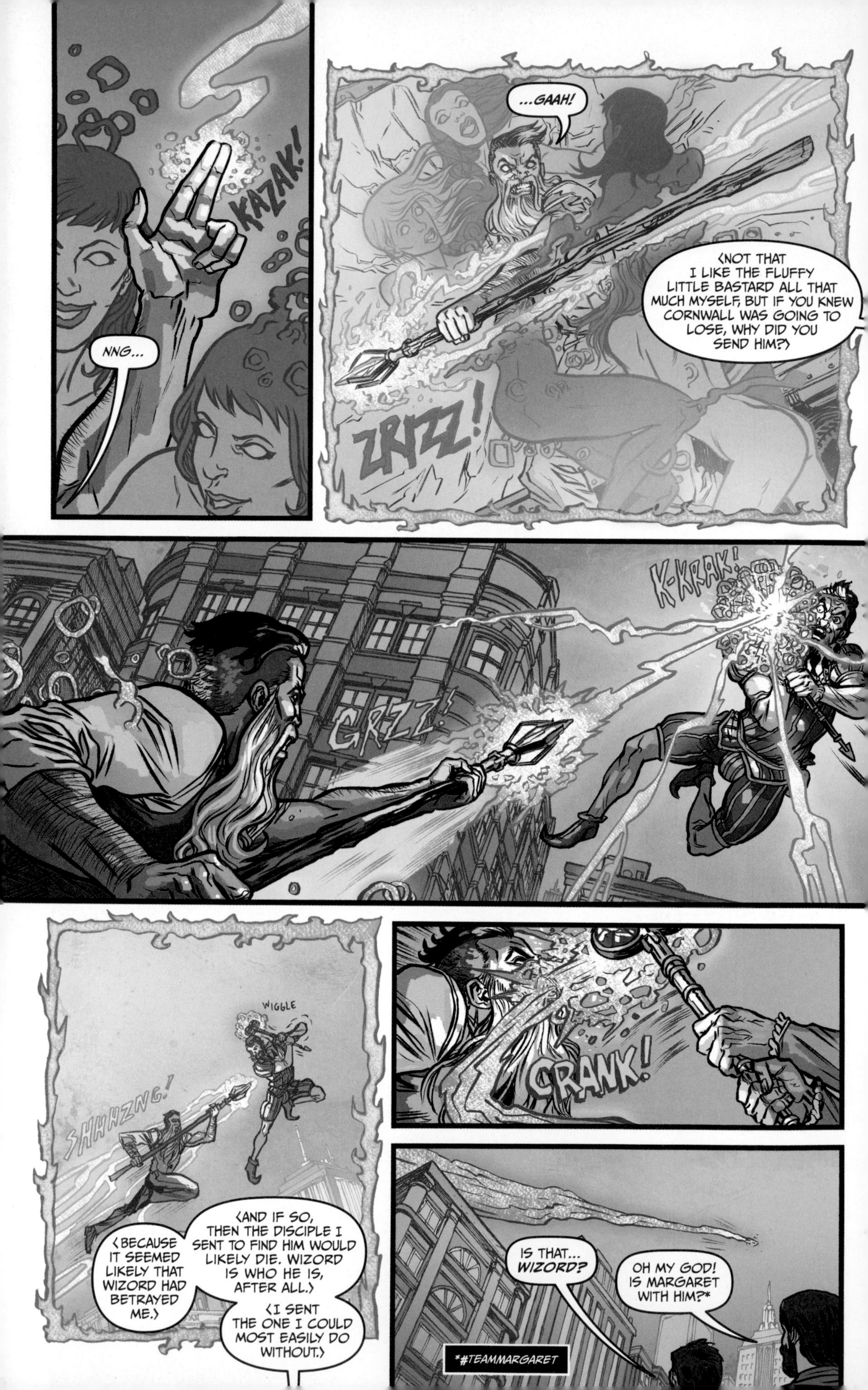
KAZAK!
NNG...
...GAAH!
<NOT THAT I LIKE THE FLUFFY LITTLE BASTARD ALL THAT MUCH MYSELF, BUT IF YOU KNEW CORNWALL WAS GOING TO LOSE, WHY DID YOU SEND HIM?>
ZRZZ!
K-KRAK!
GRZZ!
WIGGLE
SHHHZNG!
<BECAUSE IT SEEMED LIKELY THAT WIZORD HAD BETRAYED ME.>
<AND IF SO, THEN THE DISCIPLE I SENT TO FIND HIM WOULD LIKELY DIE. WIZORD IS WHO HE IS, AFTER ALL.>
<I SENT THE ONE I COULD MOST EASILY DO WITHOUT.>
CRANK!
IS THAT... WIZORD?
OH MY GOD! IS MARGARET WITH HIM?*
*#TEAMMARGARET

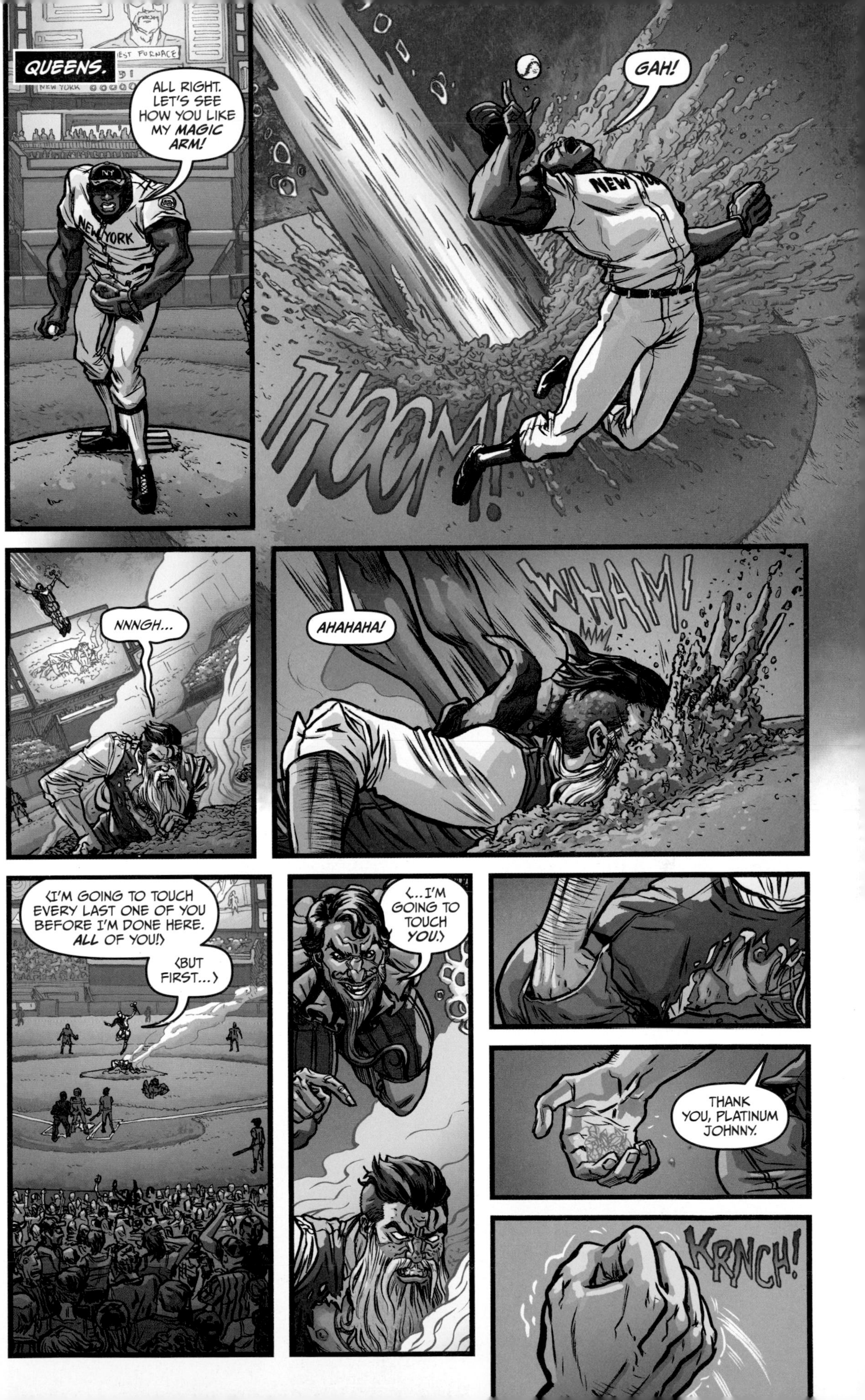
QUEENS.
NEW YORK
ALL RIGHT. LET'S SEE HOW YOU LIKE MY *MAGIC ARM!*
NEW YORK
GAH!
NEW YORK
THOOM!
NNNGH...
AHAHAHA!
WHAM!
⟨I'M GOING TO TOUCH EVERY LAST ONE OF YOU BEFORE I'M DONE HERE. *ALL* OF YOU!⟩
⟨BUT FIRST...⟩
⟨...I'M GOING TO TOUCH *YOU.*⟩
THANK YOU, PLATINUM JOHNNY.
KRNCH!

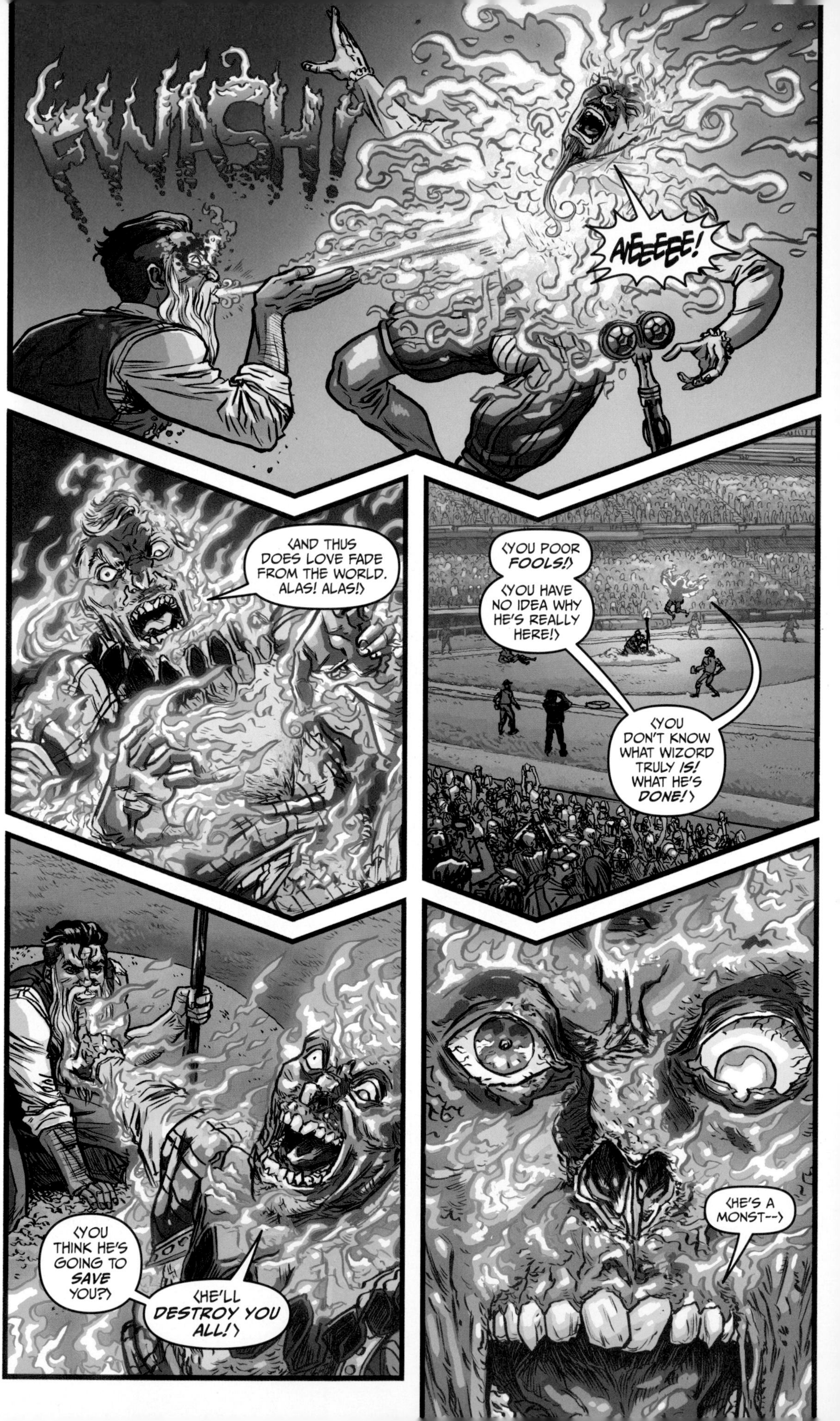
FWASH!!
AIEEEEEE!
‹AND THUS DOES LOVE FADE FROM THE WORLD. ALAS! ALAS!›
‹YOU POOR *FOOLS!*›
‹YOU HAVE NO IDEA WHY HE'S REALLY HERE!›
‹YOU DON'T KNOW WHAT WIZORD TRULY *IS!* WHAT HE'S *DONE!*›
‹YOU THINK HE'S GOING TO *SAVE* YOU?›
‹HE'LL *DESTROY YOU ALL!*›
‹HE'S A MONST--›

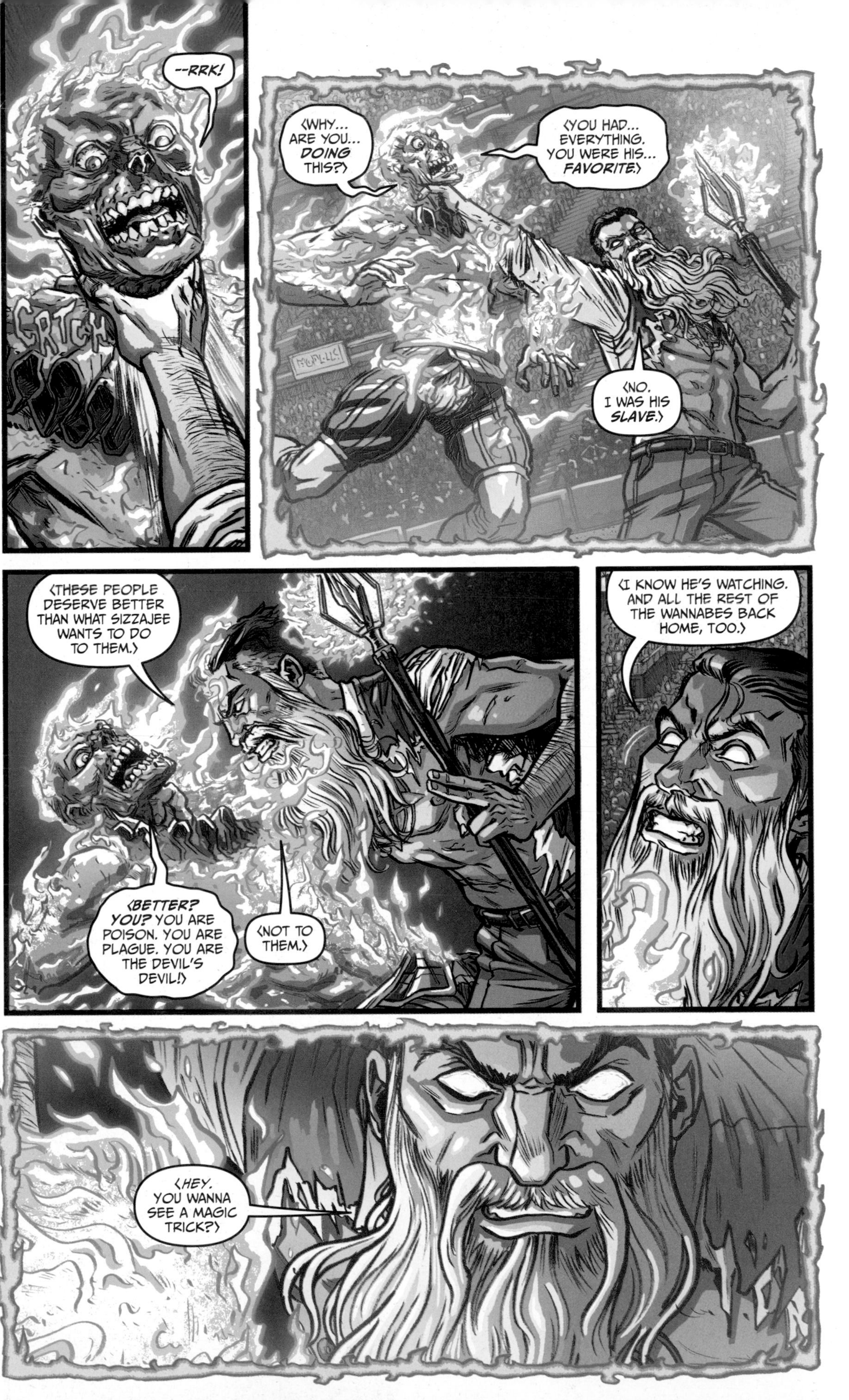
--RRK!
‹WHY... ARE YOU... DOING THIS?›
‹YOU HAD... EVERYTHING. YOU WERE HIS... FAVORITE.›
‹NO. I WAS HIS SLAVE.›
‹THESE PEOPLE DESERVE BETTER THAN WHAT SIZZAJEE WANTS TO DO TO THEM.›
‹BETTER? YOU? YOU ARE POISON. YOU ARE PLAGUE. YOU ARE THE DEVIL'S DEVIL!›
‹NOT TO THEM.›
‹I KNOW HE'S WATCHING. AND ALL THE REST OF THE WANNABES BACK HOME, TOO.›
‹HEY. YOU WANNA SEE A MAGIC TRICK?›

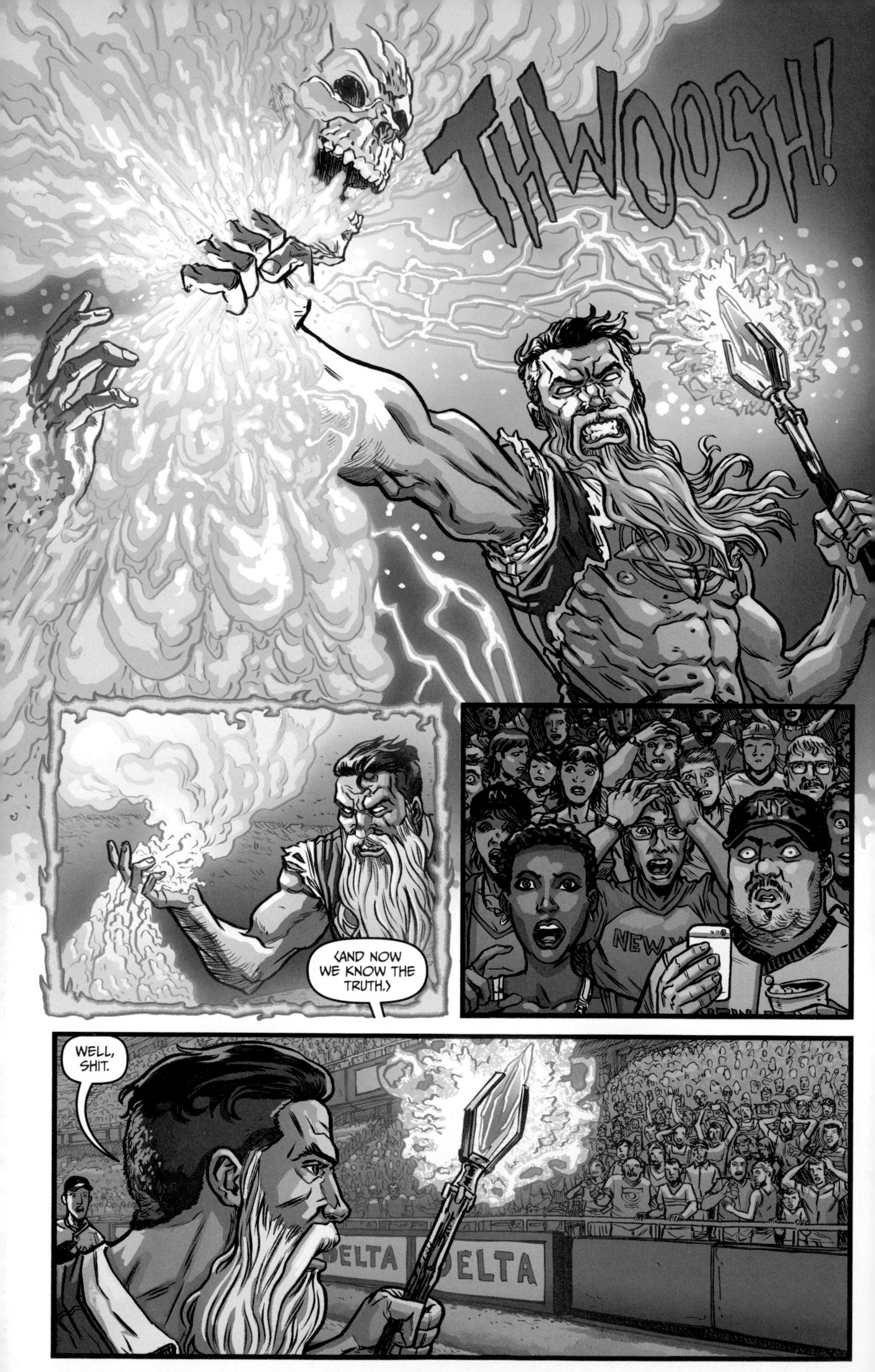
THWOOSH!
‹AND NOW WE KNOW THE TRUTH.›
NEW Y
WELL, SHIT.
DELTA
DELTA

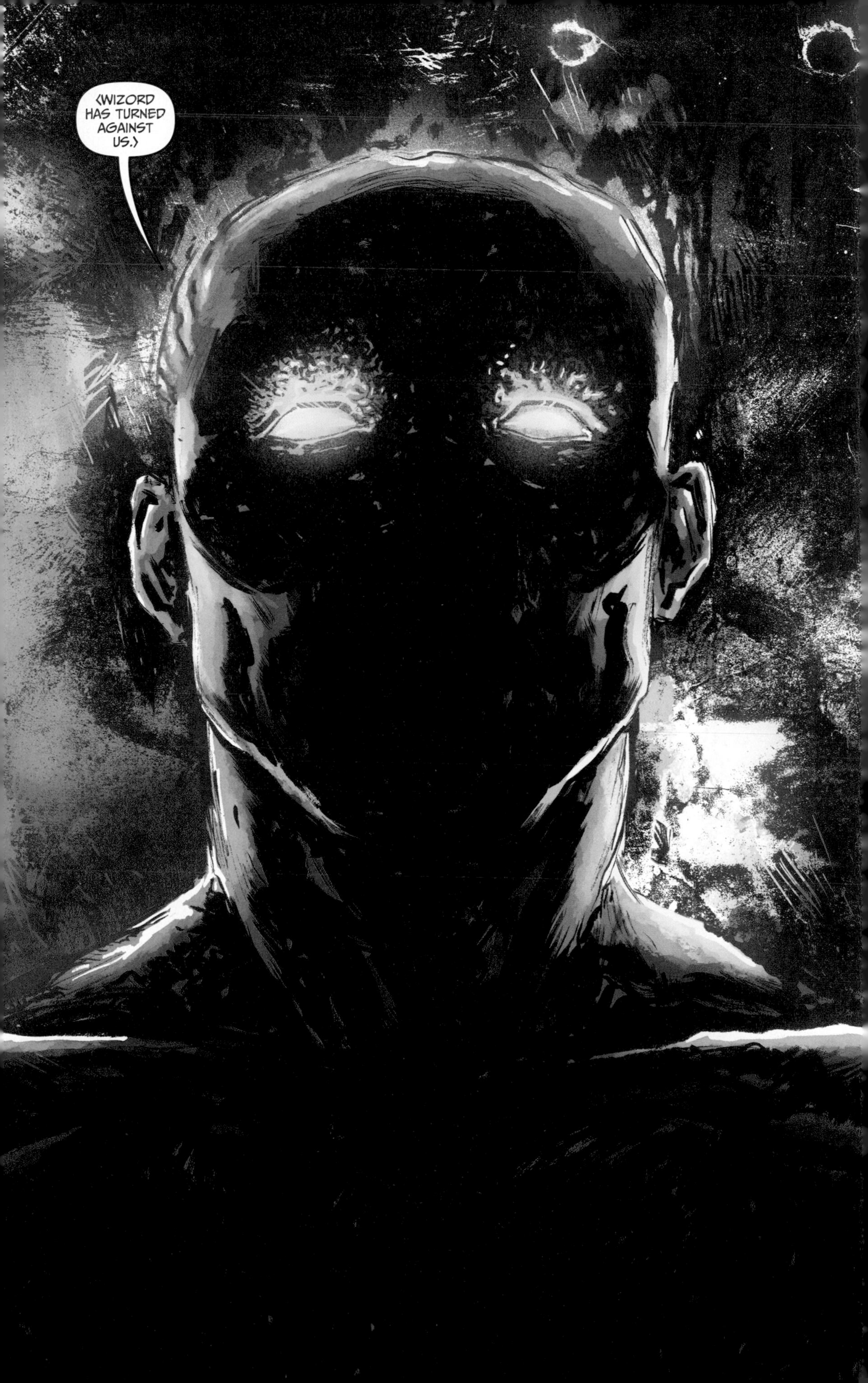
‹WIZORD HAS TURNED AGAINST US.›

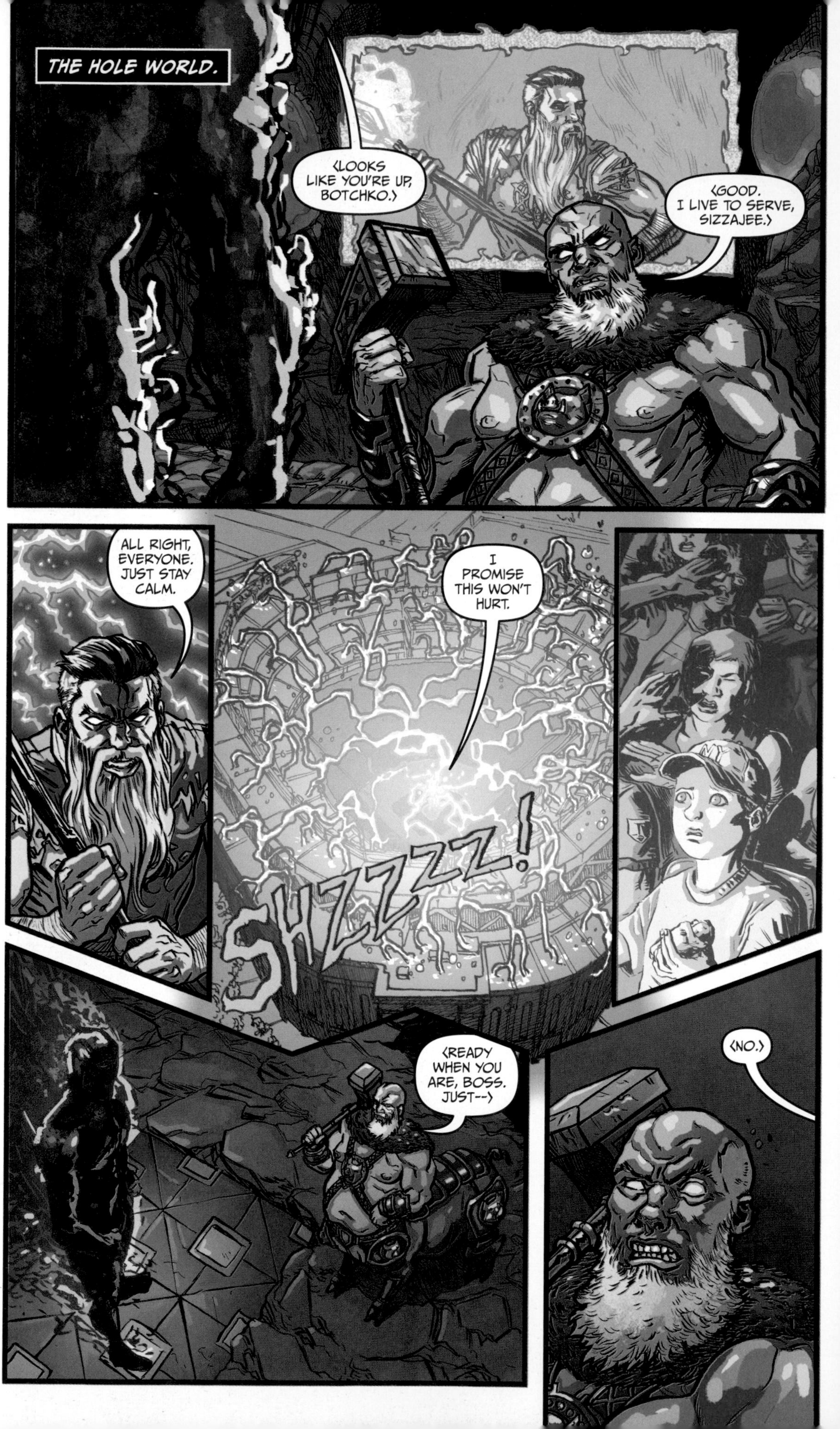
THE HOLE WORLD.
<LOOKS LIKE YOU'RE UP, BOTCHKO.>
<GOOD. I LIVE TO SERVE, SIZZAJEE.>
ALL RIGHT, EVERYONE. JUST STAY CALM.
I PROMISE THIS WON'T HURT.
SHZZZZZ!
<READY WHEN YOU ARE, BOSS. JUST-->
<NO.>

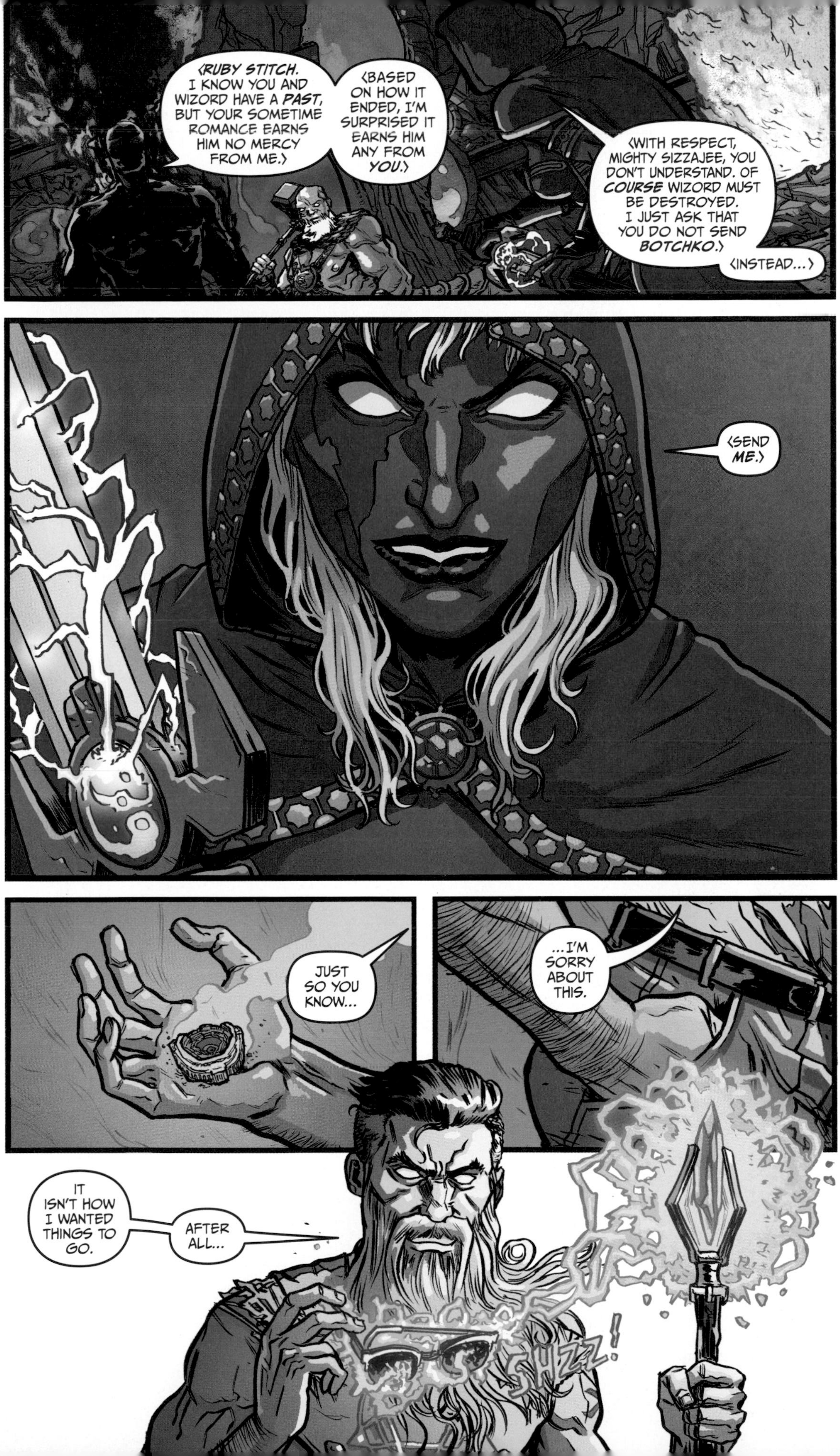
⟨RUBY STITCH. I KNOW YOU AND WIZORD HAVE A PAST, BUT YOUR SOMETIME ROMANCE EARNS HIM NO MERCY FROM ME.⟩
⟨BASED ON HOW IT ENDED, I'M SURPRISED IT EARNS HIM ANY FROM YOU.⟩
⟨WITH RESPECT, MIGHTY SIZZAJEE, YOU DON'T UNDERSTAND. OF COURSE WIZORD MUST BE DESTROYED. I JUST ASK THAT YOU DO NOT SEND BOTCHKO.⟩
⟨INSTEAD...⟩
⟨SEND ME.⟩
JUST SO YOU KNOW...
...I'M SORRY ABOUT THIS.
IT ISN'T HOW I WANTED THINGS TO GO.
AFTER ALL...
SHZZ!

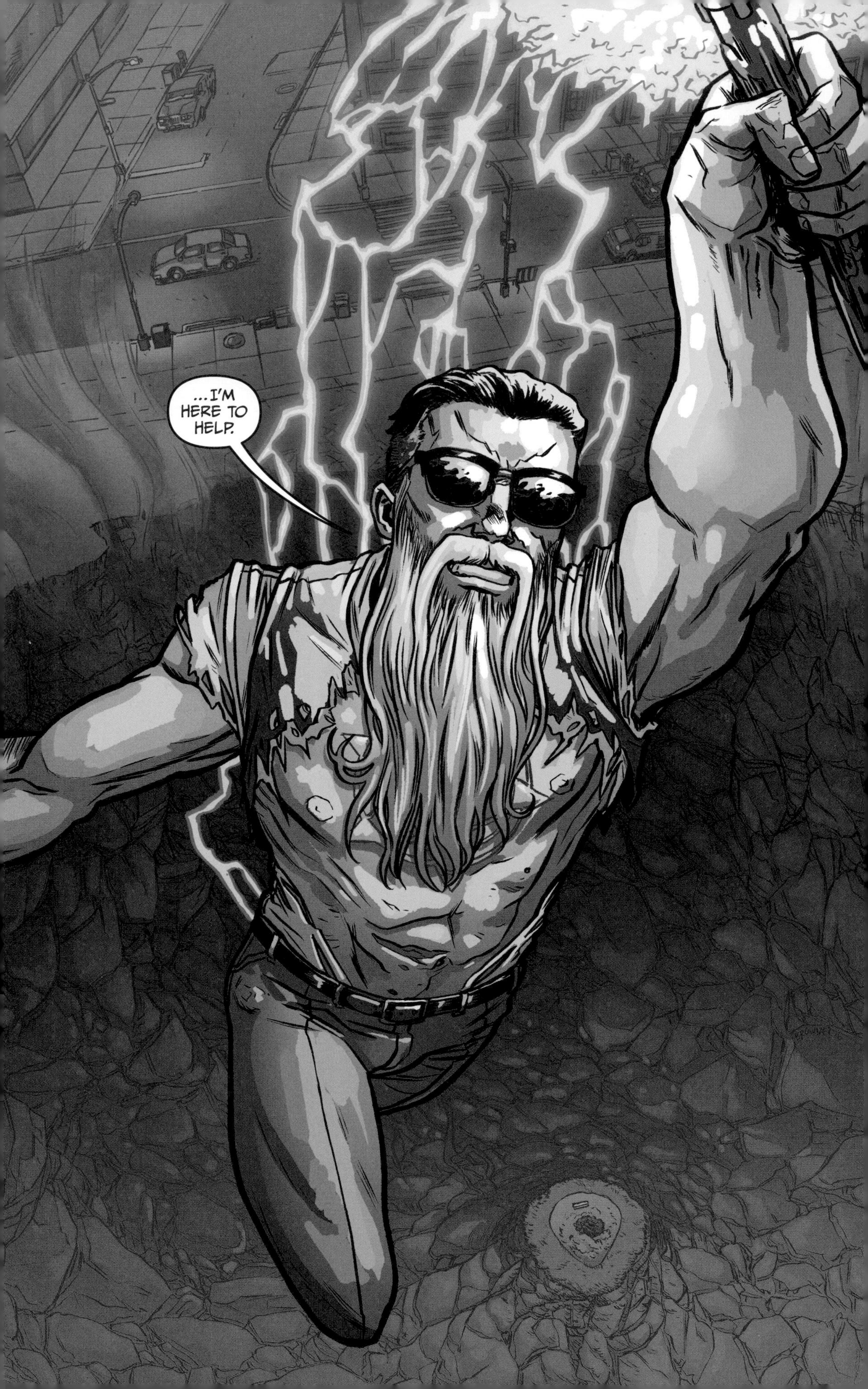
...I'M HERE TO HELP.

# TWO

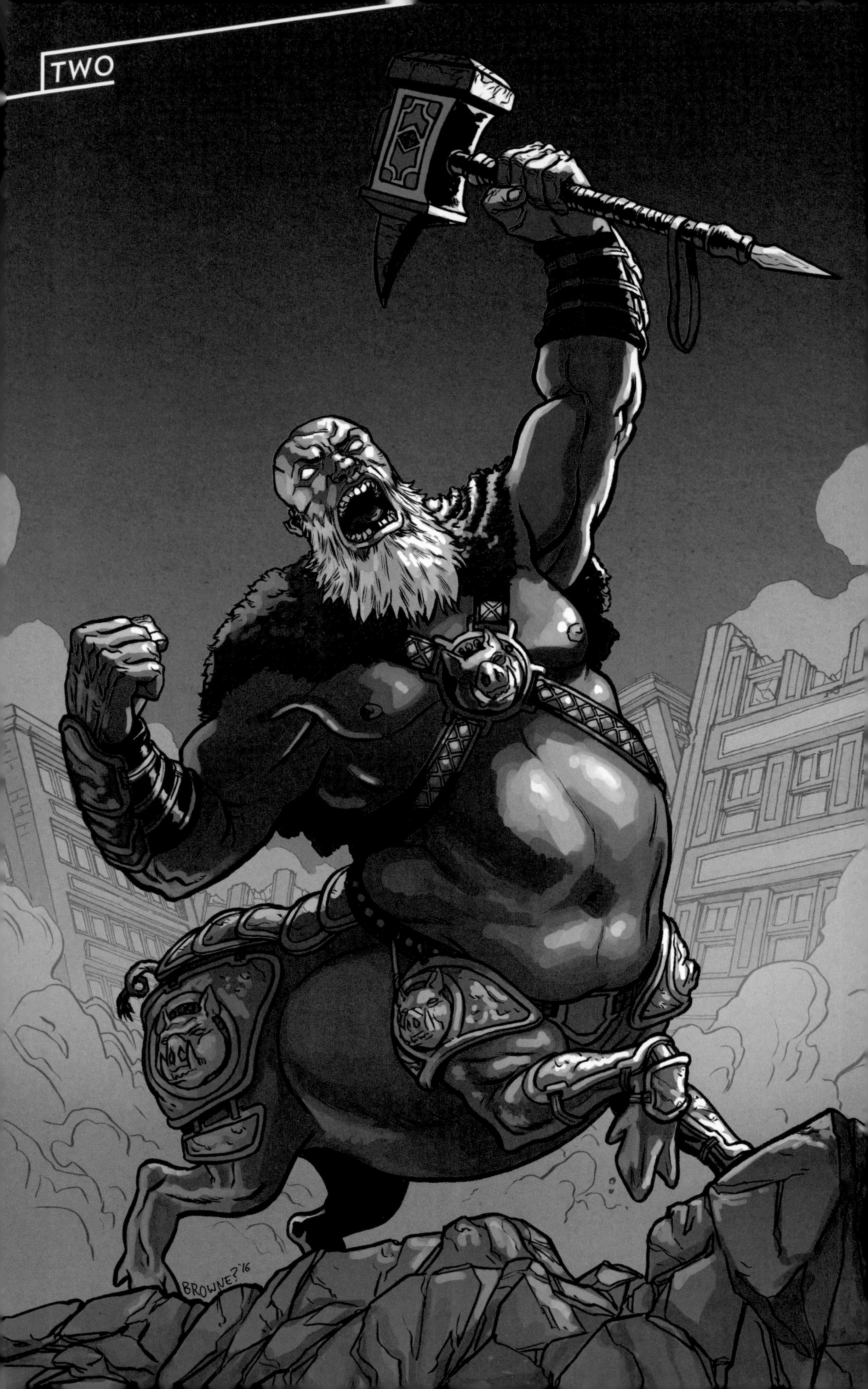
BROWNE '16

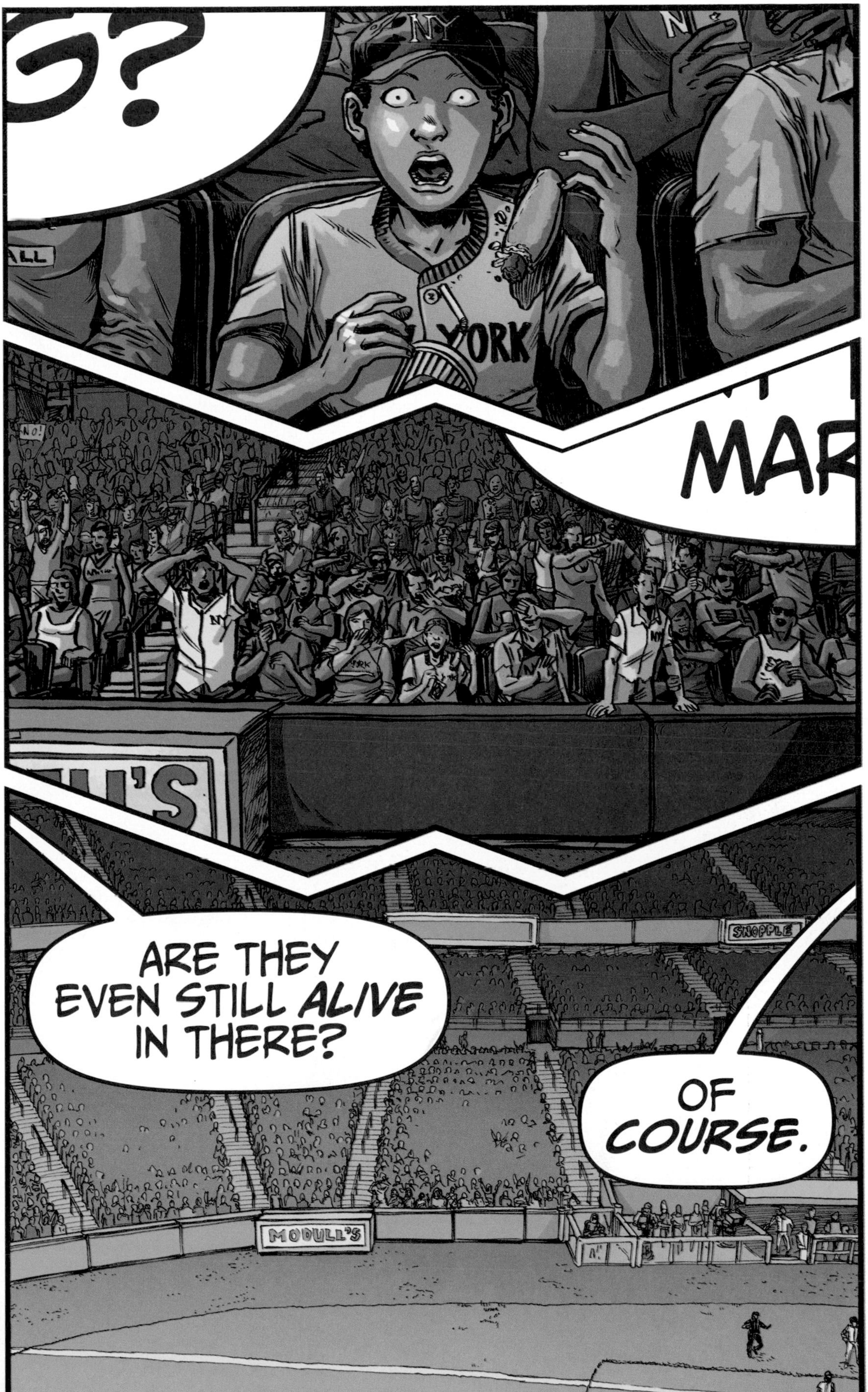
ARE THEY EVEN STILL *ALIVE* IN THERE?
OF *COURSE*.
SNOPPLE
MODULL'S

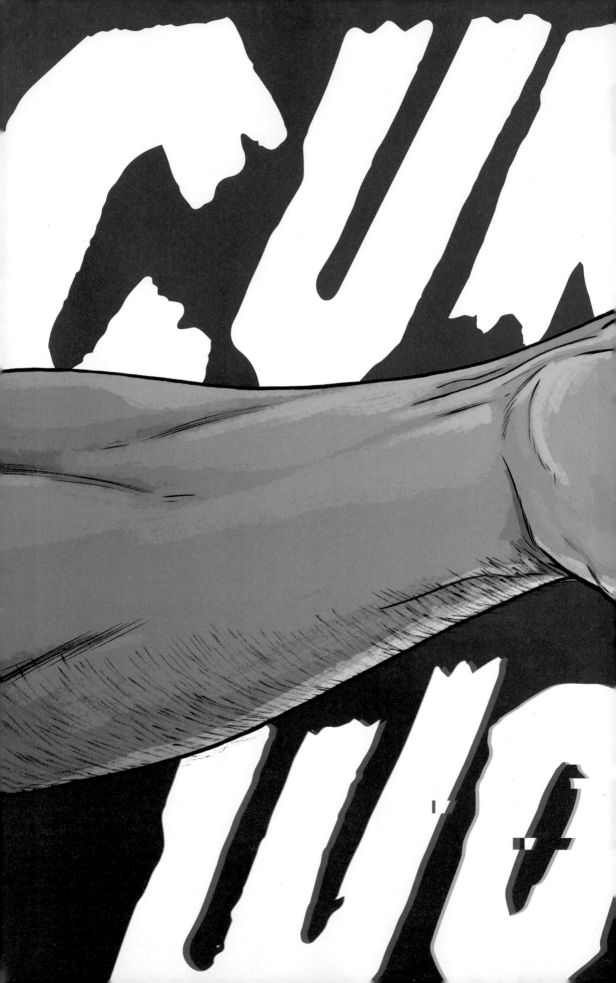

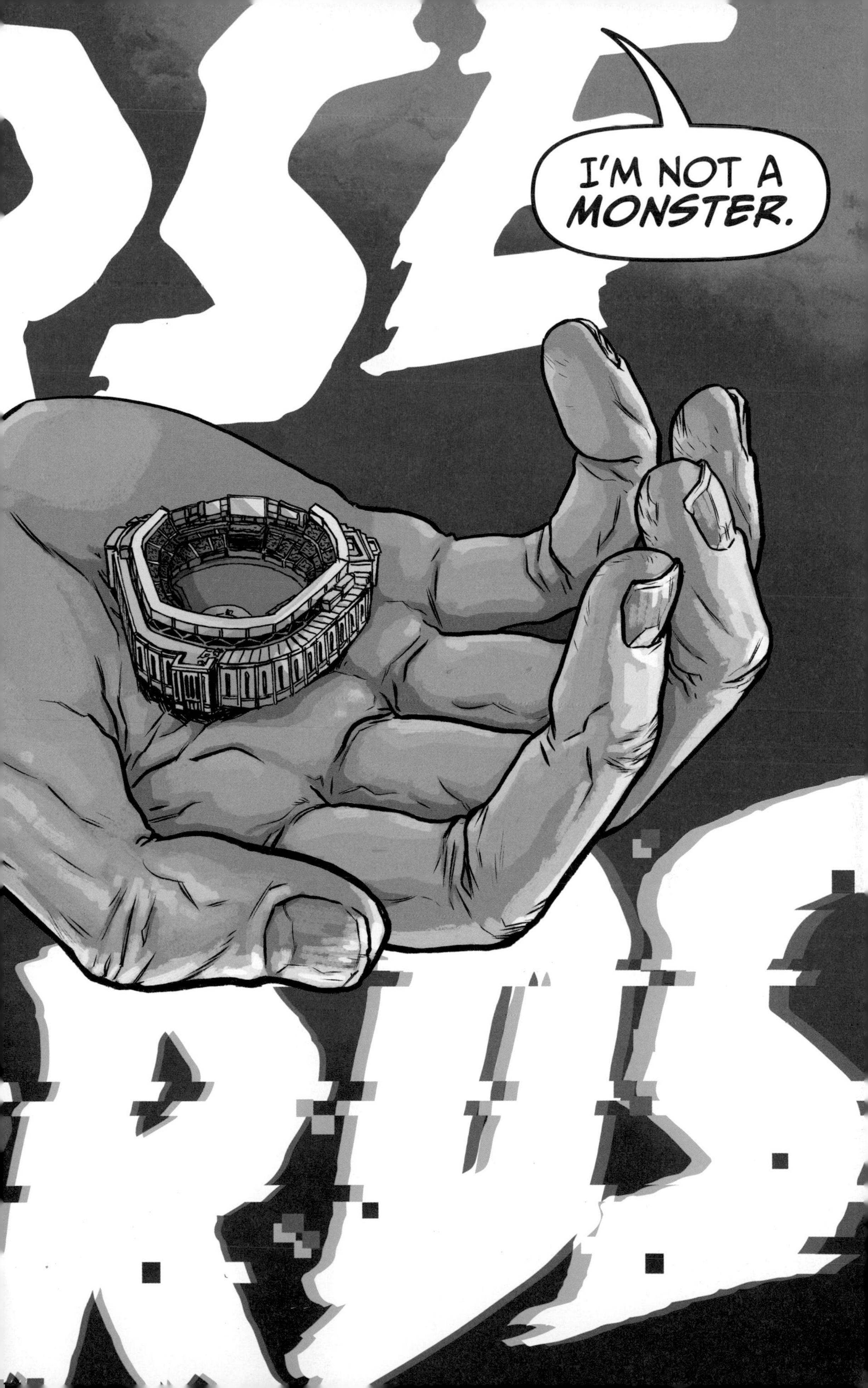
I'M NOT A MONSTER.

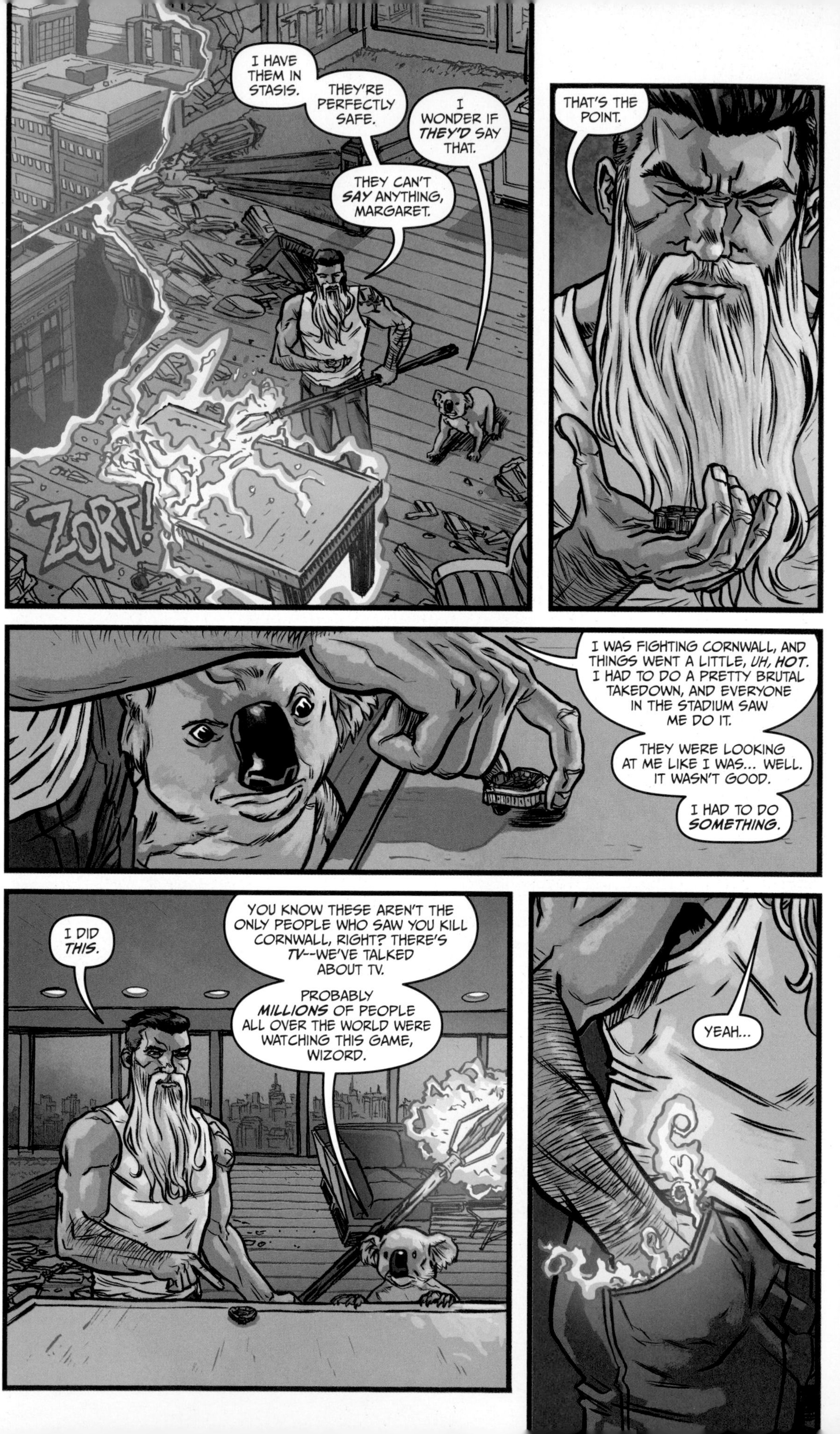
I HAVE THEM IN STASIS.
THEY'RE PERFECTLY SAFE.
I WONDER IF *THEY'D* SAY THAT.
THEY CAN'T *SAY* ANYTHING, MARGARET.
ZORT!
THAT'S THE POINT.
I WAS FIGHTING CORNWALL, AND THINGS WENT A LITTLE, *UH, HOT*. I HAD TO DO A PRETTY BRUTAL TAKEDOWN, AND EVERYONE IN THE STADIUM SAW ME DO IT.
THEY WERE LOOKING AT ME LIKE I WAS... WELL. IT WASN'T GOOD.
I HAD TO DO *SOMETHING*.
I DID *THIS*.
YOU KNOW THESE AREN'T THE ONLY PEOPLE WHO SAW YOU KILL CORNWALL, RIGHT? THERE'S *TV*--WE'VE TALKED ABOUT TV.
PROBABLY *MILLIONS* OF PEOPLE ALL OVER THE WORLD WERE WATCHING THIS GAME, WIZORD.
YEAH...

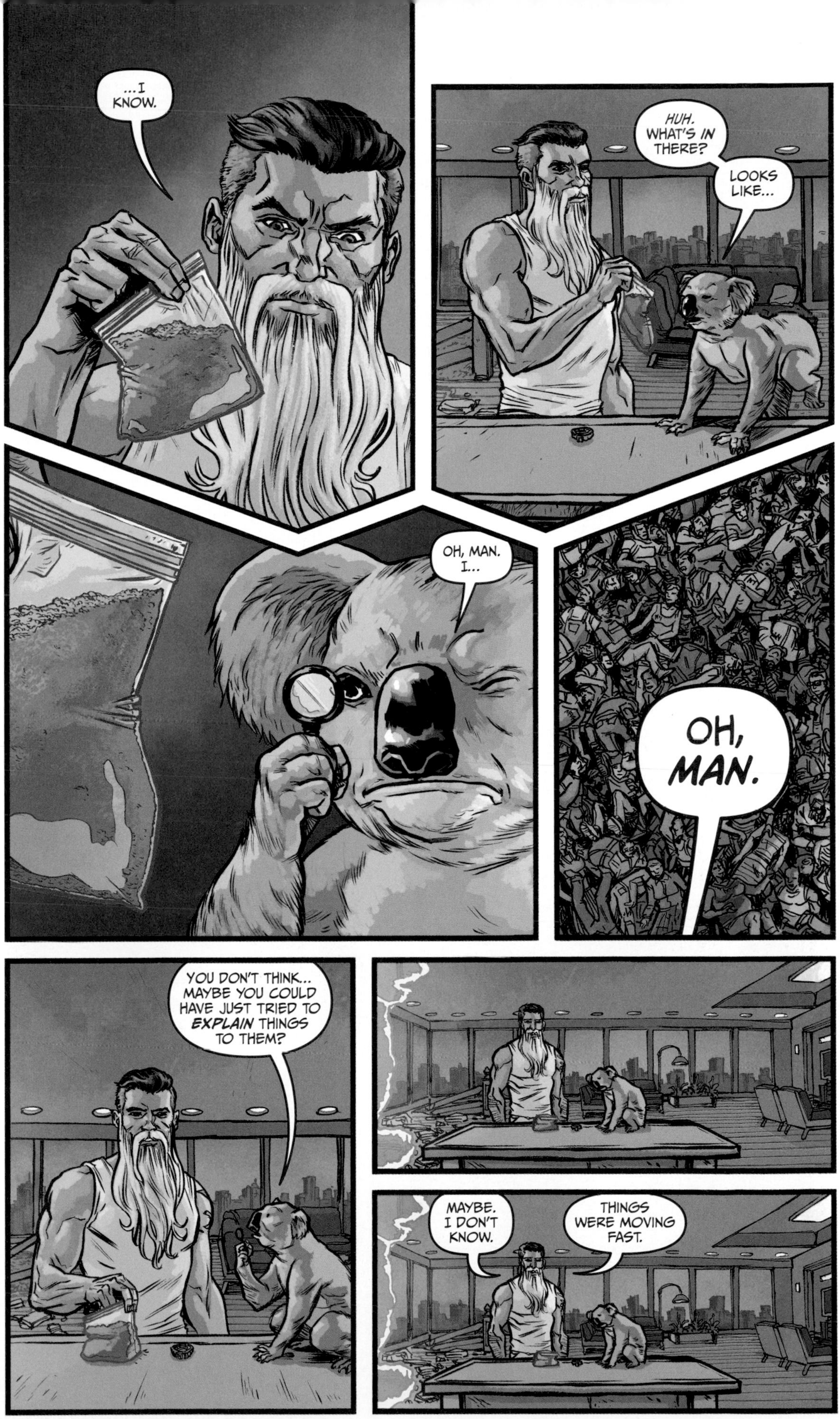
...I KNOW.
HUH. WHAT'S *IN* THERE?
LOOKS LIKE...
OH, MAN. I...
OH, *MAN.*
YOU DON'T THINK... MAYBE YOU COULD HAVE JUST TRIED TO *EXPLAIN* THINGS TO THEM?
MAYBE. I DON'T KNOW.
THINGS WERE MOVING FAST.

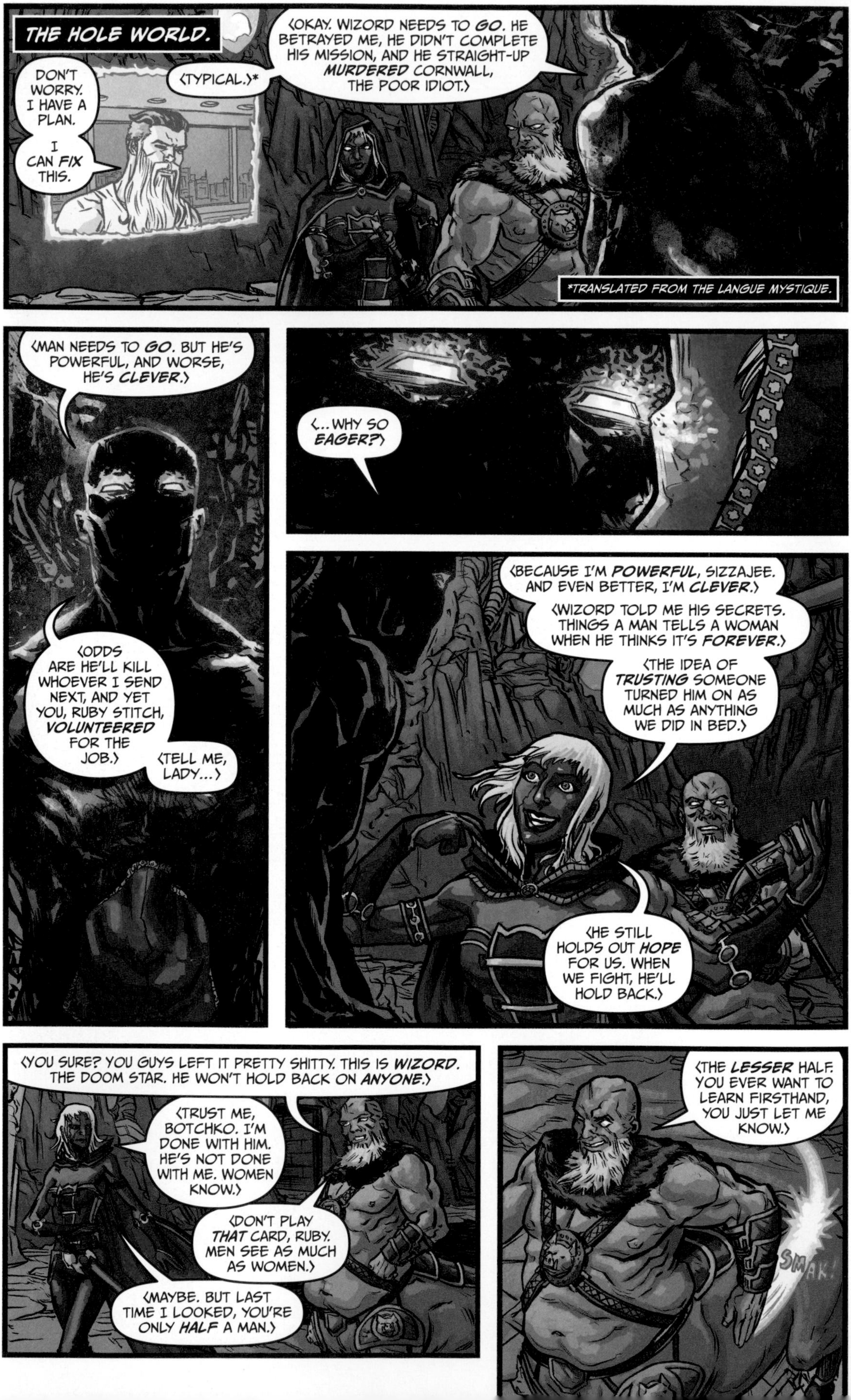
THE HOLE WORLD.
DON'T WORRY. I HAVE A PLAN.
I CAN *FIX* THIS.
<TYPICAL.>*
<OKAY. WIZORD NEEDS TO *GO*. HE BETRAYED ME, HE DIDN'T COMPLETE HIS MISSION, AND HE STRAIGHT-UP *MURDERED* CORNWALL, THE POOR IDIOT.>
*TRANSLATED FROM THE LANGUE MYSTIQUE.
<MAN NEEDS TO *GO*. BUT HE'S POWERFUL, AND WORSE, HE'S *CLEVER*.>
<ODDS ARE HE'LL KILL WHOEVER I SEND NEXT, AND YET YOU, RUBY STITCH, ***VOLUNTEERED*** FOR THE JOB.>
<TELL ME, LADY...>
<...WHY SO *EAGER?*>
<BECAUSE I'M *POWERFUL*, SIZZAJEE. AND EVEN BETTER, I'M *CLEVER*.>
<WIZORD TOLD ME HIS SECRETS. THINGS A MAN TELLS A WOMAN WHEN HE THINKS IT'S *FOREVER*.>
<THE IDEA OF *TRUSTING* SOMEONE TURNED HIM ON AS MUCH AS ANYTHING WE DID IN BED.>
<HE STILL HOLDS OUT *HOPE* FOR US. WHEN WE FIGHT, HE'LL HOLD BACK.>
<YOU SURE? YOU GUYS LEFT IT PRETTY SHITTY. THIS IS *WIZORD*. THE DOOM STAR. HE WON'T HOLD BACK ON *ANYONE*.>
<TRUST ME, BOTCHKO. I'M DONE WITH HIM. HE'S NOT DONE WITH ME. WOMEN KNOW.>
<DON'T PLAY *THAT* CARD, RUBY. MEN SEE AS MUCH AS WOMEN.>
<MAYBE. BUT LAST TIME I LOOKED, YOU'RE ONLY *HALF* A MAN.>
<THE *LESSER* HALF. YOU EVER WANT TO LEARN FIRSTHAND, YOU JUST LET ME KNOW.>
SMAK!

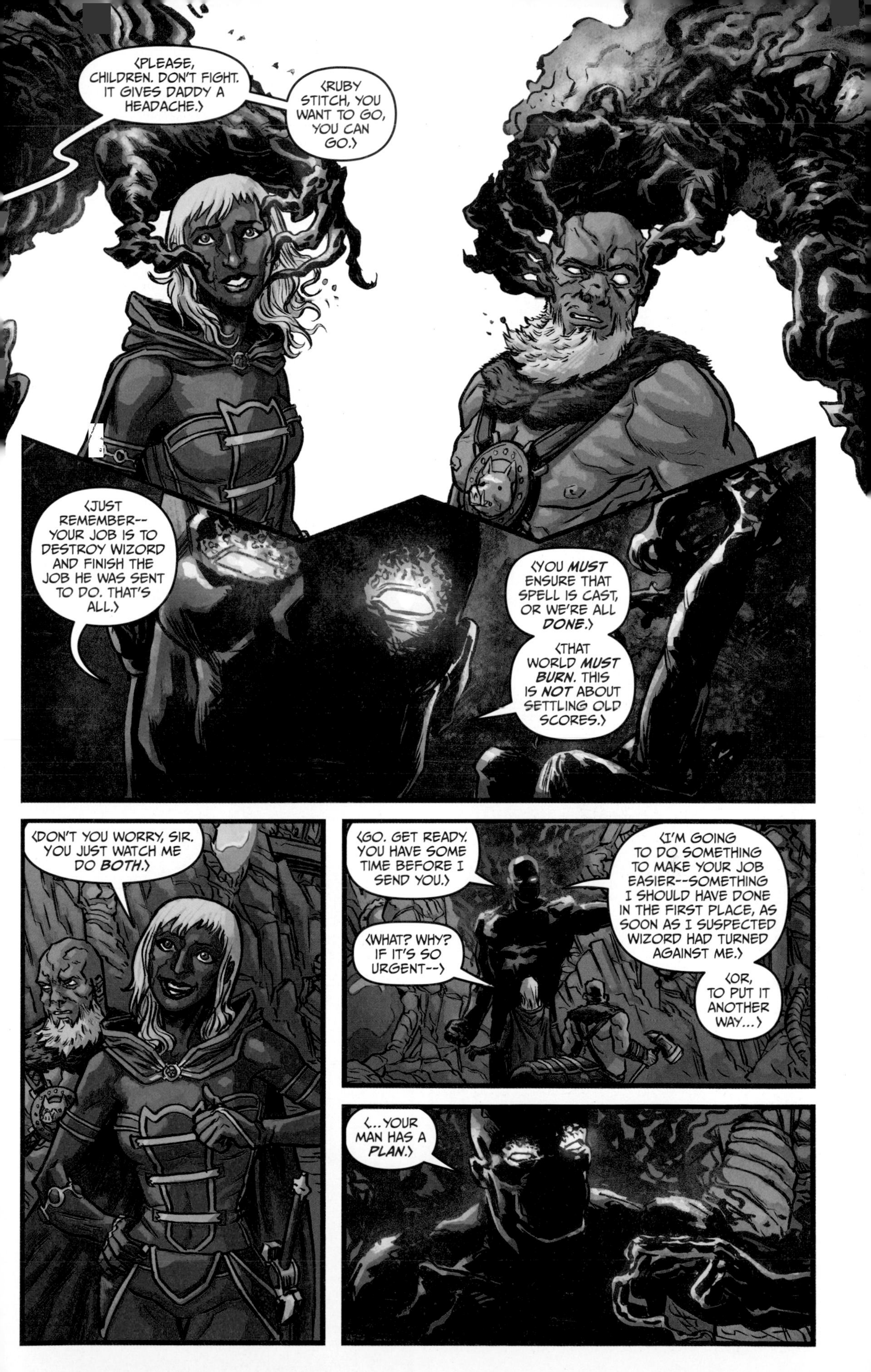
⟨PLEASE, CHILDREN. DON'T FIGHT. IT GIVES DADDY A HEADACHE.⟩
⟨RUBY STITCH, YOU WANT TO GO, YOU CAN GO.⟩
⟨JUST REMEMBER-- YOUR JOB IS TO DESTROY WIZORD AND FINISH THE JOB HE WAS SENT TO DO. THAT'S ALL.⟩
⟨YOU MUST ENSURE THAT SPELL IS CAST, OR WE'RE ALL DONE.⟩
⟨THAT WORLD MUST BURN. THIS IS NOT ABOUT SETTLING OLD SCORES.⟩
⟨DON'T YOU WORRY, SIR. YOU JUST WATCH ME DO BOTH.⟩
⟨GO. GET READY. YOU HAVE SOME TIME BEFORE I SEND YOU.⟩
⟨WHAT? WHY? IF IT'S SO URGENT--⟩
⟨I'M GOING TO DO SOMETHING TO MAKE YOUR JOB EASIER--SOMETHING I SHOULD HAVE DONE IN THE FIRST PLACE, AS SOON AS I SUSPECTED WIZORD HAD TURNED AGAINST ME.⟩
⟨OR, TO PUT IT ANOTHER WAY...⟩
⟨...YOUR MAN HAS A PLAN.⟩

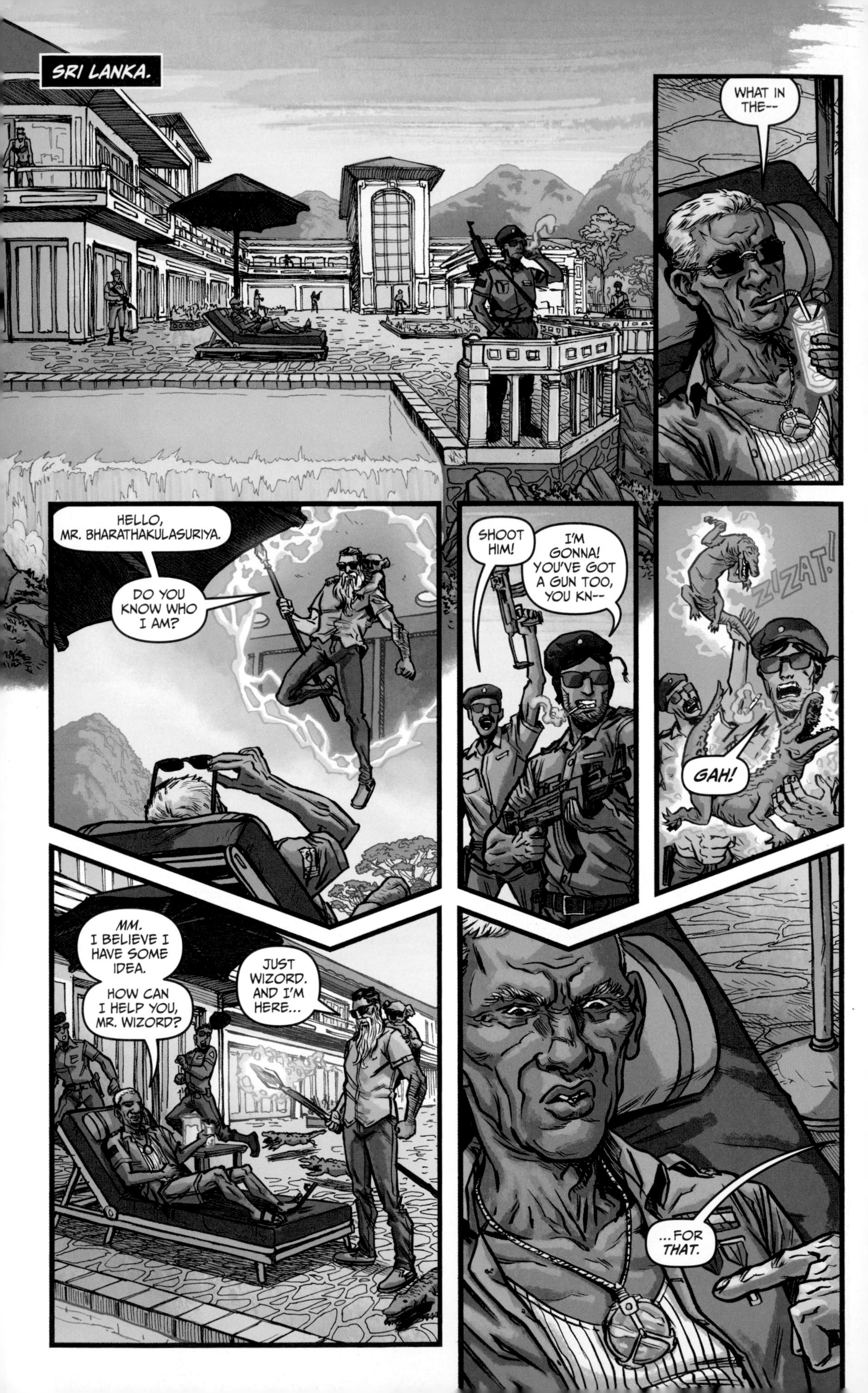
SRI LANKA.
WHAT IN THE--
HELLO, MR. BHARATHAKULASURIYA.
DO YOU KNOW WHO I AM?
SHOOT HIM!
I'M GONNA! YOU'VE GOT A GUN TOO, YOU KN--
ZIZAT!
GAH!
MM. I BELIEVE I HAVE SOME IDEA.
HOW CAN I HELP YOU, MR. WIZORD?
JUST WIZORD. AND I'M HERE...
...FOR THAT.

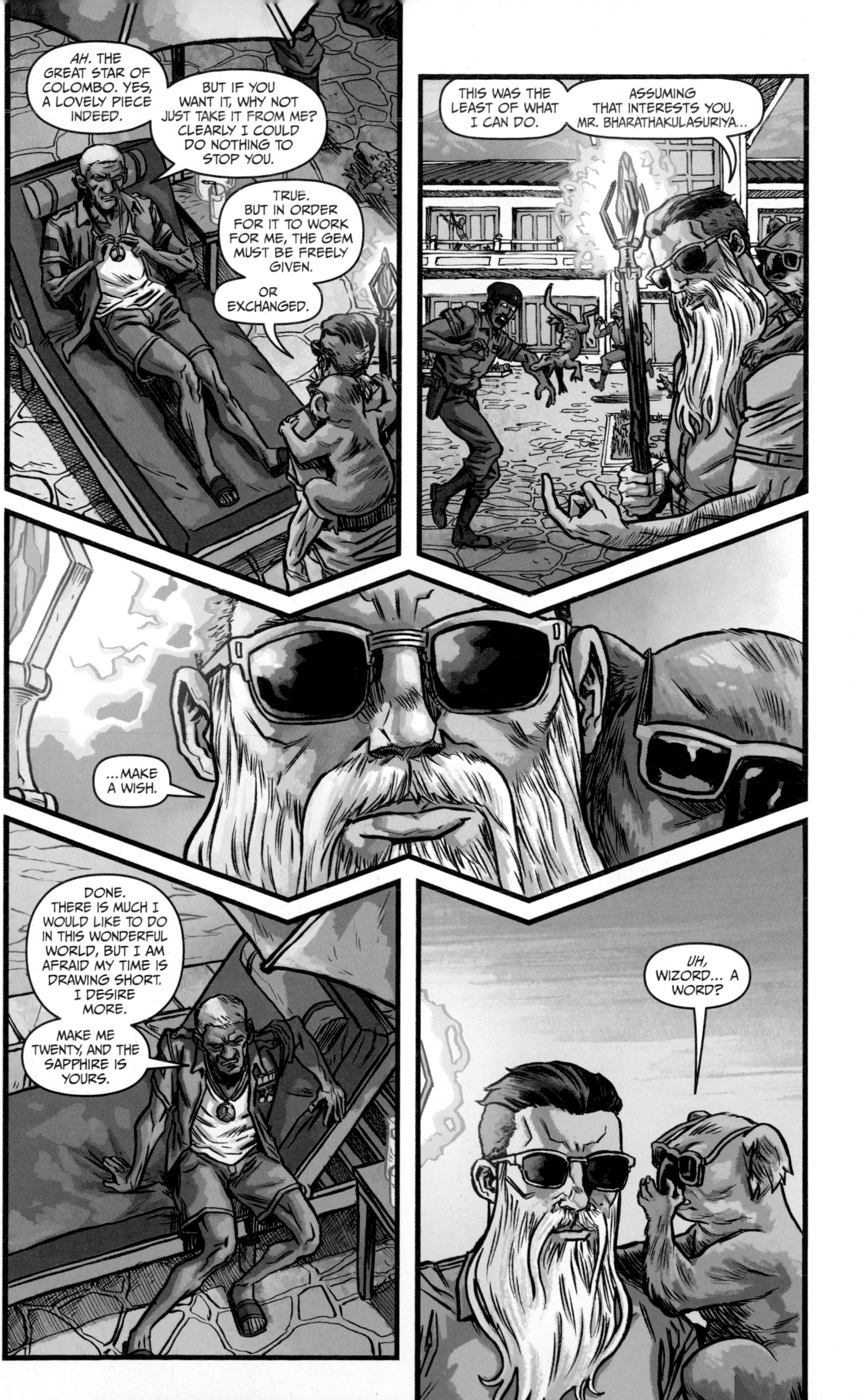

AH. THE GREAT STAR OF COLOMBO. YES, A LOVELY PIECE INDEED.
BUT IF YOU WANT IT, WHY NOT JUST TAKE IT FROM ME? CLEARLY I COULD DO NOTHING TO STOP YOU.
TRUE. BUT IN ORDER FOR IT TO WORK FOR ME, THE GEM MUST BE FREELY GIVEN.
OR EXCHANGED.
THIS WAS THE LEAST OF WHAT I CAN DO.
ASSUMING THAT INTERESTS YOU, MR. BHARATHAKULASURIYA...
...MAKE A WISH.
DONE. THERE IS MUCH I WOULD LIKE TO DO IN THIS WONDERFUL WORLD, BUT I AM AFRAID MY TIME IS DRAWING SHORT. I DESIRE MORE.
MAKE ME TWENTY, AND THE SAPPHIRE IS YOURS.
UH, WIZORD... A WORD?

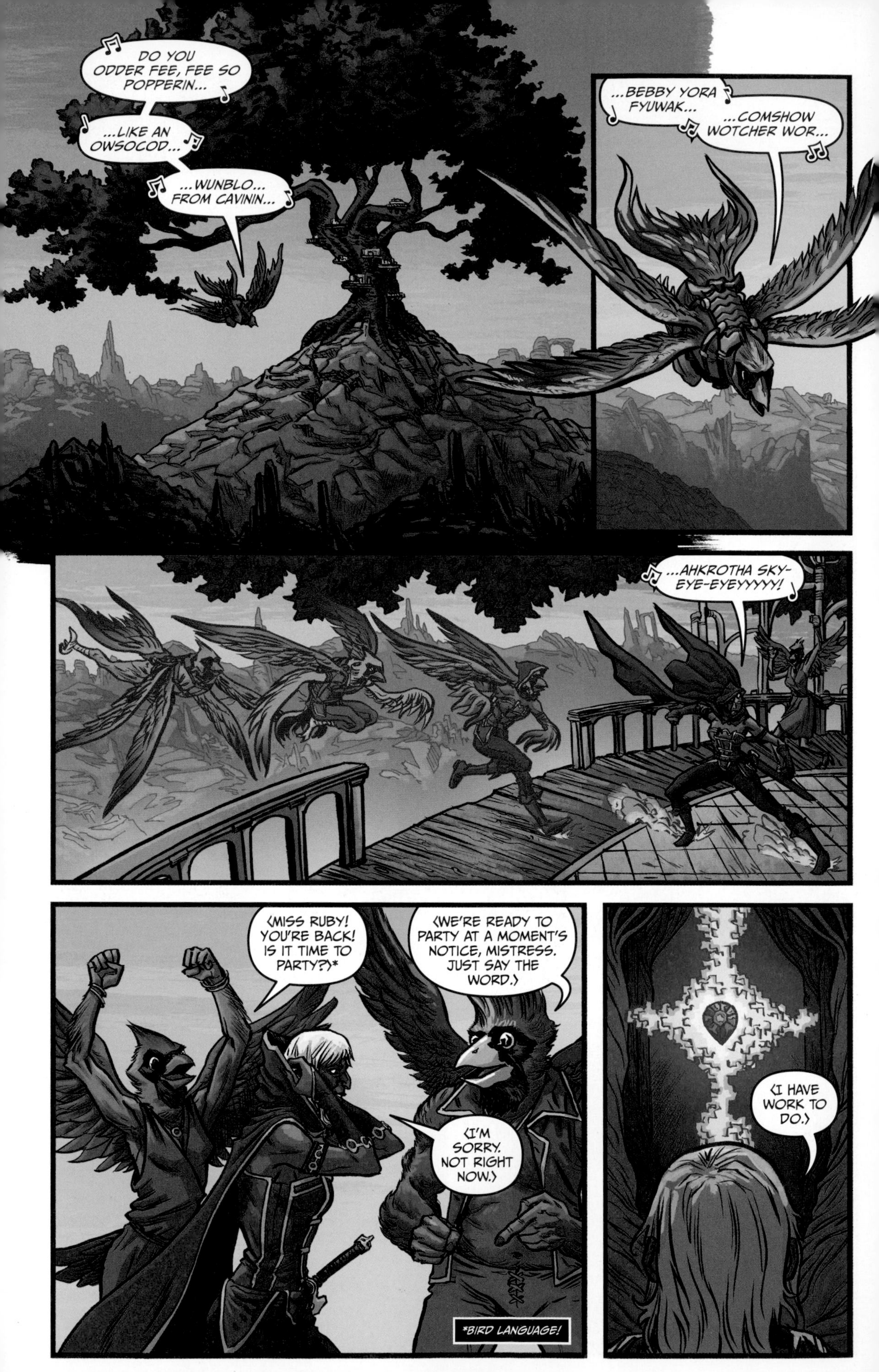
DO YOU ODDER FEE, FEE SO POPPERIN...
...LIKE AN OWSOCOD...
...WUNBLO... FROM CAVININ...
...BEBBY YORA FYUWAK...
...COMSHOW WOTCHER WOR...
...AHKROTHA SKY-EYE-EYEYYYYY!
⟨MISS RUBY! YOU'RE BACK! IS IT TIME TO PARTY?⟩*
⟨WE'RE READY TO PARTY AT A MOMENT'S NOTICE, MISTRESS. JUST SAY THE WORD.⟩
⟨I'M SORRY. NOT RIGHT NOW.⟩
*BIRD LANGUAGE!
⟨I HAVE WORK TO DO.⟩

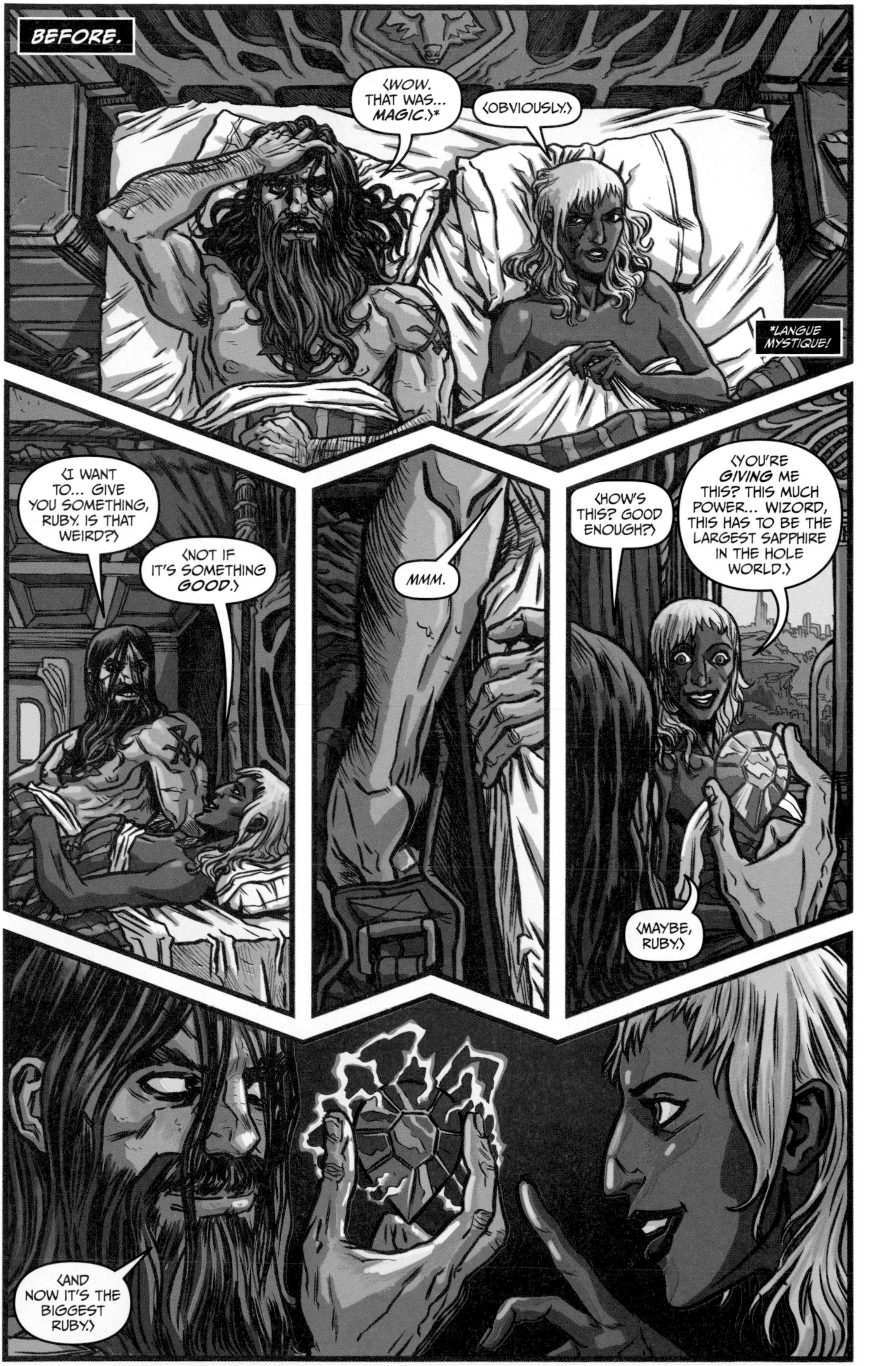
BEFORE.
⟨WOW. THAT WAS... MAGIC.⟩*
⟨OBVIOUSLY.⟩
*LANGUE MYSTIQUE!
⟨I WANT TO... GIVE YOU SOMETHING, RUBY. IS THAT WEIRD?⟩
⟨NOT IF IT'S SOMETHING GOOD.⟩
MMM.
⟨HOW'S THIS? GOOD ENOUGH?⟩
⟨YOU'RE GIVING ME THIS? THIS MUCH POWER... WIZORD, THIS HAS TO BE THE LARGEST SAPPHIRE IN THE HOLE WORLD.⟩
⟨MAYBE, RUBY.⟩
⟨AND NOW IT'S THE BIGGEST RUBY.⟩

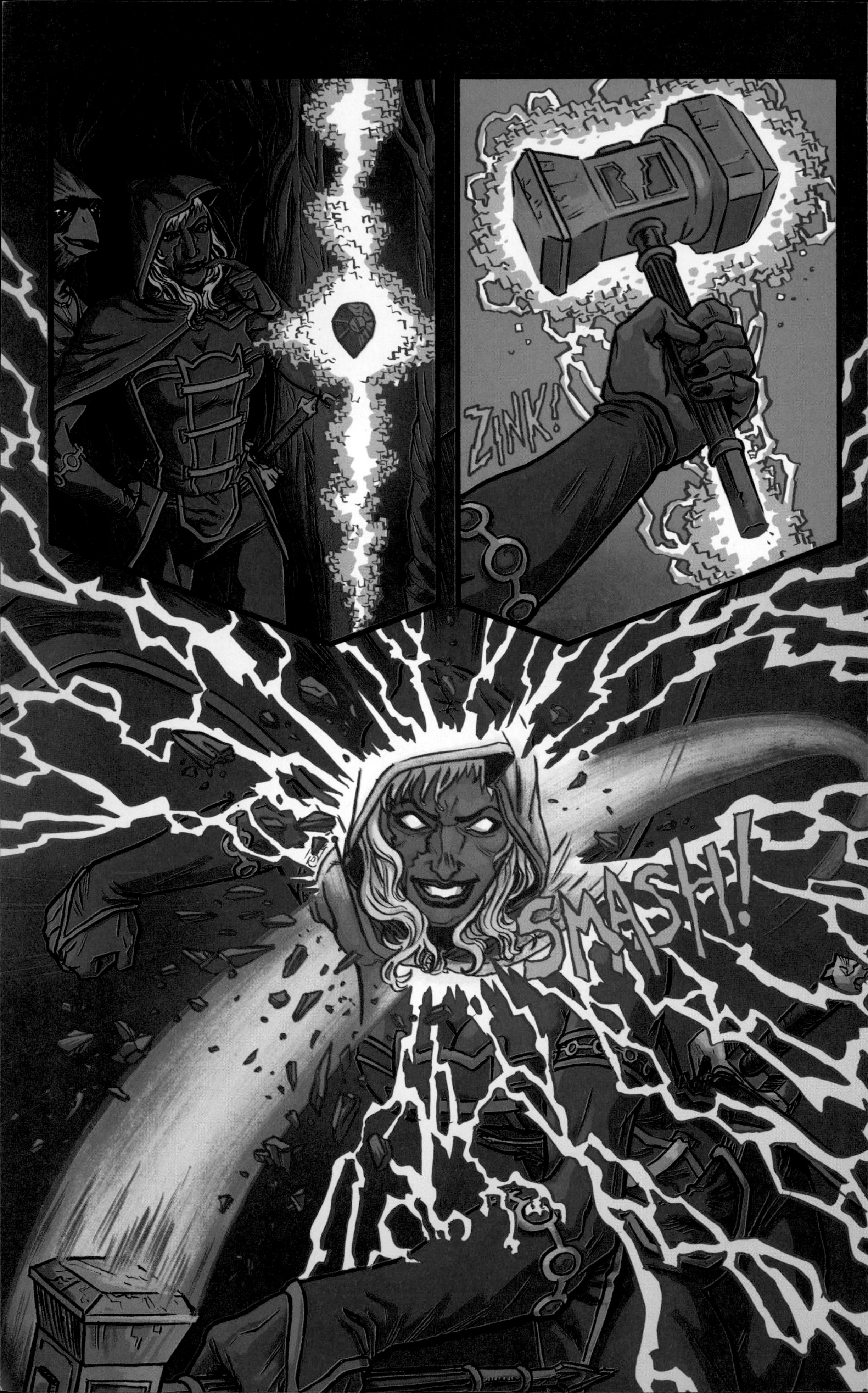
ZINK!
SMASH!

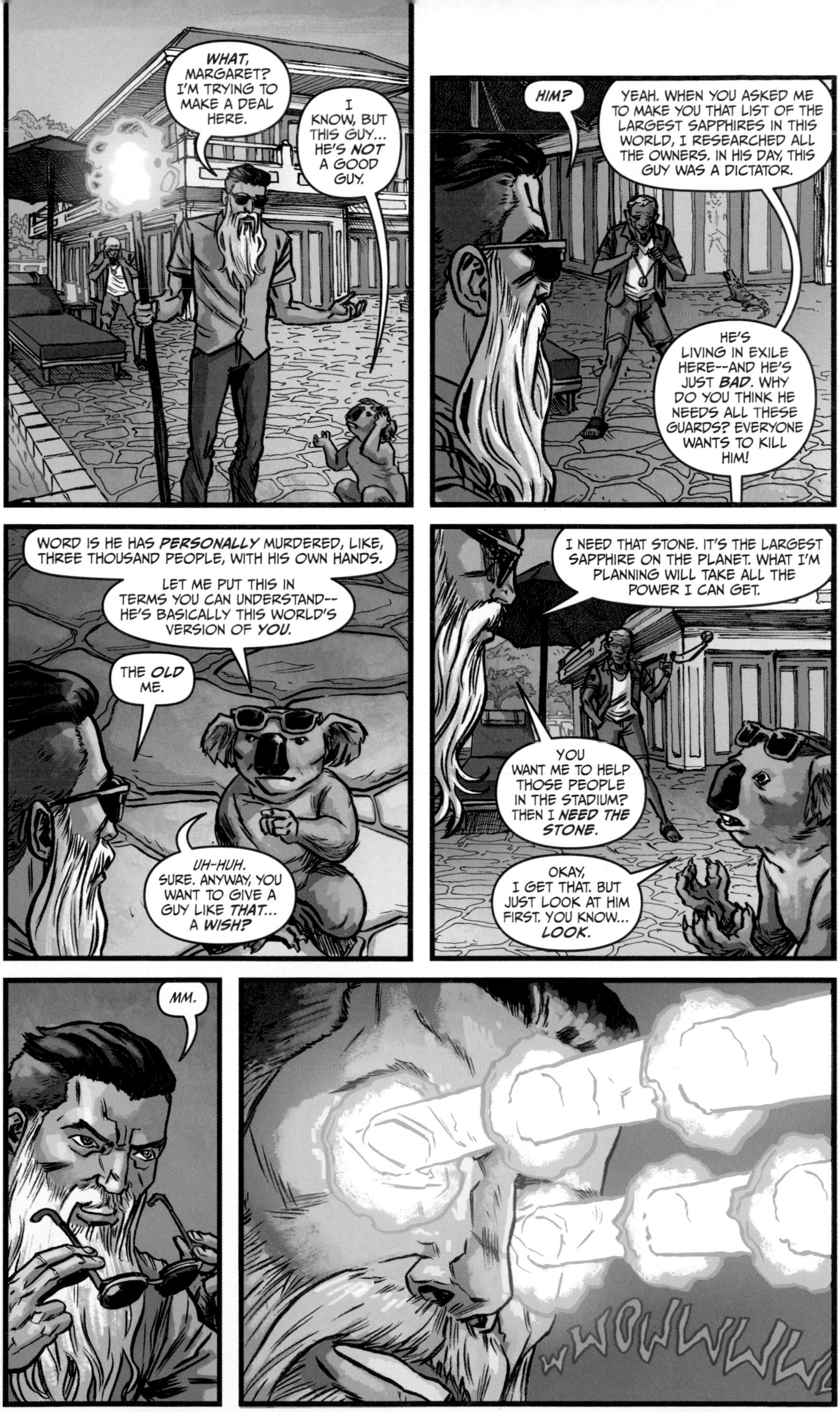
WHAT, MARGARET? I'M TRYING TO MAKE A DEAL HERE.
I KNOW, BUT THIS GUY... HE'S NOT A GOOD GUY.
HIM?
YEAH. WHEN YOU ASKED ME TO MAKE YOU THAT LIST OF THE LARGEST SAPPHIRES IN THIS WORLD, I RESEARCHED ALL THE OWNERS. IN HIS DAY, THIS GUY WAS A DICTATOR.
HE'S LIVING IN EXILE HERE--AND HE'S JUST BAD. WHY DO YOU THINK HE NEEDS ALL THESE GUARDS? EVERYONE WANTS TO KILL HIM!
WORD IS HE HAS PERSONALLY MURDERED, LIKE, THREE THOUSAND PEOPLE, WITH HIS OWN HANDS.
LET ME PUT THIS IN TERMS YOU CAN UNDERSTAND--HE'S BASICALLY THIS WORLD'S VERSION OF YOU.
THE OLD ME.
UH-HUH. SURE. ANYWAY, YOU WANT TO GIVE A GUY LIKE THAT... A WISH?
I NEED THAT STONE. IT'S THE LARGEST SAPPHIRE ON THE PLANET. WHAT I'M PLANNING WILL TAKE ALL THE POWER I CAN GET.
YOU WANT ME TO HELP THOSE PEOPLE IN THE STADIUM? THEN I NEED THE STONE.
OKAY, I GET THAT. BUT JUST LOOK AT HIM FIRST. YOU KNOW... LOOK.
MM.
WWOWWWWW

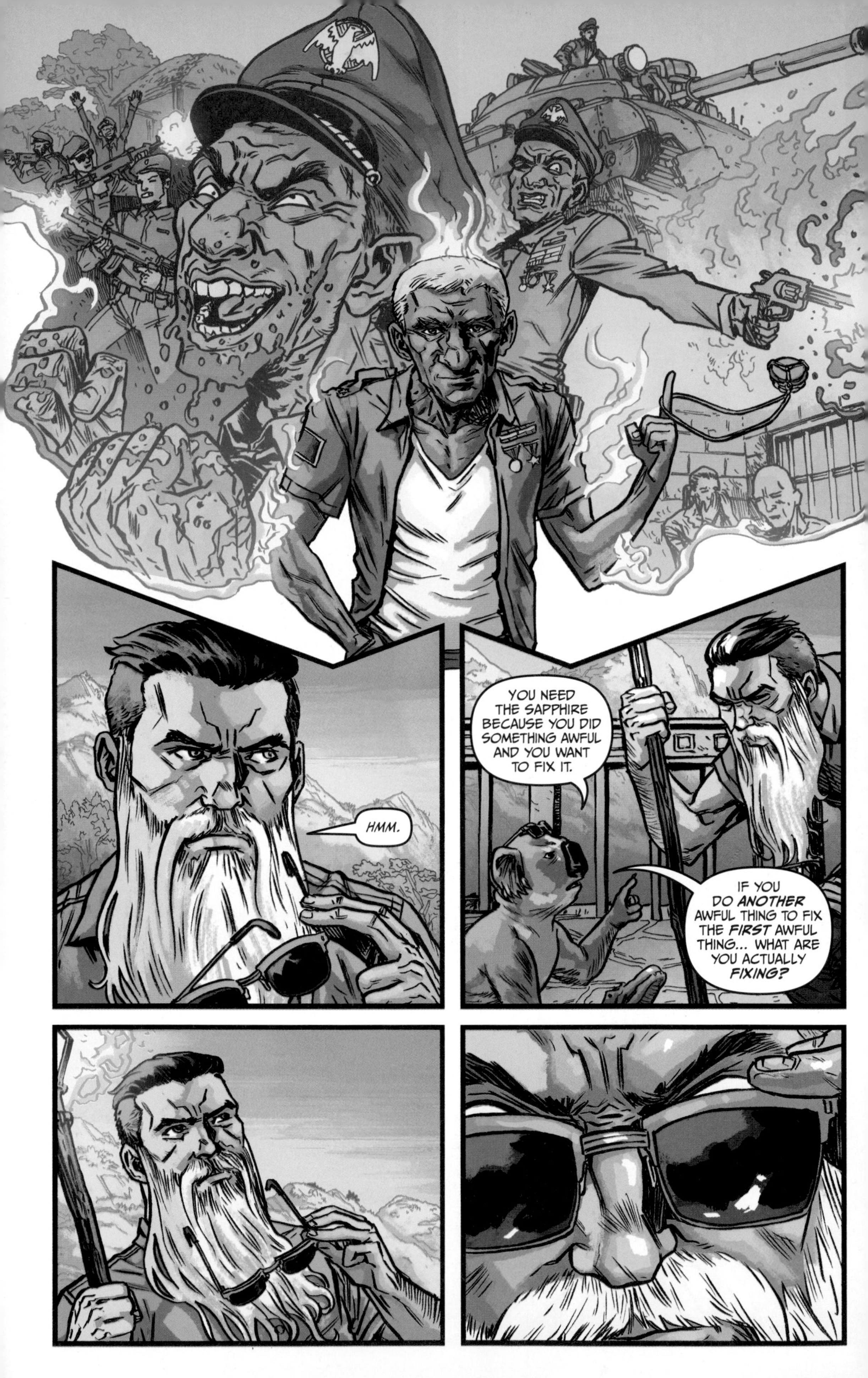
HMM.
YOU NEED THE SAPPHIRE BECAUSE YOU DID SOMETHING AWFUL AND YOU WANT TO FIX IT.
IF YOU DO ANOTHER AWFUL THING TO FIX THE FIRST AWFUL THING... WHAT ARE YOU ACTUALLY FIXING?

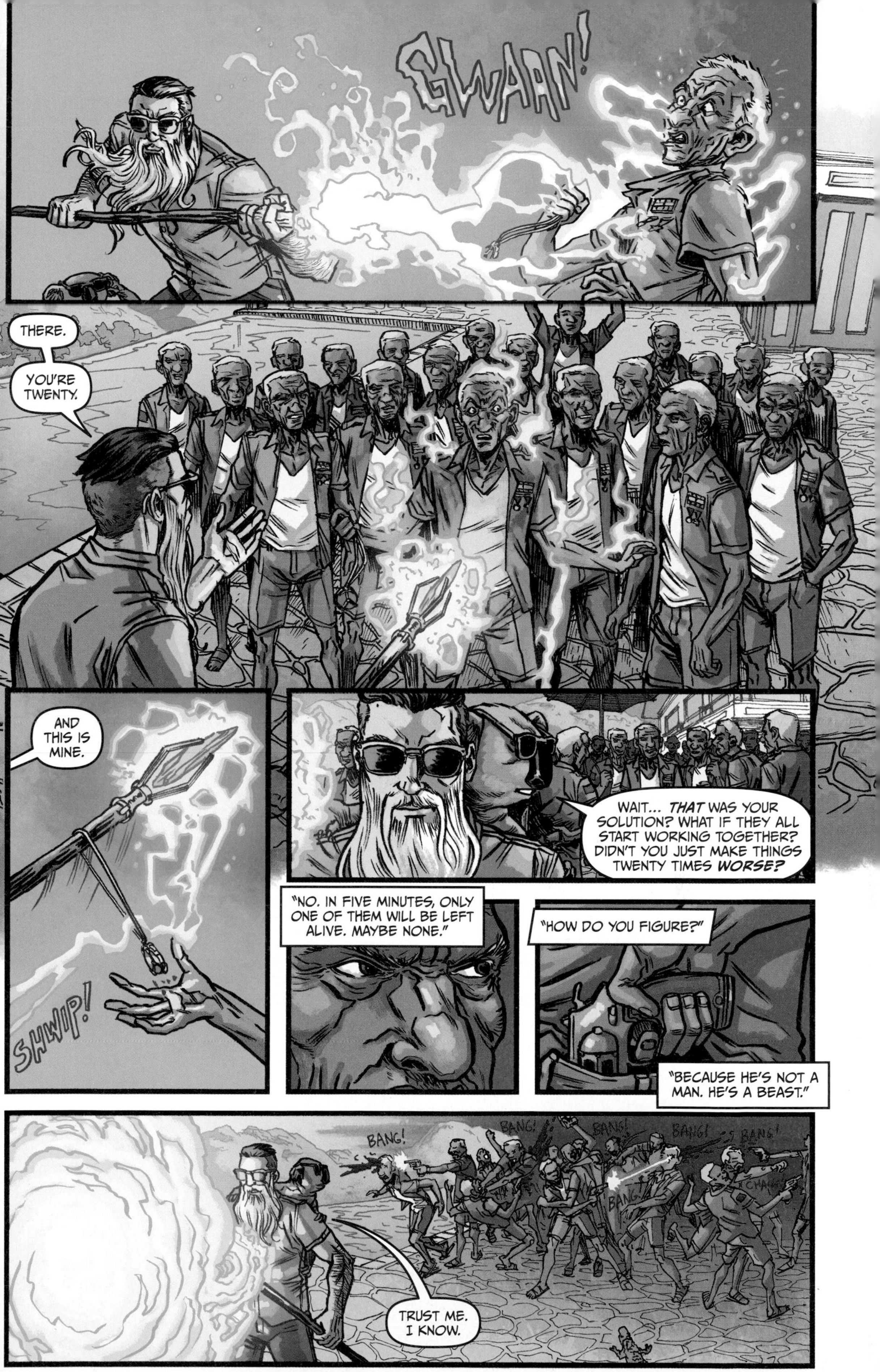
GWAAN!
THERE.
YOU'RE TWENTY.
AND THIS IS MINE.
SHWIP!
WAIT... THAT WAS YOUR SOLUTION? WHAT IF THEY ALL START WORKING TOGETHER? DIDN'T YOU JUST MAKE THINGS TWENTY TIMES WORSE?
"NO. IN FIVE MINUTES, ONLY ONE OF THEM WILL BE LEFT ALIVE. MAYBE NONE."
"HOW DO YOU FIGURE?"
"BECAUSE HE'S NOT A MAN. HE'S A BEAST."
BANG!
BANG!
BANG!
BANG!
BANG!
TRUST ME. I KNOW.

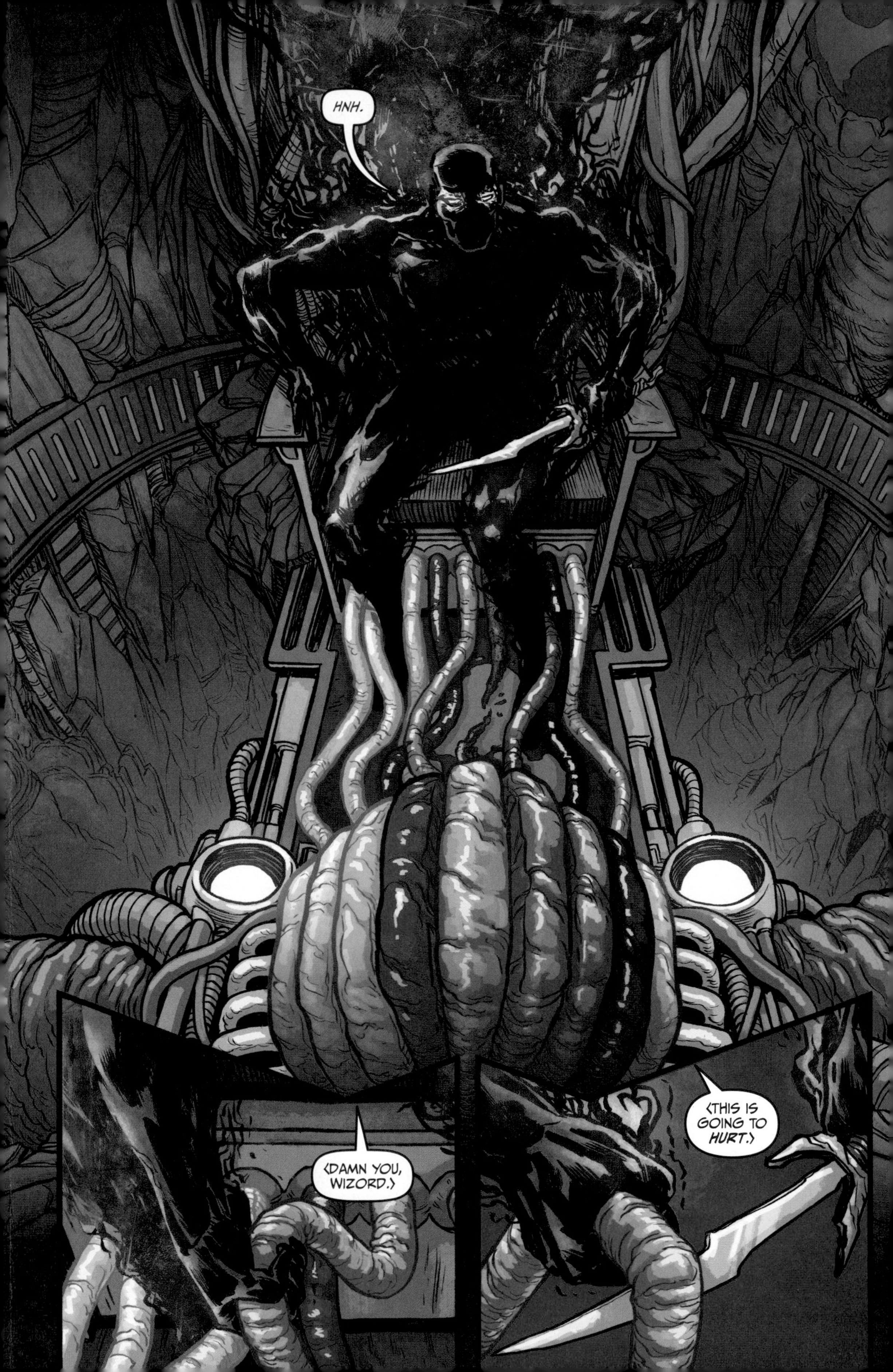
HNH.
⟨DAMN YOU, WIZORD.⟩
⟨THIS IS GOING TO HURT.⟩

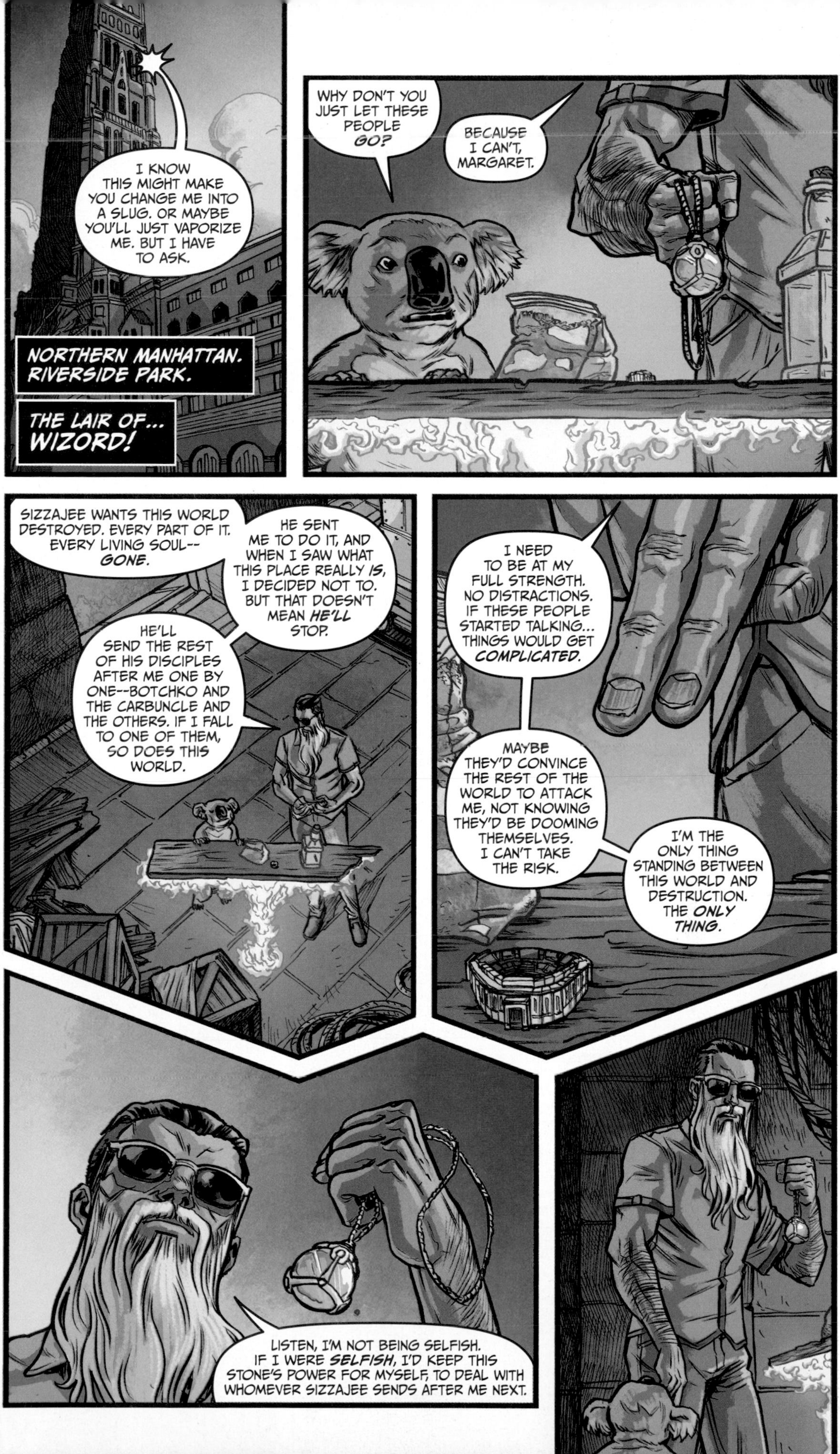
I KNOW THIS MIGHT MAKE YOU CHANGE ME INTO A SLUG. OR MAYBE YOU'LL JUST VAPORIZE ME. BUT I HAVE TO ASK.
NORTHERN MANHATTAN. RIVERSIDE PARK.
THE LAIR OF... WIZORD!
WHY DON'T YOU JUST LET THESE PEOPLE GO?
BECAUSE I CAN'T, MARGARET.
SIZZAJEE WANTS THIS WORLD DESTROYED. EVERY PART OF IT. EVERY LIVING SOUL-- GONE.
HE SENT ME TO DO IT, AND WHEN I SAW WHAT THIS PLACE REALLY IS, I DECIDED NOT TO. BUT THAT DOESN'T MEAN HE'LL STOP.
HE'LL SEND THE REST OF HIS DISCIPLES AFTER ME ONE BY ONE--BOTCHKO AND THE CARBUNCLE AND THE OTHERS. IF I FALL TO ONE OF THEM, SO DOES THIS WORLD.
I NEED TO BE AT MY FULL STRENGTH. NO DISTRACTIONS. IF THESE PEOPLE STARTED TALKING... THINGS WOULD GET COMPLICATED.
MAYBE THEY'D CONVINCE THE REST OF THE WORLD TO ATTACK ME, NOT KNOWING THEY'D BE DOOMING THEMSELVES. I CAN'T TAKE THE RISK.
I'M THE ONLY THING STANDING BETWEEN THIS WORLD AND DESTRUCTION. THE ONLY THING.
LISTEN, I'M NOT BEING SELFISH. IF I WERE SELFISH, I'D KEEP THIS STONE'S POWER FOR MYSELF, TO DEAL WITH WHOMEVER SIZZAJEE SENDS AFTER ME NEXT.

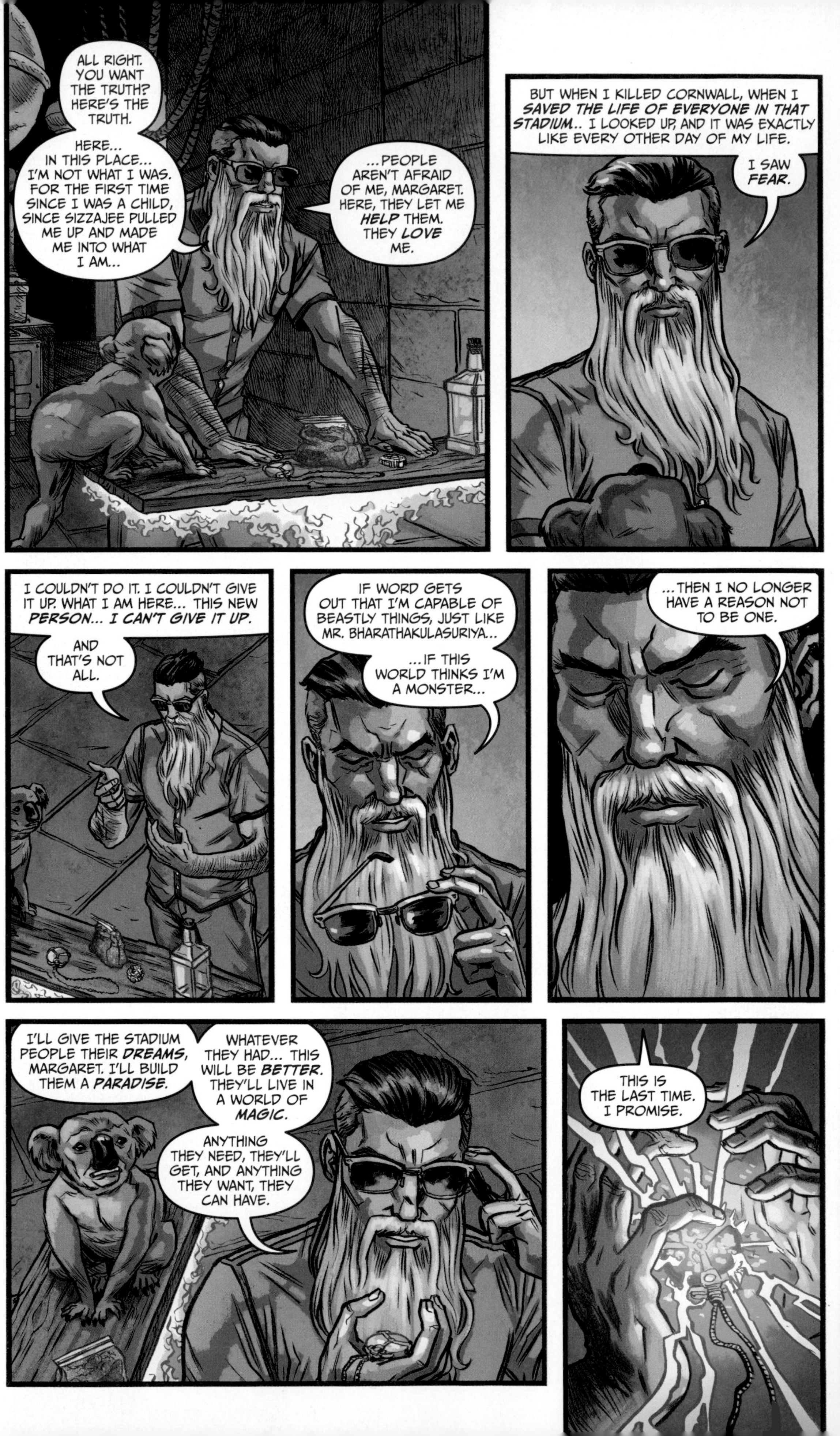
ALL RIGHT. YOU WANT THE TRUTH? HERE'S THE TRUTH.
HERE... IN THIS PLACE... I'M NOT WHAT I WAS. FOR THE FIRST TIME SINCE I WAS A CHILD, SINCE SIZZAJEE PULLED ME UP AND MADE ME INTO WHAT I AM...
...PEOPLE AREN'T AFRAID OF ME, MARGARET. HERE, THEY LET ME *HELP* THEM. THEY *LOVE* ME.
BUT WHEN I KILLED CORNWALL, WHEN I *SAVED THE LIFE OF EVERYONE IN THAT STADIUM*.. I LOOKED UP, AND IT WAS EXACTLY LIKE EVERY OTHER DAY OF MY LIFE.
I SAW *FEAR.*
I COULDN'T DO IT. I COULDN'T GIVE IT UP. WHAT I AM HERE... THIS NEW *PERSON... I CAN'T GIVE IT UP.*
AND THAT'S NOT ALL.
IF WORD GETS OUT THAT I'M CAPABLE OF BEASTLY THINGS, JUST LIKE MR. BHARATHAKULASURIYA...
...IF THIS WORLD THINKS I'M A MONSTER...
...THEN I NO LONGER HAVE A REASON NOT TO BE ONE.
I'LL GIVE THE STADIUM PEOPLE THEIR *DREAMS*, MARGARET. I'LL BUILD THEM A *PARADISE*.
WHATEVER THEY HAD... THIS WILL BE *BETTER*. THEY'LL LIVE IN A WORLD OF *MAGIC*.
ANYTHING THEY NEED, THEY'LL GET, AND ANYTHING THEY WANT, THEY CAN HAVE.
THIS IS THE LAST TIME. I PROMISE.

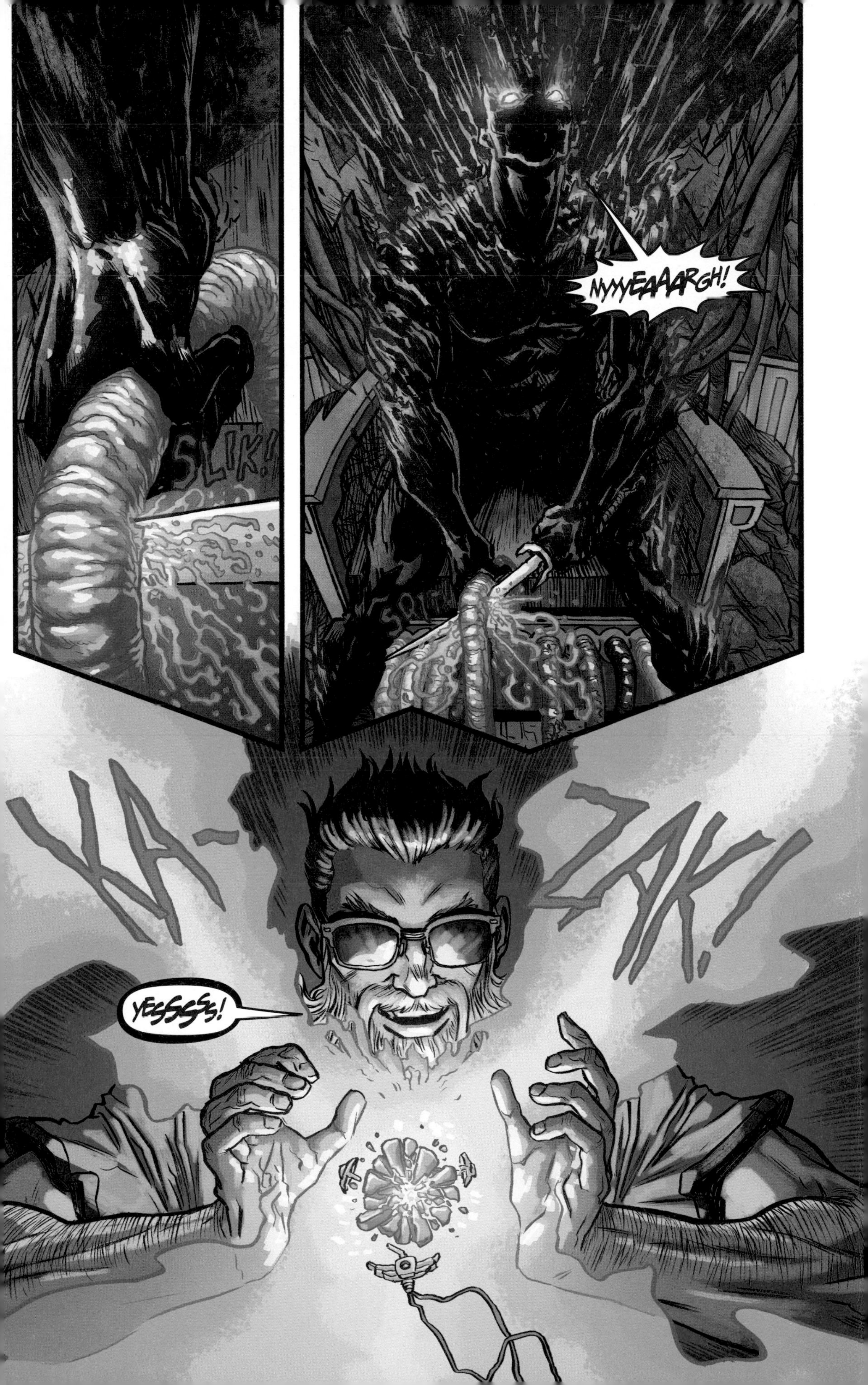
SLIK!
NYYYEAAARGH!
KA-ZAK!
YESSSSS!

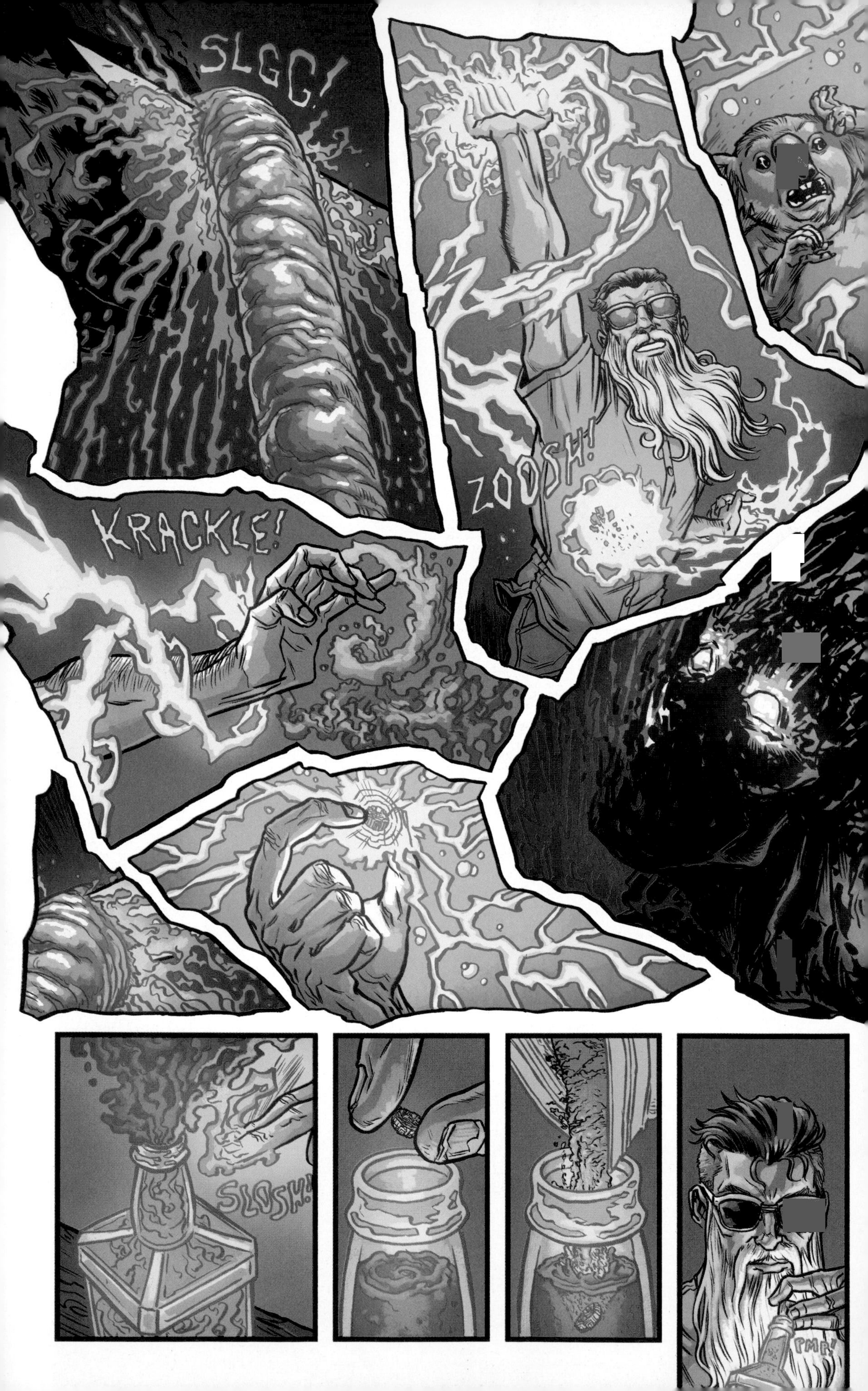
SLGG!
ZOOSH!
KRACKLE!
SLOSH!
PMP!

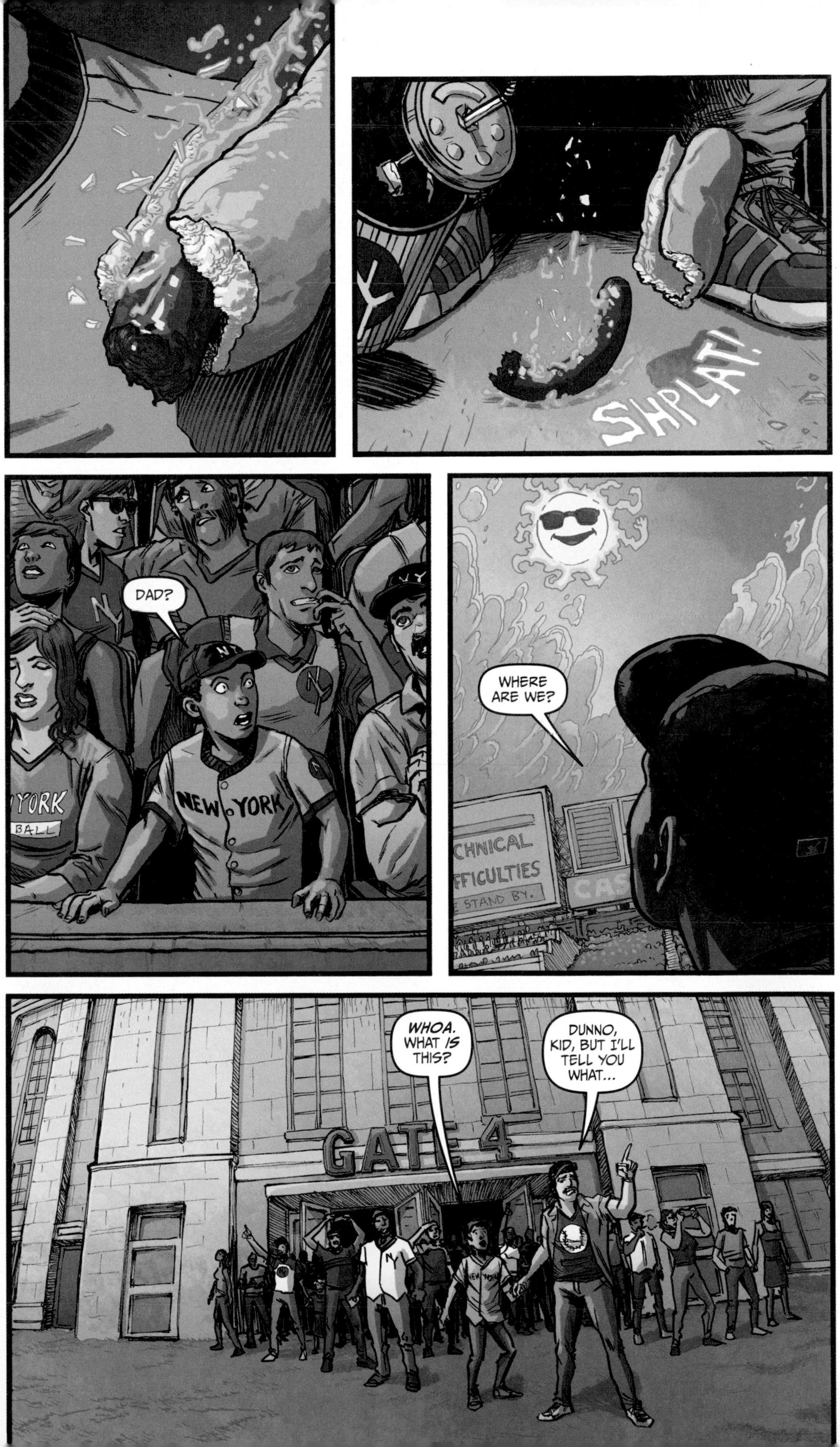
SHPLAT!
DAD?
NEW YORK
WHERE ARE WE?
GATE 4
WHOA. WHAT IS THIS?
DUNNO, KID, BUT I'LL TELL YOU WHAT...

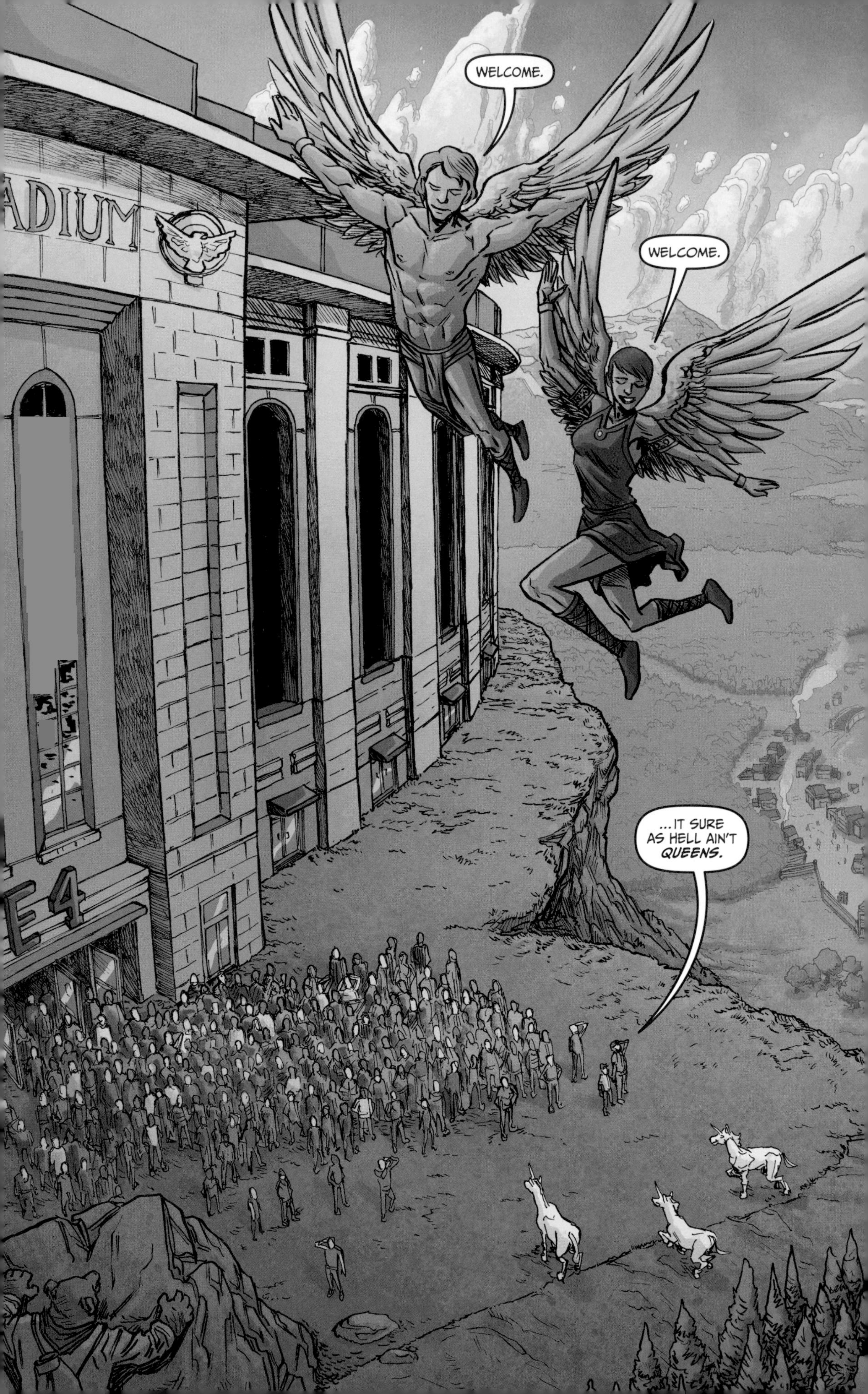
ADIUM
E4
WELCOME.
WELCOME.
...IT SURE AS HELL AIN'T *QUEENS.*

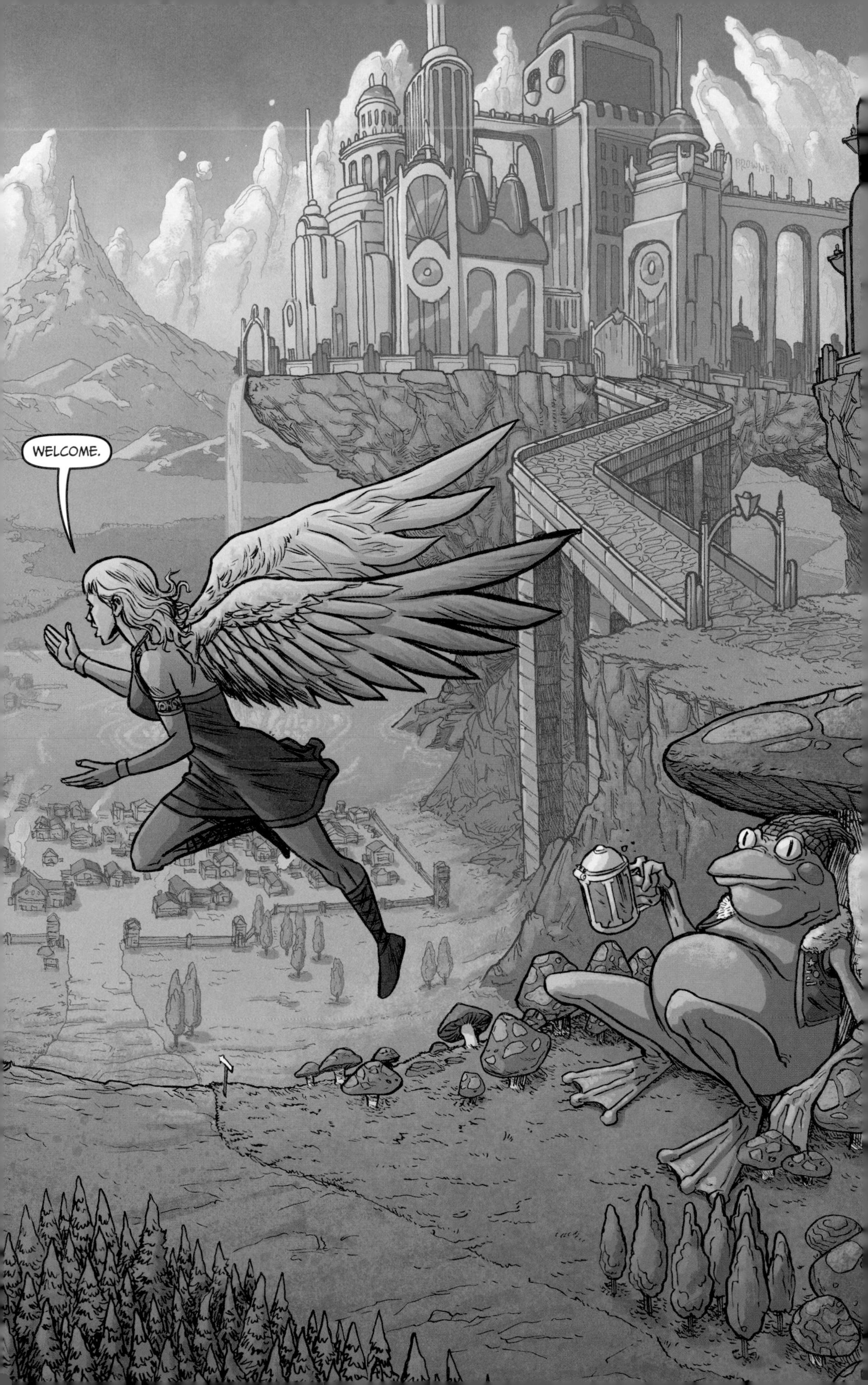
WELCOME.

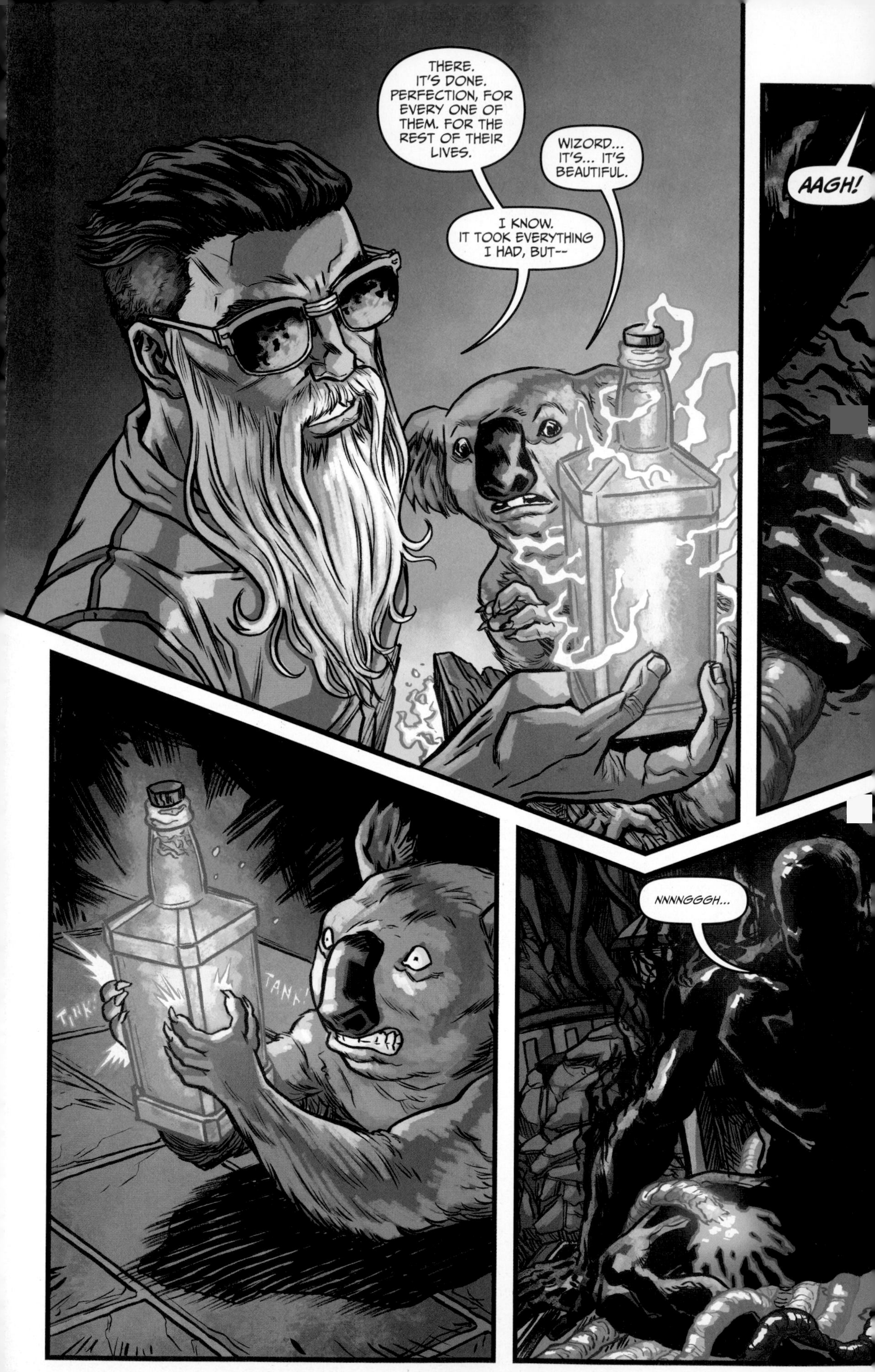
THERE. IT'S DONE. PERFECTION, FOR EVERY ONE OF THEM. FOR THE REST OF THEIR LIVES.
WIZORD... IT'S... IT'S BEAUTIFUL.
I KNOW. IT TOOK EVERYTHING I HAD, BUT--
AAGH!
TINK!
TANK!
NNNNGGGH...

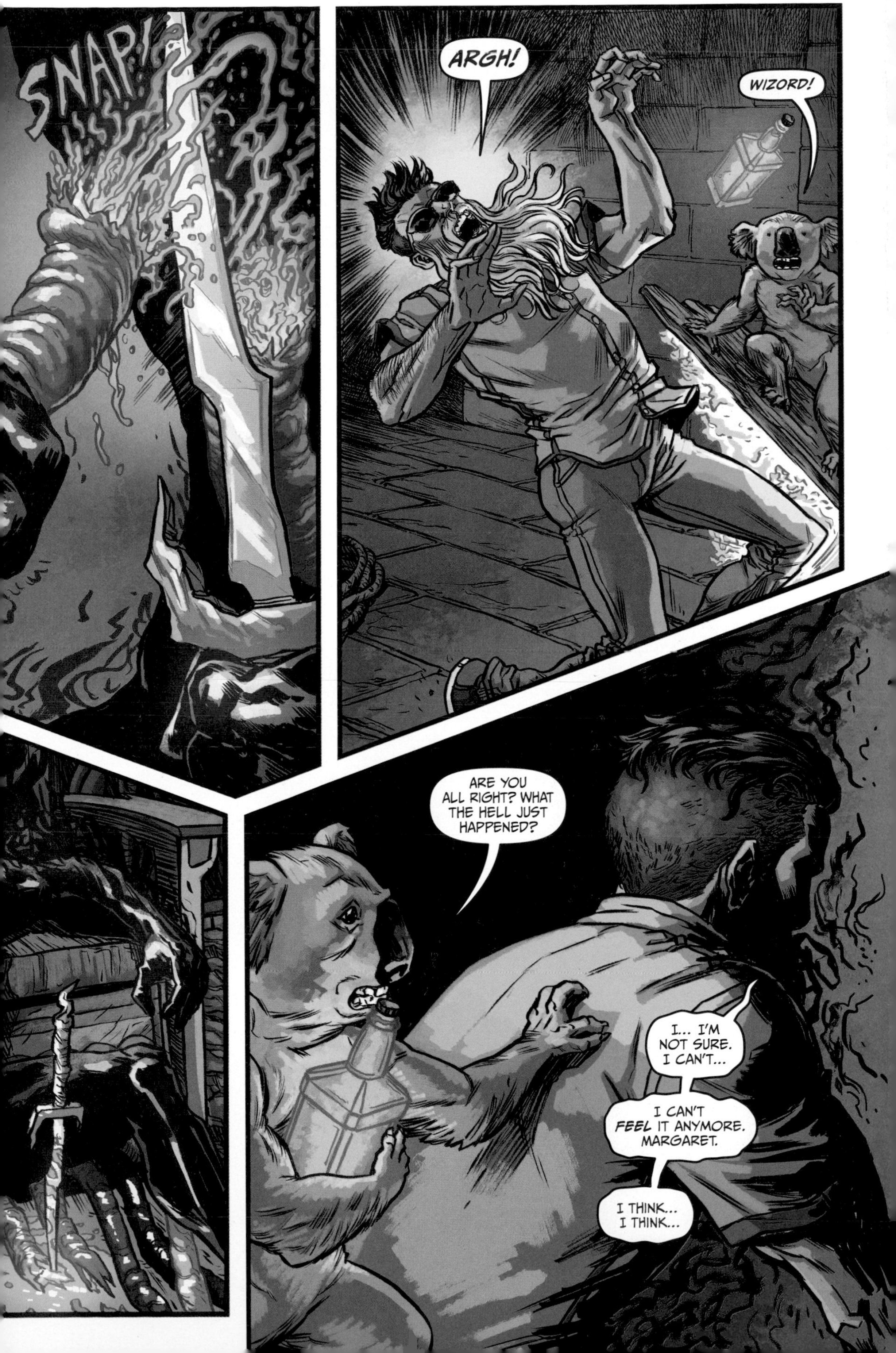
SNAP!
ARGH!
WIZORD!
ARE YOU ALL RIGHT? WHAT THE HELL JUST HAPPENED?
I... I'M NOT SURE. I CAN'T...
I CAN'T *FEEL* IT ANYMORE. MARGARET.
I THINK... I THINK...

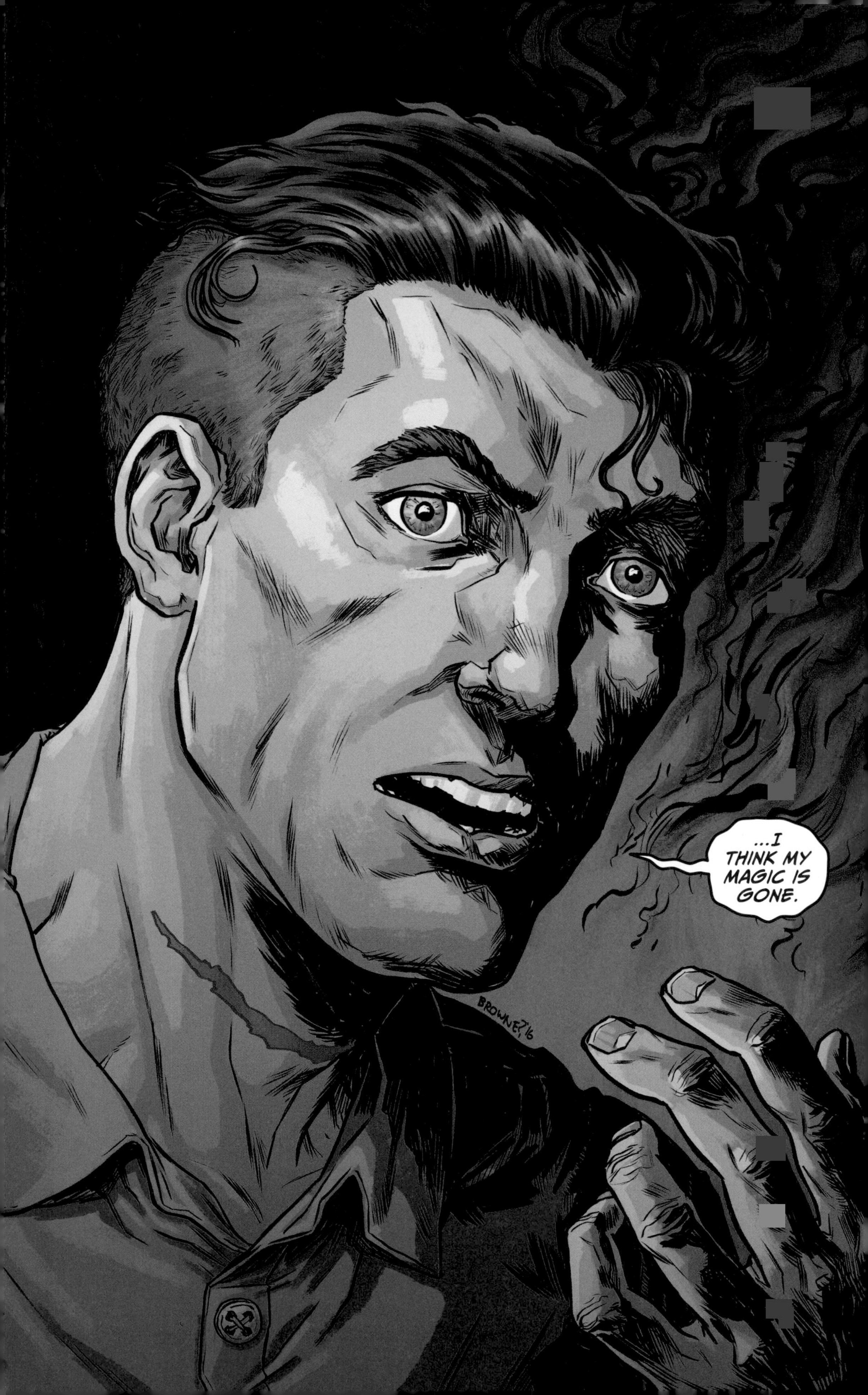
...I THINK MY MAGIC IS GONE.

# THREE

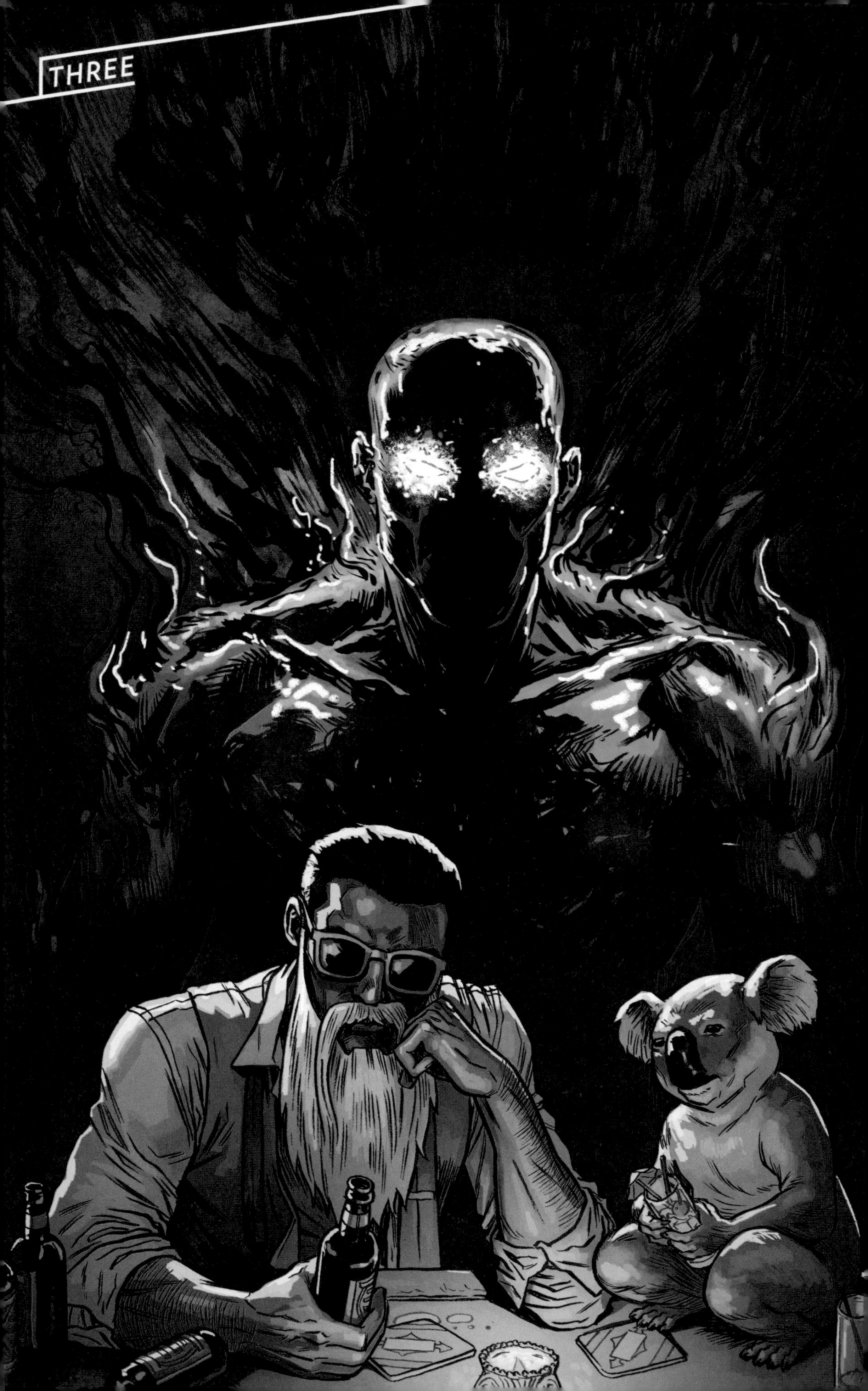

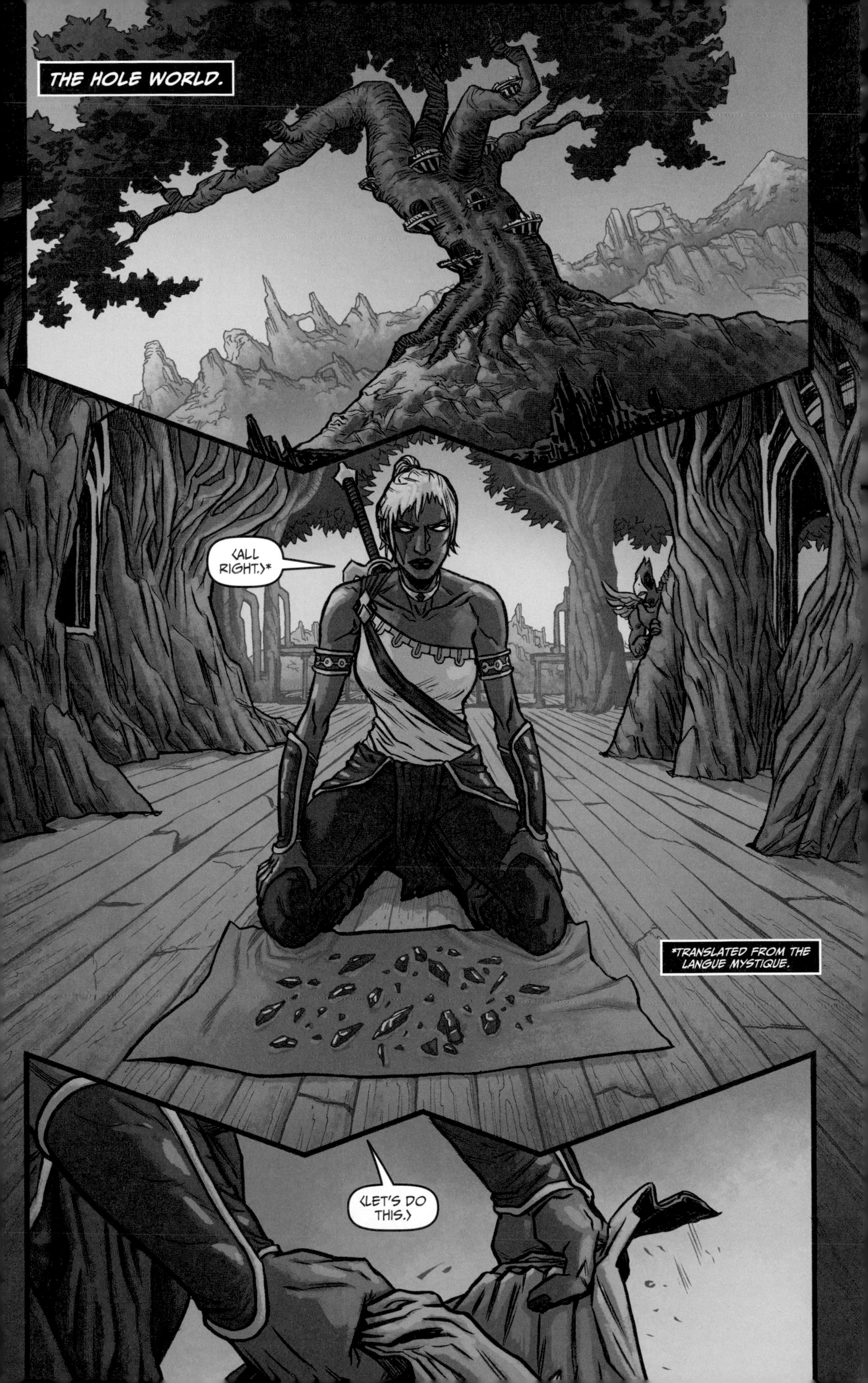
THE HOLE WORLD.
‹ALL RIGHT.›*
*TRANSLATED FROM THE LANGUE MYSTIQUE.
‹LET'S DO THIS.›

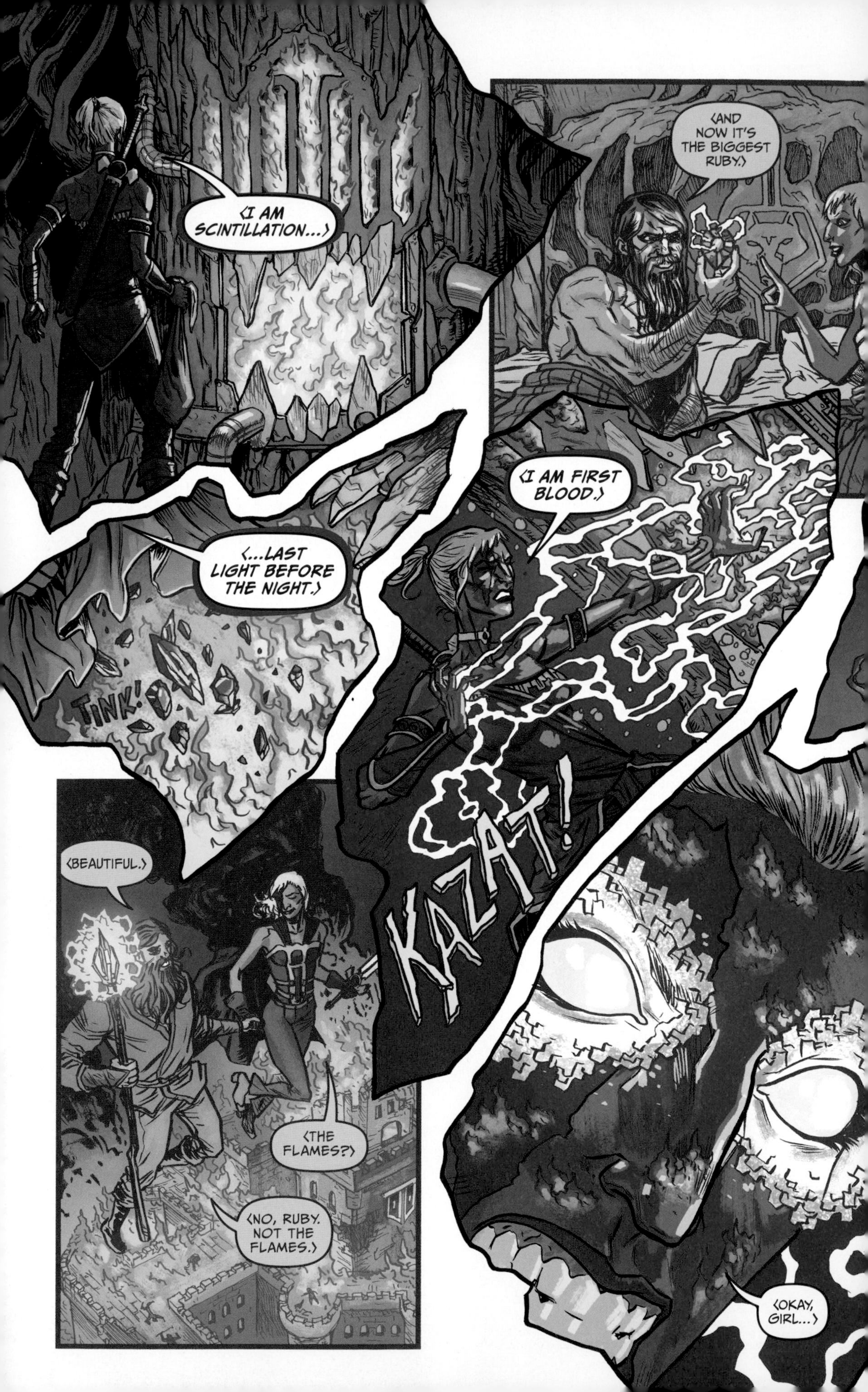

‹I AM SCINTILLATION...›
‹AND NOW IT'S THE BIGGEST RUBY.›
‹...LAST LIGHT BEFORE THE NIGHT.›
TINK!
‹I AM FIRST BLOOD.›
KAZAT!
‹BEAUTIFUL.›
‹THE FLAMES?›
‹NO, RUBY. NOT THE FLAMES.›
‹OKAY, GIRL...›

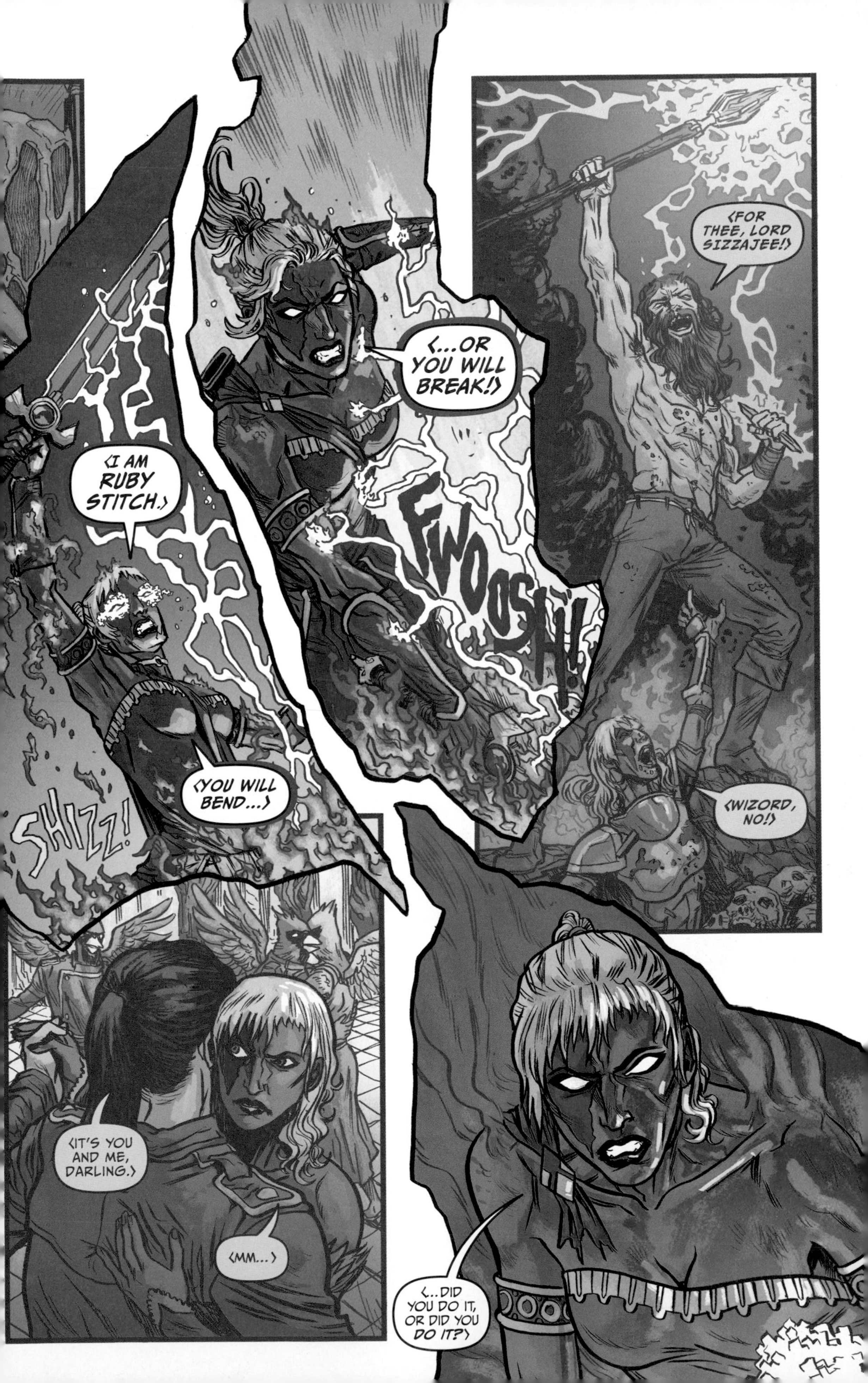
‹I AM RUBY STITCH.›
‹YOU WILL BEND...›
SHIZZ!
‹...OR YOU WILL BREAK!›
FWOOSH!
‹FOR THEE, LORD SIZZAJEE!›
‹WIZORD, NO!›
‹IT'S YOU AND ME, DARLING.›
‹MM...›
‹...DID YOU DO IT, OR DID YOU DO IT?›

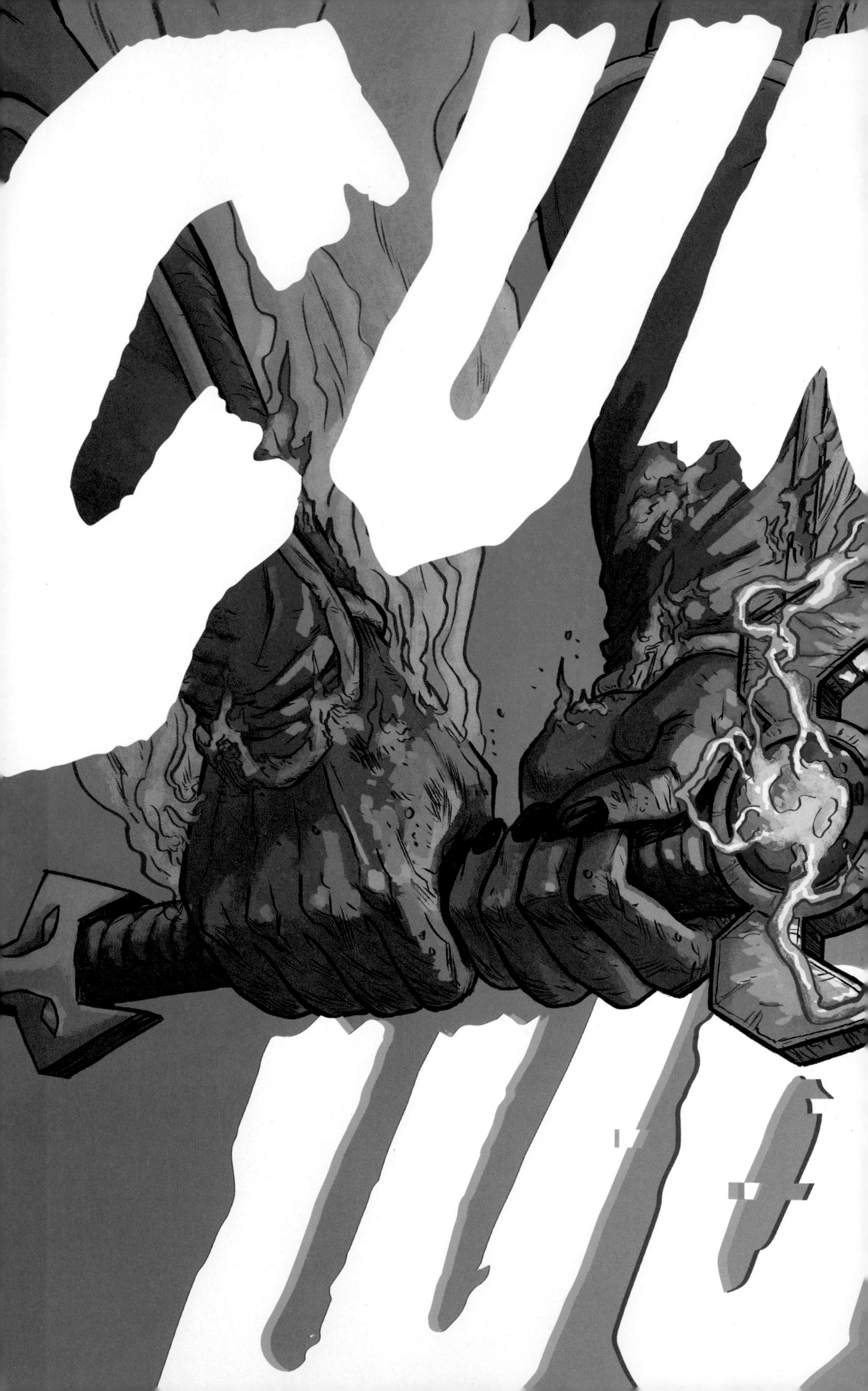

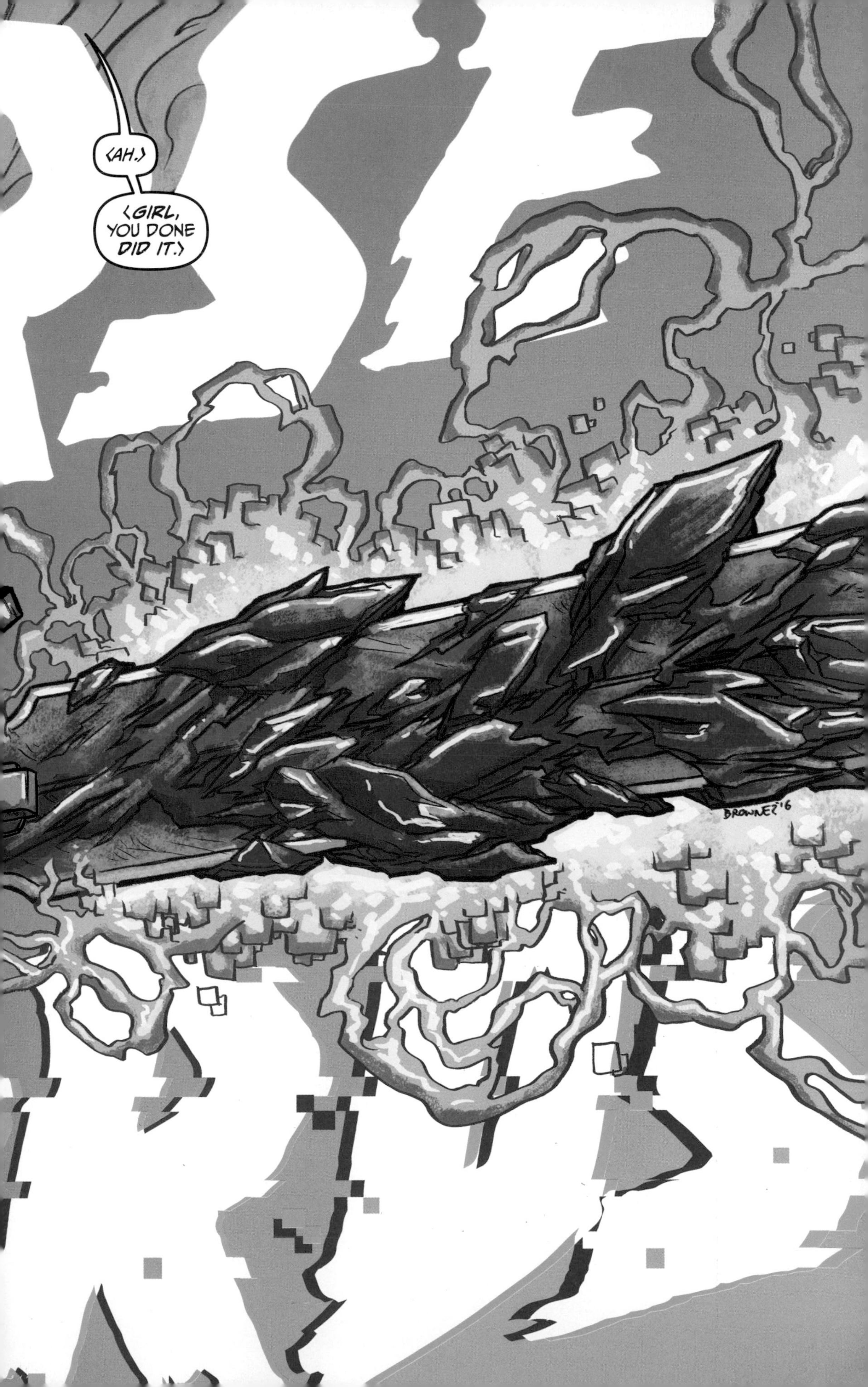
⟨AH.⟩
⟨GIRL, YOU DONE DID IT.⟩
BROWNE '16

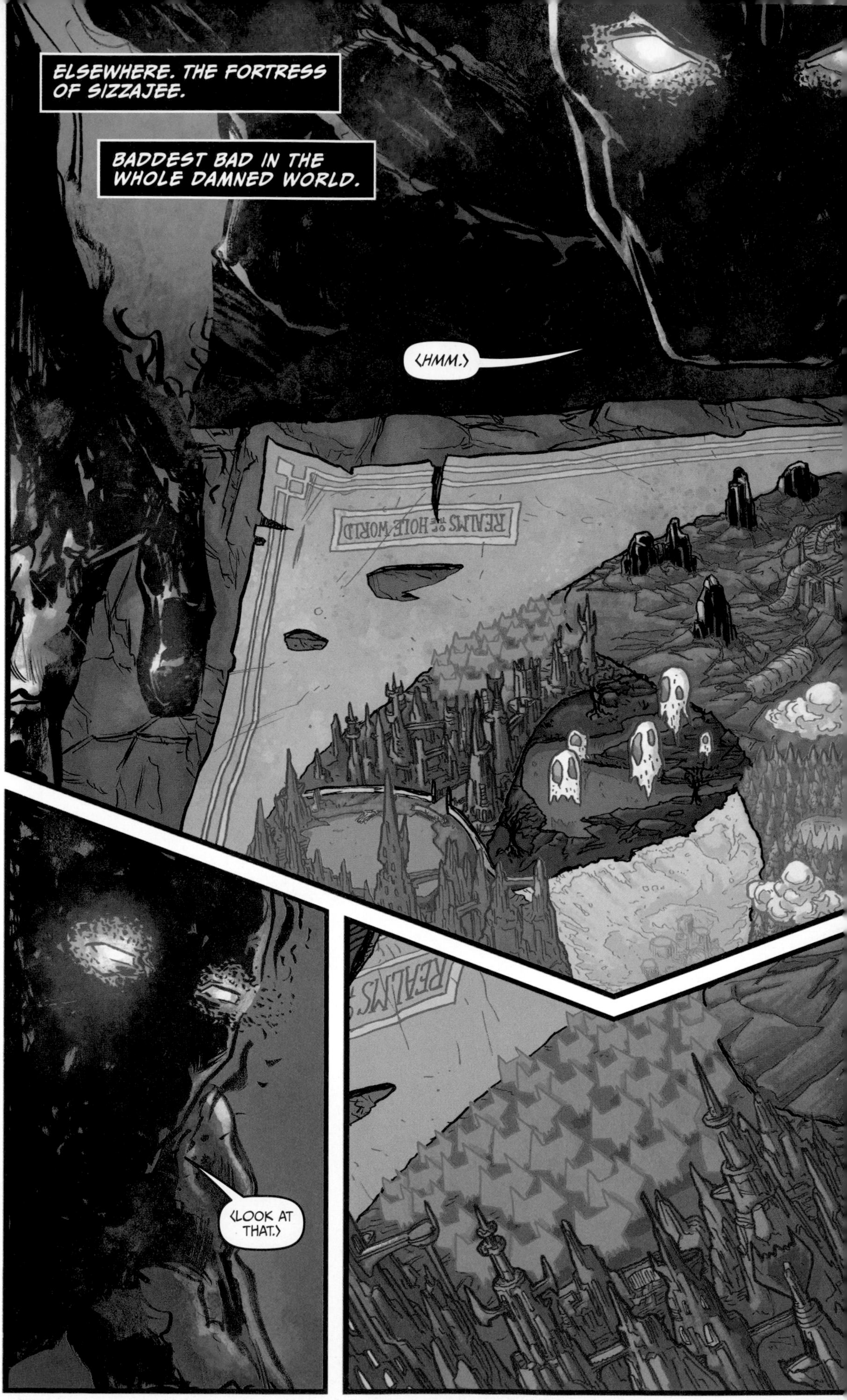
ELSEWHERE. THE FORTRESS OF SIZZAJEE.
BADDEST BAD IN THE WHOLE DAMNED WORLD.
‹HMM.›
‹LOOK AT THAT.›

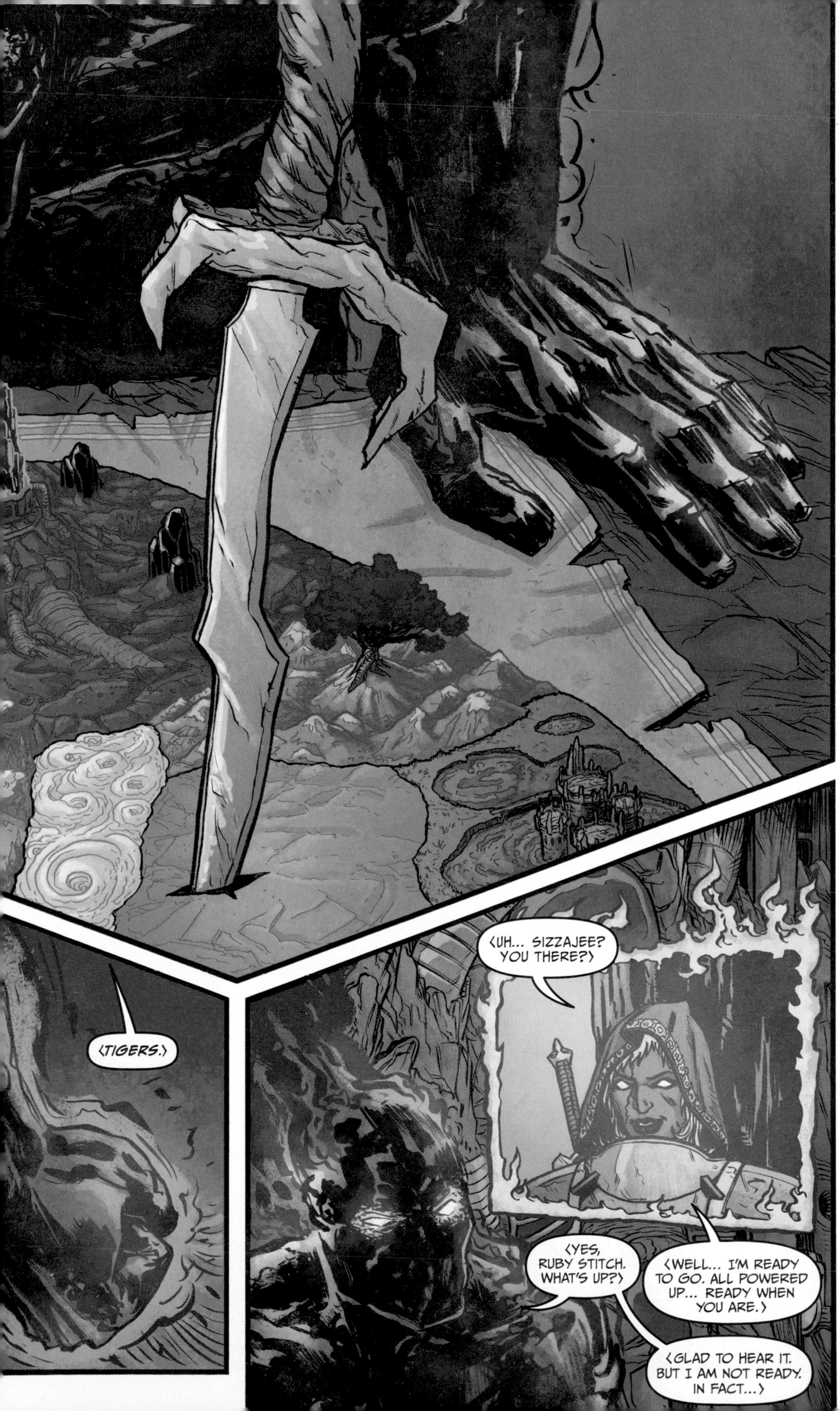

‹TIGERS.›
‹UH... SIZZAJEE? YOU THERE?›
‹YES, RUBY STITCH. WHAT'S UP?›
‹WELL... I'M READY TO GO. ALL POWERED UP... READY WHEN YOU ARE.›
‹GLAD TO HEAR IT. BUT I AM NOT READY. IN FACT...›

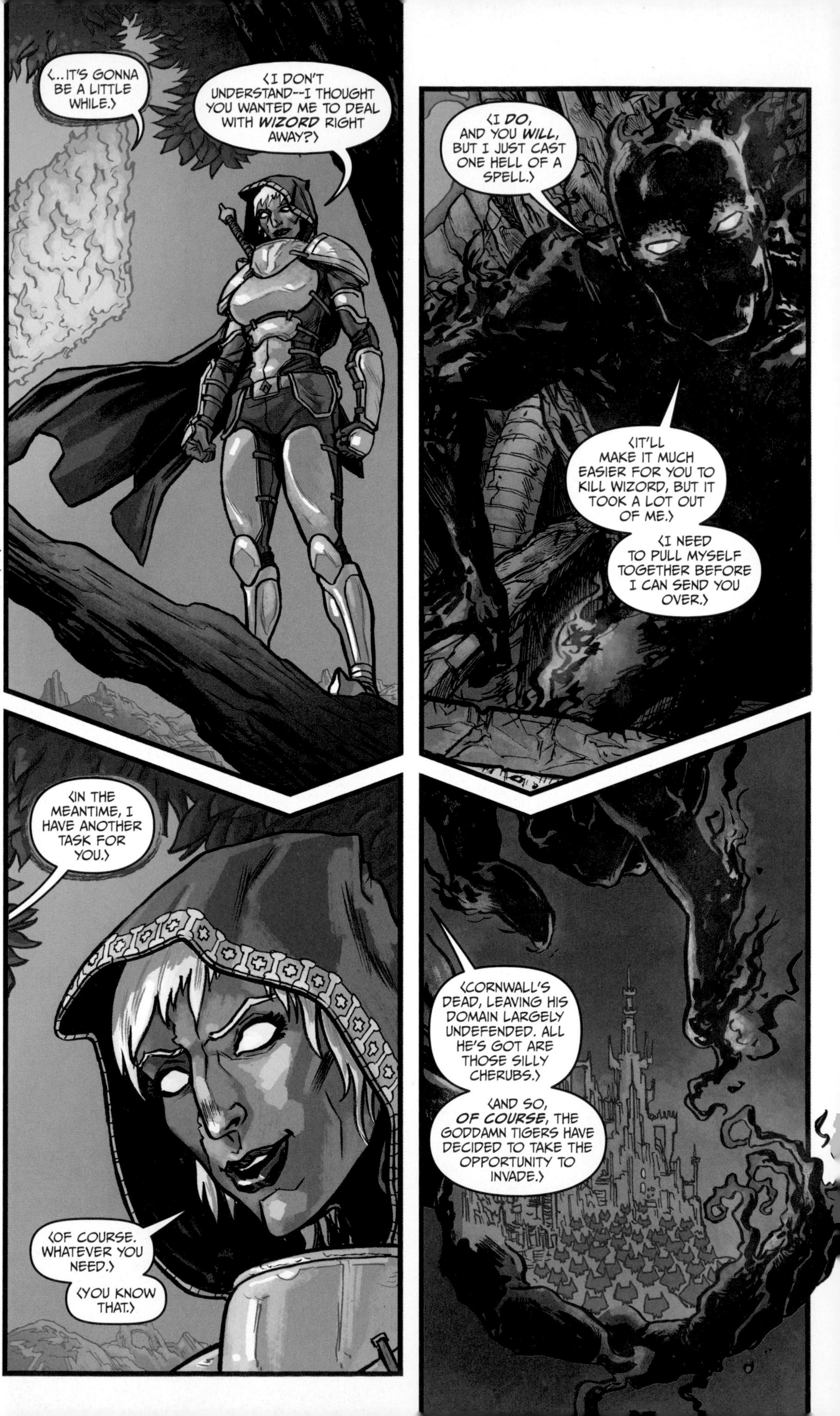
<...IT'S GONNA BE A LITTLE WHILE.>
<I DON'T UNDERSTAND--I THOUGHT YOU WANTED ME TO DEAL WITH ***WIZORD*** RIGHT AWAY?>
<I ***DO***, AND YOU ***WILL***, BUT I JUST CAST ONE HELL OF A SPELL.>
<IT'LL MAKE IT MUCH EASIER FOR YOU TO KILL WIZORD, BUT IT TOOK A LOT OUT OF ME.>
<I NEED TO PULL MYSELF TOGETHER BEFORE I CAN SEND YOU OVER.>
<IN THE MEANTIME, I HAVE ANOTHER TASK FOR YOU.>
<OF COURSE. WHATEVER YOU NEED.>
<YOU KNOW THAT.>
<CORNWALL'S DEAD, LEAVING HIS DOMAIN LARGELY UNDEFENDED. ALL HE'S GOT ARE THOSE SILLY CHERUBS.>
<AND SO, ***OF COURSE***, THE GODDAMN TIGERS HAVE DECIDED TO TAKE THE OPPORTUNITY TO INVADE.>

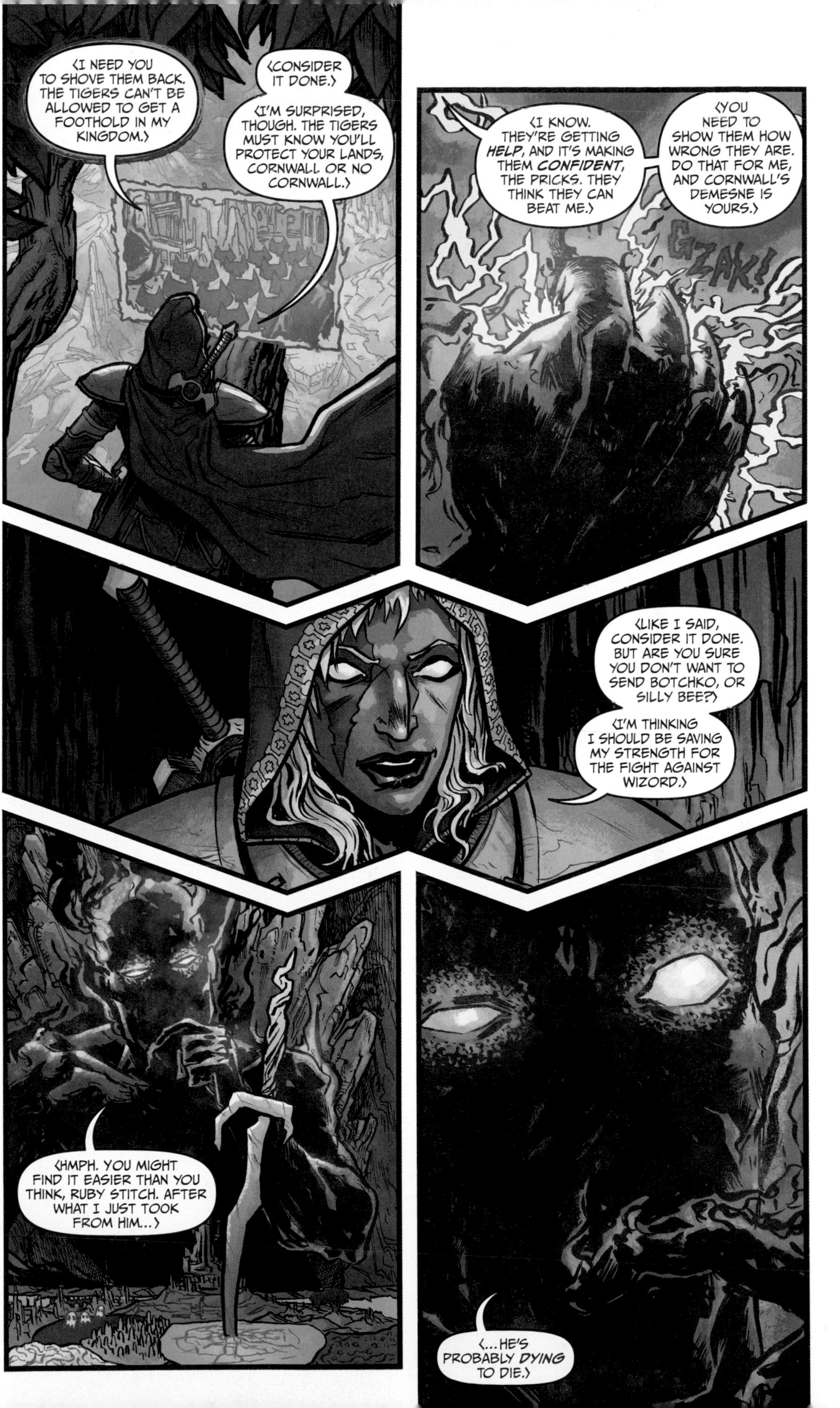

⟨I NEED YOU TO SHOVE THEM BACK. THE TIGERS CAN'T BE ALLOWED TO GET A FOOTHOLD IN MY KINGDOM.⟩
⟨CONSIDER IT DONE.⟩
⟨I'M SURPRISED, THOUGH. THE TIGERS MUST KNOW YOU'LL PROTECT YOUR LANDS, CORNWALL OR NO CORNWALL.⟩
⟨I KNOW. THEY'RE GETTING *HELP*, AND IT'S MAKING THEM *CONFIDENT*, THE PRICKS. THEY THINK THEY CAN BEAT ME.⟩
⟨YOU NEED TO SHOW THEM HOW WRONG THEY ARE. DO THAT FOR ME, AND CORNWALL'S DEMESNE IS YOURS.⟩
GZAK!
⟨LIKE I SAID, CONSIDER IT DONE. BUT ARE YOU SURE YOU DON'T WANT TO SEND BOTCHKO, OR SILLY BEE?⟩
⟨I'M THINKING I SHOULD BE SAVING MY STRENGTH FOR THE FIGHT AGAINST WIZORD.⟩
⟨HMPH. YOU MIGHT FIND IT EASIER THAN YOU THINK, RUBY STITCH. AFTER WHAT I JUST TOOK FROM HIM...⟩
⟨...HE'S PROBABLY *DYING* TO DIE.⟩

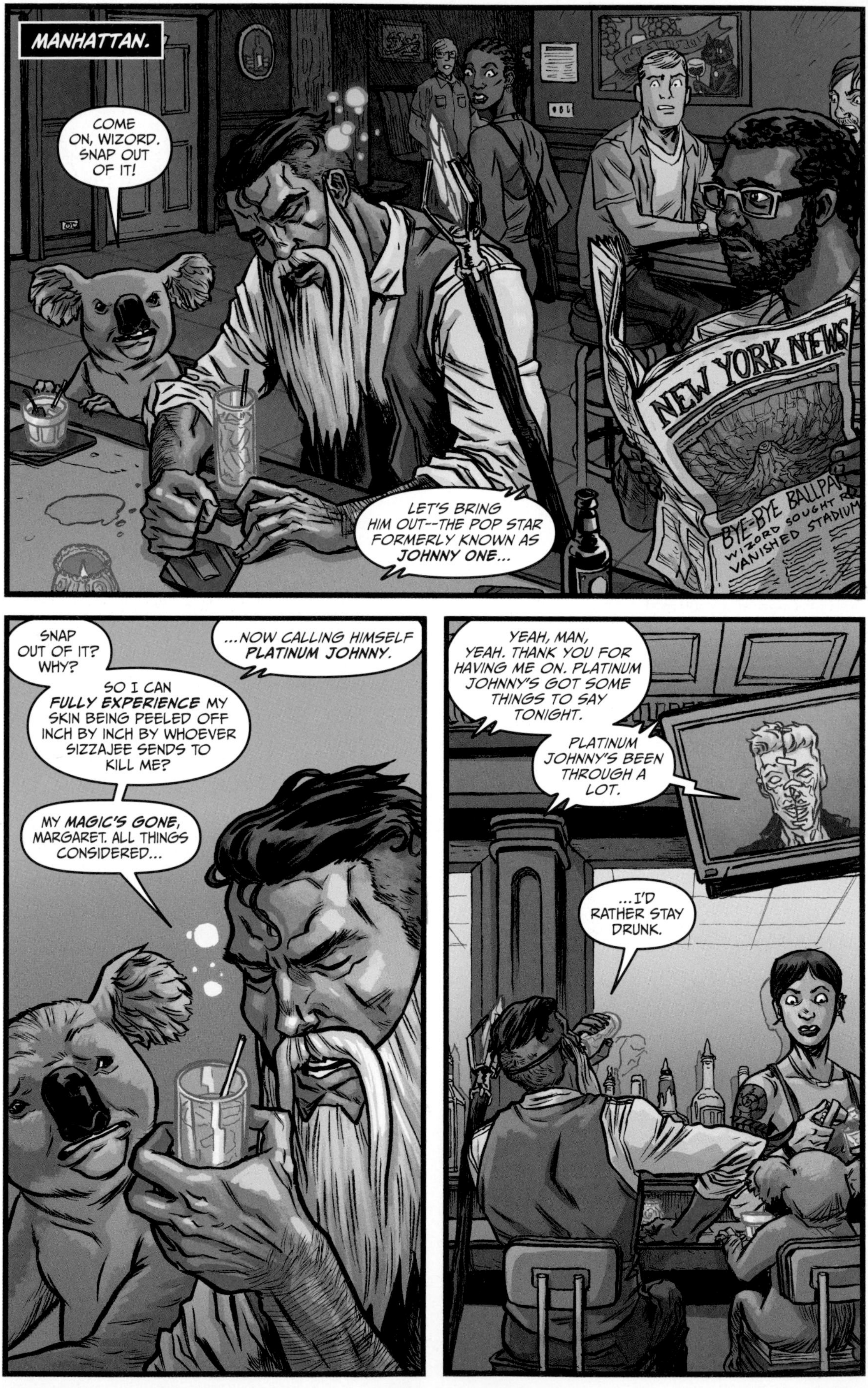
MANHATTAN.
COME ON, WIZORD. SNAP OUT OF IT!
NEW YORK NEWS
WIZORD SOUGHT
VANISHED STADIUM
LET'S BRING HIM OUT--THE POP STAR FORMERLY KNOWN AS JOHNNY ONE...
SNAP OUT OF IT? WHY?
...NOW CALLING HIMSELF PLATINUM JOHNNY.
SO I CAN FULLY EXPERIENCE MY SKIN BEING PEELED OFF INCH BY INCH BY WHOEVER SIZZAJEE SENDS TO KILL ME?
MY MAGIC'S GONE, MARGARET. ALL THINGS CONSIDERED...
YEAH, MAN, YEAH. THANK YOU FOR HAVING ME ON. PLATINUM JOHNNY'S GOT SOME THINGS TO SAY TONIGHT.
PLATINUM JOHNNY'S BEEN THROUGH A LOT.
...I'D RATHER STAY DRUNK.

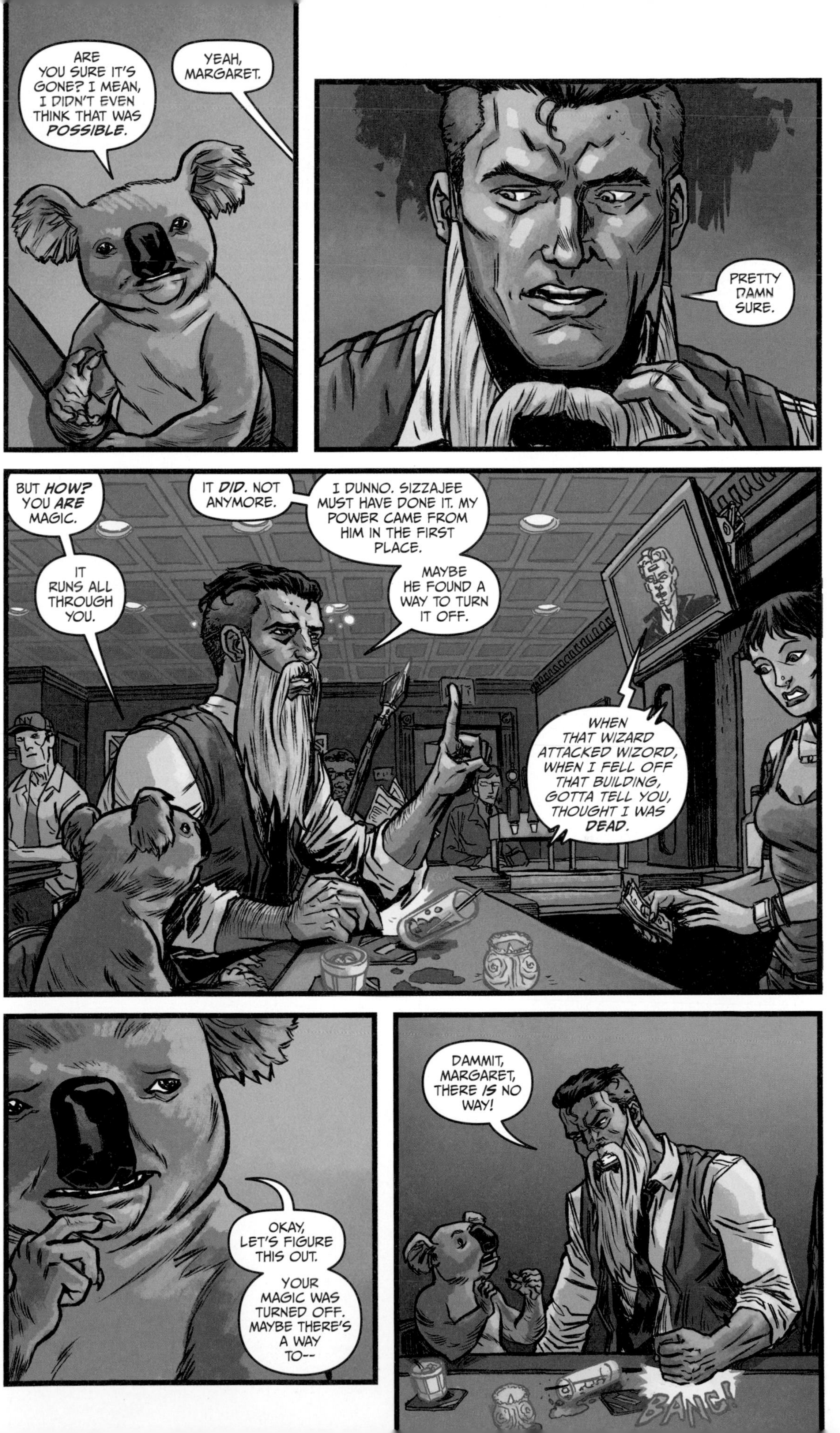
ARE YOU SURE IT'S GONE? I MEAN, I DIDN'T EVEN THINK THAT WAS POSSIBLE.
YEAH, MARGARET.
PRETTY DAMN SURE.
BUT HOW? YOU ARE MAGIC.
IT RUNS ALL THROUGH YOU.
IT DID. NOT ANYMORE.
I DUNNO. SIZZAJEE MUST HAVE DONE IT. MY POWER CAME FROM HIM IN THE FIRST PLACE.
MAYBE HE FOUND A WAY TO TURN IT OFF.
WHEN THAT WIZARD ATTACKED WIZORD, WHEN I FELL OFF THAT BUILDING, GOTTA TELL YOU, THOUGHT I WAS DEAD.
OKAY, LET'S FIGURE THIS OUT.
YOUR MAGIC WAS TURNED OFF. MAYBE THERE'S A WAY TO--
DAMMIT, MARGARET, THERE IS NO WAY!
BANG!

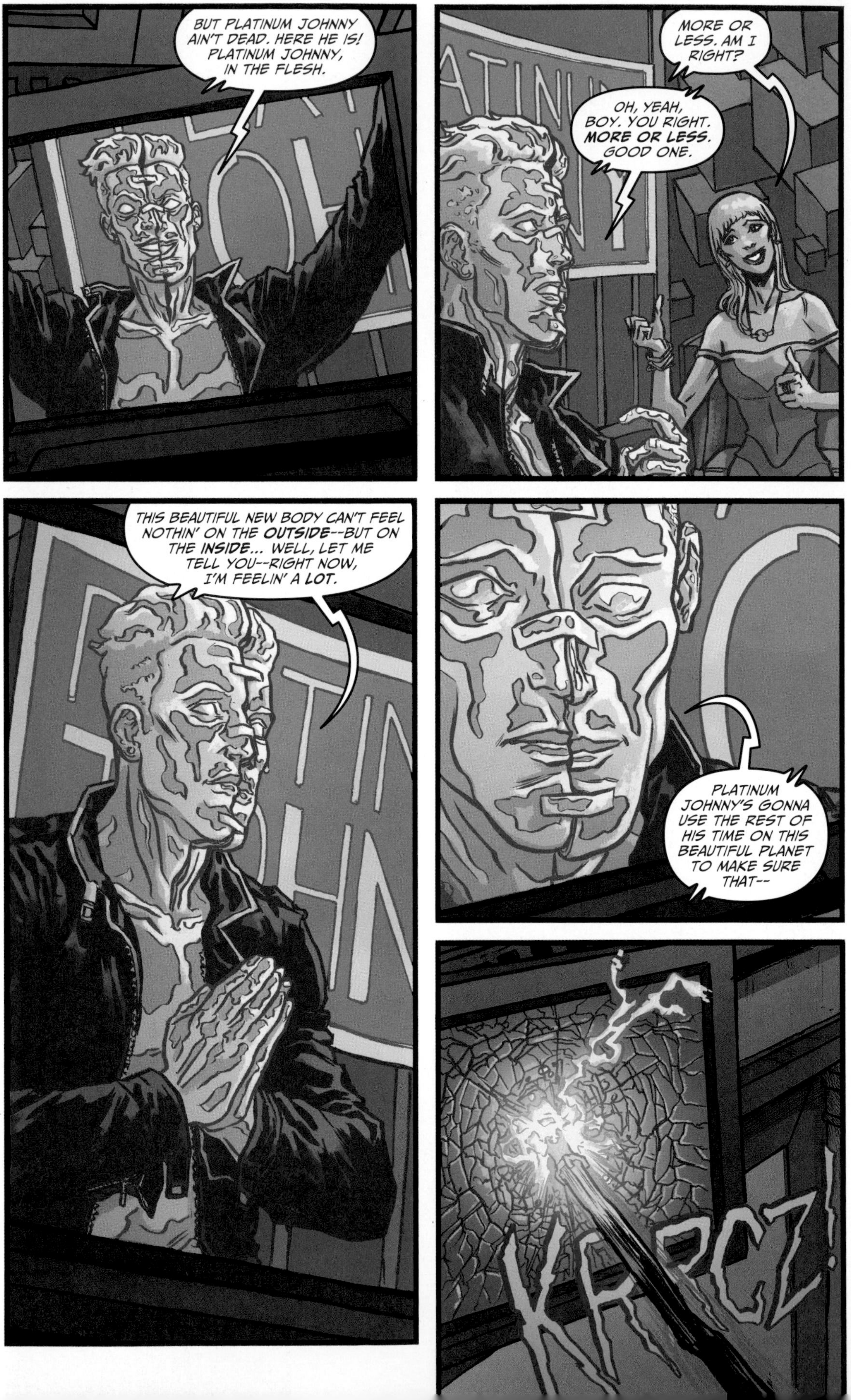
BUT PLATINUM JOHNNY AIN'T DEAD. HERE HE IS! PLATINUM JOHNNY, IN THE FLESH.
MORE OR LESS. AM I RIGHT?
OH, YEAH, BOY. YOU RIGHT. MORE OR LESS. GOOD ONE.
THIS BEAUTIFUL NEW BODY CAN'T FEEL NOTHIN' ON THE OUTSIDE--BUT ON THE INSIDE... WELL, LET ME TELL YOU--RIGHT NOW, I'M FEELIN' A LOT.
PLATINUM JOHNNY'S GONNA USE THE REST OF HIS TIME ON THIS BEAUTIFUL PLANET TO MAKE SURE THAT--
KRRRCZ!

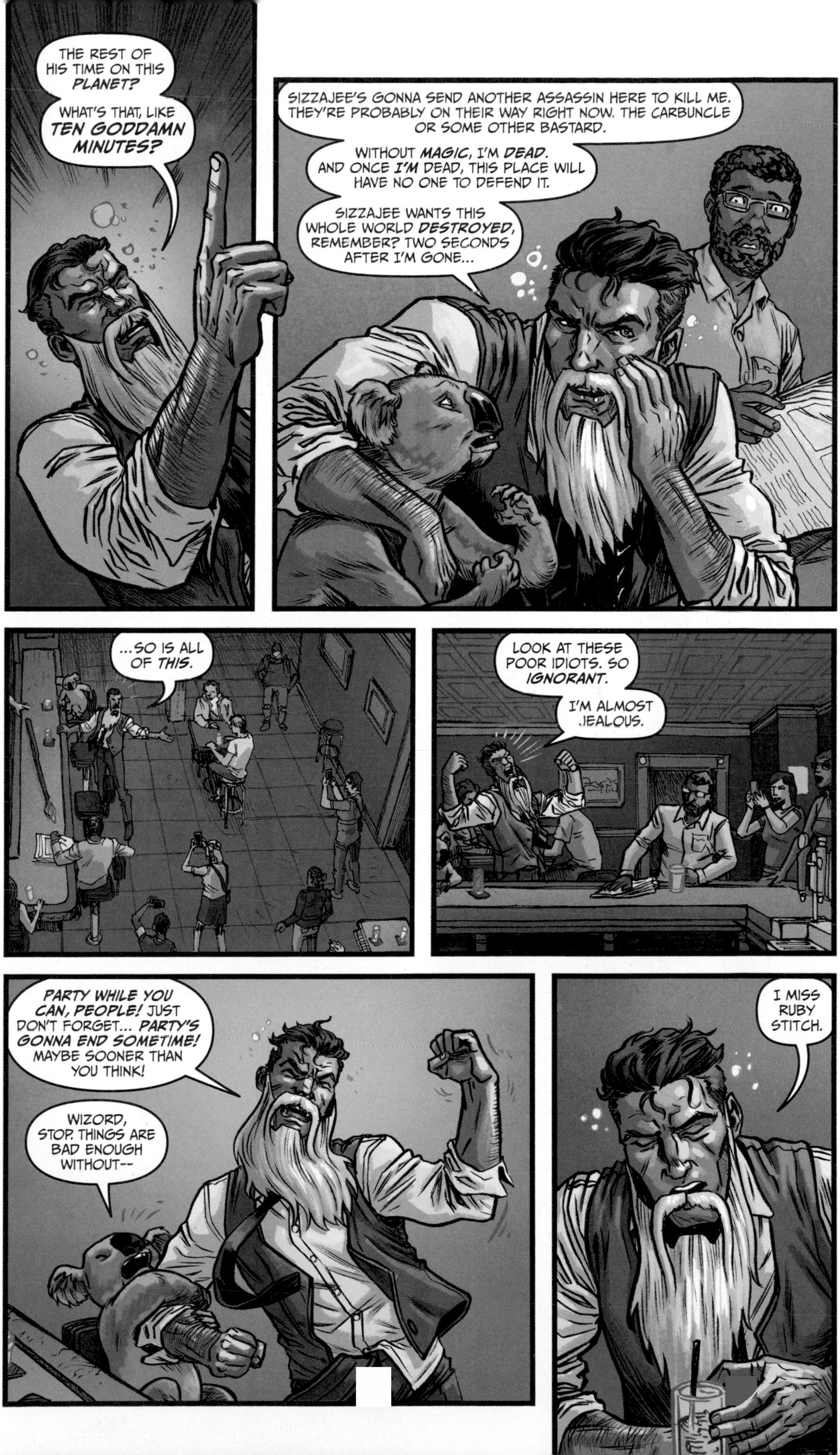
THE REST OF HIS TIME ON THIS PLANET?
WHAT'S THAT, LIKE TEN GODDAMN MINUTES?
SIZZAJEE'S GONNA SEND ANOTHER ASSASSIN HERE TO KILL ME. THEY'RE PROBABLY ON THEIR WAY RIGHT NOW. THE CARBUNCLE OR SOME OTHER BASTARD.
WITHOUT MAGIC, I'M DEAD. AND ONCE I'M DEAD, THIS PLACE WILL HAVE NO ONE TO DEFEND IT.
SIZZAJEE WANTS THIS WHOLE WORLD DESTROYED, REMEMBER? TWO SECONDS AFTER I'M GONE...
...SO IS ALL OF THIS.
LOOK AT THESE POOR IDIOTS. SO IGNORANT.
I'M ALMOST JEALOUS.
PARTY WHILE YOU CAN, PEOPLE! JUST DON'T FORGET... PARTY'S GONNA END SOMETIME! MAYBE SOONER THAN YOU THINK!
WIZORD, STOP. THINGS ARE BAD ENOUGH WITHOUT--
I MISS RUBY STITCH.

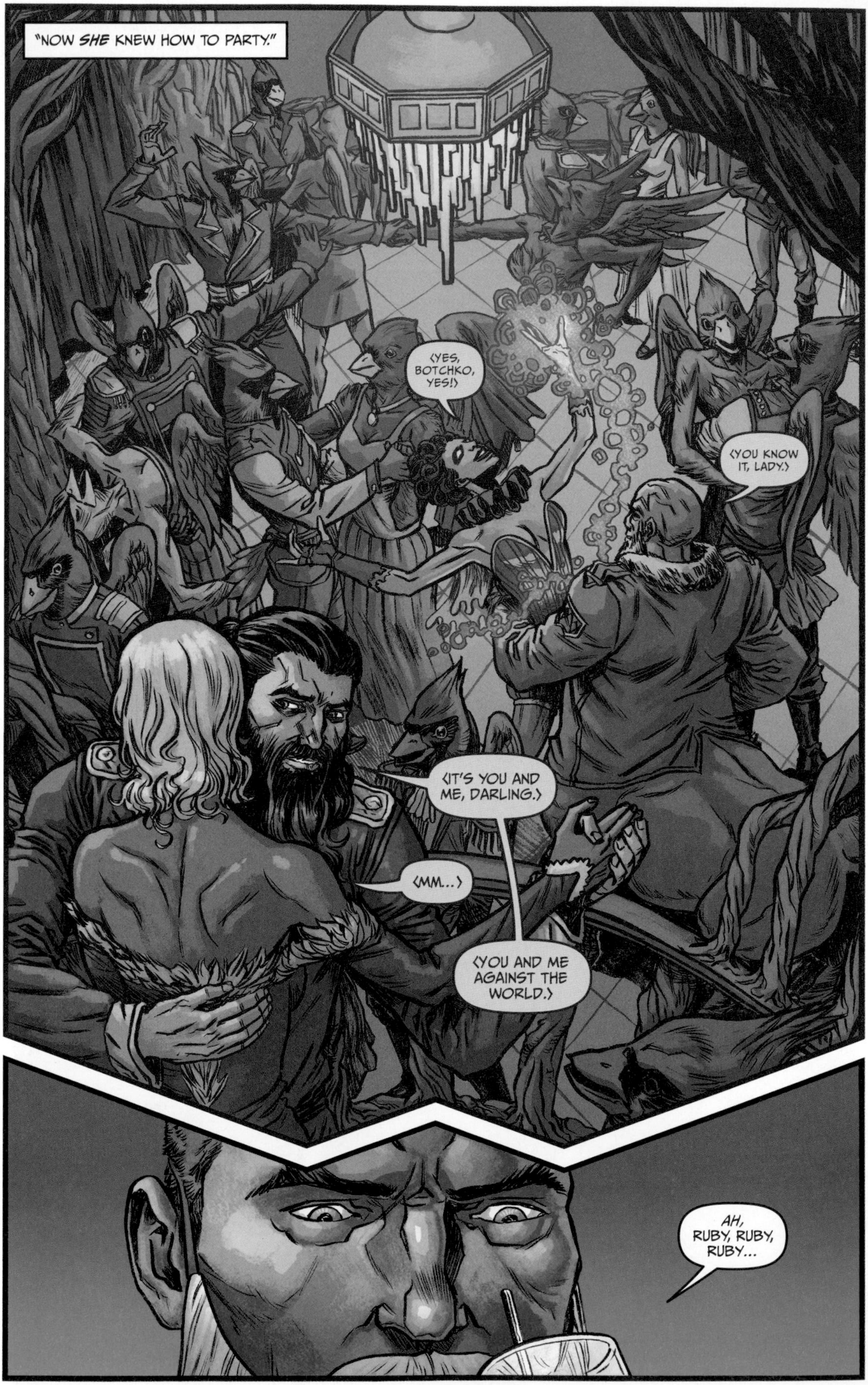
"NOW SHE KNEW HOW TO PARTY."
‹YES, BOTCHKO, YES!›
‹YOU KNOW IT, LADY.›
‹IT'S YOU AND ME, DARLING.›
‹MM...›
‹YOU AND ME AGAINST THE WORLD.›
AH, RUBY, RUBY, RUBY...

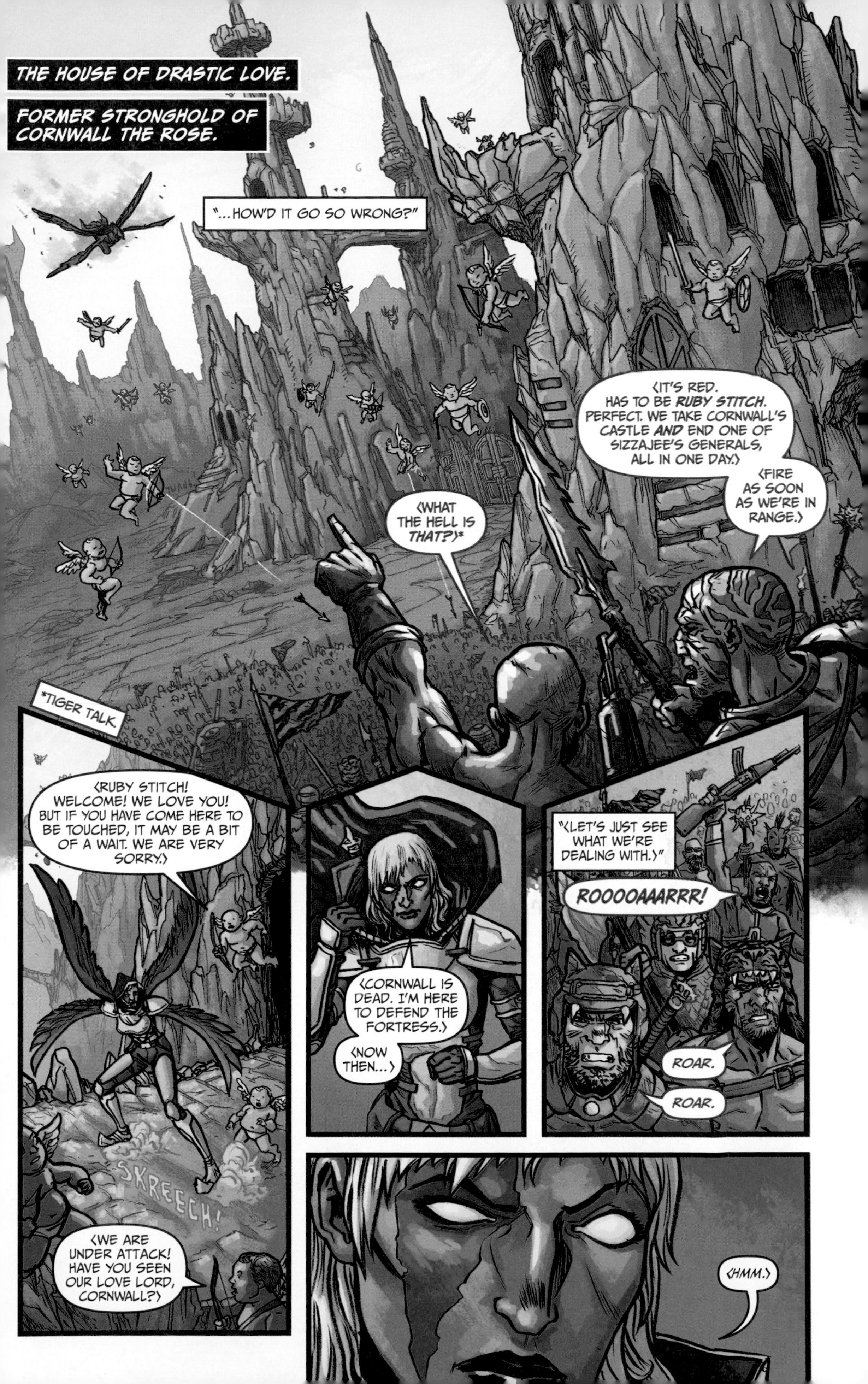
THE HOUSE OF DRASTIC LOVE.
FORMER STRONGHOLD OF CORNWALL THE ROSE.
"...HOW'D IT GO SO WRONG?"
‹IT'S RED. HAS TO BE RUBY STITCH. PERFECT. WE TAKE CORNWALL'S CASTLE AND END ONE OF SIZZAJEE'S GENERALS, ALL IN ONE DAY.›
‹FIRE AS SOON AS WE'RE IN RANGE.›
‹WHAT THE HELL IS THAT?›*
*TIGER TALK.
‹RUBY STITCH! WELCOME! WE LOVE YOU! BUT IF YOU HAVE COME HERE TO BE TOUCHED, IT MAY BE A BIT OF A WAIT. WE ARE VERY SORRY.›
SKREECH!
‹WE ARE UNDER ATTACK! HAVE YOU SEEN OUR LOVE LORD, CORNWALL?›
‹CORNWALL IS DEAD. I'M HERE TO DEFEND THE FORTRESS.›
‹NOW THEN...›
"‹LET'S JUST SEE WHAT WE'RE DEALING WITH.›"
ROOOOAAARRR!
ROAR.
ROAR.
‹HMM.›

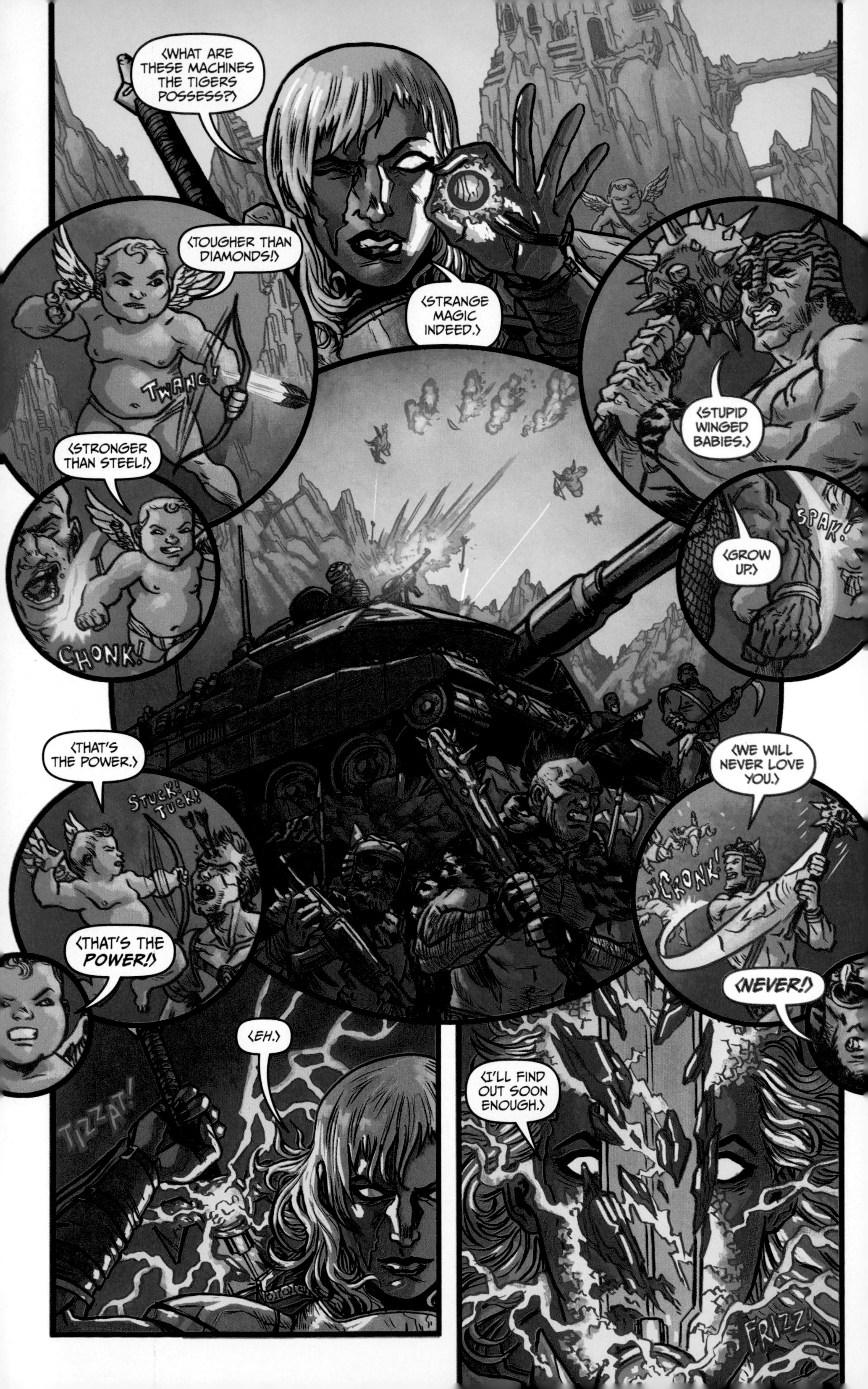
‹WHAT ARE THESE MACHINES THE TIGERS POSSESS?›
‹TOUGHER THAN DIAMONDS!›
‹STRANGE MAGIC INDEED.›
TWANG!
‹STUPID WINGED BABIES.›
‹STRONGER THAN STEEL!›
CHONK!
SPAK!
‹GROW UP.›
‹THAT'S THE POWER.›
STUCK! TUCK!
‹WE WILL NEVER LOVE YOU.›
CRONK!
‹THAT'S THE *POWER!*›
‹*NEVER!*›
‹EH.›
TIZZAT!
‹I'LL FIND OUT SOON ENOUGH.›
FRIZZ!

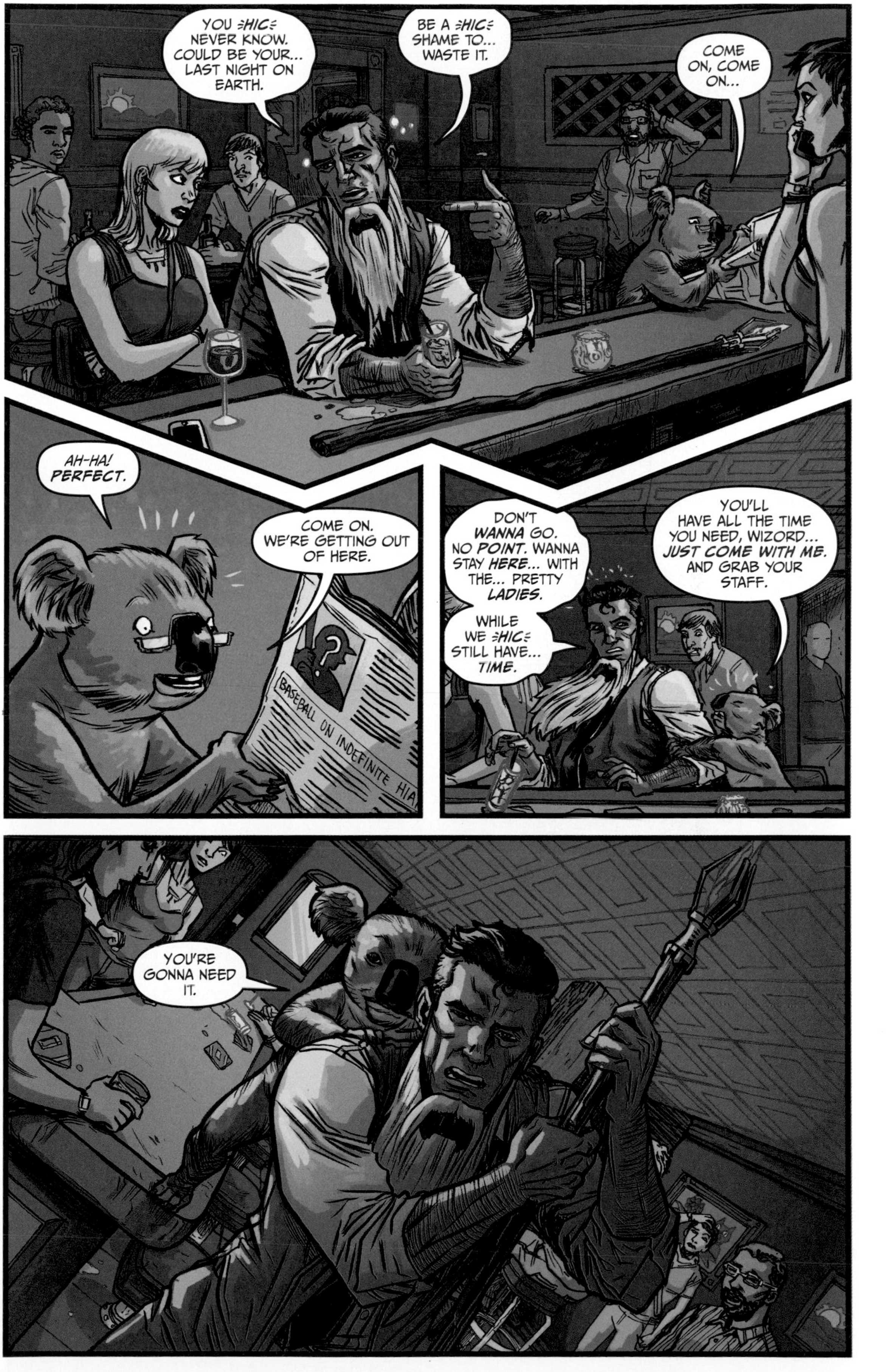
YOU =HIC= NEVER KNOW. COULD BE YOUR... LAST NIGHT ON EARTH.
BE A =HIC= SHAME TO... WASTE IT.
COME ON, COME ON...
AH-HA! PERFECT.
COME ON. WE'RE GETTING OUT OF HERE.
BASEBALL ON INDEFINITE HIA
DON'T WANNA GO. NO POINT. WANNA STAY HERE... WITH THE... PRETTY LADIES.
WHILE WE =HIC= STILL HAVE... TIME.
YOU'LL HAVE ALL THE TIME YOU NEED, WIZORD... JUST COME WITH ME. AND GRAB YOUR STAFF.
YOU'RE GONNA NEED IT.

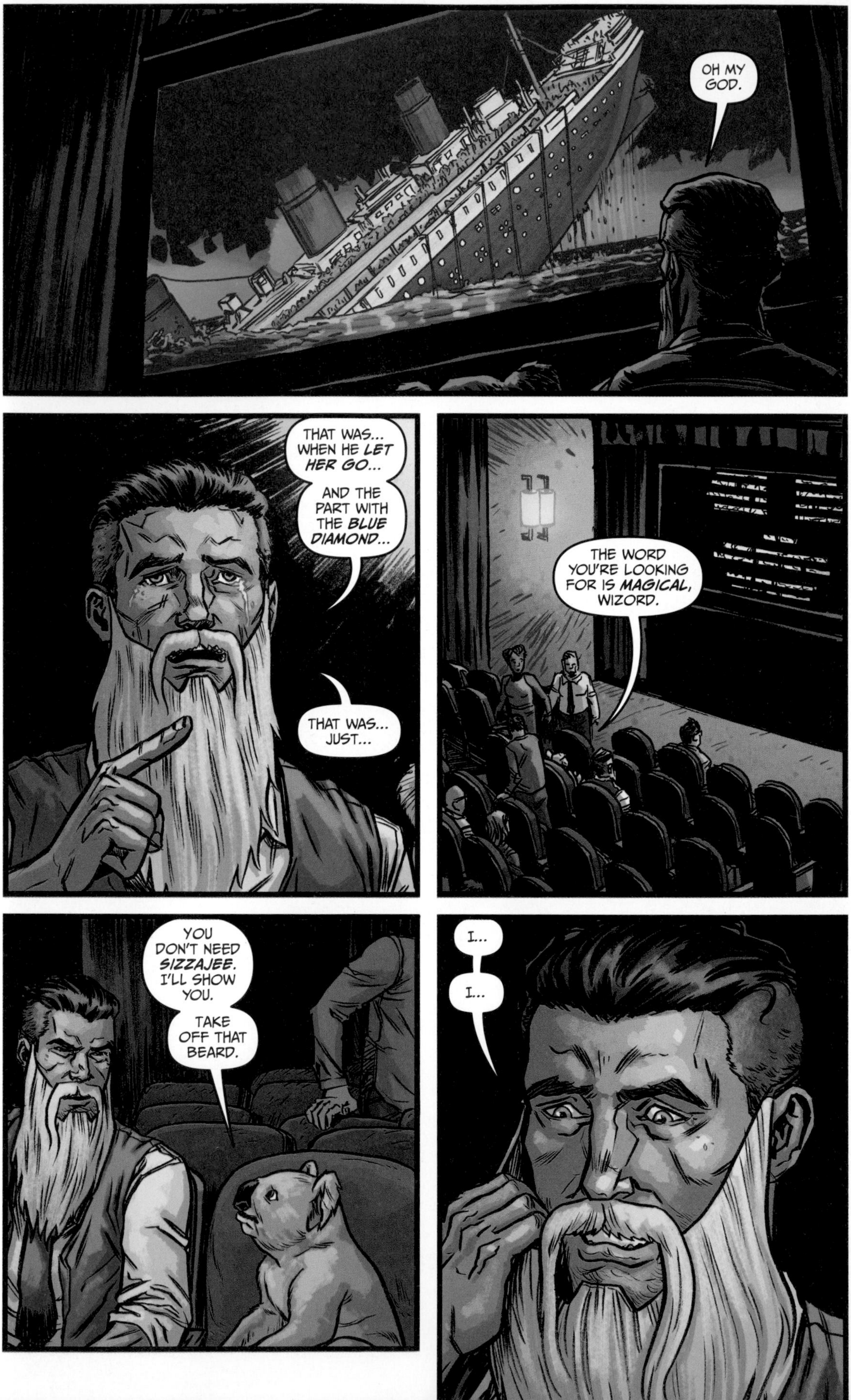
OH MY GOD.
THAT WAS... WHEN HE LET HER GO...
AND THE PART WITH THE BLUE DIAMOND...
THAT WAS... JUST...
THE WORD YOU'RE LOOKING FOR IS MAGICAL, WIZORD.
YOU DON'T NEED SIZZAJEE. I'LL SHOW YOU.
TAKE OFF THAT BEARD.
I...
I...

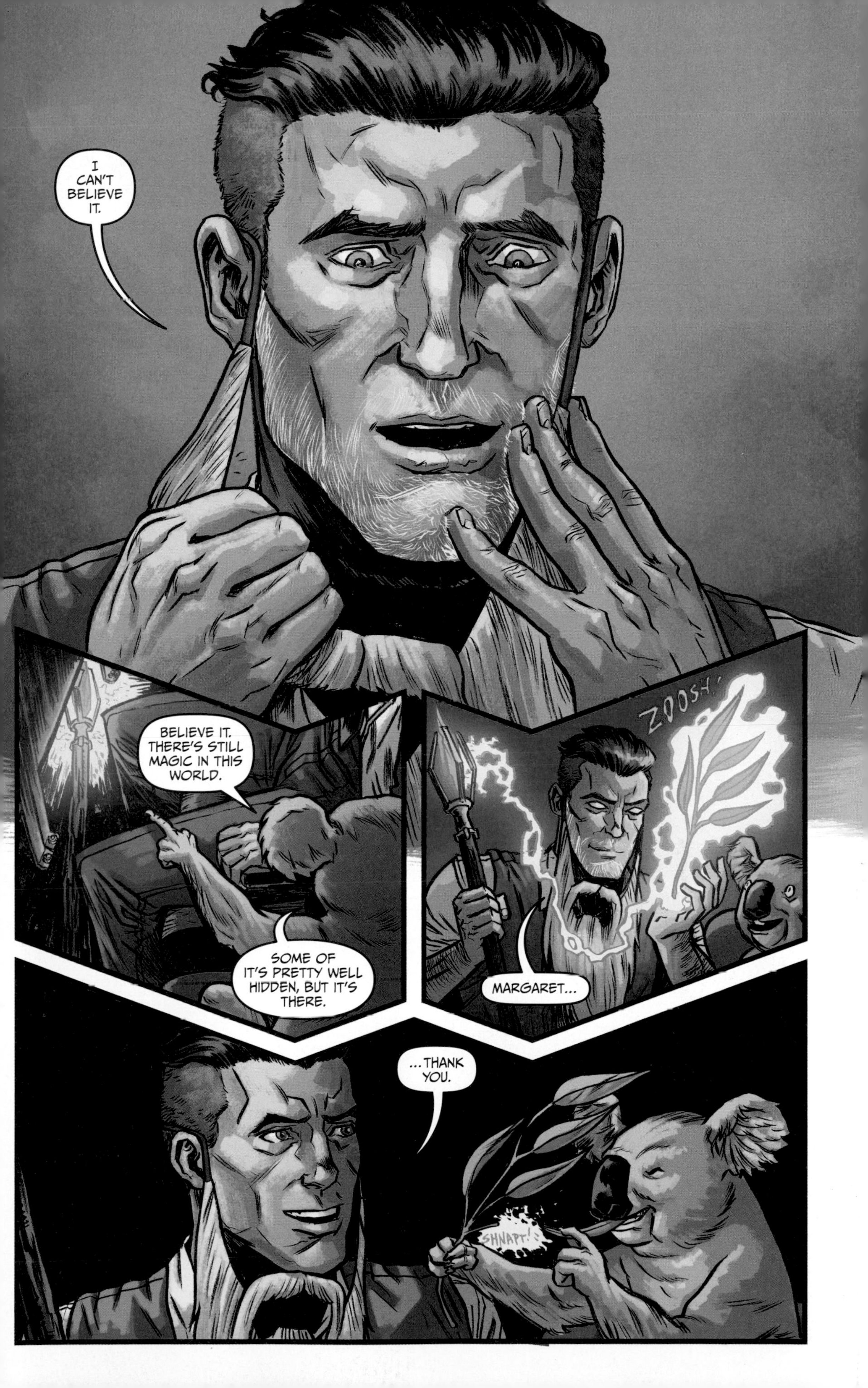
I CAN'T BELIEVE IT.
BELIEVE IT. THERE'S STILL MAGIC IN THIS WORLD.
SOME OF IT'S PRETTY WELL HIDDEN, BUT IT'S THERE.
ZOOSH!
MARGARET...
...THANK YOU.
SHNAPT!

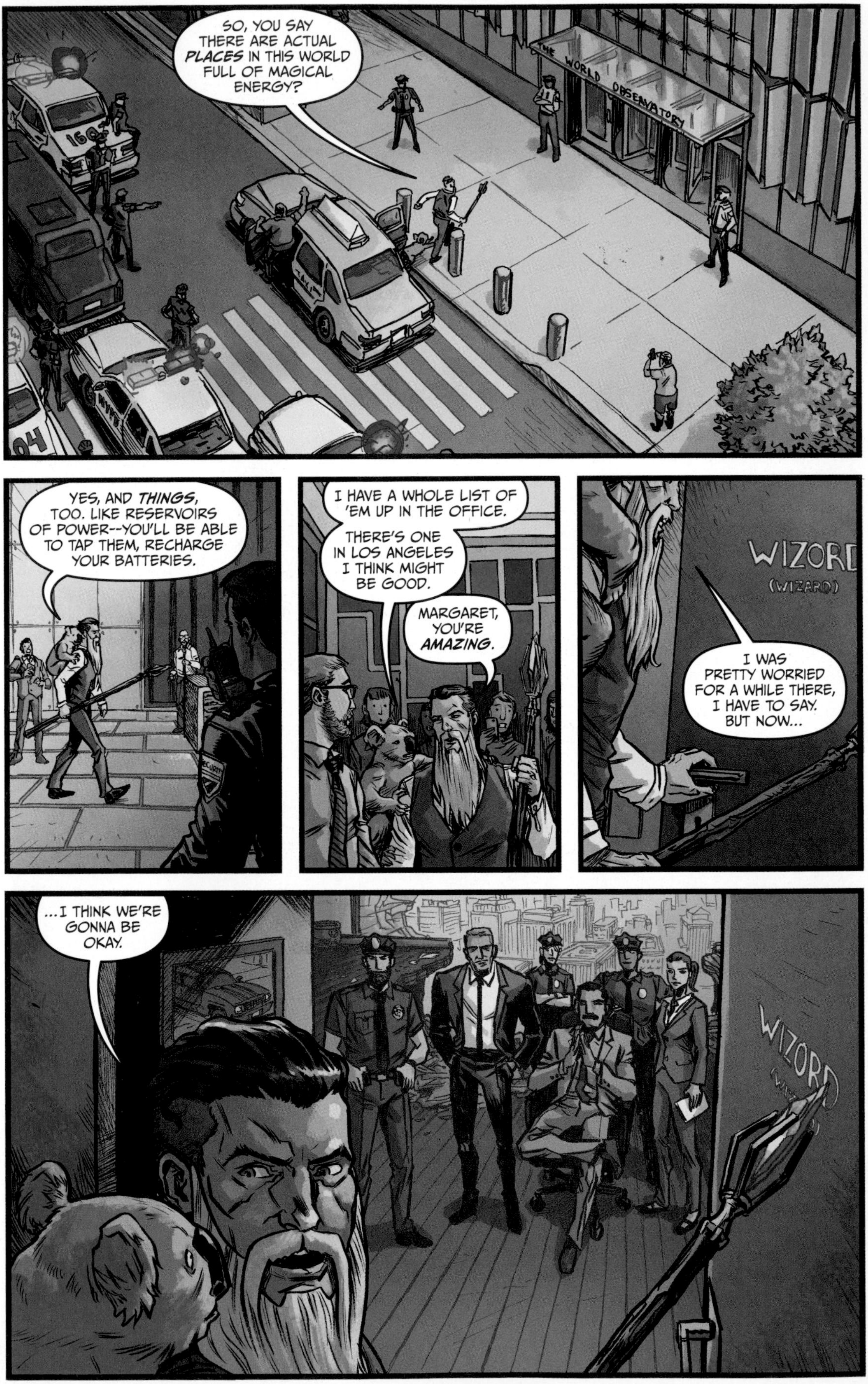
SO, YOU SAY THERE ARE ACTUAL *PLACES* IN THIS WORLD FULL OF MAGICAL ENERGY?
THE WORLD OBSERVATORY
YES, AND *THINGS*, TOO. LIKE RESERVOIRS OF POWER--YOU'LL BE ABLE TO TAP THEM, RECHARGE YOUR BATTERIES.
I HAVE A WHOLE LIST OF 'EM UP IN THE OFFICE.
THERE'S ONE IN LOS ANGELES I THINK MIGHT BE GOOD.
MARGARET, YOU'RE *AMAZING*.
WIZORD
(WIZARD)
I WAS PRETTY WORRIED FOR A WHILE THERE, I HAVE TO SAY. BUT NOW...
...I THINK WE'RE GONNA BE OKAY.
WIZORD

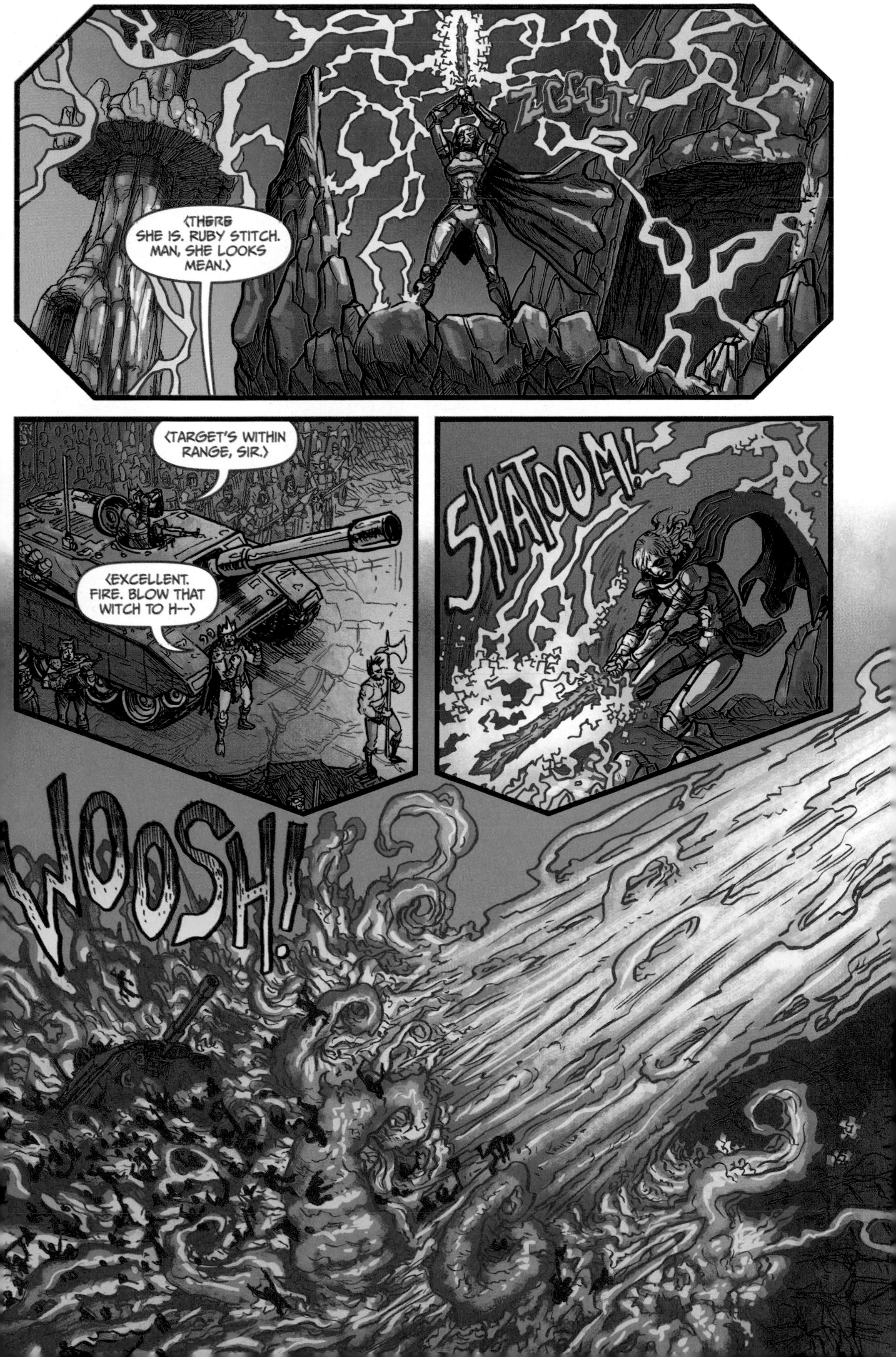
ZGGGT!
⟨THERE SHE IS. RUBY STITCH. MAN, SHE LOOKS MEAN.⟩
⟨TARGET'S WITHIN RANGE, SIR.⟩
⟨EXCELLENT. FIRE. BLOW THAT WITCH TO H--⟩
SHATOOM!
WOOSH!

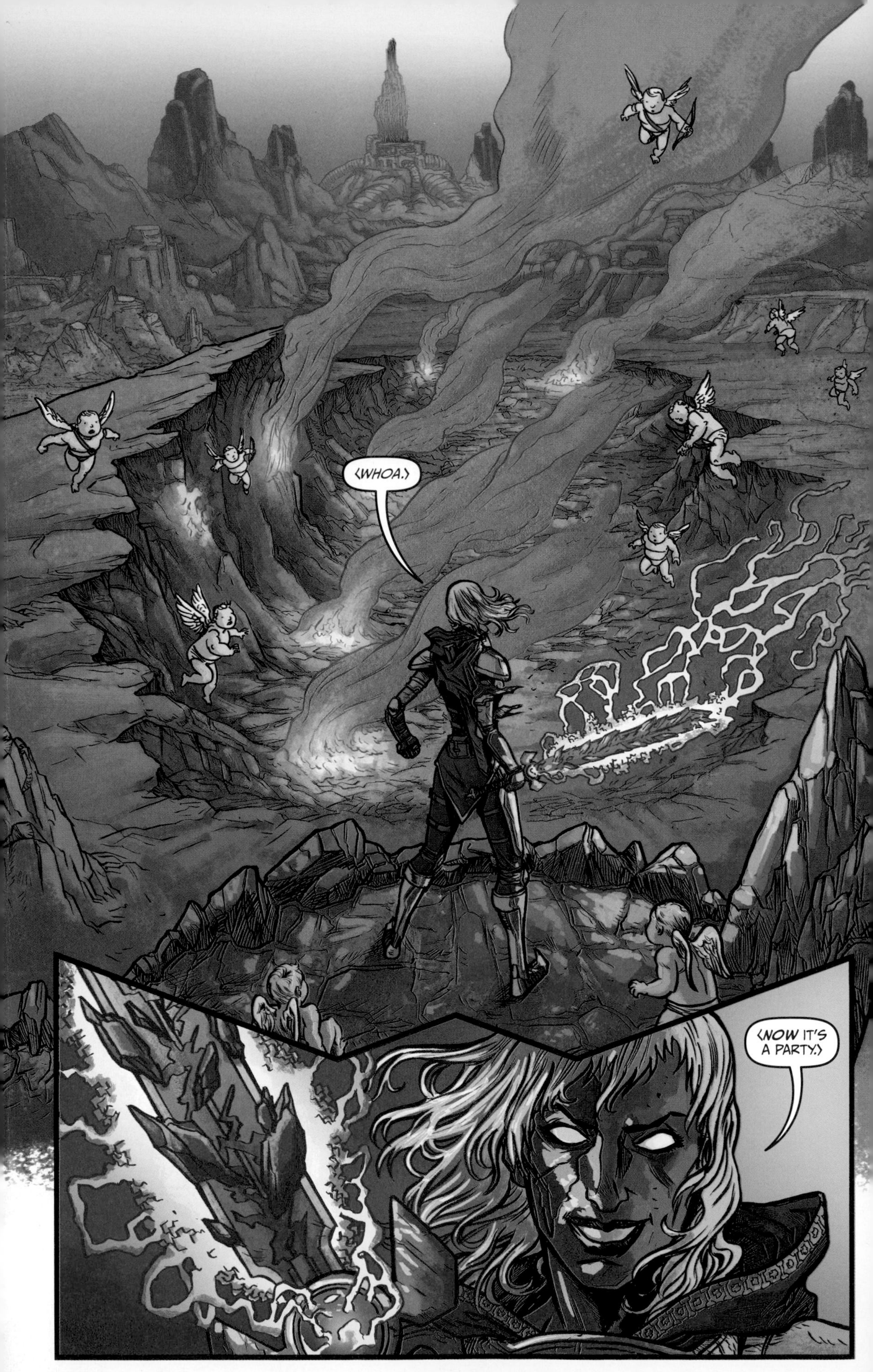
‹WHOA.›
‹NOW IT'S A PARTY.›

# FOUR

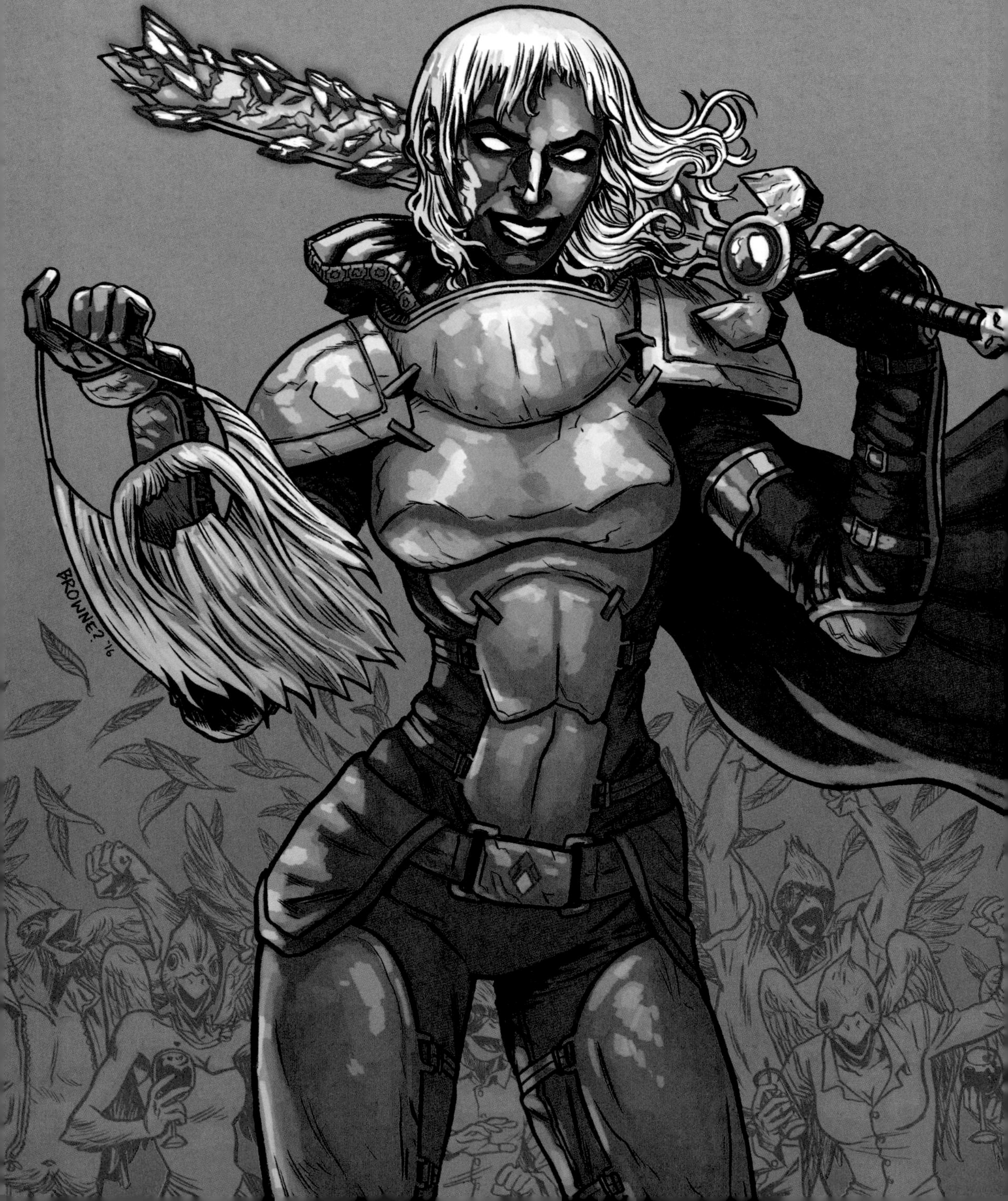
BROWNE? '16

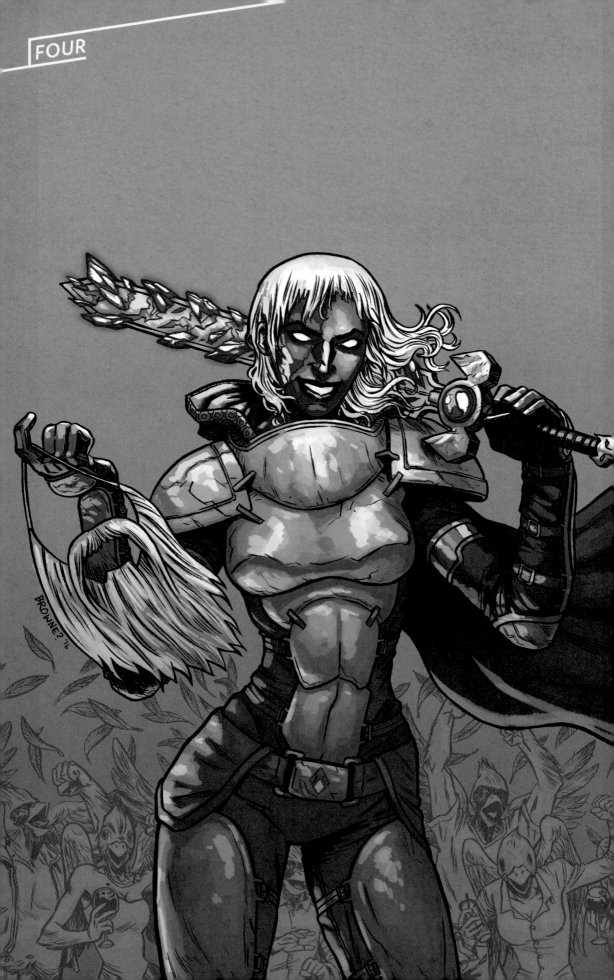

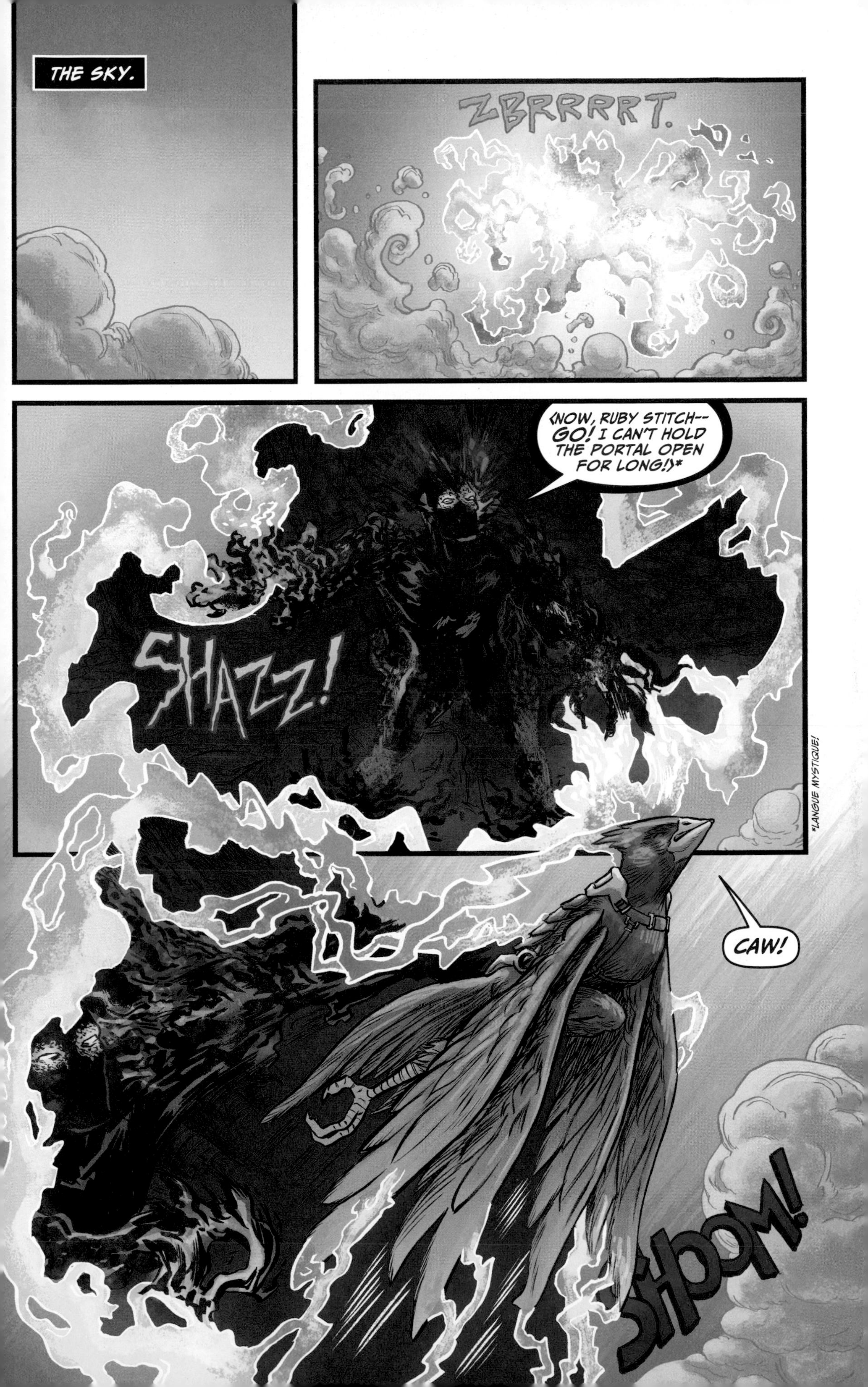
THE SKY.
ZBRRRRT.
‹NOW, RUBY STITCH-- GO! I CAN'T HOLD THE PORTAL OPEN FOR LONG!›*
SHAZZ!
CAW!
SHOOM!
*LANGUE MYSTIQUE!

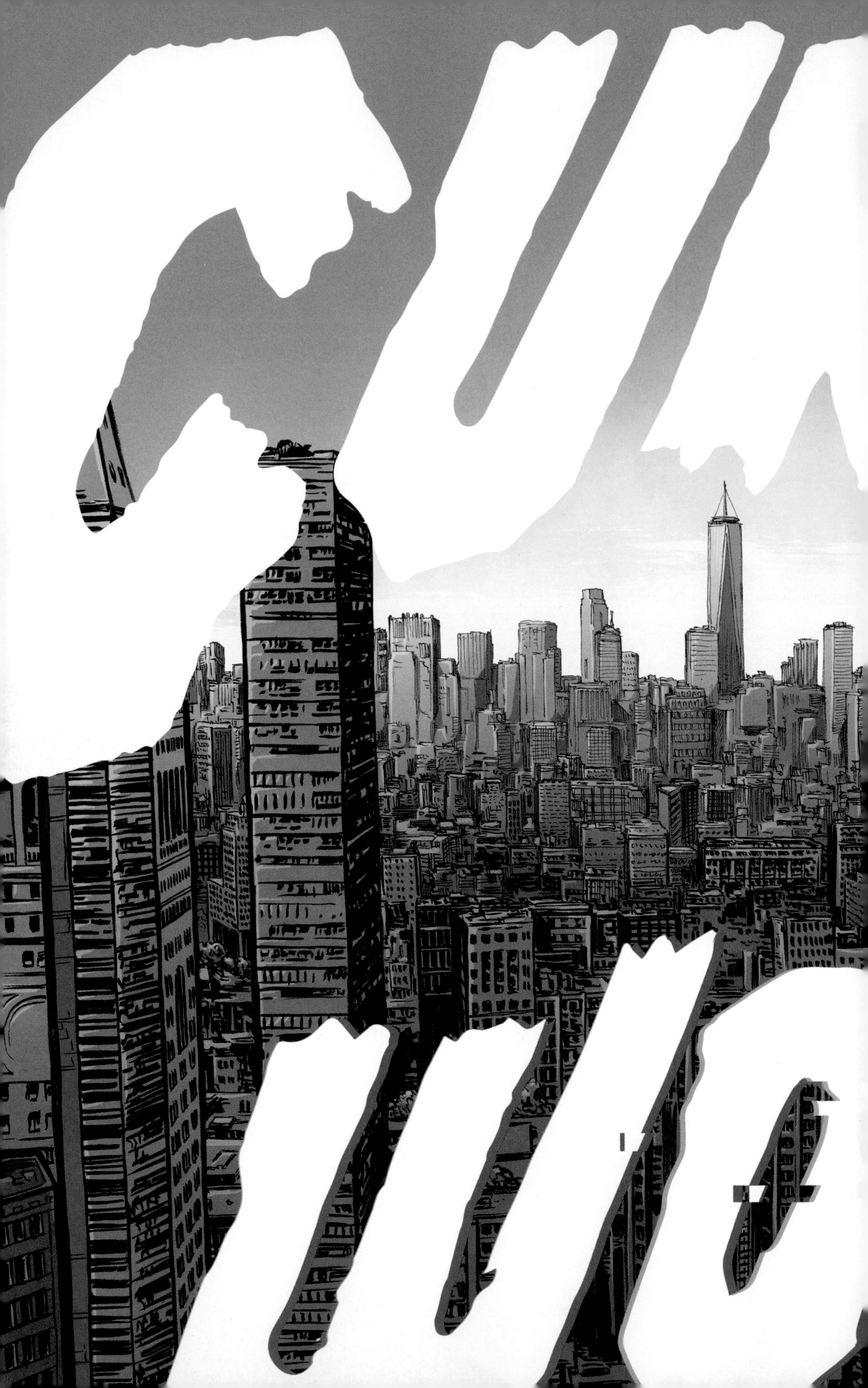

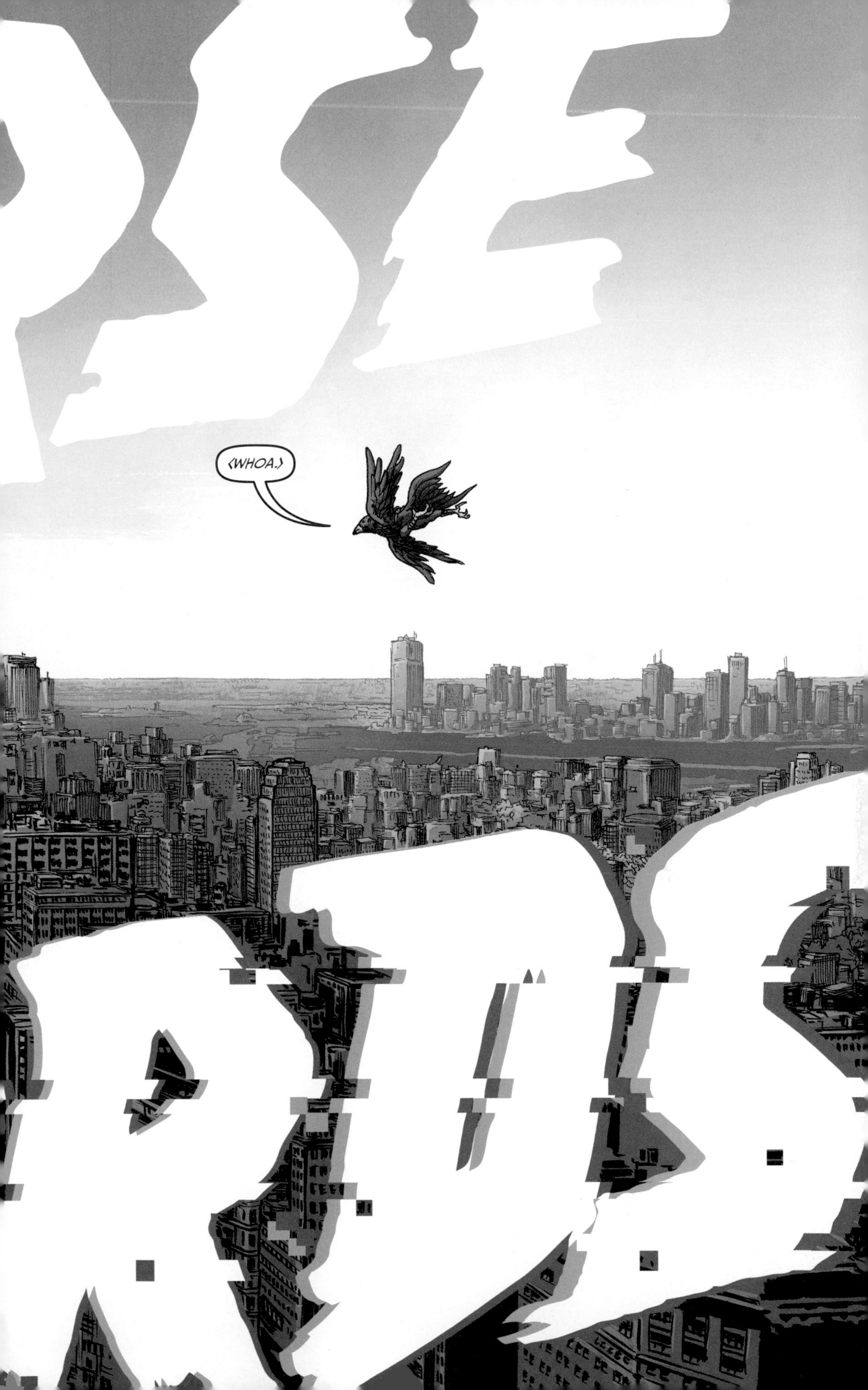
<WHOA.>

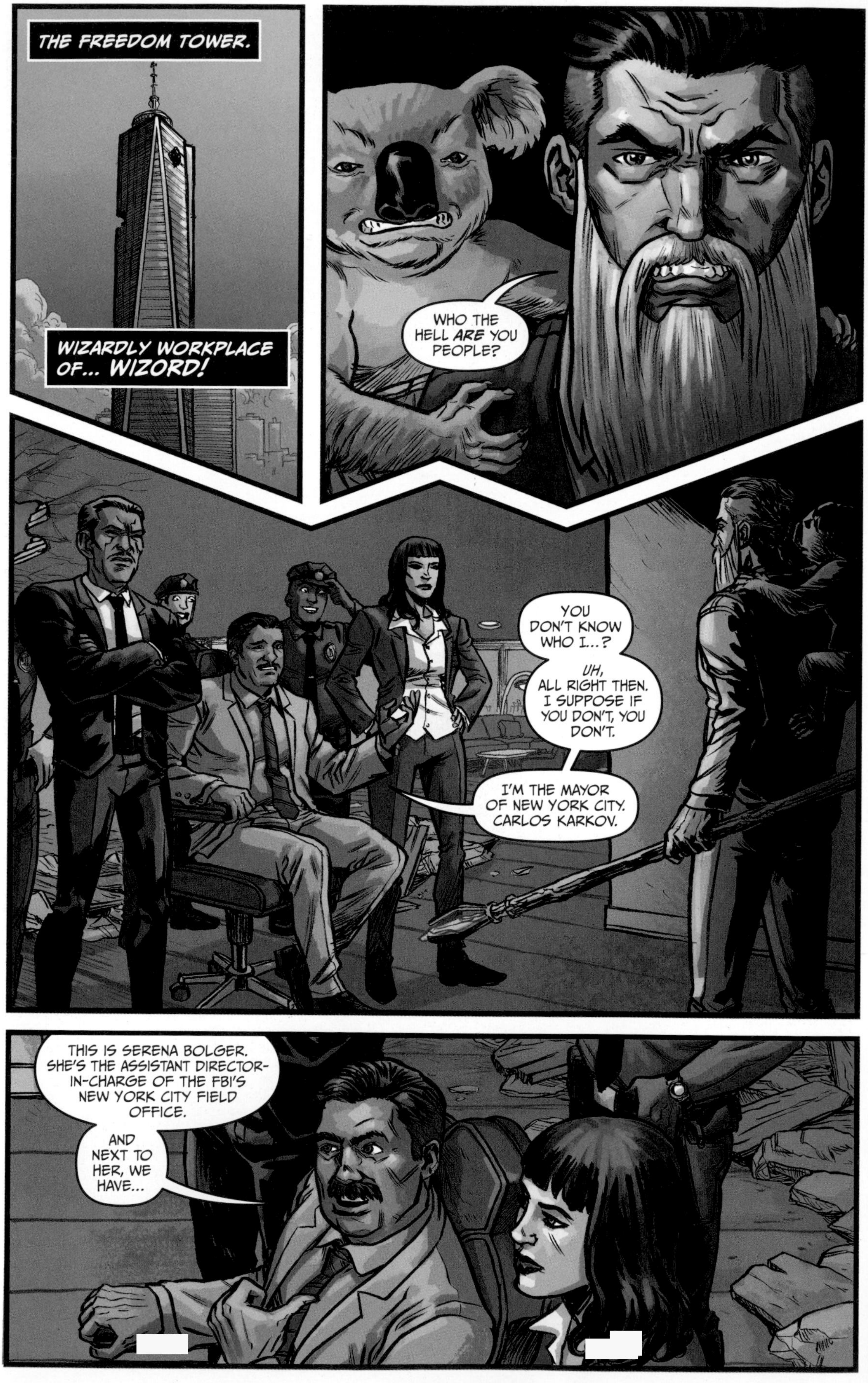
THE FREEDOM TOWER.
WIZARDLY WORKPLACE OF... WIZORD!
WHO THE HELL ARE YOU PEOPLE?
YOU DON'T KNOW WHO I...?
UH, ALL RIGHT THEN. I SUPPOSE IF YOU DON'T, YOU DON'T.
I'M THE MAYOR OF NEW YORK CITY. CARLOS KARKOV.
THIS IS SERENA BOLGER. SHE'S THE ASSISTANT DIRECTOR-IN-CHARGE OF THE FBI'S NEW YORK CITY FIELD OFFICE.
AND NEXT TO HER, WE HAVE...

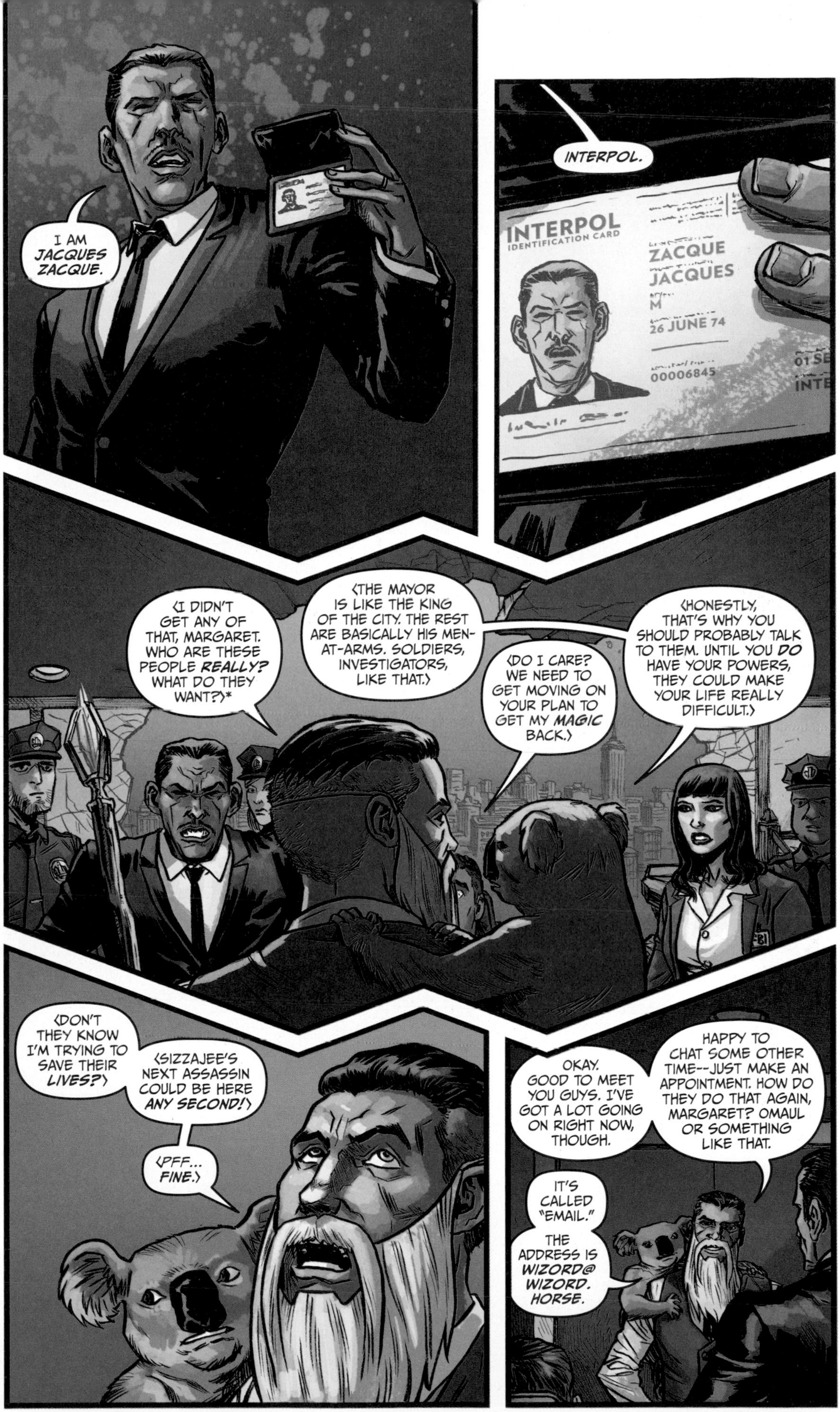
I AM JACQUES ZACQUE.
INTERPOL.
INTERPOL
IDENTIFICATION CARD
ZACQUE
JACQUES
M
26 JUNE 74
00006845
‹I DIDN'T GET ANY OF THAT, MARGARET. WHO ARE THESE PEOPLE REALLY? WHAT DO THEY WANT?›*
‹THE MAYOR IS LIKE THE KING OF THE CITY. THE REST ARE BASICALLY HIS MEN-AT-ARMS. SOLDIERS, INVESTIGATORS, LIKE THAT.›
‹DO I CARE? WE NEED TO GET MOVING ON YOUR PLAN TO GET MY MAGIC BACK.›
‹HONESTLY, THAT'S WHY YOU SHOULD PROBABLY TALK TO THEM. UNTIL YOU DO HAVE YOUR POWERS, THEY COULD MAKE YOUR LIFE REALLY DIFFICULT.›
FBI
‹DON'T THEY KNOW I'M TRYING TO SAVE THEIR LIVES?›
‹SIZZAJEE'S NEXT ASSASSIN COULD BE HERE ANY SECOND!›
‹PFF... FINE.›
OKAY. GOOD TO MEET YOU GUYS. I'VE GOT A LOT GOING ON RIGHT NOW, THOUGH.
HAPPY TO CHAT SOME OTHER TIME--JUST MAKE AN APPOINTMENT. HOW DO THEY DO THAT AGAIN, MARGARET? OMAUL OR SOMETHING LIKE THAT.
IT'S CALLED "EMAIL."
THE ADDRESS IS WIZORD@WIZORD.HORSE.

*ALSO LANGUE MYSTIQUE!

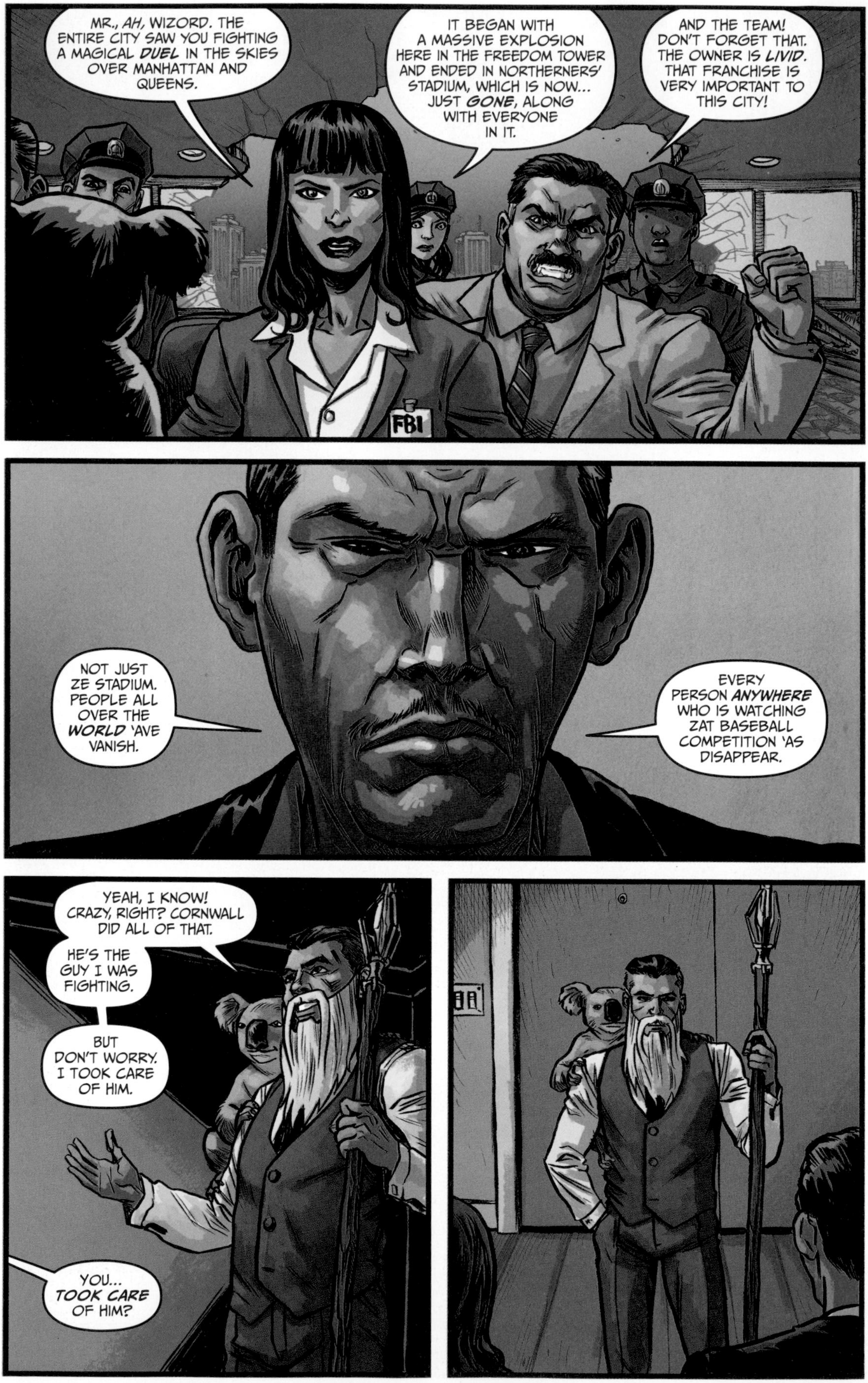
MR., AH, WIZORD. THE ENTIRE CITY SAW YOU FIGHTING A MAGICAL DUEL IN THE SKIES OVER MANHATTAN AND QUEENS.
IT BEGAN WITH A MASSIVE EXPLOSION HERE IN THE FREEDOM TOWER AND ENDED IN NORTHERNERS' STADIUM, WHICH IS NOW... JUST GONE, ALONG WITH EVERYONE IN IT.
AND THE TEAM! DON'T FORGET THAT. THE OWNER IS LIVID. THAT FRANCHISE IS VERY IMPORTANT TO THIS CITY!
FBI
NOT JUST ZE STADIUM. PEOPLE ALL OVER THE WORLD 'AVE VANISH.
EVERY PERSON ANYWHERE WHO IS WATCHING ZAT BASEBALL COMPETITION 'AS DISAPPEAR.
YEAH, I KNOW! CRAZY, RIGHT? CORNWALL DID ALL OF THAT.
HE'S THE GUY I WAS FIGHTING.
BUT DON'T WORRY. I TOOK CARE OF HIM.
YOU... TOOK CARE OF HIM?

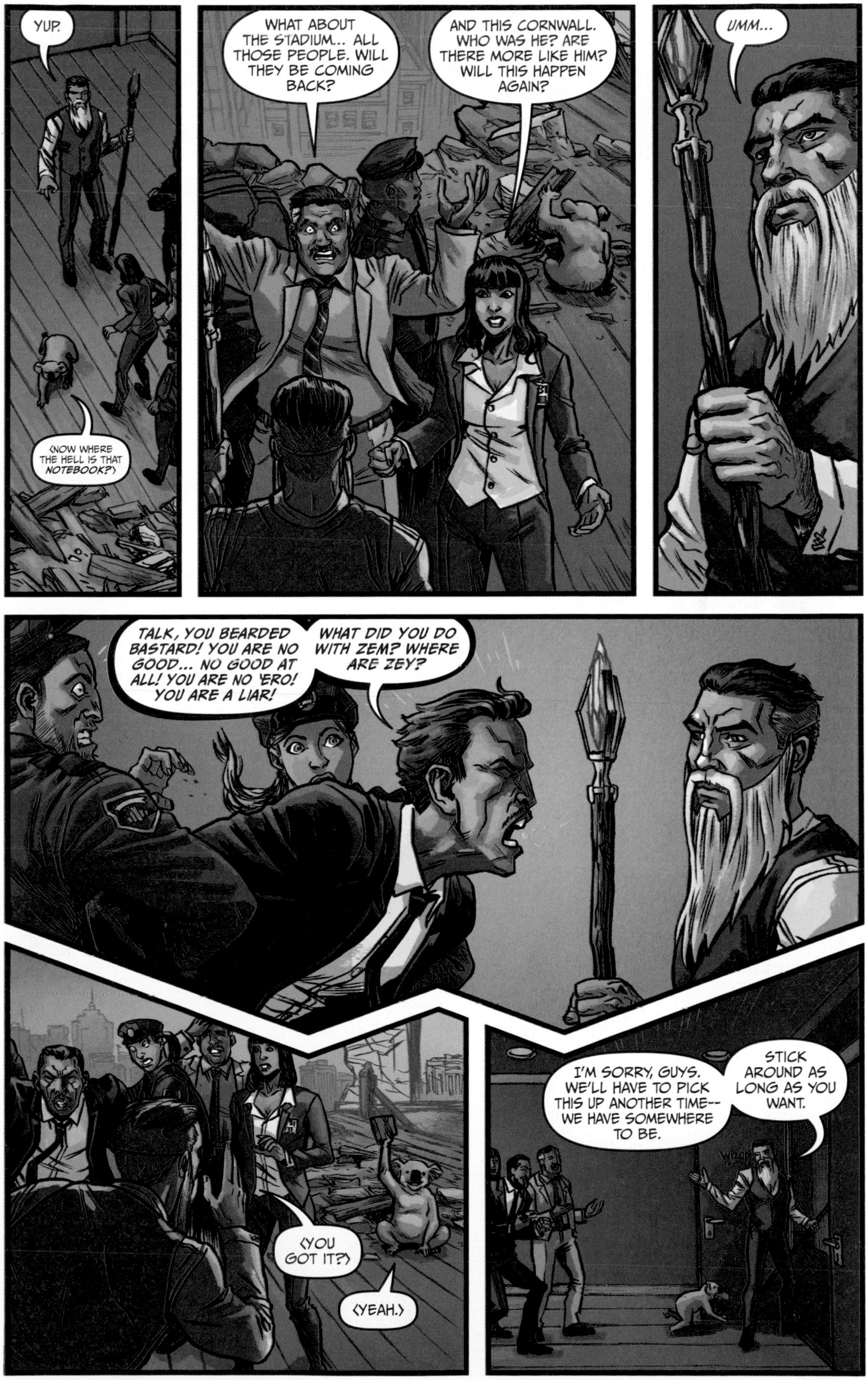
YUP.
<NOW WHERE THE HELL IS THAT NOTEBOOK?>
WHAT ABOUT THE STADIUM... ALL THOSE PEOPLE. WILL THEY BE COMING BACK?
AND THIS CORNWALL. WHO WAS HE? ARE THERE MORE LIKE HIM? WILL THIS HAPPEN AGAIN?
UMM...
TALK, YOU BEARDED BASTARD! YOU ARE NO GOOD... NO GOOD AT ALL! YOU ARE NO 'ERO! YOU ARE A LIAR!
WHAT DID YOU DO WITH ZEM? WHERE ARE ZEY?
<YOU GOT IT?>
<YEAH.>
I'M SORRY, GUYS. WE'LL HAVE TO PICK THIS UP ANOTHER TIME-- WE HAVE SOMEWHERE TO BE.
STICK AROUND AS LONG AS YOU WANT.

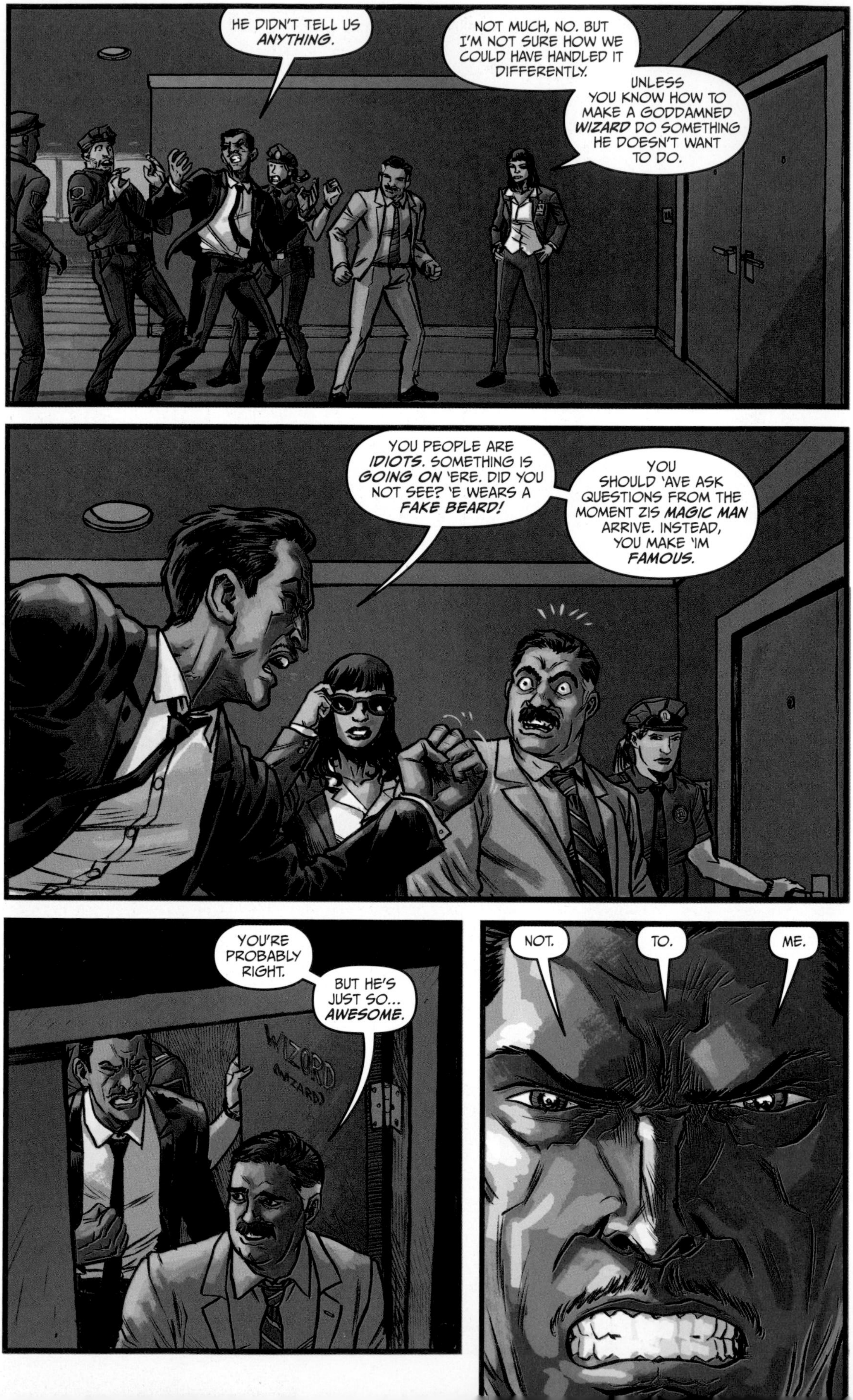
HE DIDN'T TELL US ANYTHING.
NOT MUCH, NO. BUT I'M NOT SURE HOW WE COULD HAVE HANDLED IT DIFFERENTLY.
UNLESS YOU KNOW HOW TO MAKE A GODDAMNED WIZARD DO SOMETHING HE DOESN'T WANT TO DO.
YOU PEOPLE ARE IDIOTS. SOMETHING IS GOING ON 'ERE. DID YOU NOT SEE? 'E WEARS A FAKE BEARD!
YOU SHOULD 'AVE ASK QUESTIONS FROM THE MOMENT ZIS MAGIC MAN ARRIVE. INSTEAD, YOU MAKE 'IM FAMOUS.
YOU'RE PROBABLY RIGHT.
BUT HE'S JUST SO... AWESOME.
NOT.
TO.
ME.

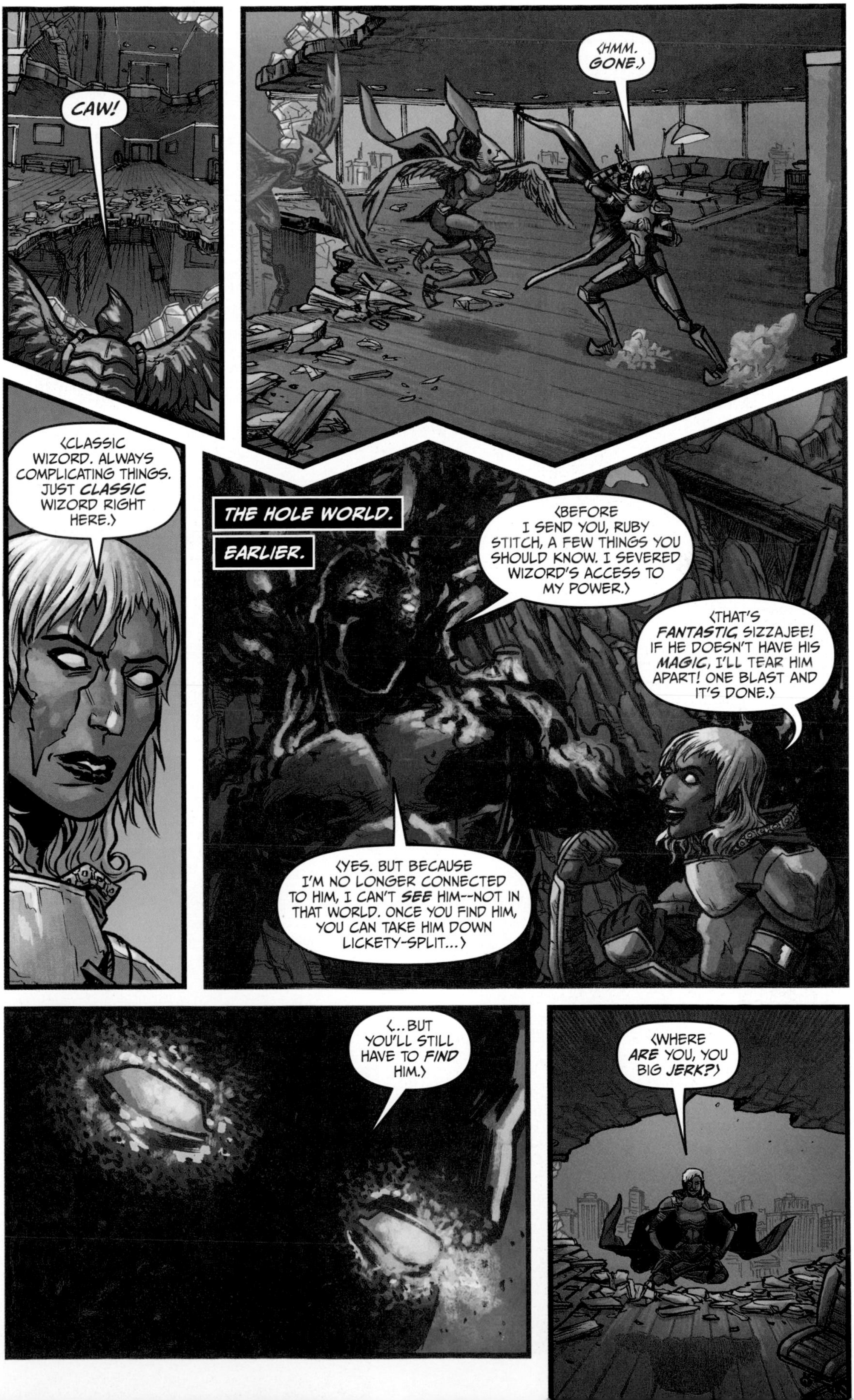
CAW!
‹HMM. GONE.›
‹CLASSIC WIZORD. ALWAYS COMPLICATING THINGS. JUST CLASSIC WIZORD RIGHT HERE.›
THE HOLE WORLD.
EARLIER.
‹BEFORE I SEND YOU, RUBY STITCH, A FEW THINGS YOU SHOULD KNOW. I SEVERED WIZORD'S ACCESS TO MY POWER.›
‹THAT'S FANTASTIC SIZZAJEE! IF HE DOESN'T HAVE HIS MAGIC, I'LL TEAR HIM APART! ONE BLAST AND IT'S DONE.›
‹YES. BUT BECAUSE I'M NO LONGER CONNECTED TO HIM, I CAN'T SEE HIM--NOT IN THAT WORLD. ONCE YOU FIND HIM, YOU CAN TAKE HIM DOWN LICKETY-SPLIT...›
‹...BUT YOU'LL STILL HAVE TO FIND HIM.›
‹WHERE ARE YOU, YOU BIG JERK?›

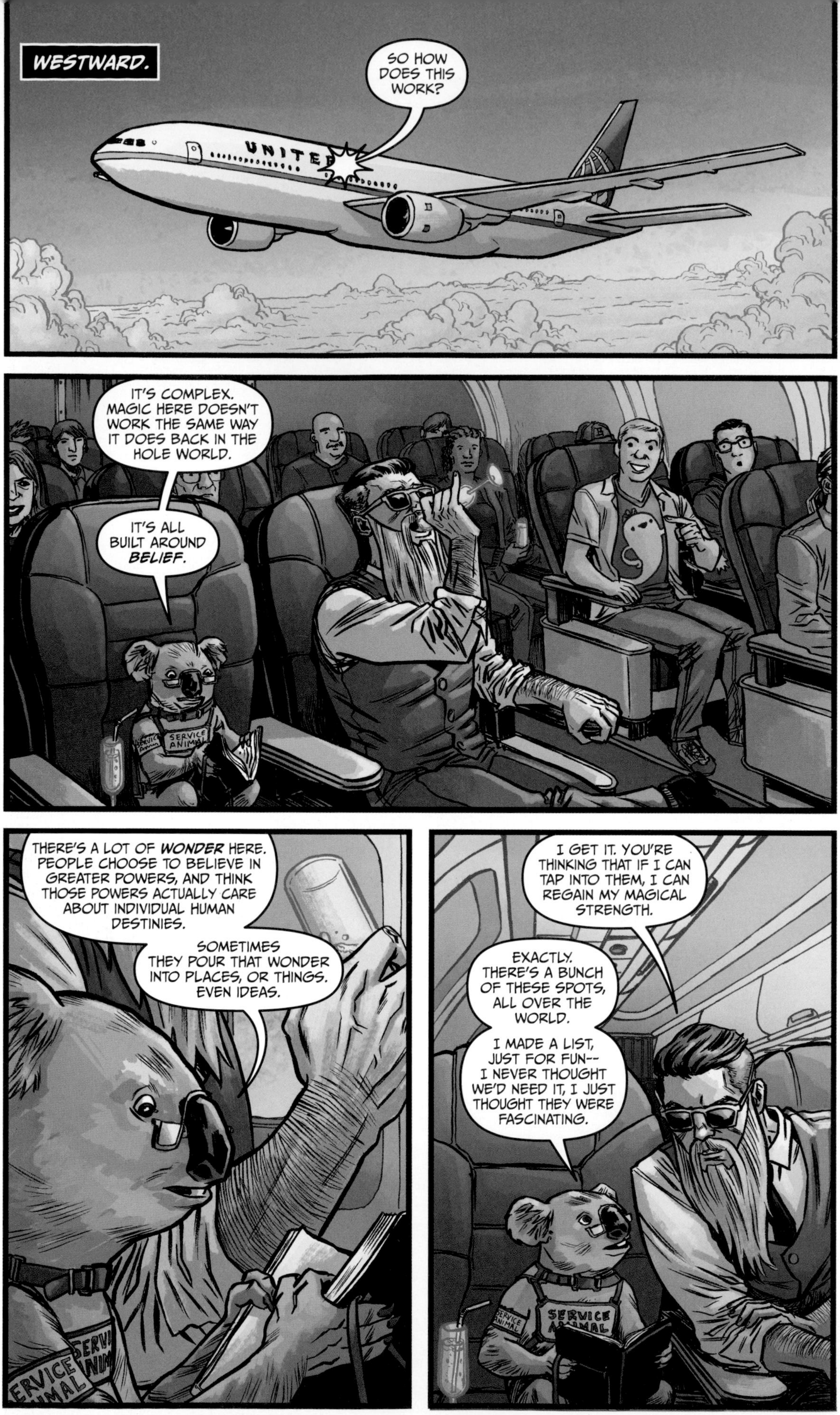

WESTWARD.
SO HOW DOES THIS WORK?
UNITED
IT'S COMPLEX. MAGIC HERE DOESN'T WORK THE SAME WAY IT DOES BACK IN THE HOLE WORLD.
IT'S ALL BUILT AROUND BELIEF.
SERVICE ANIMAL
THERE'S A LOT OF WONDER HERE. PEOPLE CHOOSE TO BELIEVE IN GREATER POWERS, AND THINK THOSE POWERS ACTUALLY CARE ABOUT INDIVIDUAL HUMAN DESTINIES.
SOMETIMES THEY POUR THAT WONDER INTO PLACES, OR THINGS. EVEN IDEAS.
I GET IT. YOU'RE THINKING THAT IF I CAN TAP INTO THEM, I CAN REGAIN MY MAGICAL STRENGTH.
EXACTLY. THERE'S A BUNCH OF THESE SPOTS, ALL OVER THE WORLD.
I MADE A LIST, JUST FOR FUN-- I NEVER THOUGHT WE'D NEED IT, I JUST THOUGHT THEY WERE FASCINATING.
SERVICE ANIMAL

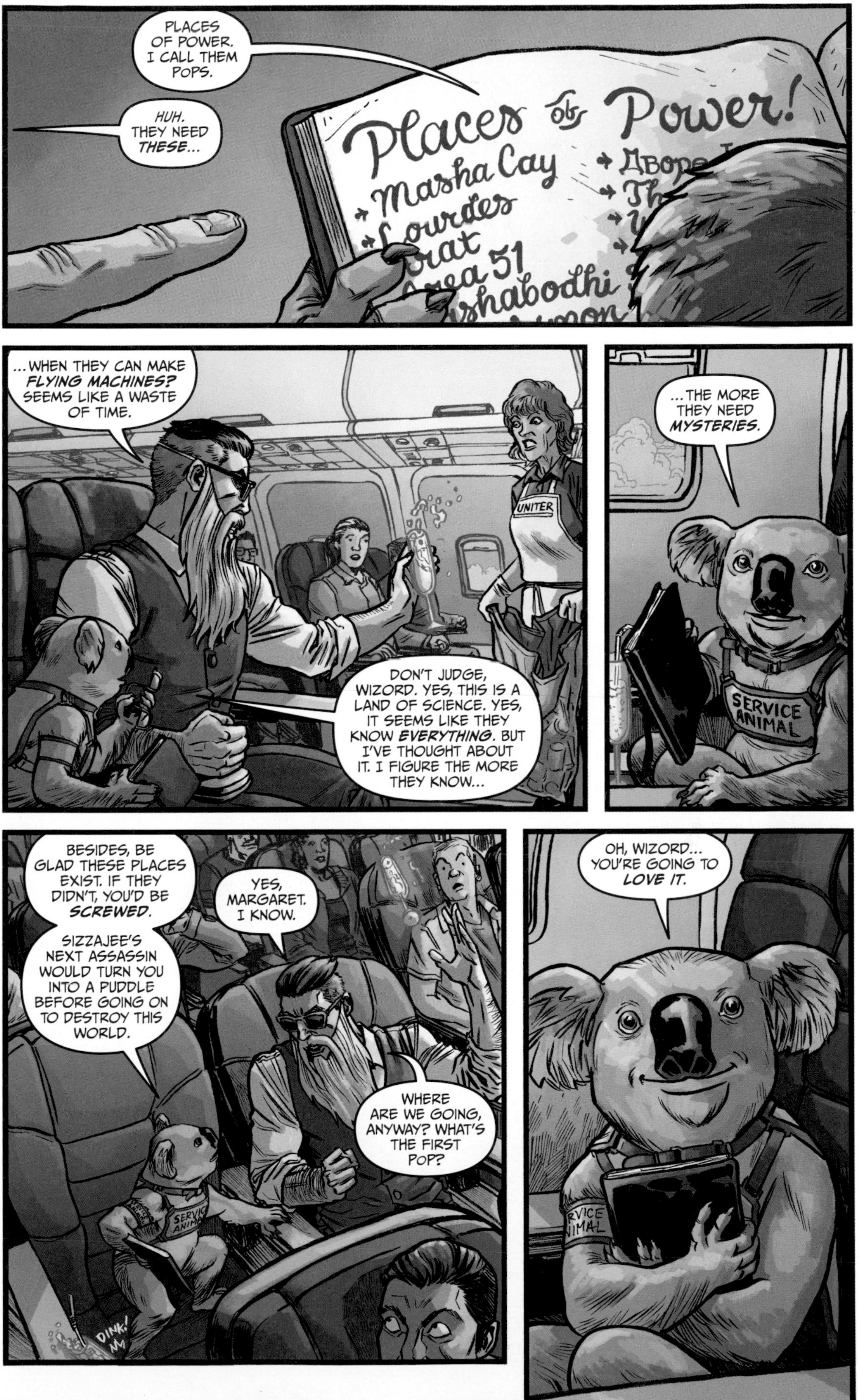
PLACES OF POWER. I CALL THEM POPS.
HUH. THEY NEED THESE...
Places of Power!
Masha Cay
Lourdes
Area 51
...WHEN THEY CAN MAKE FLYING MACHINES? SEEMS LIKE A WASTE OF TIME.
UNITER
DON'T JUDGE, WIZORD. YES, THIS IS A LAND OF SCIENCE. YES, IT SEEMS LIKE THEY KNOW EVERYTHING. BUT I'VE THOUGHT ABOUT IT. I FIGURE THE MORE THEY KNOW...
...THE MORE THEY NEED MYSTERIES.
SERVICE ANIMAL
BESIDES, BE GLAD THESE PLACES EXIST. IF THEY DIDN'T, YOU'D BE SCREWED.
SIZZAJEE'S NEXT ASSASSIN WOULD TURN YOU INTO A PUDDLE BEFORE GOING ON TO DESTROY THIS WORLD.
YES, MARGARET. I KNOW.
WHERE ARE WE GOING, ANYWAY? WHAT'S THE FIRST POP?
SERVICE ANIMAL
DINK!
OH, WIZORD... YOU'RE GOING TO LOVE IT.
SERVICE ANIMAL

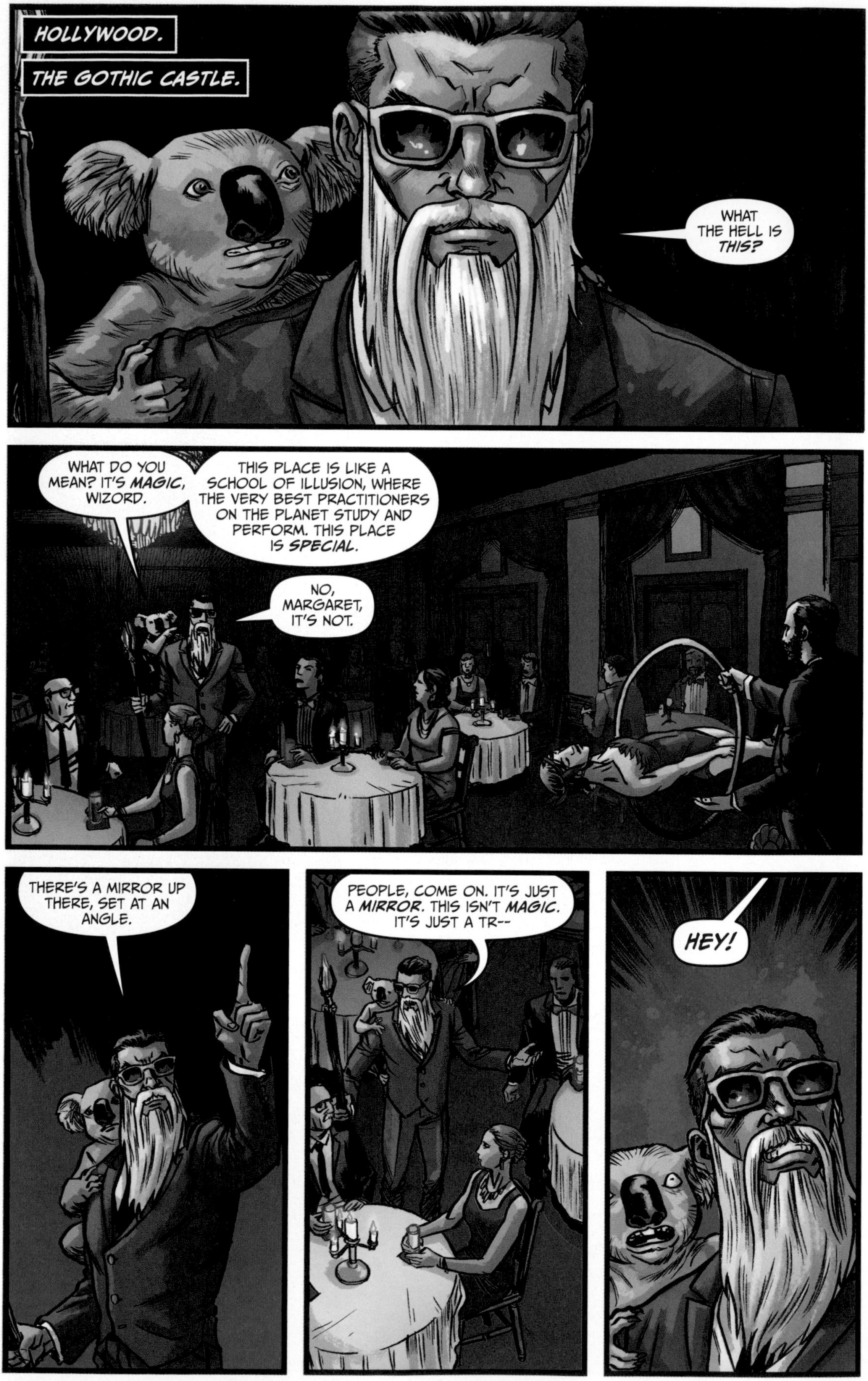
HOLLYWOOD.
THE GOTHIC CASTLE.
WHAT THE HELL IS THIS?
WHAT DO YOU MEAN? IT'S MAGIC, WIZORD.
THIS PLACE IS LIKE A SCHOOL OF ILLUSION, WHERE THE VERY BEST PRACTITIONERS ON THE PLANET STUDY AND PERFORM. THIS PLACE IS SPECIAL.
NO, MARGARET, IT'S NOT.
THERE'S A MIRROR UP THERE, SET AT AN ANGLE.
PEOPLE, COME ON. IT'S JUST A MIRROR. THIS ISN'T MAGIC. IT'S JUST A TR--
HEY!

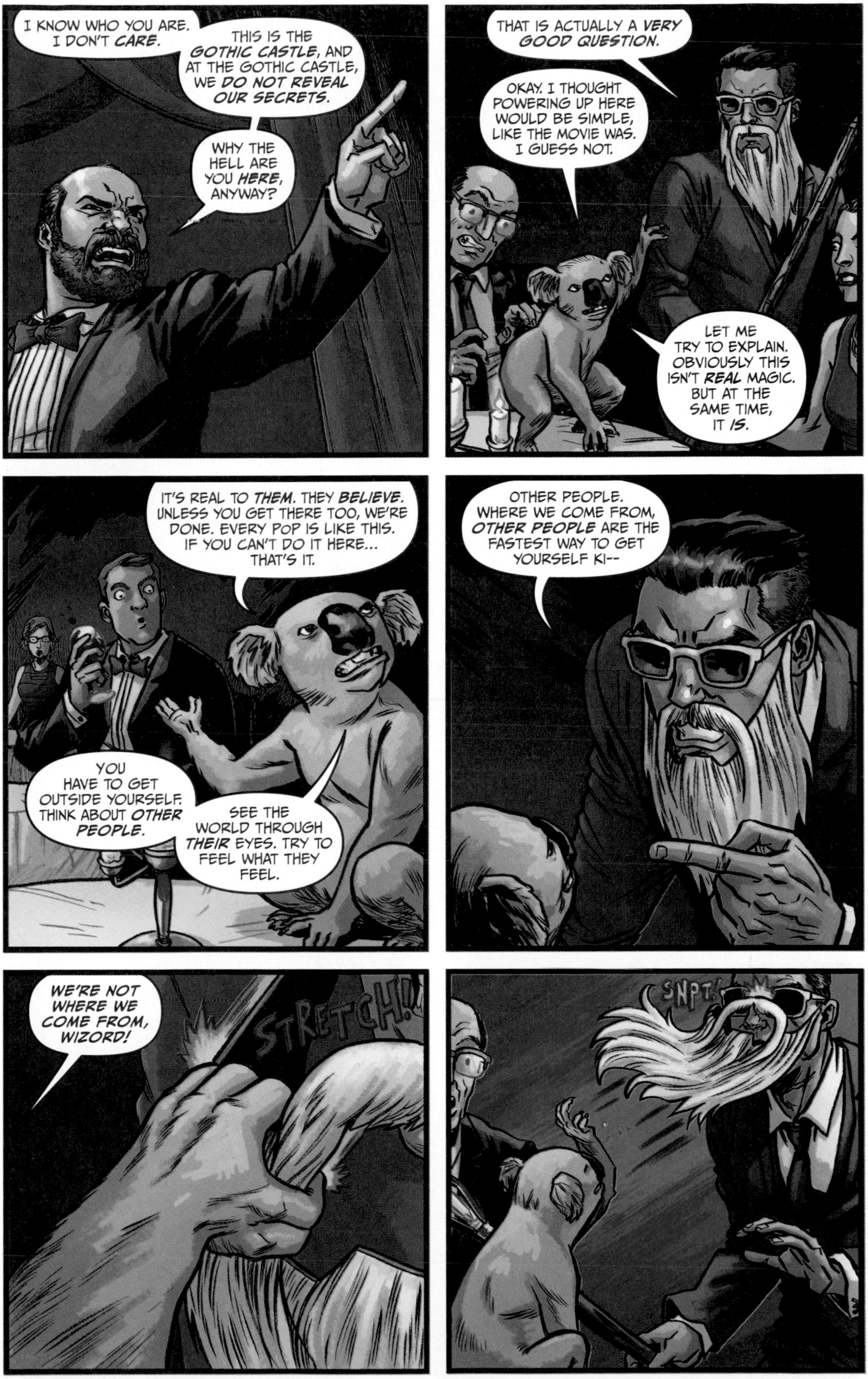
I KNOW WHO YOU ARE. I DON'T CARE.
THIS IS THE GOTHIC CASTLE, AND AT THE GOTHIC CASTLE, WE DO NOT REVEAL OUR SECRETS.
WHY THE HELL ARE YOU HERE, ANYWAY?
THAT IS ACTUALLY A VERY GOOD QUESTION.
OKAY. I THOUGHT POWERING UP HERE WOULD BE SIMPLE, LIKE THE MOVIE WAS. I GUESS NOT.
LET ME TRY TO EXPLAIN. OBVIOUSLY THIS ISN'T REAL MAGIC. BUT AT THE SAME TIME, IT IS.
IT'S REAL TO THEM. THEY BELIEVE. UNLESS YOU GET THERE TOO, WE'RE DONE. EVERY POP IS LIKE THIS. IF YOU CAN'T DO IT HERE... THAT'S IT.
YOU HAVE TO GET OUTSIDE YOURSELF. THINK ABOUT OTHER PEOPLE.
SEE THE WORLD THROUGH THEIR EYES. TRY TO FEEL WHAT THEY FEEL.
OTHER PEOPLE. WHERE WE COME FROM, OTHER PEOPLE ARE THE FASTEST WAY TO GET YOURSELF KI--
WE'RE NOT WHERE WE COME FROM, WIZORD!
STRETCH!!
SNPT!

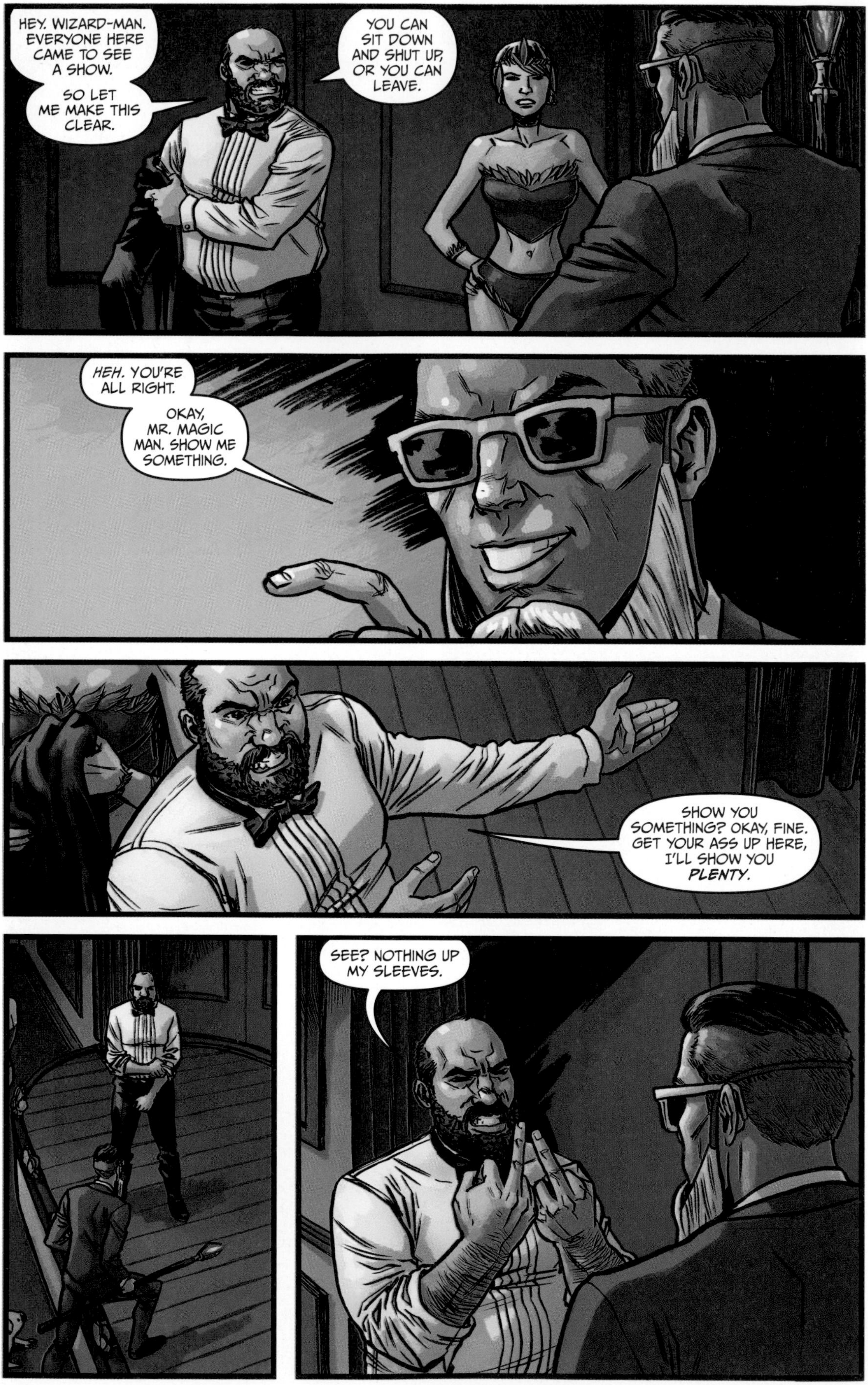
HEY. WIZARD-MAN. EVERYONE HERE CAME TO SEE A SHOW.
SO LET ME MAKE THIS CLEAR.
YOU CAN SIT DOWN AND SHUT UP, OR YOU CAN LEAVE.
HEH. YOU'RE ALL RIGHT.
OKAY, MR. MAGIC MAN. SHOW ME SOMETHING.
SHOW YOU SOMETHING? OKAY, FINE. GET YOUR ASS UP HERE, I'LL SHOW YOU *PLENTY*.
SEE? NOTHING UP MY SLEEVES.

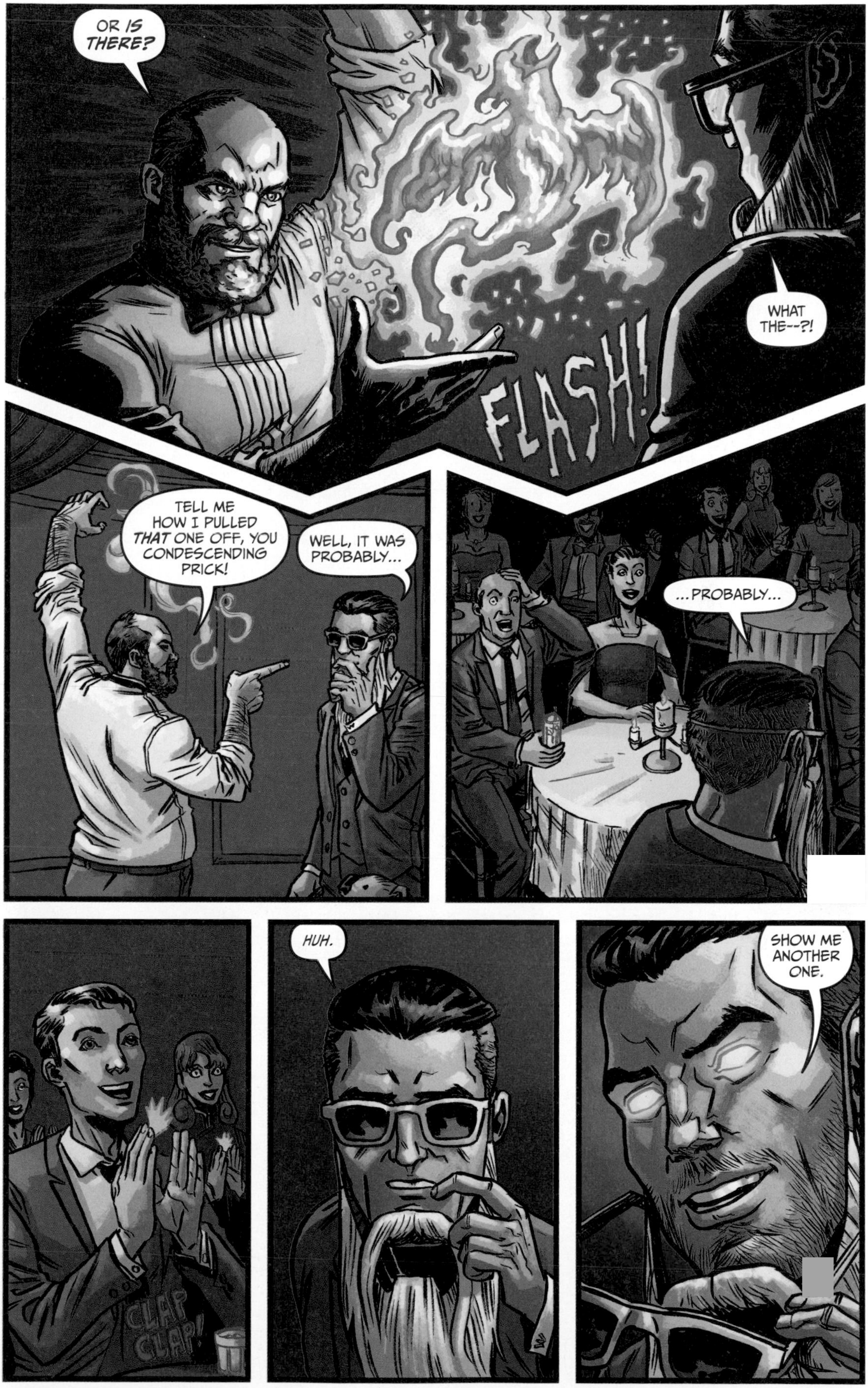
OR *IS* *THERE?*
WHAT THE--?!
FLASH!
TELL ME HOW I PULLED *THAT* ONE OFF, YOU CONDESCENDING PRICK!
WELL, IT WAS PROBABLY...
...PROBABLY...
CLAP CLAP!
*HUH.*
SHOW ME ANOTHER ONE.

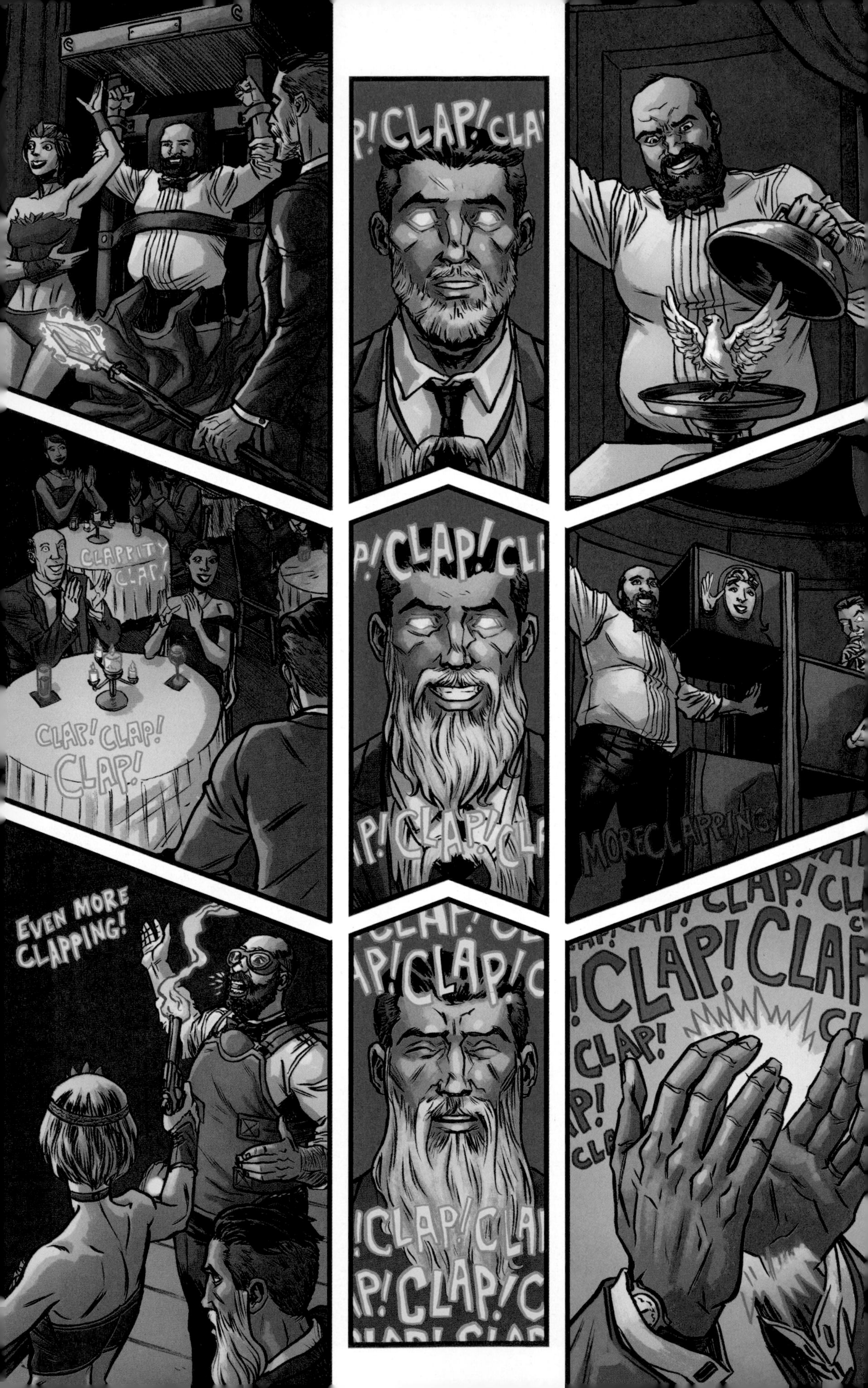

P! CLAP! CLA
CLAPPITY CLAP!
CLAP! CLAP! CLAP!
P! CLAP! CL
P! CLAP! CLA
MORE CLAPPING!
EVEN MORE CLAPPING!
AP! CLAP! C
! CLAP! CLA
P! CLAP! C
CLAP! CLAP!
! CLAP! CLAP
CLAP!
P!

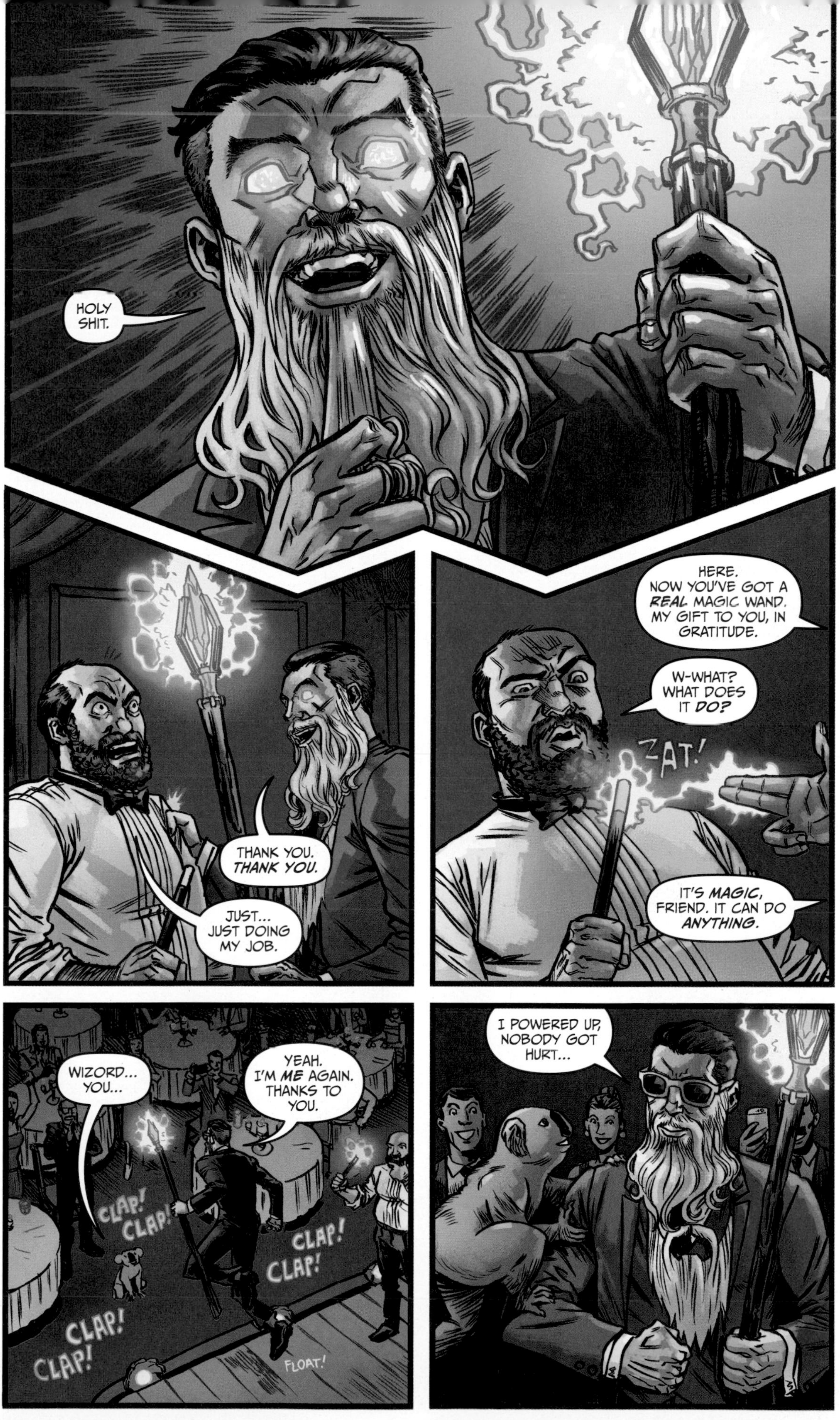
HOLY SHIT.
THANK YOU. THANK YOU.
JUST... JUST DOING MY JOB.
HERE. NOW YOU'VE GOT A REAL MAGIC WAND. MY GIFT TO YOU, IN GRATITUDE.
W-WHAT? WHAT DOES IT DO?
ZAT!
IT'S MAGIC, FRIEND. IT CAN DO ANYTHING.
WIZORD... YOU...
YEAH. I'M ME AGAIN. THANKS TO YOU.
CLAP! CLAP!
CLAP! CLAP!
CLAP! CLAP!
FLOAT!
I POWERED UP, NOBODY GOT HURT...

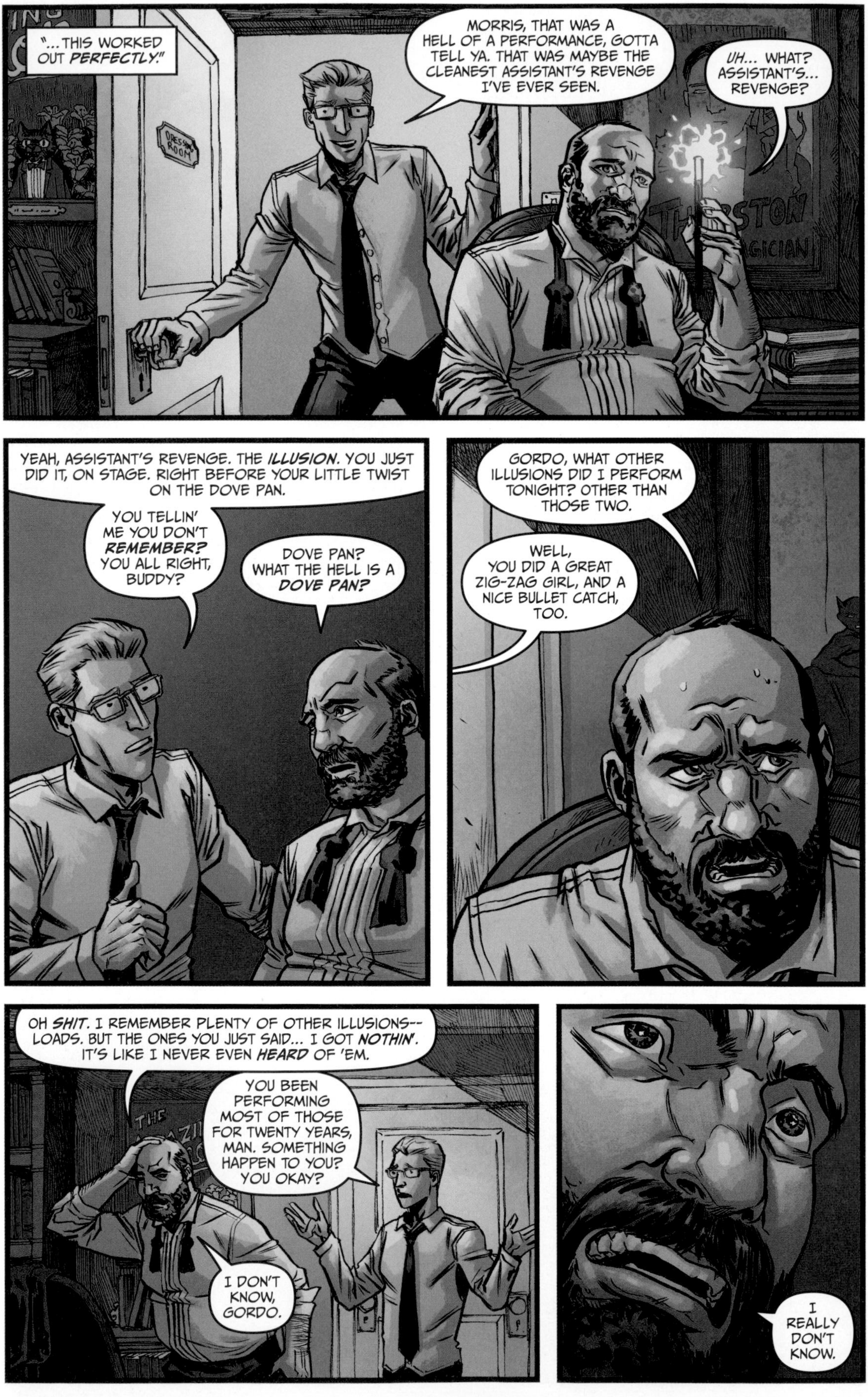
"...THIS WORKED OUT PERFECTLY."
MORRIS, THAT WAS A HELL OF A PERFORMANCE, GOTTA TELL YA. THAT WAS MAYBE THE CLEANEST ASSISTANT'S REVENGE I'VE EVER SEEN.
UH... WHAT? ASSISTANT'S... REVENGE?
DRESSING ROOM
THURSTON
MAGICIAN
YEAH, ASSISTANT'S REVENGE. THE ILLUSION. YOU JUST DID IT, ON STAGE. RIGHT BEFORE YOUR LITTLE TWIST ON THE DOVE PAN.
YOU TELLIN' ME YOU DON'T REMEMBER? YOU ALL RIGHT, BUDDY?
DOVE PAN? WHAT THE HELL IS A DOVE PAN?
GORDO, WHAT OTHER ILLUSIONS DID I PERFORM TONIGHT? OTHER THAN THOSE TWO.
WELL, YOU DID A GREAT ZIG-ZAG GIRL, AND A NICE BULLET CATCH, TOO.
OH SHIT. I REMEMBER PLENTY OF OTHER ILLUSIONS-- LOADS. BUT THE ONES YOU JUST SAID... I GOT NOTHIN'. IT'S LIKE I NEVER EVEN HEARD OF 'EM.
YOU BEEN PERFORMING MOST OF THOSE FOR TWENTY YEARS, MAN. SOMETHING HAPPEN TO YOU? YOU OKAY?
I DON'T KNOW, GORDO.
I REALLY DON'T KNOW.

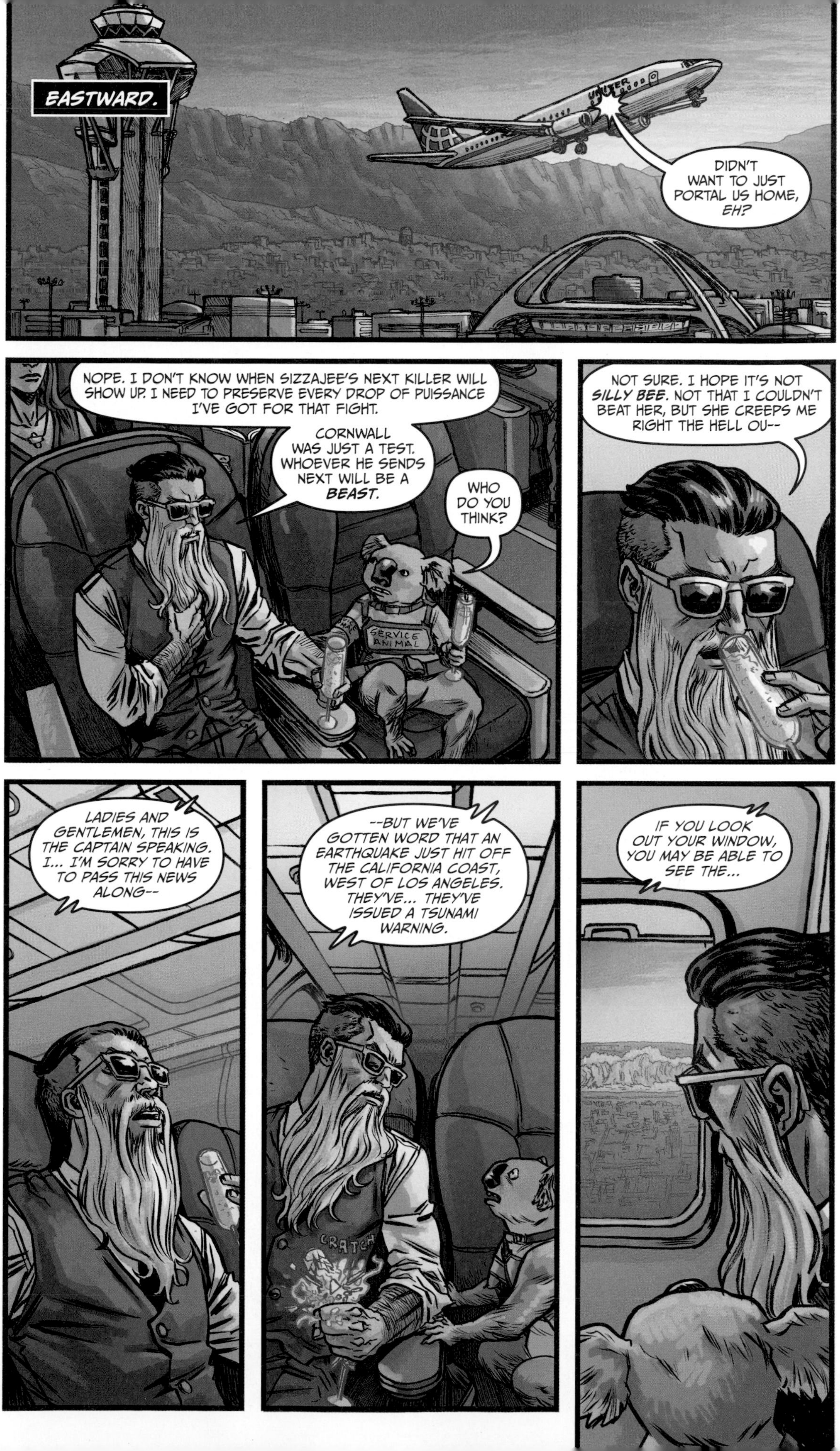
EASTWARD.
DIDN'T WANT TO JUST PORTAL US HOME, EH?
NOPE. I DON'T KNOW WHEN SIZZAJEE'S NEXT KILLER WILL SHOW UP. I NEED TO PRESERVE EVERY DROP OF PUISSANCE I'VE GOT FOR THAT FIGHT.
CORNWALL WAS JUST A TEST. WHOEVER HE SENDS NEXT WILL BE A BEAST.
WHO DO YOU THINK?
SERVICE ANIMAL
NOT SURE. I HOPE IT'S NOT SILLY BEE. NOT THAT I COULDN'T BEAT HER, BUT SHE CREEPS ME RIGHT THE HELL OU--
LADIES AND GENTLEMEN, THIS IS THE CAPTAIN SPEAKING. I... I'M SORRY TO HAVE TO PASS THIS NEWS ALONG--
--BUT WE'VE GOTTEN WORD THAT AN EARTHQUAKE JUST HIT OFF THE CALIFORNIA COAST, WEST OF LOS ANGELES. THEY'VE... THEY'VE ISSUED A TSUNAMI WARNING.
IF YOU LOOK OUT YOUR WINDOW, YOU MAY BE ABLE TO SEE THE...

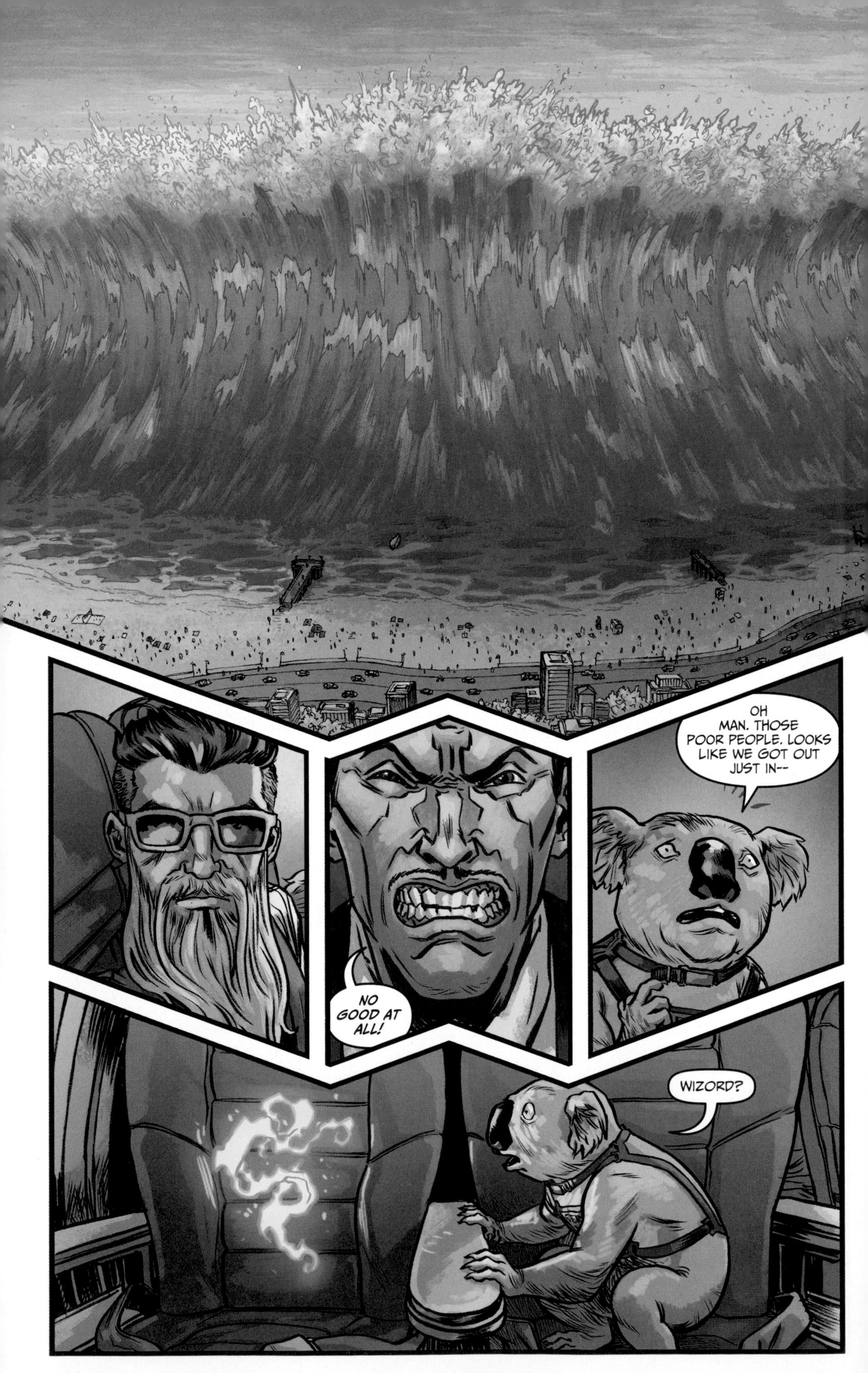
OH MAN. THOSE POOR PEOPLE. LOOKS LIKE WE GOT OUT JUST IN--
NO GOOD AT ALL!
WIZORD?

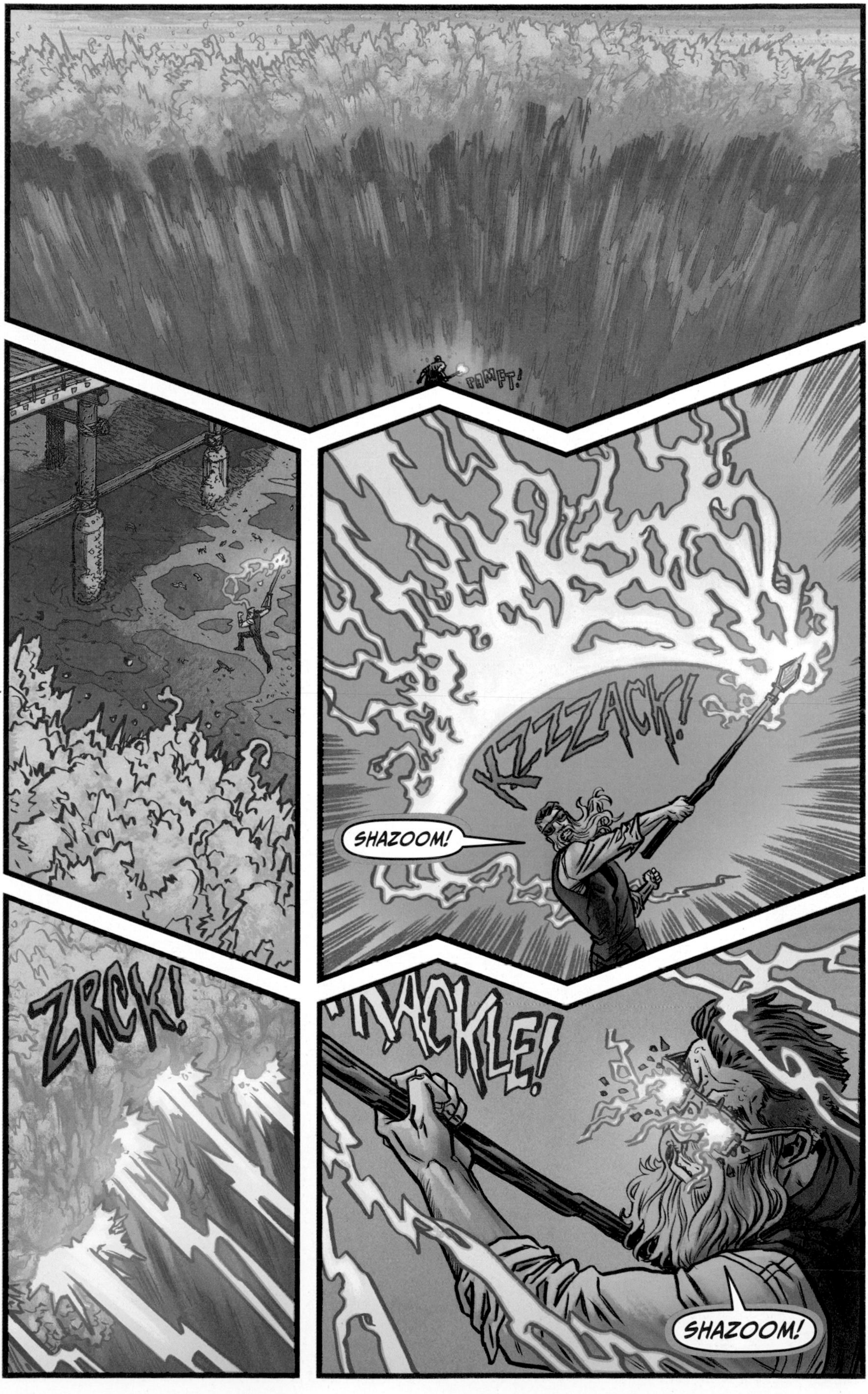
PAMFT!
KZZZZACK!
SHAZOOM!
ZRCK!
RACKLE!
SHAZOOM!

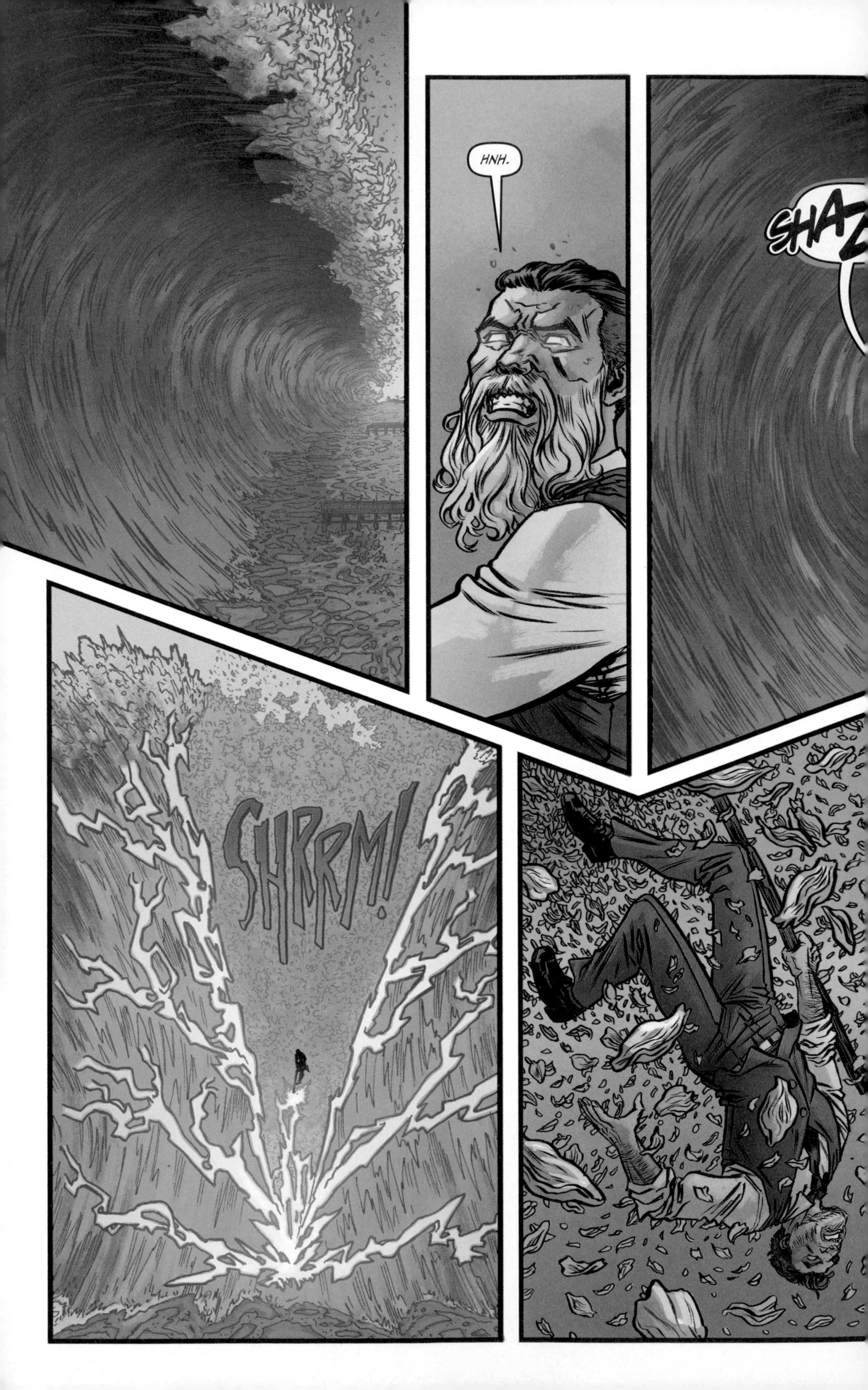
HNH.
SHRRM!

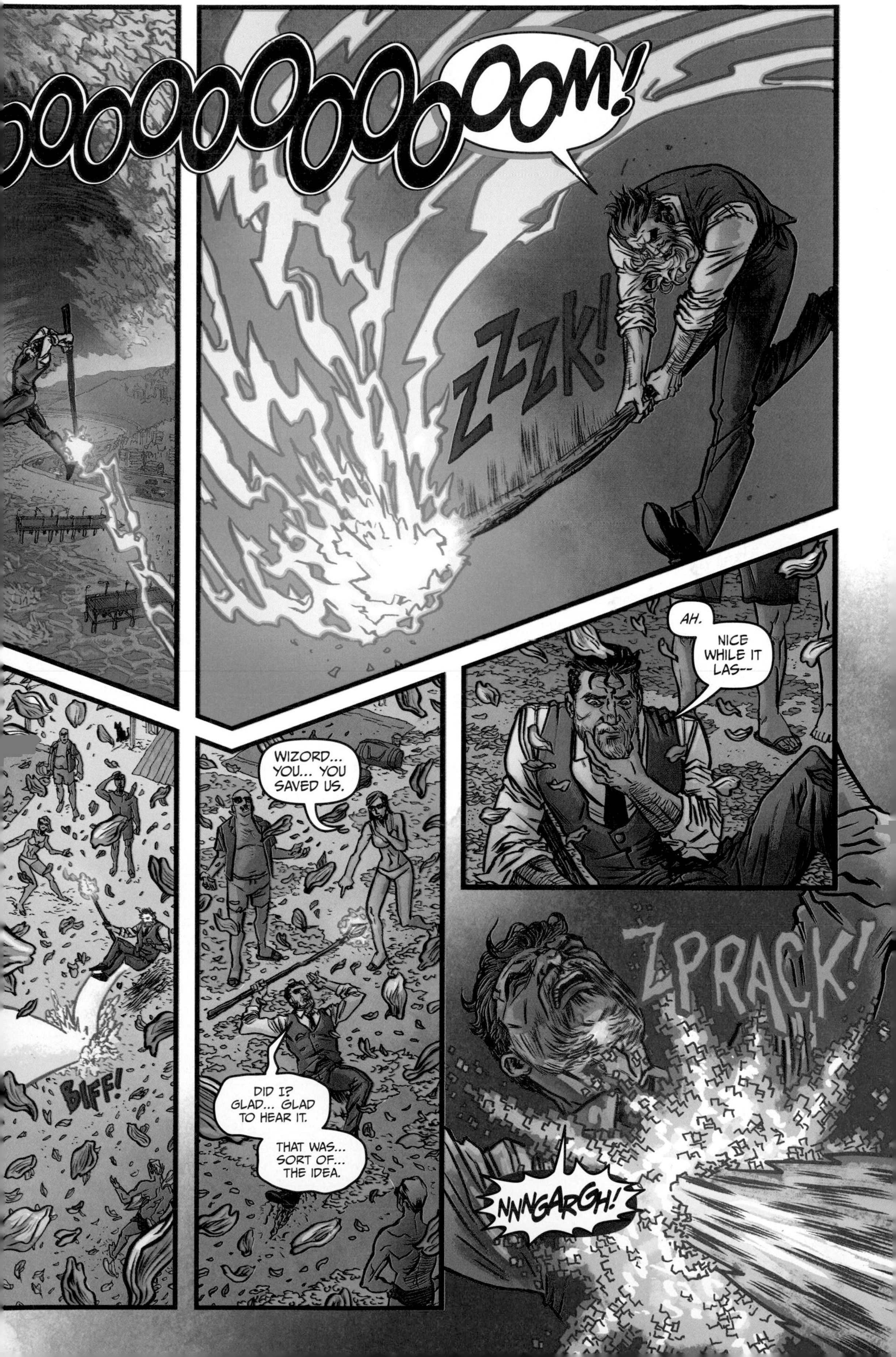
OOOOOOOOOOOOOM!
ZZZK!
BIFF!
WIZORD... YOU... YOU SAVED US.
DID I? GLAD... GLAD TO HEAR IT.
THAT WAS... SORT OF... THE IDEA.
AH.
NICE WHILE IT LAS--
ZPRACK!
NNNGARGH!

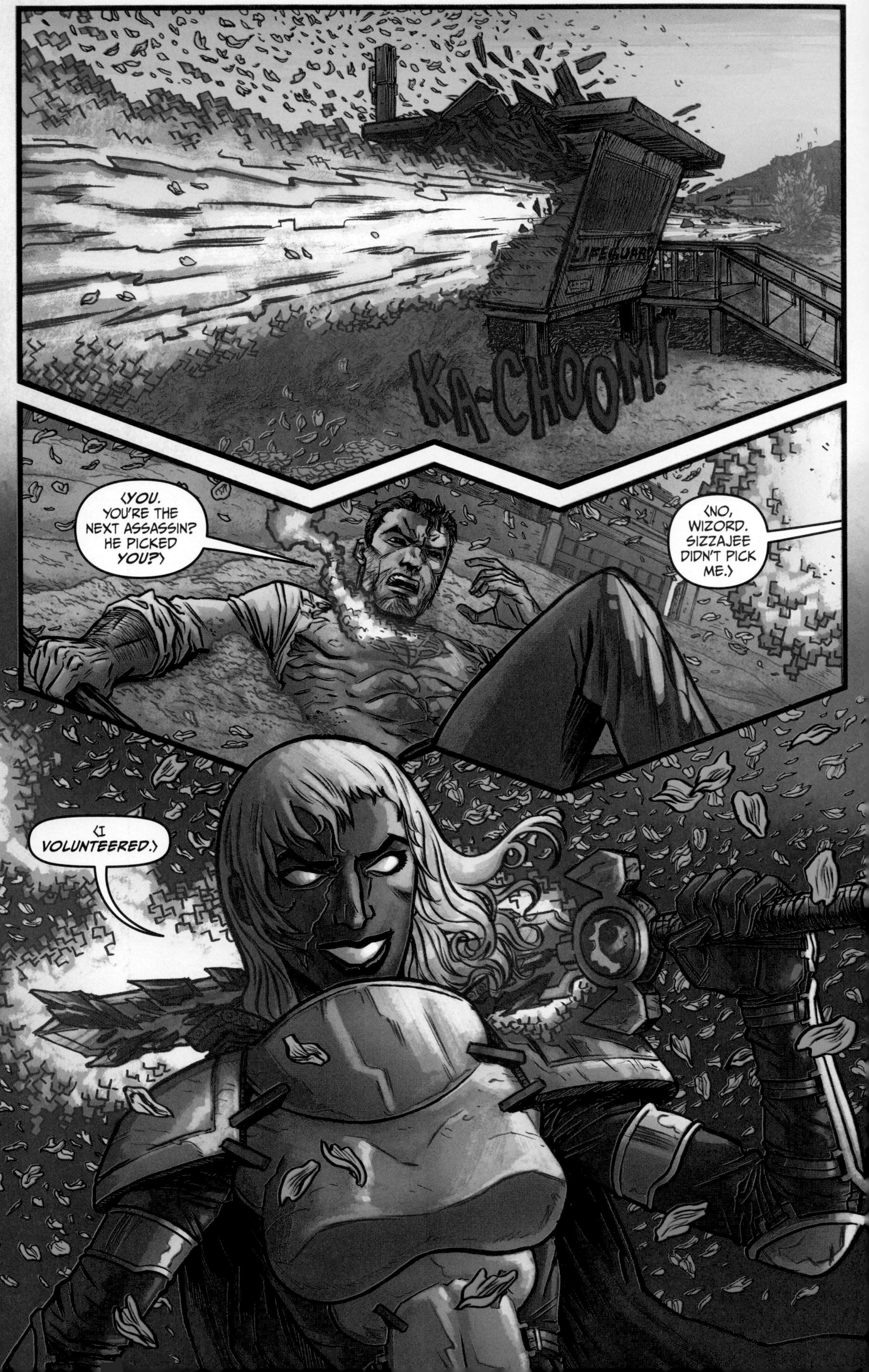
LIFEGUARD
KA-CHOOM!
‹YOU. YOU'RE THE NEXT ASSASSIN? HE PICKED YOU?›
‹NO, WIZORD. SIZZAJEE DIDN'T PICK ME.›
‹I VOLUNTEERED.›

# FIVE

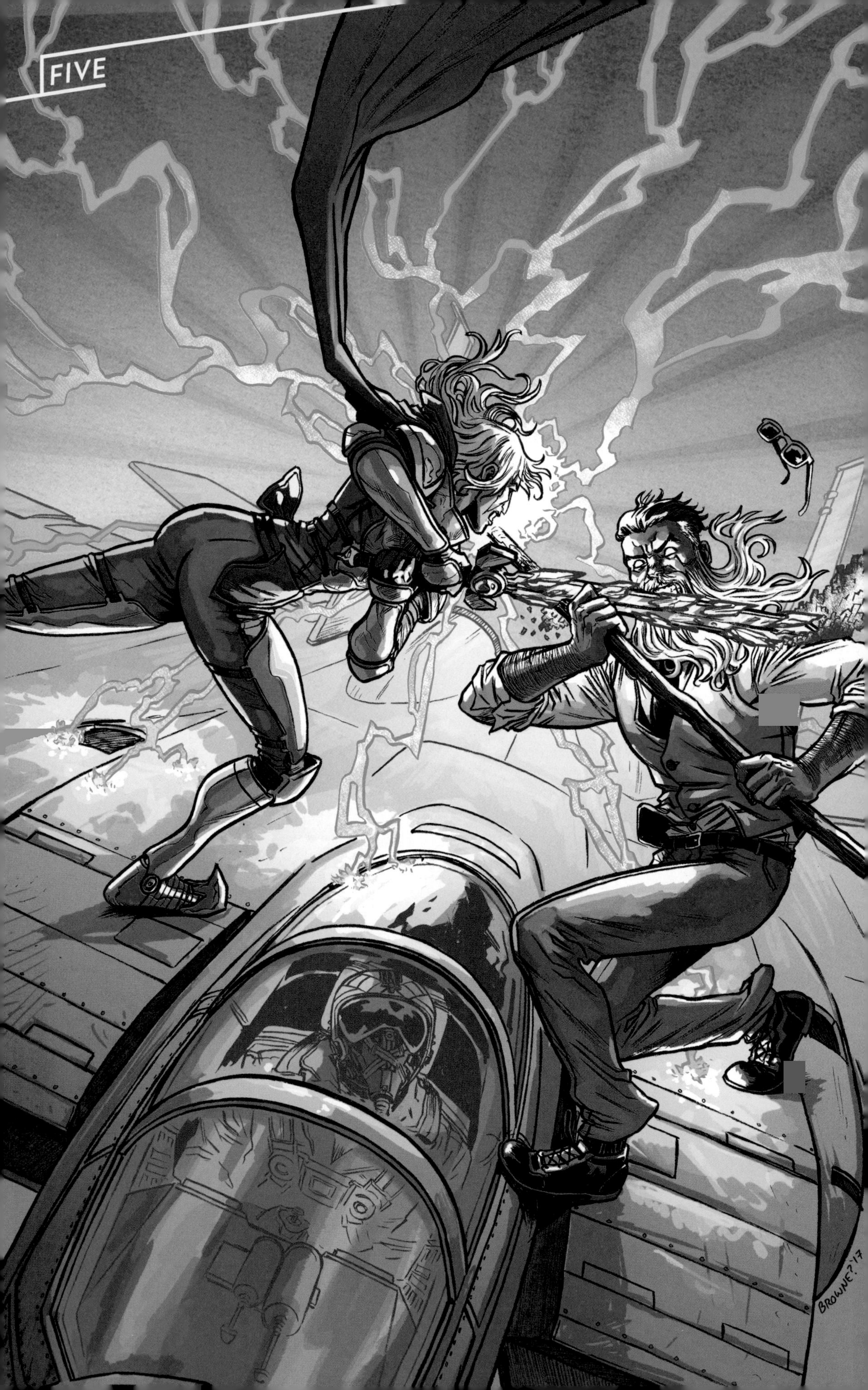
BROWNE? '17

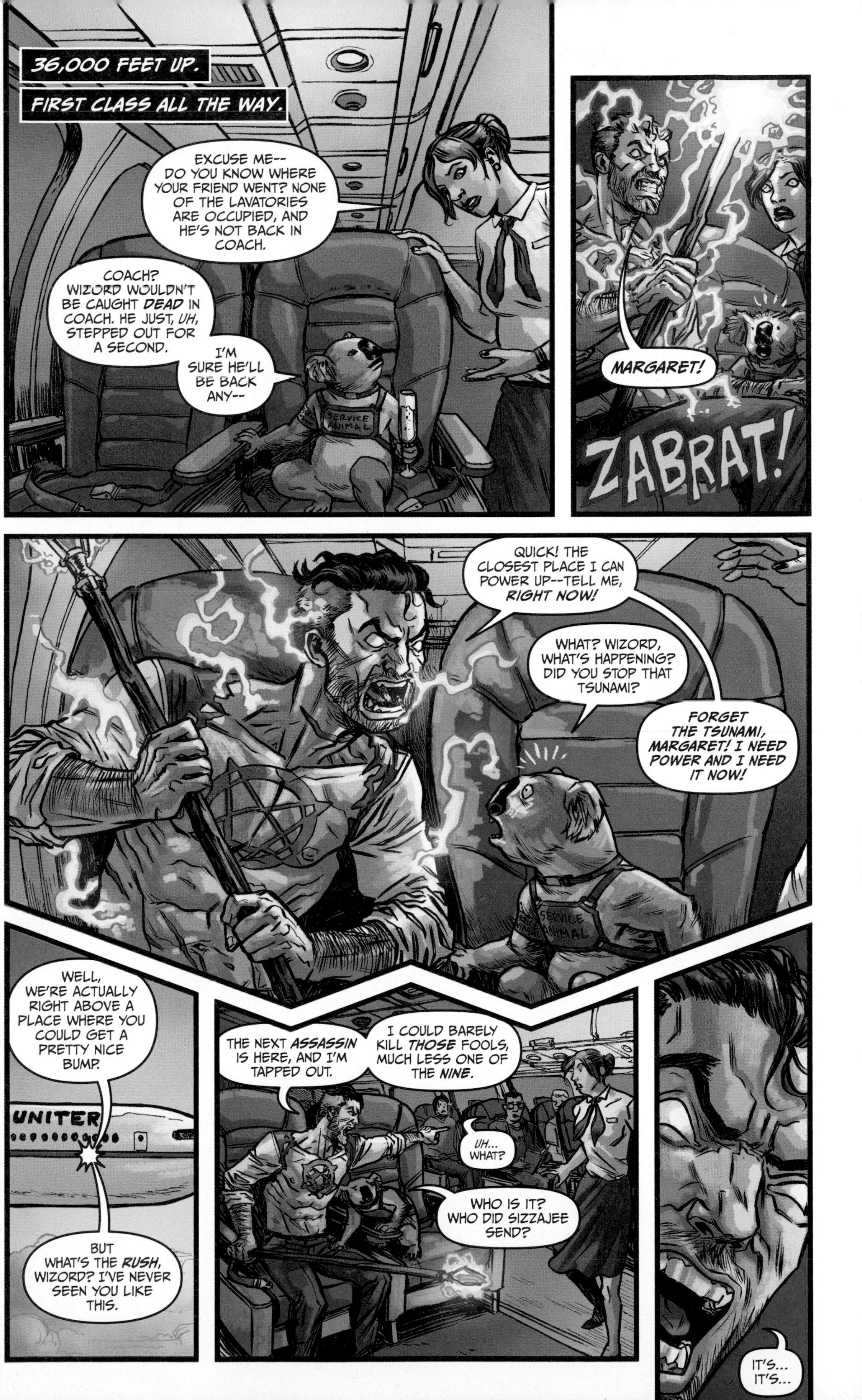
36,000 FEET UP.
FIRST CLASS ALL THE WAY.
EXCUSE ME-- DO YOU KNOW WHERE YOUR FRIEND WENT? NONE OF THE LAVATORIES ARE OCCUPIED, AND HE'S NOT BACK IN COACH.
COACH? WIZORD WOULDN'T BE CAUGHT *DEAD* IN COACH. HE JUST, *UH*, STEPPED OUT FOR A SECOND.
I'M SURE HE'LL BE BACK ANY--
SERVICE ANIMAL
*MARGARET!*
ZABRAT!
QUICK! THE CLOSEST PLACE I CAN POWER UP--TELL ME, *RIGHT NOW!*
WHAT? WIZORD, WHAT'S HAPPENING? DID YOU STOP THAT TSUNAMI?
*FORGET THE TSUNAMI, MARGARET! I NEED POWER AND I NEED IT NOW!*
SERVICE ANIMAL
WELL, WE'RE ACTUALLY RIGHT ABOVE A PLACE WHERE YOU COULD GET A PRETTY NICE BUMP.
UNITER
BUT WHAT'S THE *RUSH*, WIZORD? I'VE NEVER SEEN YOU LIKE THIS.
THE NEXT *ASSASSIN* IS HERE, AND I'M TAPPED OUT.
I COULD BARELY KILL *THOSE* FOOLS, MUCH LESS ONE OF THE *NINE*.
*UH...* WHAT?
WHO IS IT? WHO DID SIZZAJEE SEND?
IT'S... IT'S...

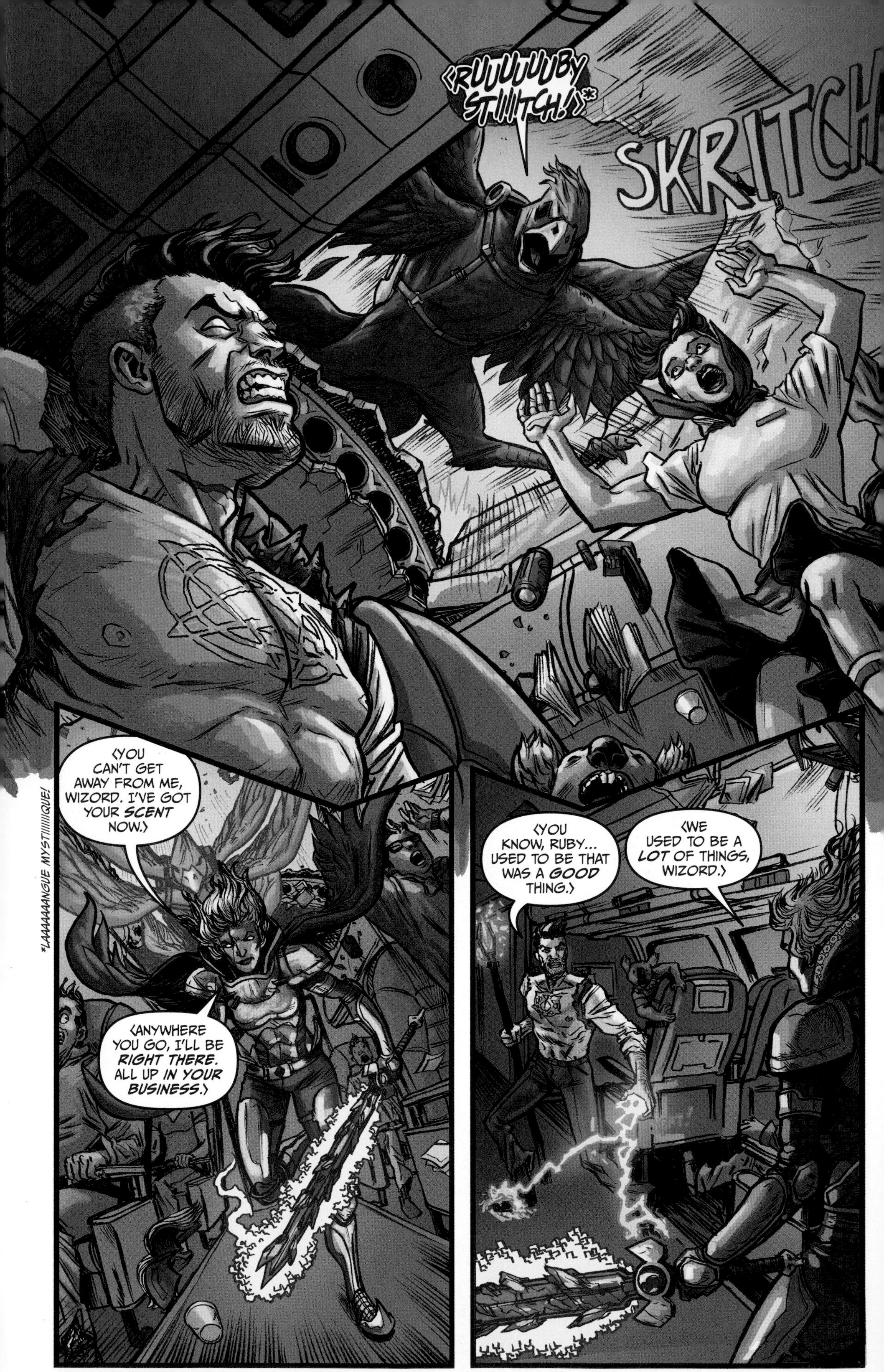
‹RUUUUUUBY STIIIITCH!›*
SKRITCH
‹YOU CAN'T GET AWAY FROM ME, WIZORD. I'VE GOT YOUR *SCENT* NOW.›
‹ANYWHERE YOU GO, I'LL BE ***RIGHT THERE.*** ALL UP ***IN YOUR BUSINESS.***›
‹YOU KNOW, RUBY... USED TO BE THAT WAS A *GOOD* THING.›
‹WE USED TO BE A *LOT* OF THINGS, WIZORD.›

*LAAAAAAANGUE MYSTIIIIIIIQUE!

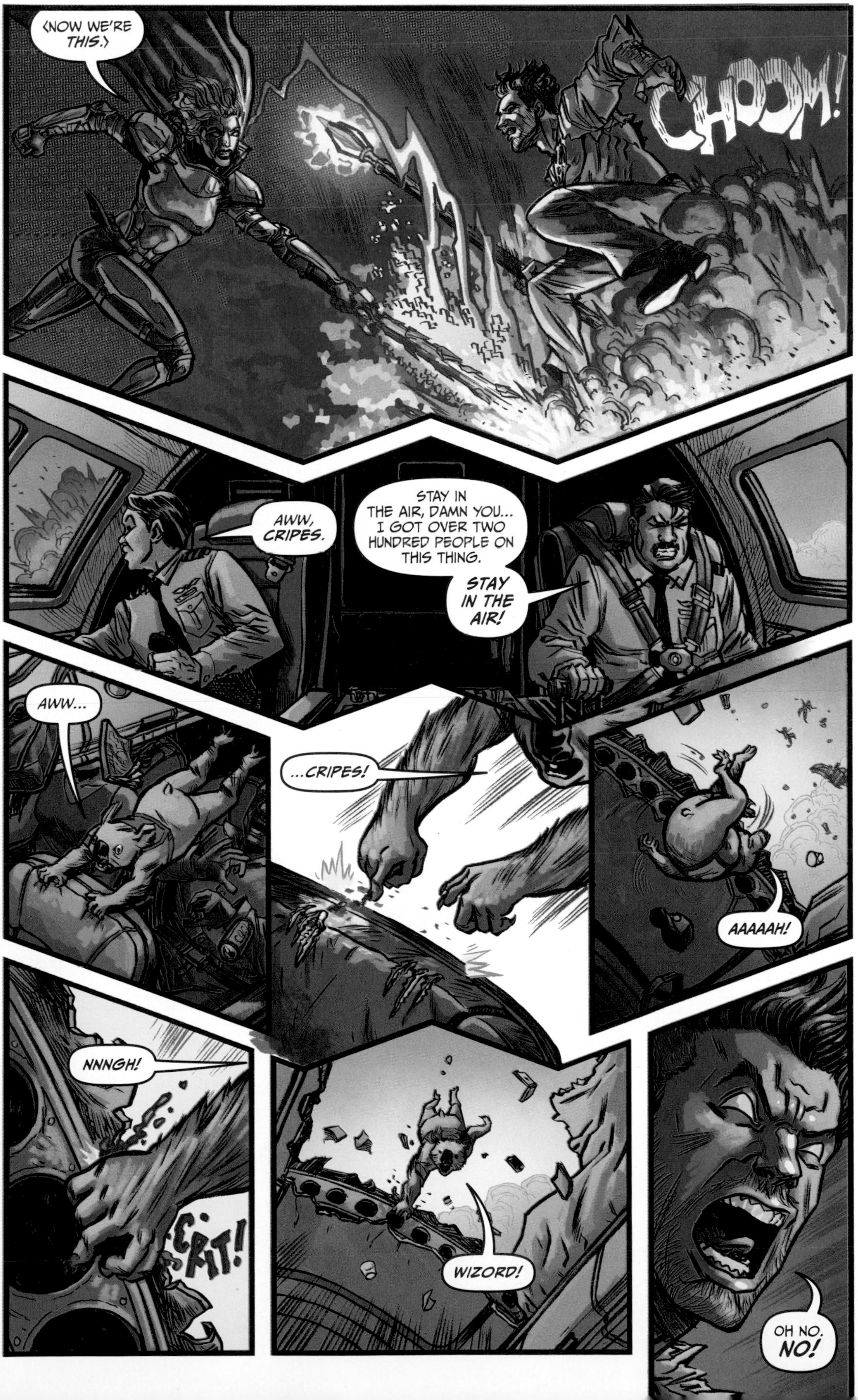
‹NOW WE'RE THIS.›
CHOOM!
AWW, CRIPES.
STAY IN THE AIR, DAMN YOU... I GOT OVER TWO HUNDRED PEOPLE ON THIS THING.
STAY IN THE AIR!
AWW...
...CRIPES!
AAAAAH!
NNNGH!
CRIT!
WIZORD!
OH NO. NO!

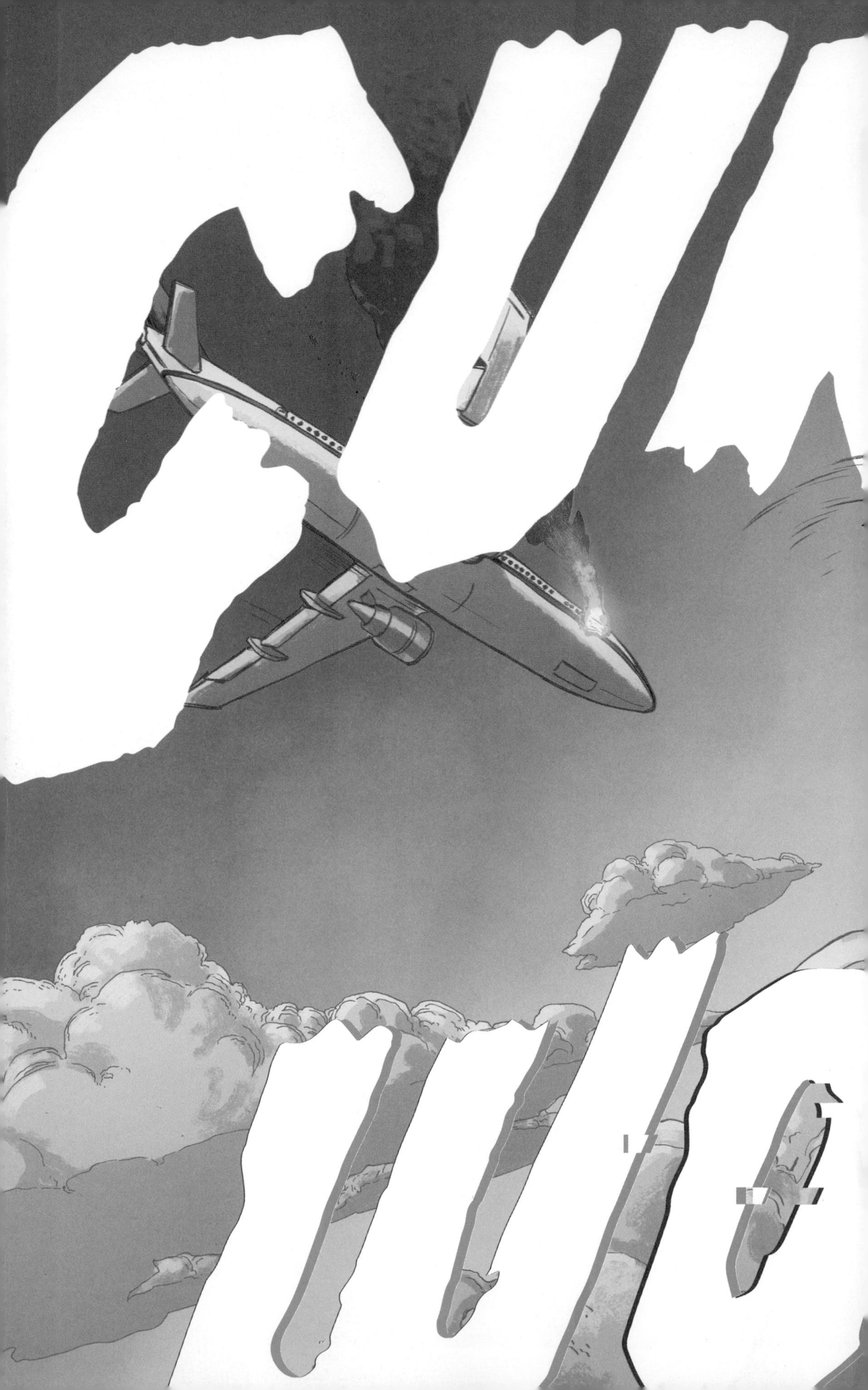

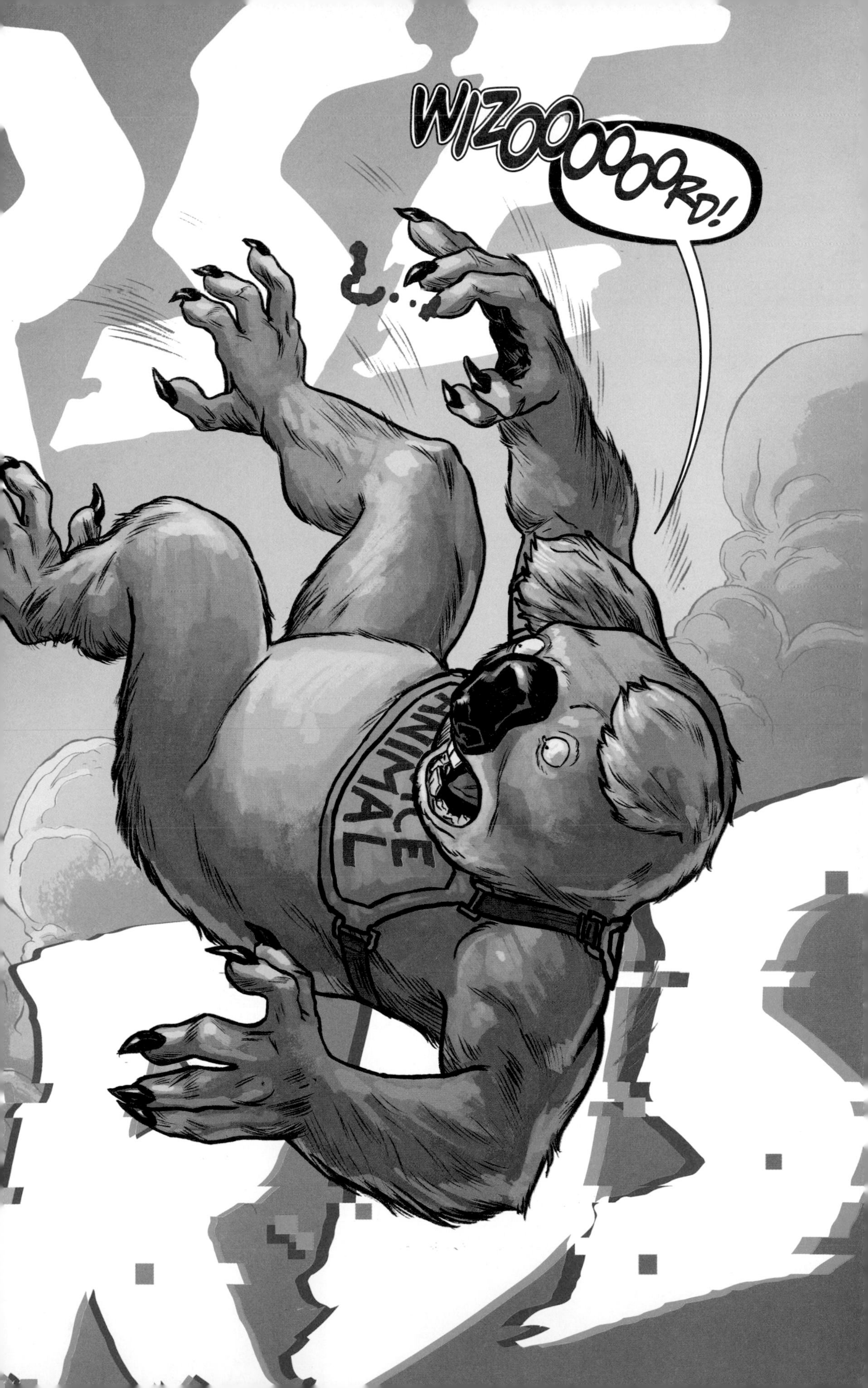
WIZOOOOOORD!

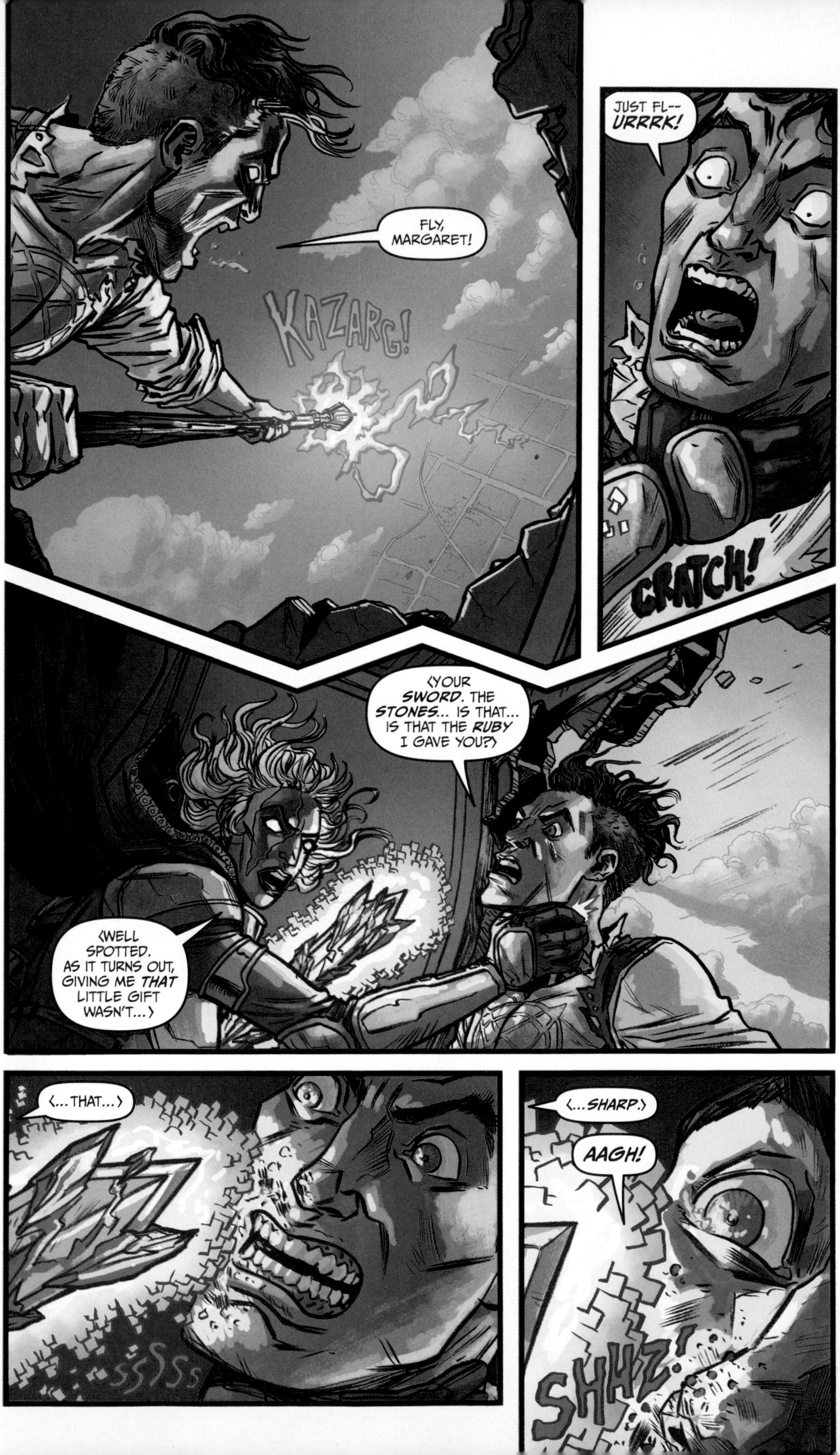
FLY, MARGARET!
KAZARG!
JUST FL-- URRRK!
CRATCH!
‹YOUR SWORD. THE STONES... IS THAT... IS THAT THE RUBY I GAVE YOU?›
‹WELL SPOTTED. AS IT TURNS OUT, GIVING ME THAT LITTLE GIFT WASN'T...›
‹...THAT...›
SSSSS
‹...SHARP.›
AAGH!
SHHZ!

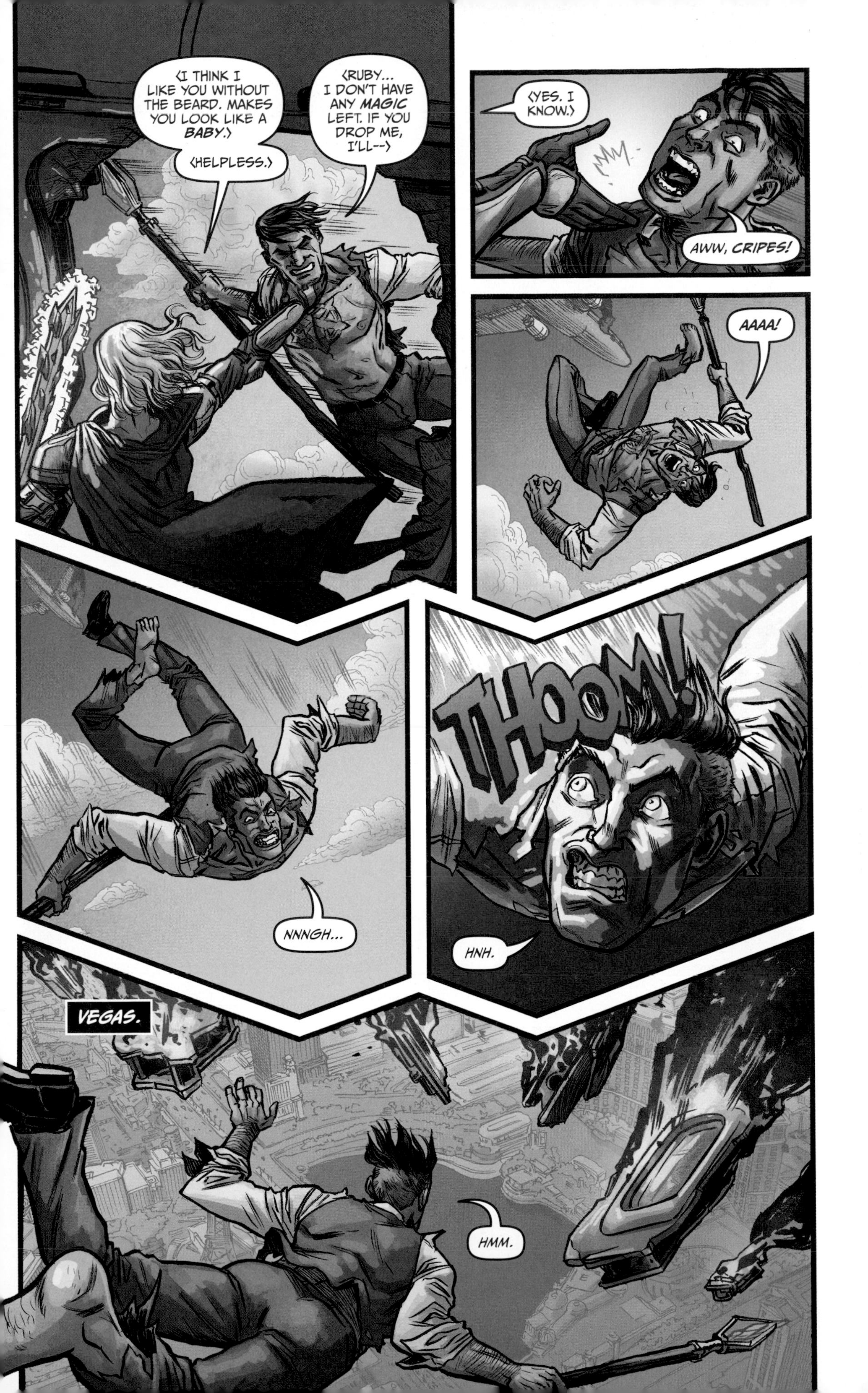

‹I THINK I LIKE YOU WITHOUT THE BEARD. MAKES YOU LOOK LIKE A BABY.›
‹HELPLESS.›
‹RUBY... I DON'T HAVE ANY MAGIC LEFT. IF YOU DROP ME, I'LL--›
‹YES. I KNOW.›
AWW, CRIPES!
AAAA!
NNNGH...
THOOM!
HNH.
VEGAS.
HMM.

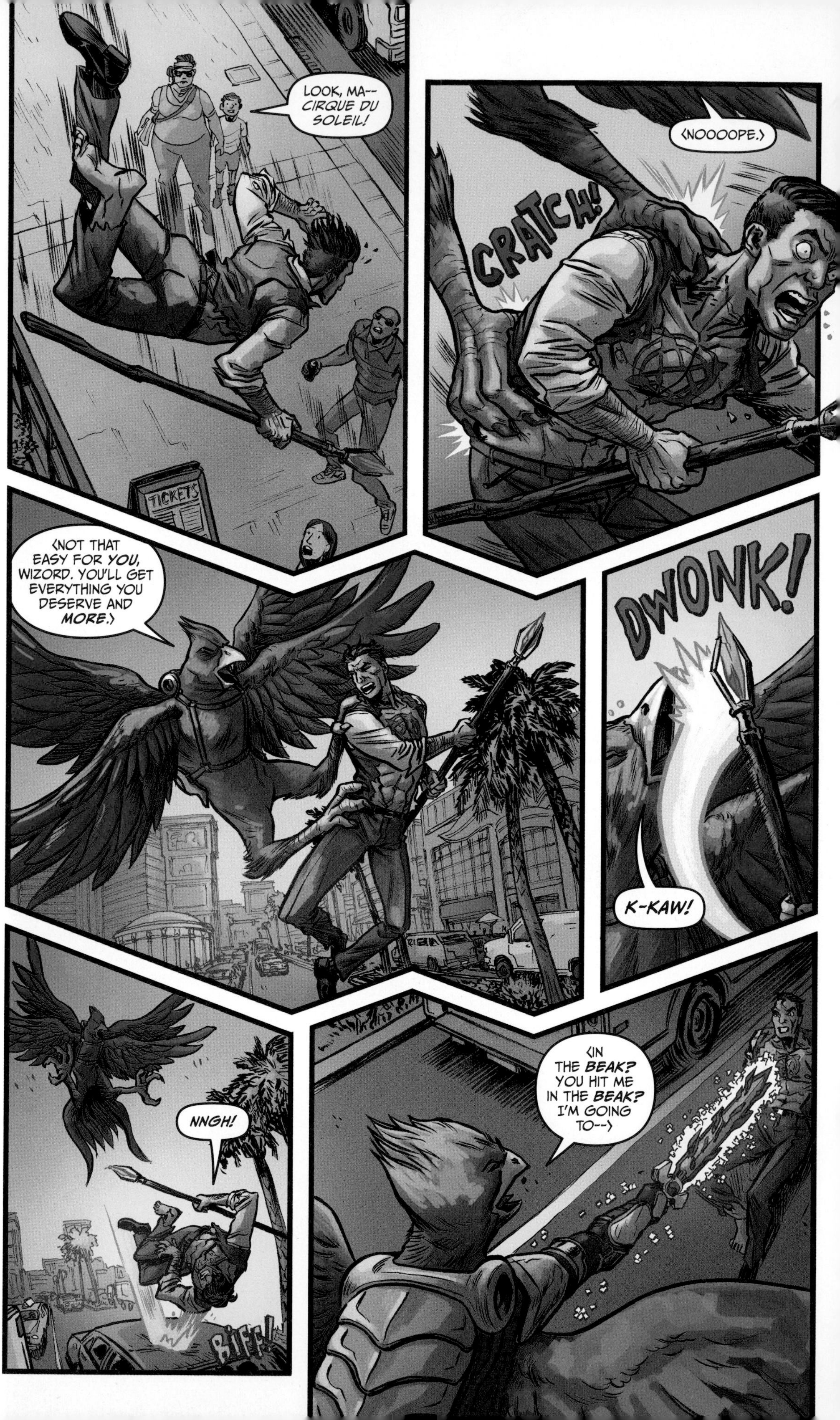
LOOK, MA-- CIRQUE DU SOLEIL!
TICKETS
‹NOOOOPE.›
CRATCH!
‹NOT THAT EASY FOR YOU, WIZORD. YOU'LL GET EVERYTHING YOU DESERVE AND MORE.›
DWONK!
K-KAW!
NNGH!
BIFF!
‹IN THE BEAK? YOU HIT ME IN THE BEAK? I'M GOING TO--›

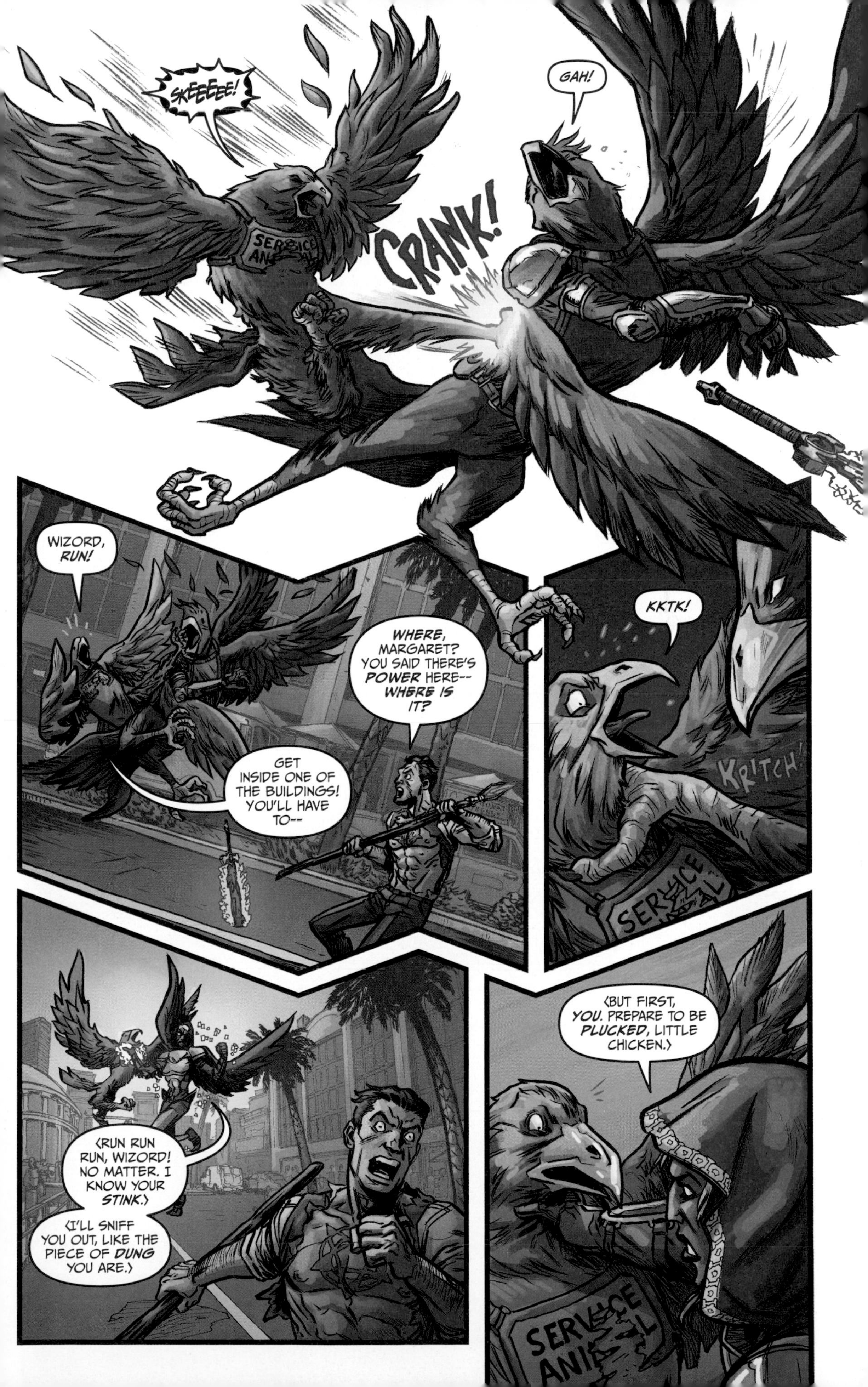
SKEEEEEE!
GAH!
CRANK!
SERVICE ANI
WIZORD, RUN!
WHERE, MARGARET? YOU SAID THERE'S POWER HERE-- WHERE IS IT?
GET INSIDE ONE OF THE BUILDINGS! YOU'LL HAVE TO--
KKTK!
KRITCH!
SERVICE
‹RUN RUN RUN, WIZORD! NO MATTER. I KNOW YOUR STINK.›
‹I'LL SNIFF YOU OUT, LIKE THE PIECE OF DUNG YOU ARE.›
‹BUT FIRST, YOU. PREPARE TO BE PLUCKED, LITTLE CHICKEN.›
SERVICE ANI

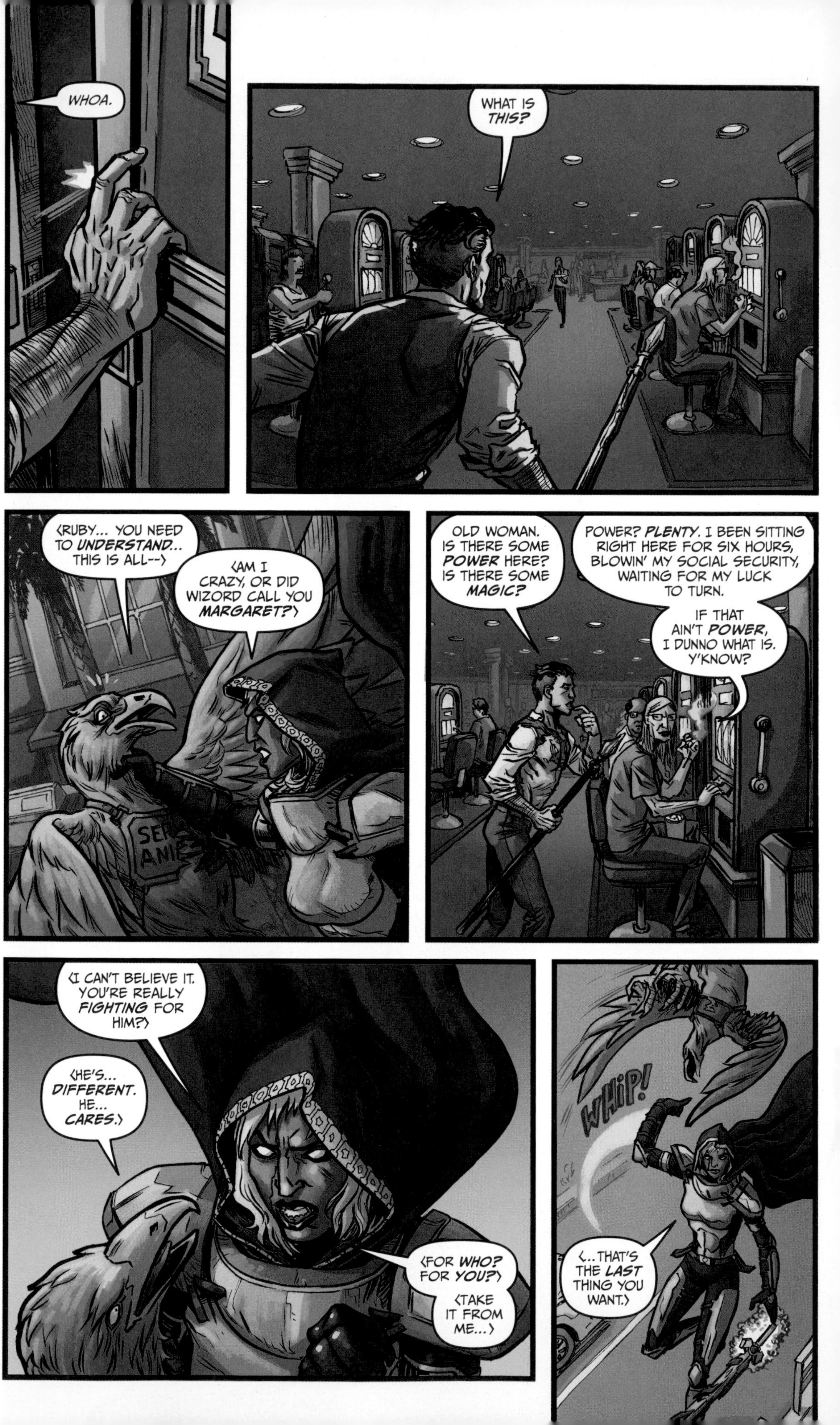
WHOA.
WHAT IS THIS?
<RUBY... YOU NEED TO UNDERSTAND... THIS IS ALL-->
<AM I CRAZY, OR DID WIZORD CALL YOU MARGARET?>
OLD WOMAN. IS THERE SOME POWER HERE? IS THERE SOME MAGIC?
POWER? PLENTY. I BEEN SITTING RIGHT HERE FOR SIX HOURS, BLOWIN' MY SOCIAL SECURITY, WAITING FOR MY LUCK TO TURN.
IF THAT AIN'T POWER, I DUNNO WHAT IS. Y'KNOW?
<I CAN'T BELIEVE IT. YOU'RE REALLY FIGHTING FOR HIM?>
<HE'S... DIFFERENT. HE... CARES.>
<FOR WHO? FOR YOU?>
<TAKE IT FROM ME...>
WHIP!
<...THAT'S THE LAST THING YOU WANT.>

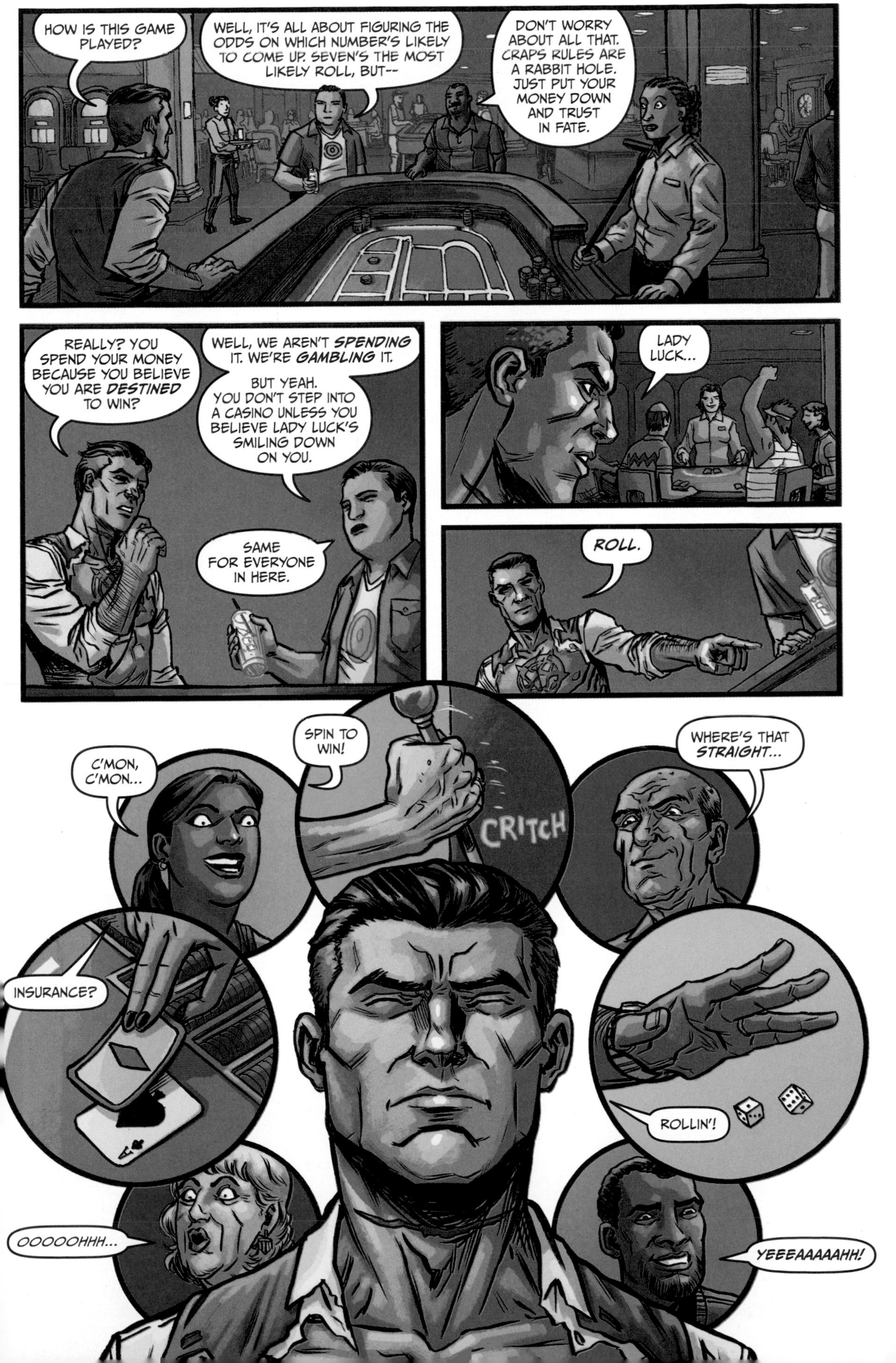
HOW IS THIS GAME PLAYED?
WELL, IT'S ALL ABOUT FIGURING THE ODDS ON WHICH NUMBER'S LIKELY TO COME UP. SEVEN'S THE MOST LIKELY ROLL, BUT--
DON'T WORRY ABOUT ALL THAT. CRAPS RULES ARE A RABBIT HOLE. JUST PUT YOUR MONEY DOWN AND TRUST IN FATE.
REALLY? YOU SPEND YOUR MONEY BECAUSE YOU BELIEVE YOU ARE *DESTINED* TO WIN?
WELL, WE AREN'T *SPENDING* IT. WE'RE *GAMBLING* IT.
BUT YEAH. YOU DON'T STEP INTO A CASINO UNLESS YOU BELIEVE LADY LUCK'S SMILING DOWN ON YOU.
SAME FOR EVERYONE IN HERE.
LADY LUCK...
*ROLL.*
C'MON, C'MON...
SPIN TO WIN!
CRITCH
WHERE'S THAT *STRAIGHT*...
INSURANCE?
ROLLIN'!
OOOOOHHH...
YEEEAAAAAHH!

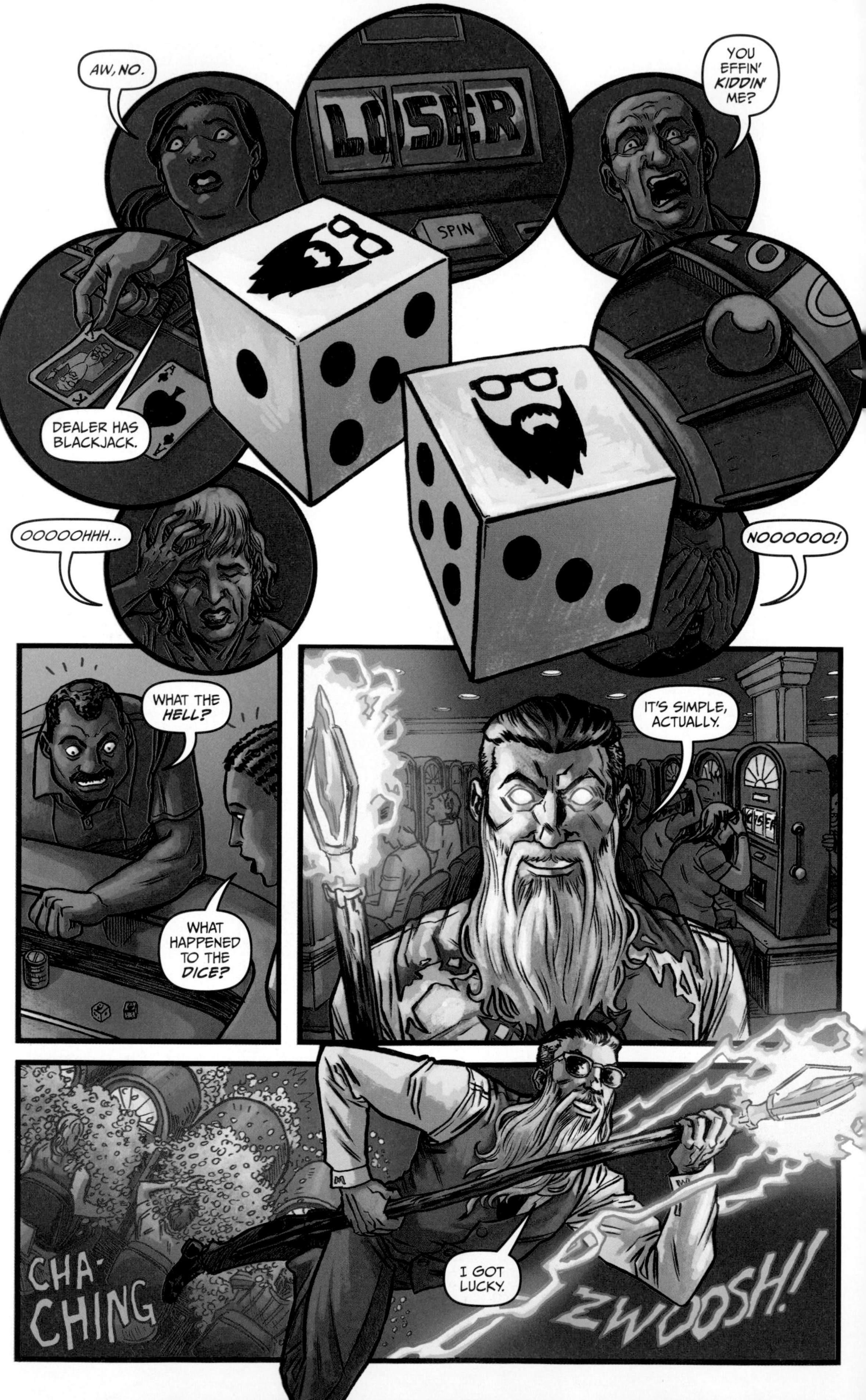
AW, NO.
LOSER
SPIN
YOU EFFIN' *KIDDIN'* ME?
DEALER HAS BLACKJACK.
OOOOOHHH...
NOOOOOO!
WHAT THE *HELL?*
WHAT HAPPENED TO THE *DICE?*
IT'S SIMPLE, ACTUALLY.
I GOT LUCKY.
CHA-CHING
ZWOOSH!

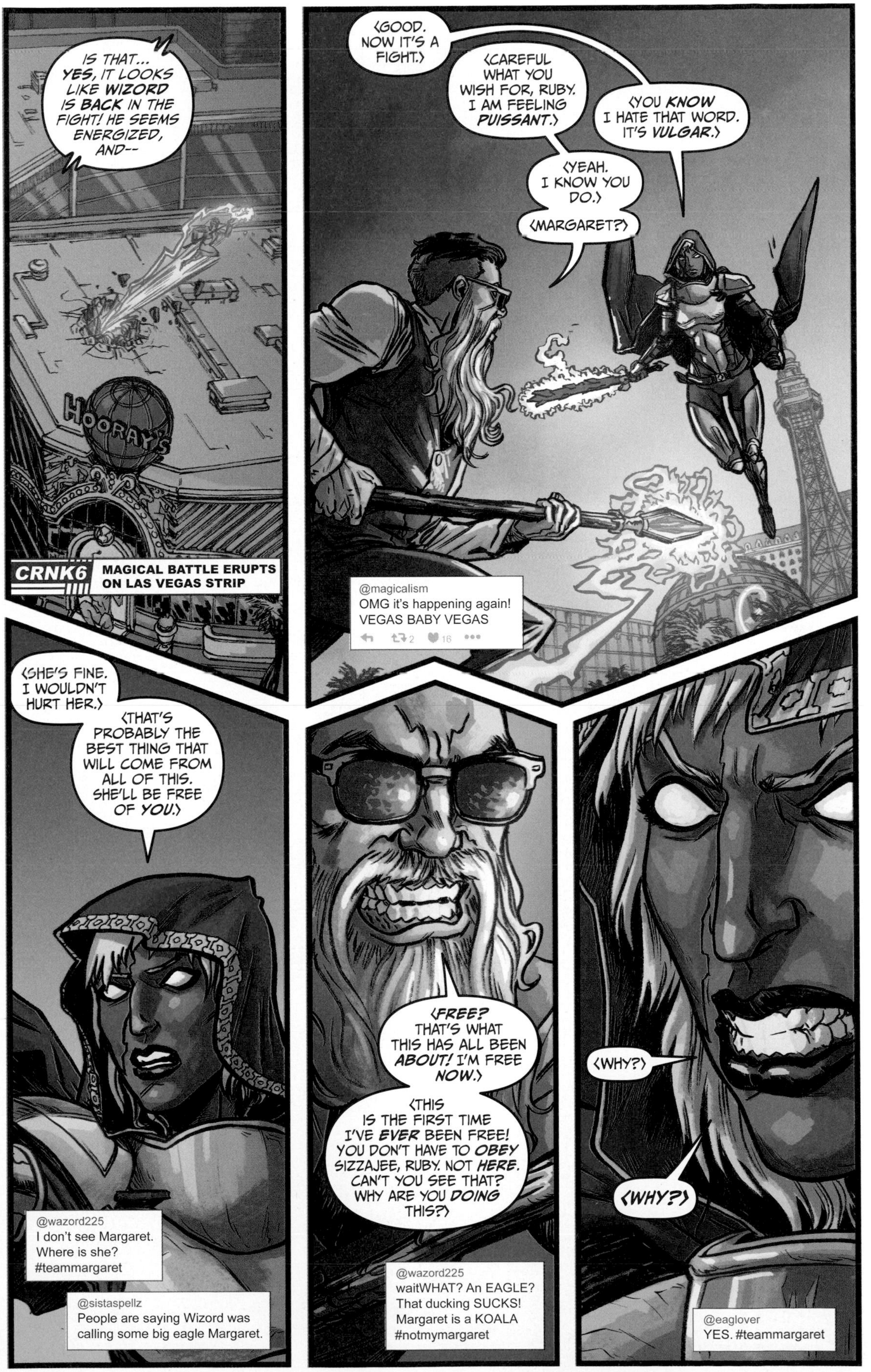
IS THAT... YES, IT LOOKS LIKE WIZORD IS BACK IN THE FIGHT! HE SEEMS ENERGIZED, AND--
HOORAY'S
CRNK6 MAGICAL BATTLE ERUPTS ON LAS VEGAS STRIP
‹GOOD. NOW IT'S A FIGHT.›
‹CAREFUL WHAT YOU WISH FOR, RUBY. I AM FEELING PUISSANT.›
‹YOU KNOW I HATE THAT WORD. IT'S VULGAR.›
‹YEAH. I KNOW YOU DO.›
‹MARGARET?›
@magicalism
OMG it's happening again! VEGAS BABY VEGAS
2 16
‹SHE'S FINE. I WOULDN'T HURT HER.›
‹THAT'S PROBABLY THE BEST THING THAT WILL COME FROM ALL OF THIS. SHE'LL BE FREE OF YOU.›
@wazord225
I don't see Margaret. Where is she? #teammargaret
@sistaspellz
People are saying Wizord was calling some big eagle Margaret.
‹FREE? THAT'S WHAT THIS HAS ALL BEEN ABOUT! I'M FREE NOW.›
‹THIS IS THE FIRST TIME I'VE EVER BEEN FREE! YOU DON'T HAVE TO OBEY SIZZAJEE, RUBY. NOT HERE. CAN'T YOU SEE THAT? WHY ARE YOU DOING THIS?›
@wazord225
waitWHAT? An EAGLE? That ducking SUCKS! Margaret is a KOALA #notmymargaret
‹WHY?›
‹WHY?›
@eaglover
YES. #teammargaret

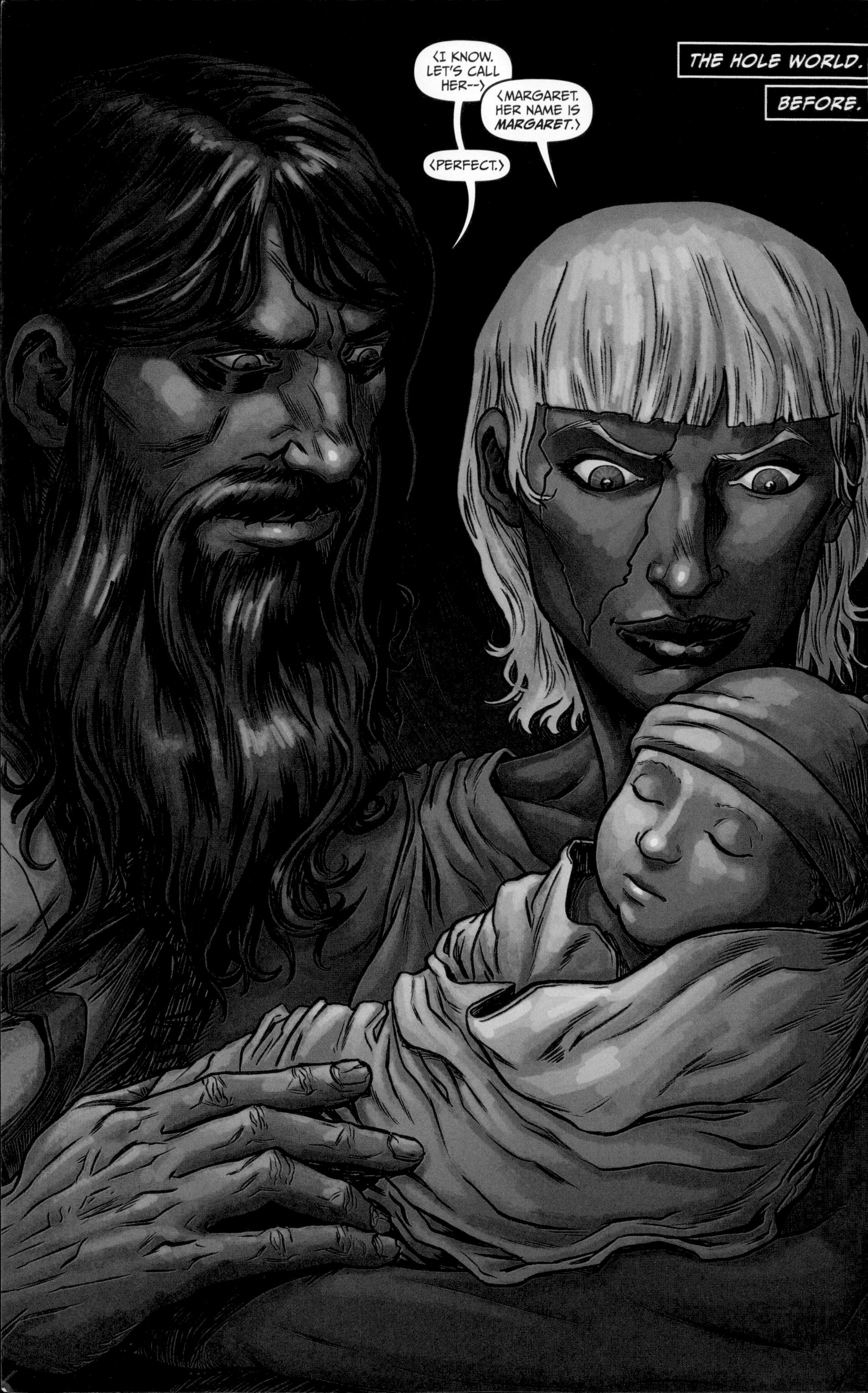
THE HOLE WORLD.
BEFORE.
‹I KNOW. LET'S CALL HER--›
‹MARGARET. HER NAME IS MARGARET.›
‹PERFECT.›

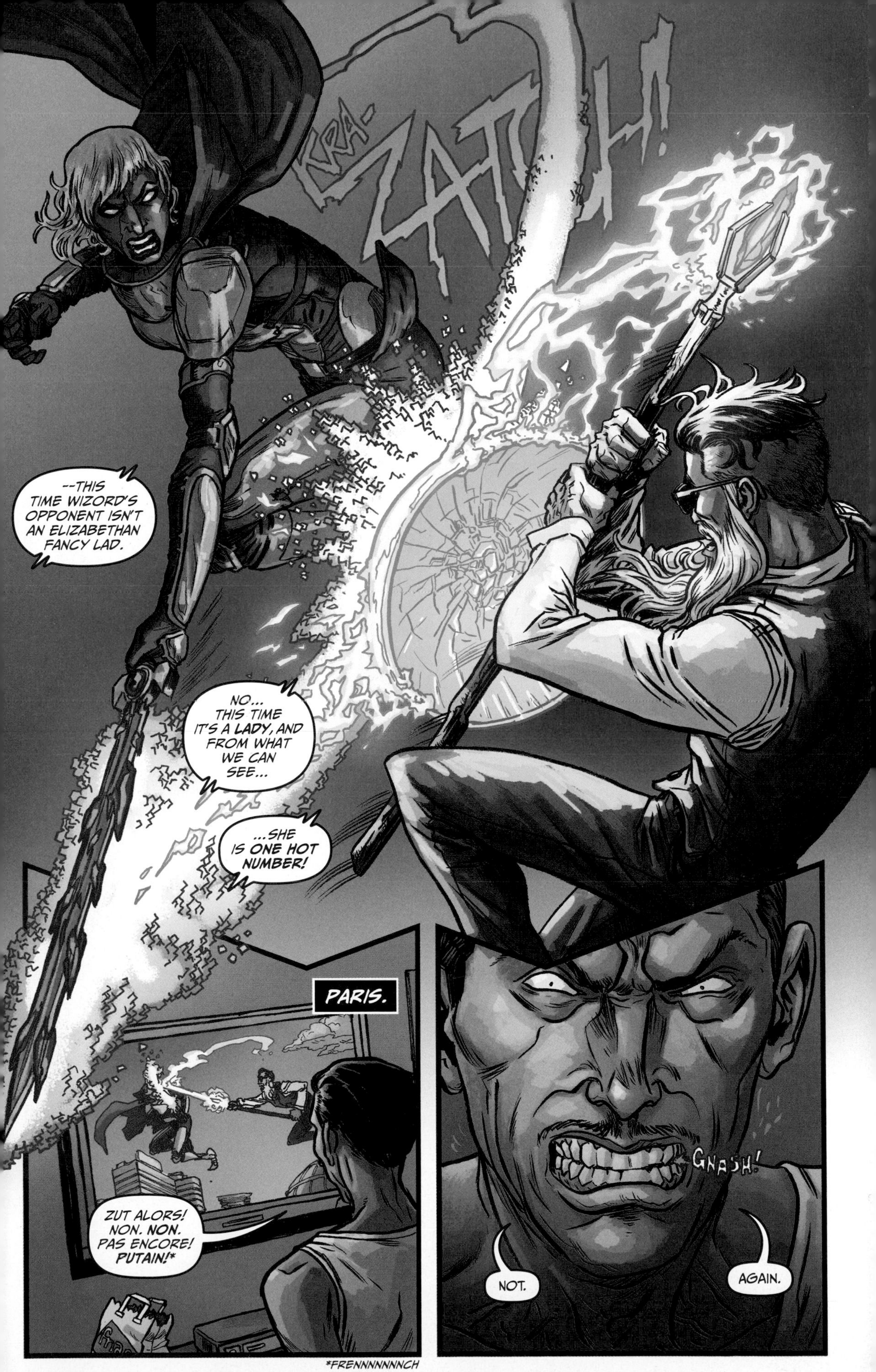
CRA-ZATCH!
--THIS TIME WIZORD'S OPPONENT ISN'T AN ELIZABETHAN FANCY LAD.
NO... THIS TIME IT'S A **LADY**, AND FROM WHAT WE CAN SEE...
...SHE IS **ONE HOT NUMBER!**
PARIS.
ZUT ALORS! NON. **NON.** PAS ENCORE! **PUTAIN!***
GNASH!
NOT.
AGAIN.

*FRENNNNNNNCH

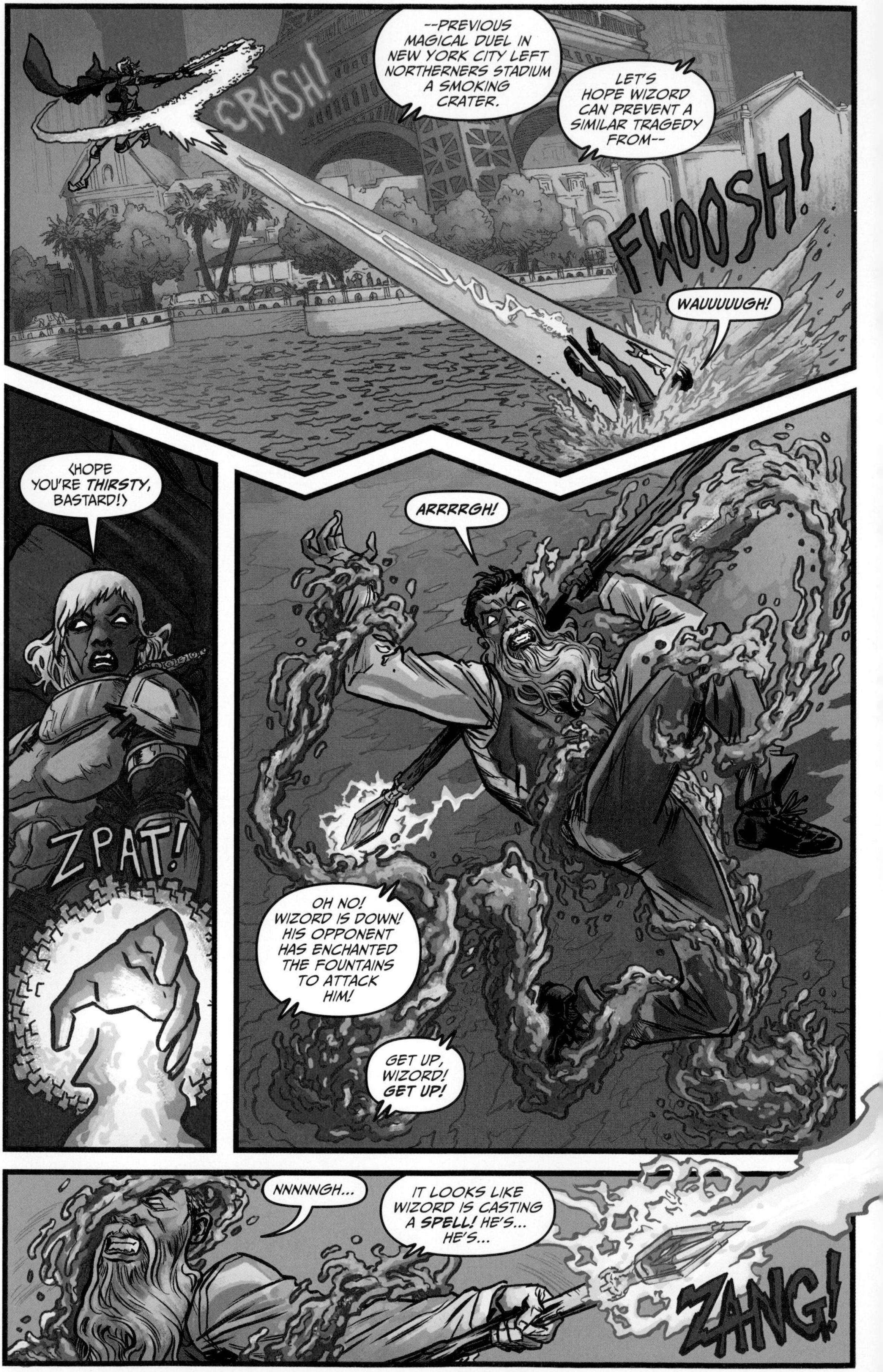
CRASH!
--PREVIOUS MAGICAL DUEL IN NEW YORK CITY LEFT NORTHERNERS STADIUM A SMOKING CRATER.
LET'S HOPE WIZORD CAN PREVENT A SIMILAR TRAGEDY FROM--
FWOOSH!
WAUUUUUGH!
⟨HOPE YOU'RE THIRSTY, BASTARD!⟩
ZPAT!
ARRRRGH!
OH NO! WIZORD IS DOWN! HIS OPPONENT HAS ENCHANTED THE FOUNTAINS TO ATTACK HIM!
GET UP, WIZORD! GET UP!
NNNNNGH...
IT LOOKS LIKE WIZORD IS CASTING A SPELL! HE'S... HE'S...
ZANG!

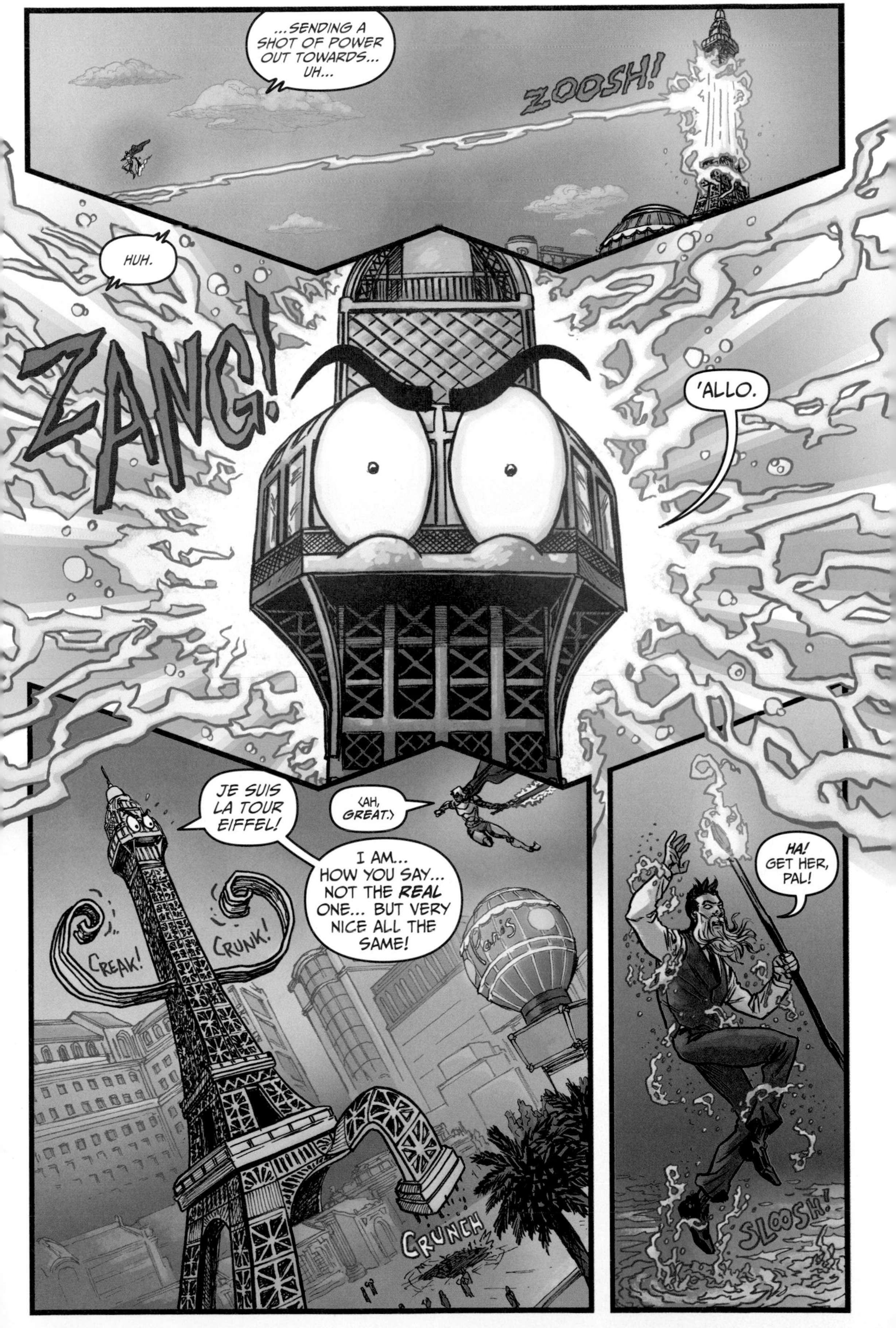
...SENDING A SHOT OF POWER OUT TOWARDS... UH...
ZOOSH!
HUH.
ZANG!
'ALLO.
JE SUIS LA TOUR EIFFEL!
‹AH, GREAT.›
I AM... HOW YOU SAY... NOT THE **REAL** ONE... BUT VERY NICE ALL THE SAME!
CREAK!
CRUNK!
CRUNCH
**HA!** GET HER, PAL!
SLOOSH!

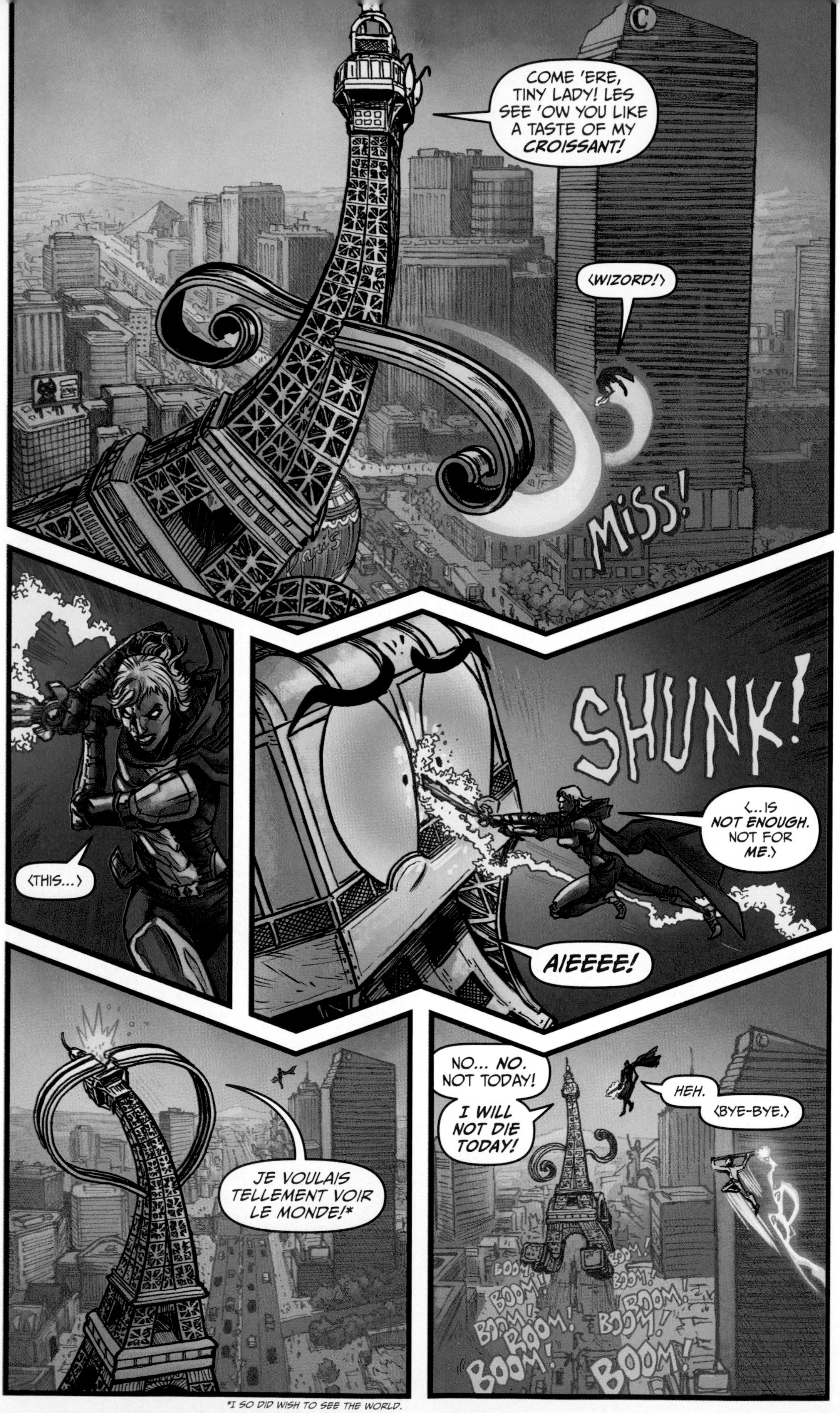
COME 'ERE, TINY LADY! LES SEE 'OW YOU LIKE A TASTE OF MY CROISSANT!
⟨WIZORD!⟩
MISS!
⟨THIS...⟩
SHUNK!
⟨...IS NOT ENOUGH. NOT FOR ME.⟩
AIEEEE!
JE VOULAIS TELLEMENT VOIR LE MONDE!*
NO... NO. NOT TODAY!
I WILL NOT DIE TODAY!
HEH.
⟨BYE-BYE.⟩
BOOM! BOOM! BOOM! BOOM! BOOM! BOOM! BOOM! BOOM! BOOM! BOOM!

*I SO DID WISH TO SEE THE WORLD.

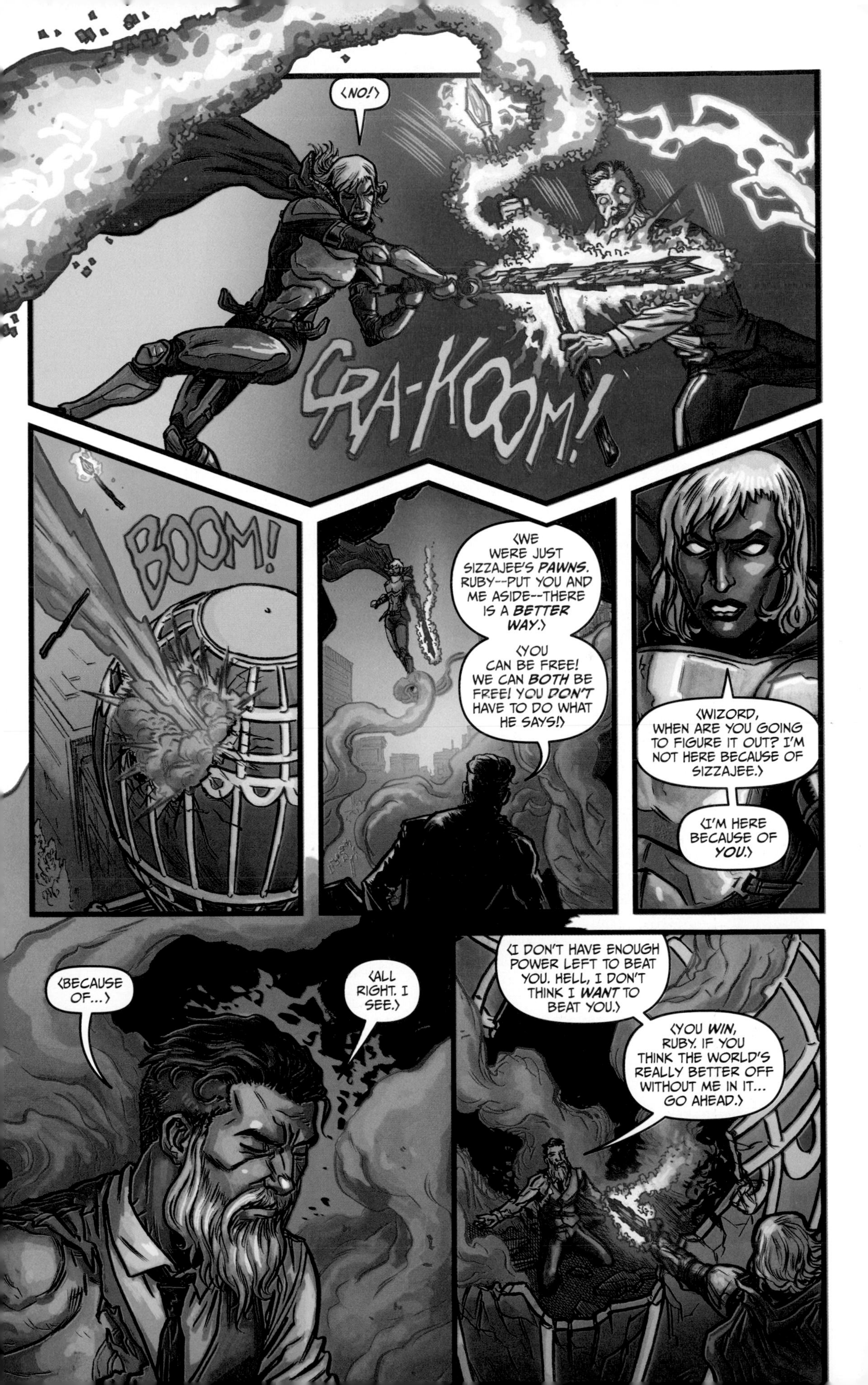

<NO!>
CRA-KOOM!
BOOM!
<WE WERE JUST SIZZAJEE'S PAWNS. RUBY--PUT YOU AND ME ASIDE--THERE IS A BETTER WAY.>
<YOU CAN BE FREE! WE CAN BOTH BE FREE! YOU DON'T HAVE TO DO WHAT HE SAYS!>
<WIZORD, WHEN ARE YOU GOING TO FIGURE IT OUT? I'M NOT HERE BECAUSE OF SIZZAJEE.>
<I'M HERE BECAUSE OF YOU.>
<BECAUSE OF...>
<ALL RIGHT. I SEE.>
<I DON'T HAVE ENOUGH POWER LEFT TO BEAT YOU. HELL, I DON'T THINK I WANT TO BEAT YOU.>
<YOU WIN, RUBY. IF YOU THINK THE WORLD'S REALLY BETTER OFF WITHOUT ME IN IT... GO AHEAD.>

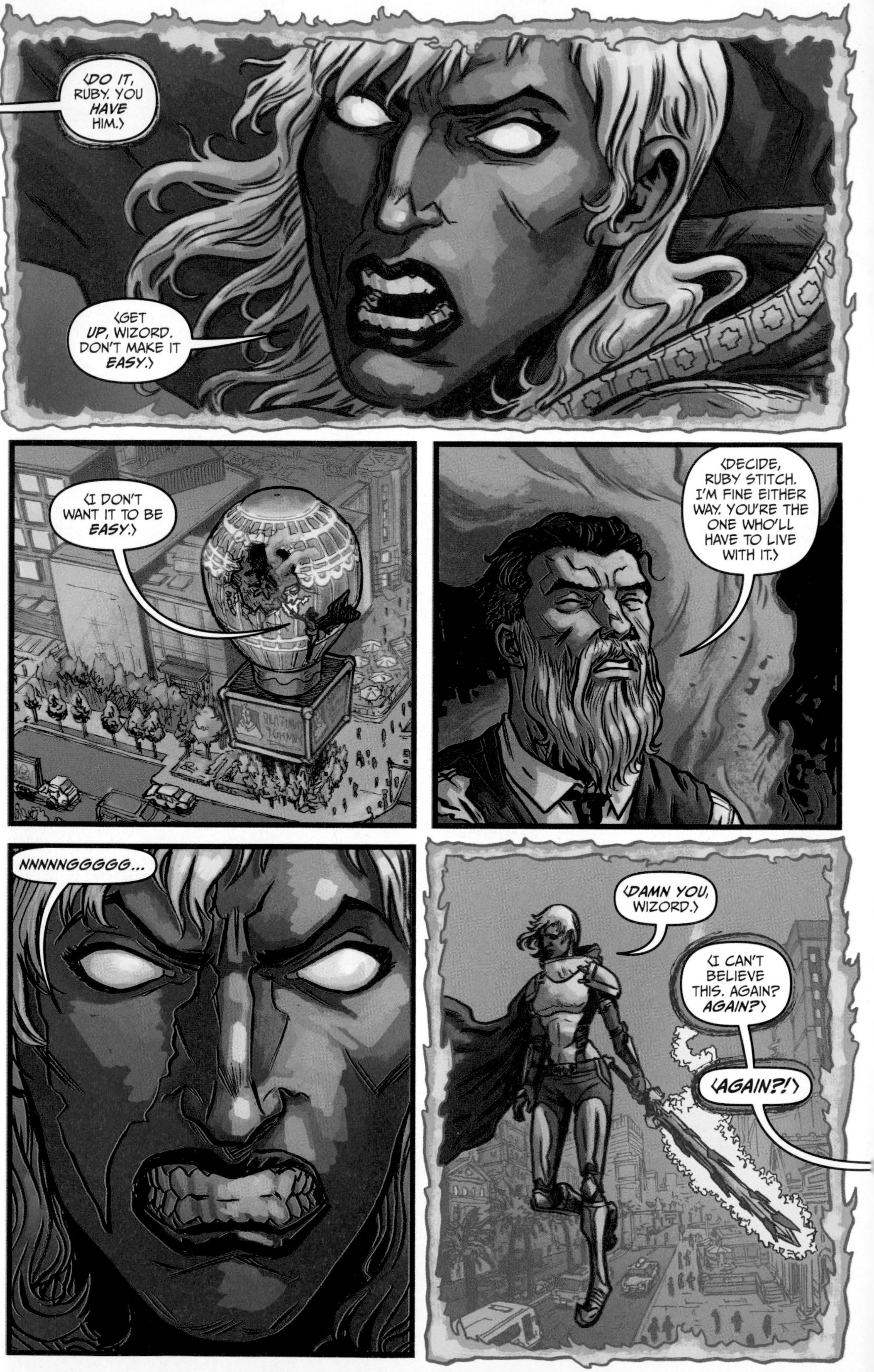

‹DO IT, RUBY. YOU HAVE HIM.›
‹GET UP, WIZORD. DON'T MAKE IT EASY.›
‹I DON'T WANT IT TO BE EASY.›
‹DECIDE, RUBY STITCH. I'M FINE EITHER WAY. YOU'RE THE ONE WHO'LL HAVE TO LIVE WITH IT.›
NNNNNGGGGG...
‹DAMN YOU, WIZORD.›
‹I CAN'T BELIEVE THIS. AGAIN? AGAIN?›
‹AGAIN?!›

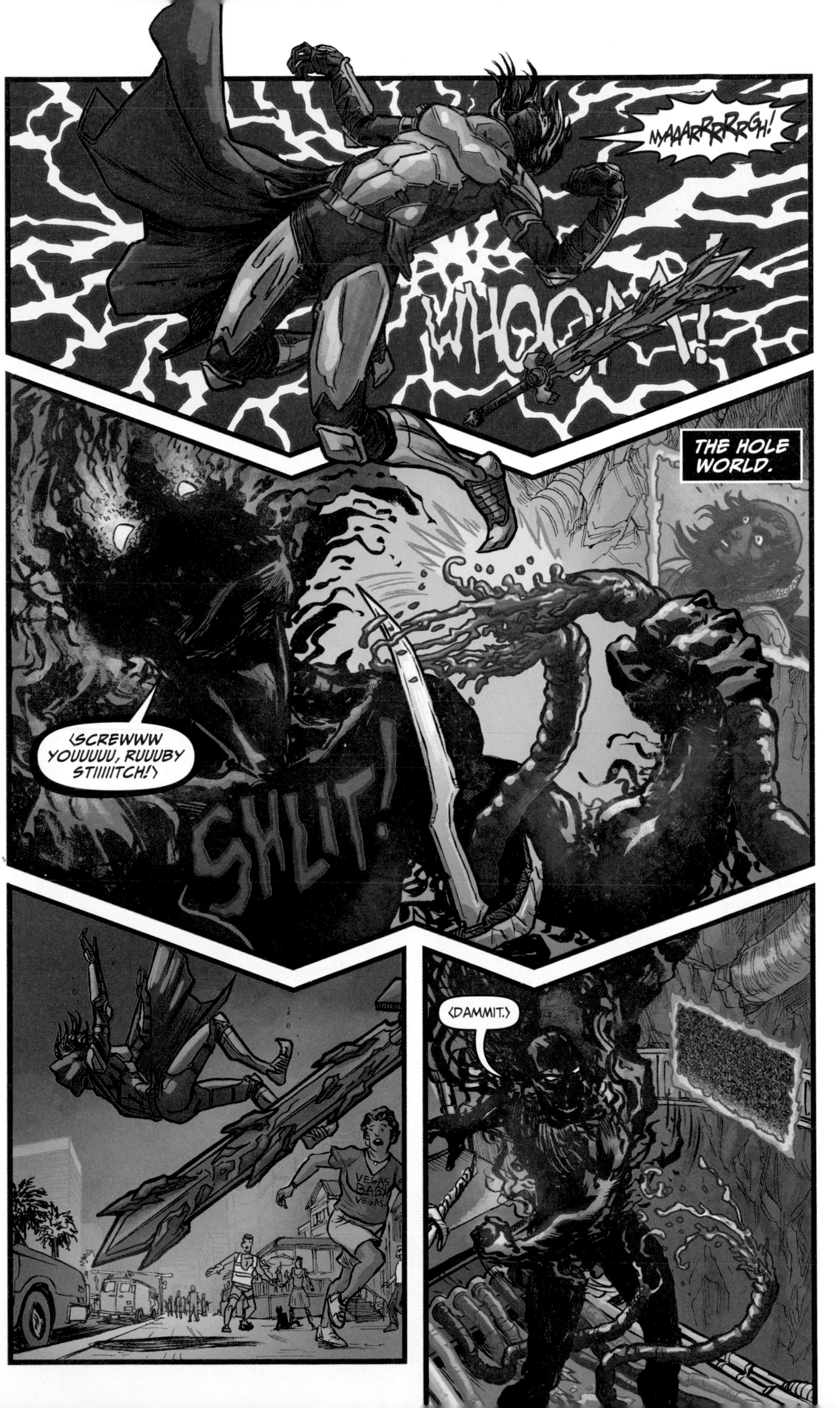
NYAAARRRRRGH!
WHOOAA!
THE HOLE WORLD.
‹SCREWWW YOUUUUU, RUUUBY STIIIIITCH!›
SHLIT!
VEGAS BABY VEGAS
‹DAMMIT.›

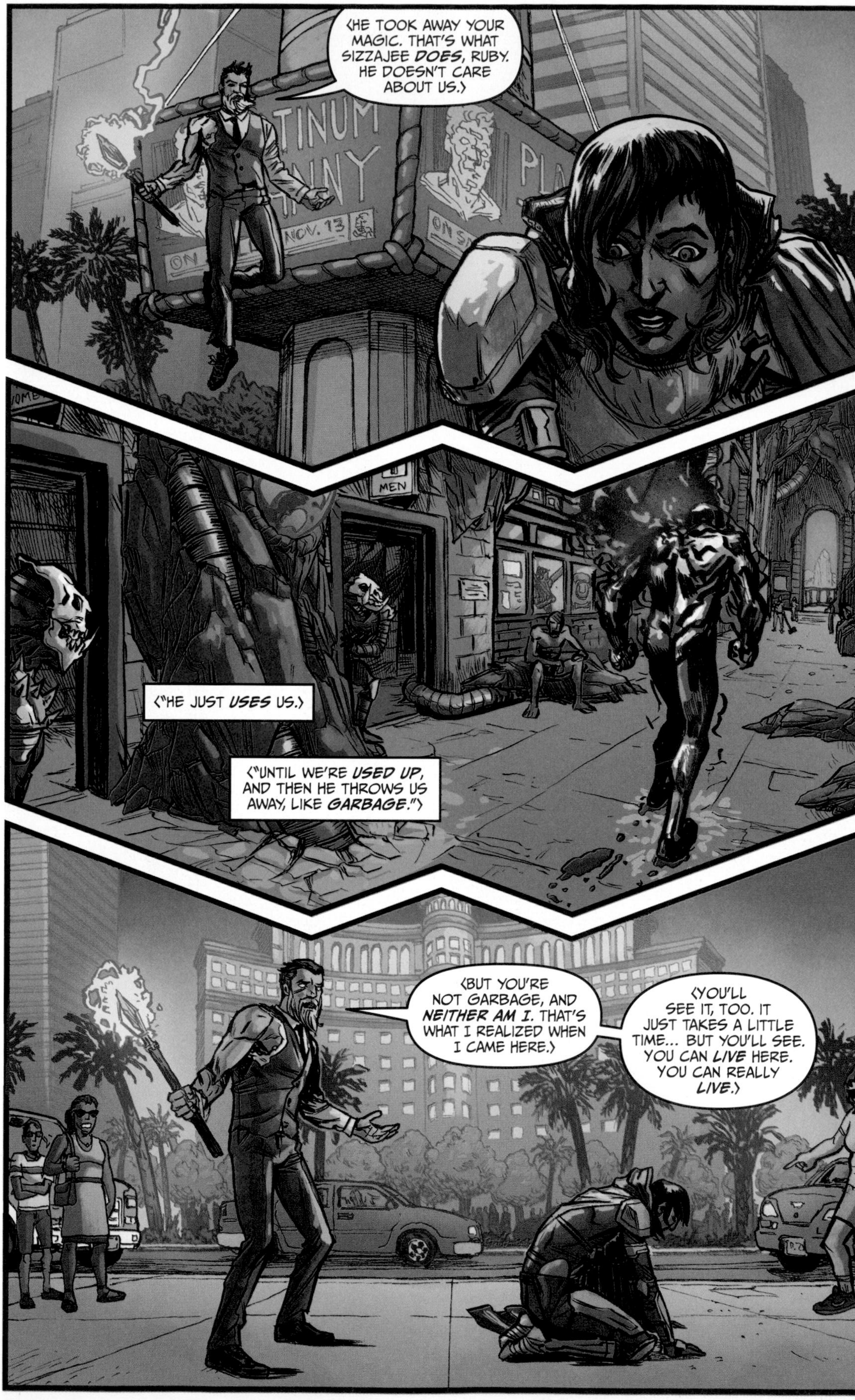
‹HE TOOK AWAY YOUR MAGIC. THAT'S WHAT SIZZAJEE DOES, RUBY. HE DOESN'T CARE ABOUT US.›
TINUM
NNY
NOV. 13
ON
ON S
MEN
‹"HE JUST USES US.›
‹"UNTIL WE'RE USED UP, AND THEN HE THROWS US AWAY, LIKE GARBAGE."›
‹BUT YOU'RE NOT GARBAGE, AND NEITHER AM I. THAT'S WHAT I REALIZED WHEN I CAME HERE.›
‹YOU'LL SEE IT, TOO. IT JUST TAKES A LITTLE TIME... BUT YOU'LL SEE. YOU CAN LIVE HERE. YOU CAN REALLY LIVE.›

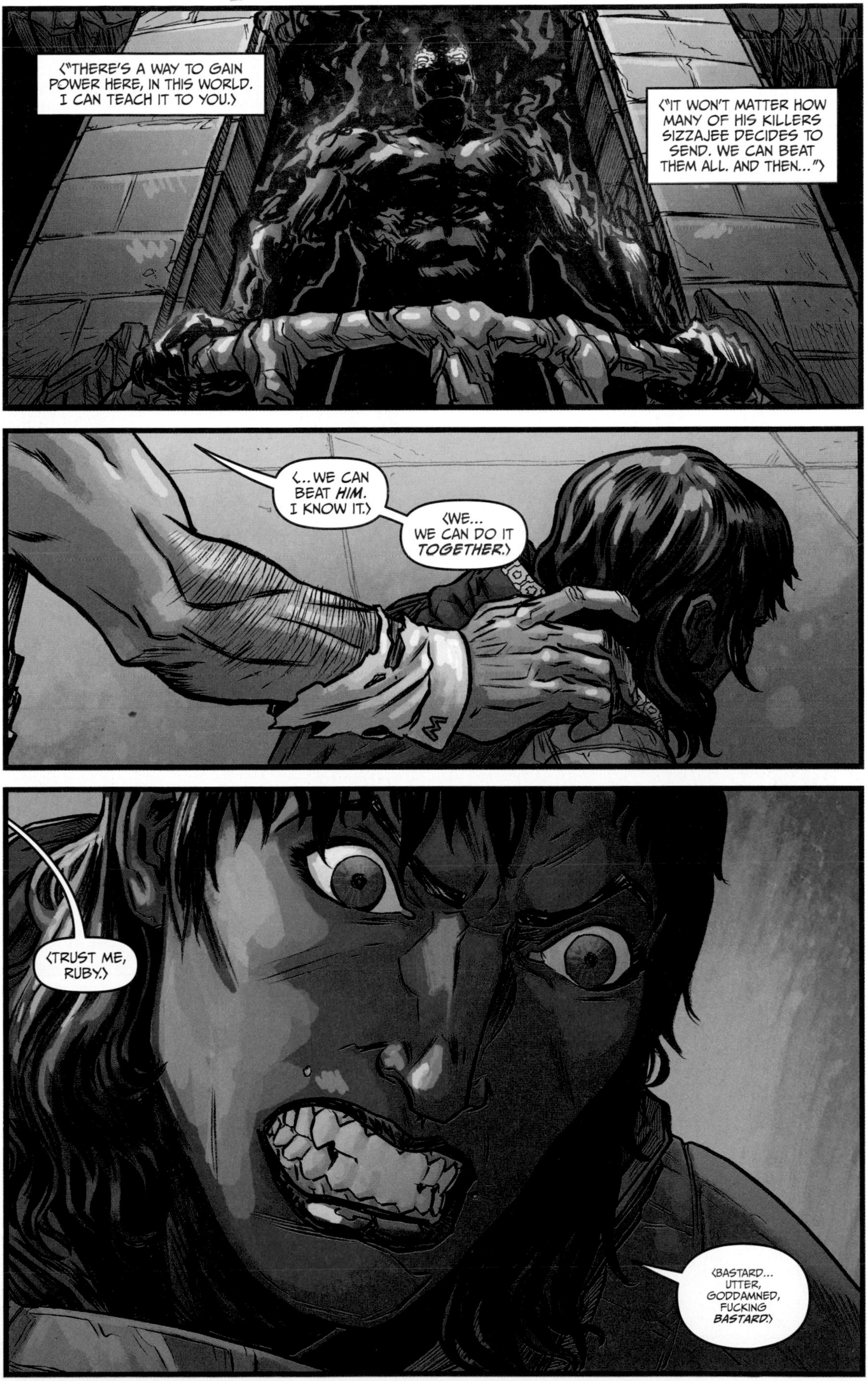
‹"THERE'S A WAY TO GAIN POWER HERE, IN THIS WORLD. I CAN TEACH IT TO YOU.›
‹"IT WON'T MATTER HOW MANY OF HIS KILLERS SIZZAJEE DECIDES TO SEND. WE CAN BEAT THEM ALL. AND THEN..."›
‹...WE CAN BEAT *HIM*. I KNOW IT.›
‹WE... WE CAN DO IT *TOGETHER*.›
‹TRUST ME, RUBY.›
‹BASTARD... UTTER, GODDAMNED, FUCKING *BASTARD*.›

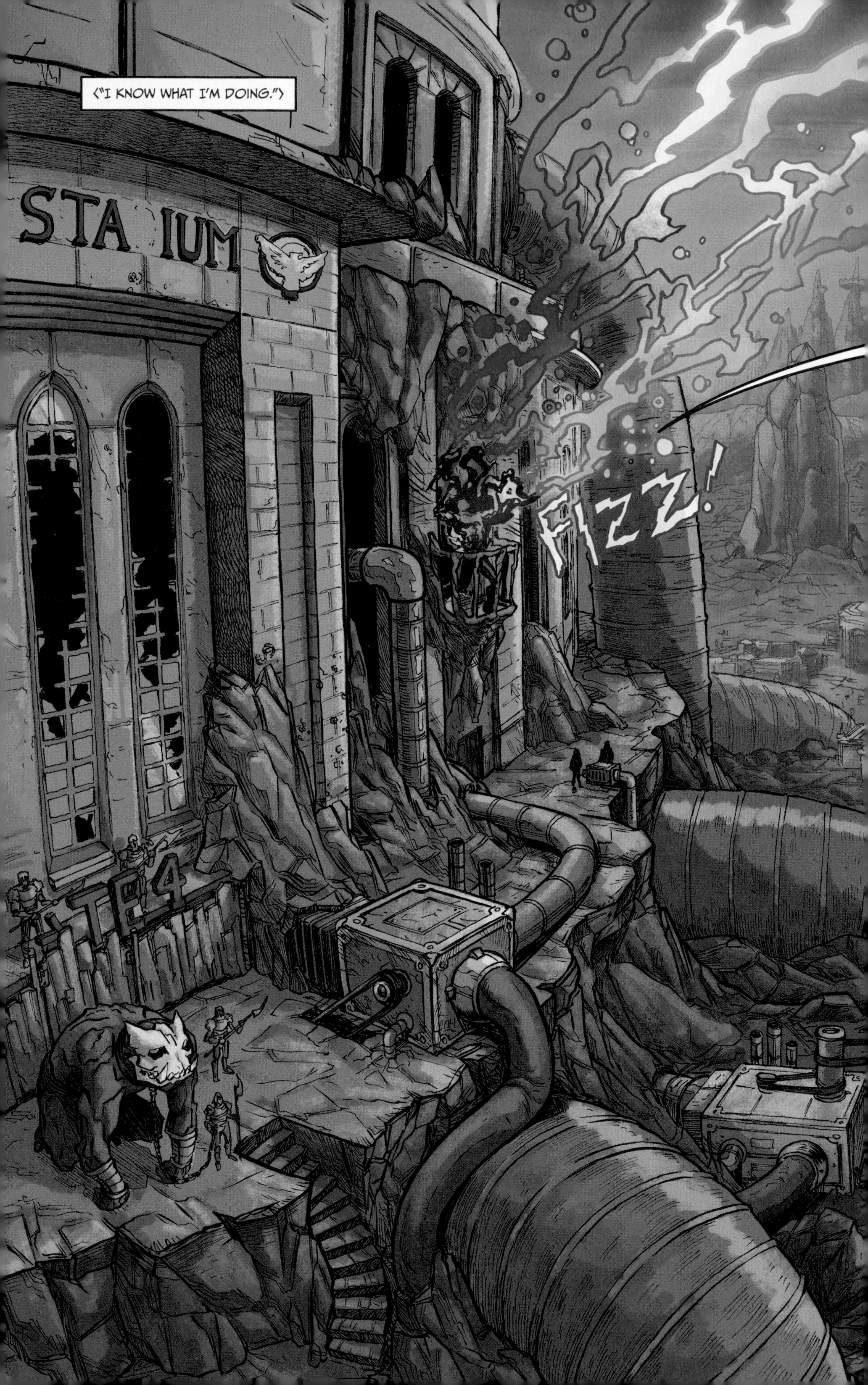
<"I KNOW WHAT I'M DOING.">
STA IUM
TE 4
FIZZ!

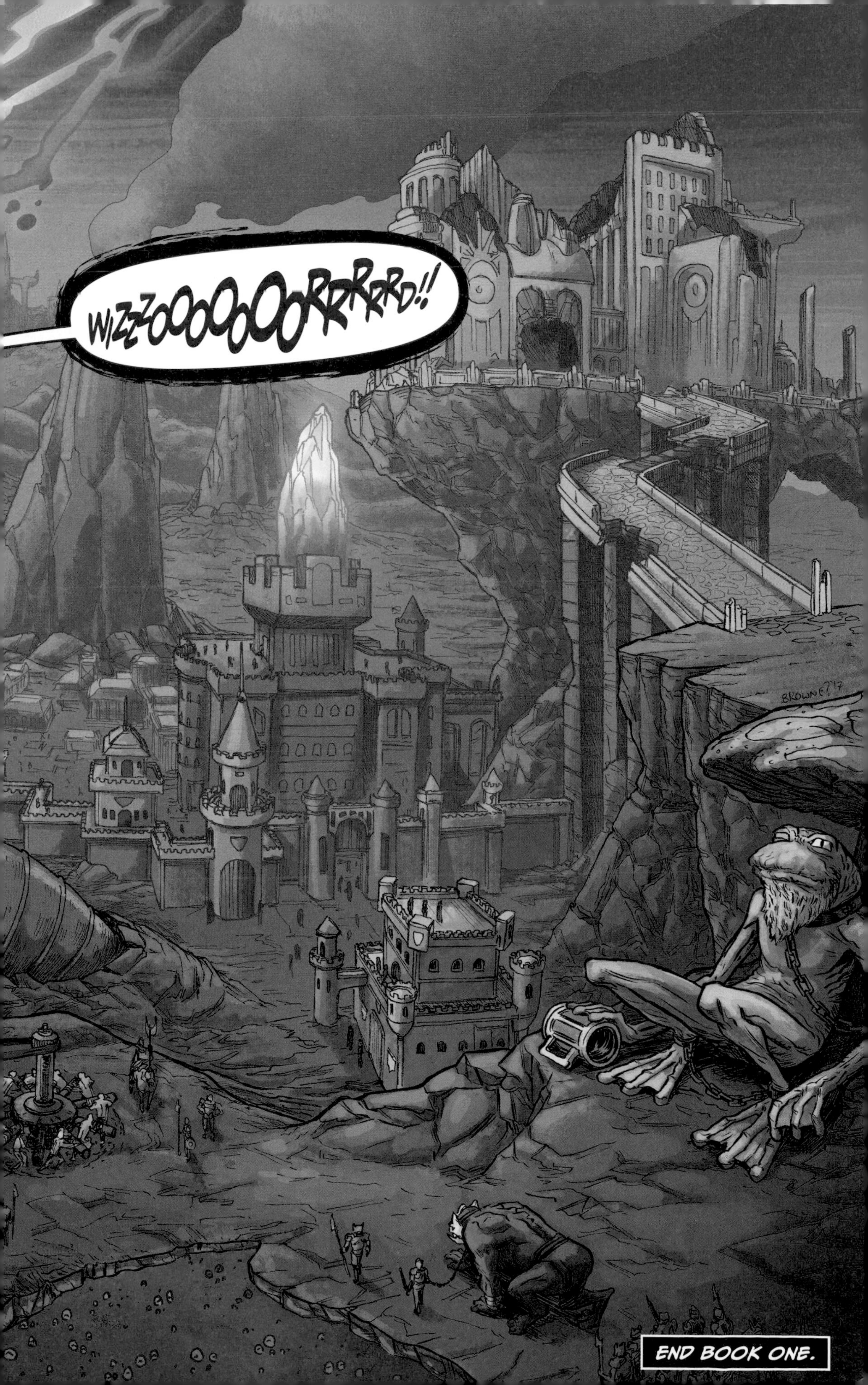
WIZZZOOOOOOORRRRRD!!
BROWNE '17
END BOOK ONE.

ISSUE ONE VARIANT COVER
BY **SKOTTIE YOUNG**

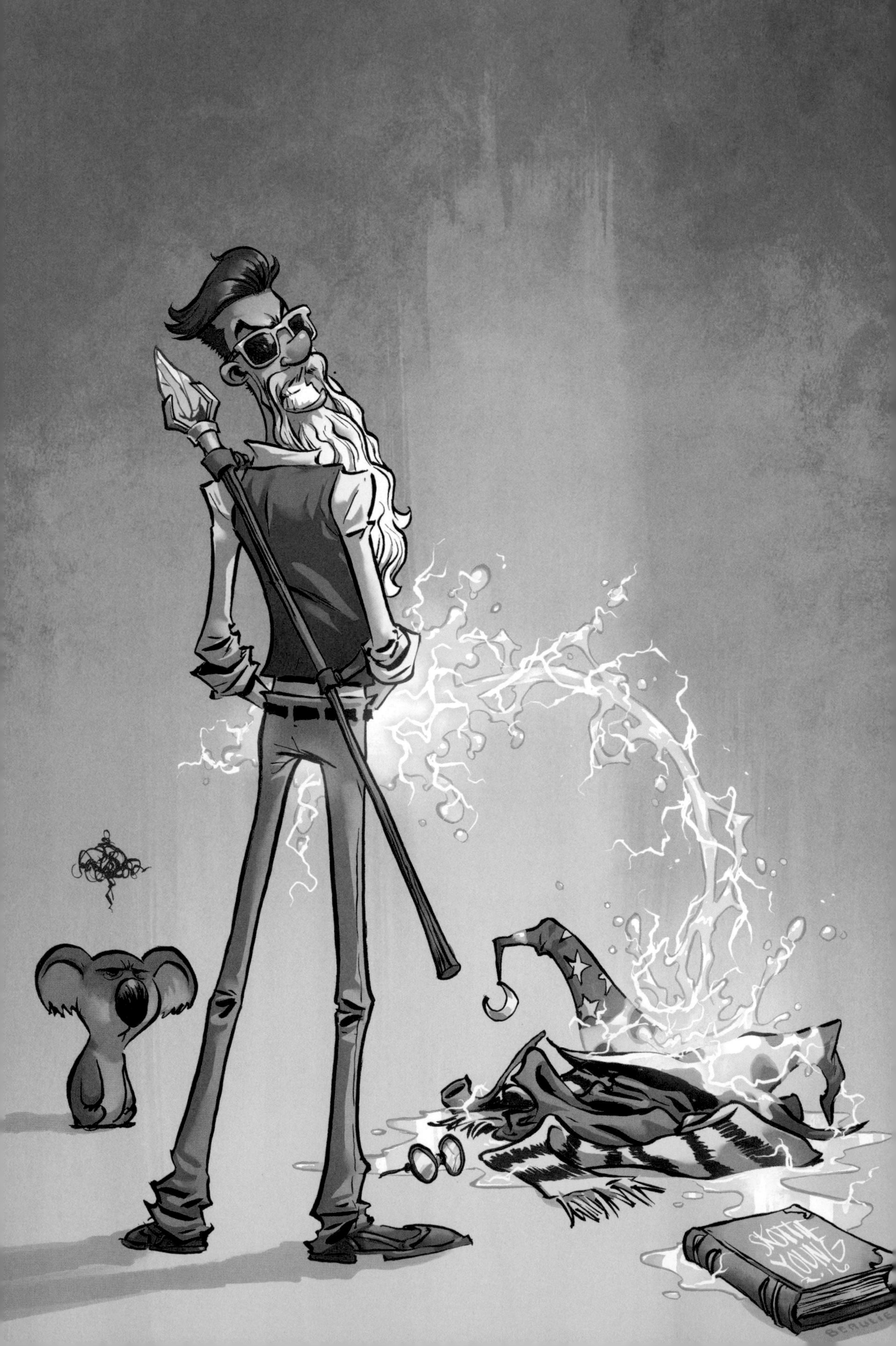
SKOTTIE YOUNG

ISSUE TWO VARIANT COVER
BY **CHIP ZDARSKY**

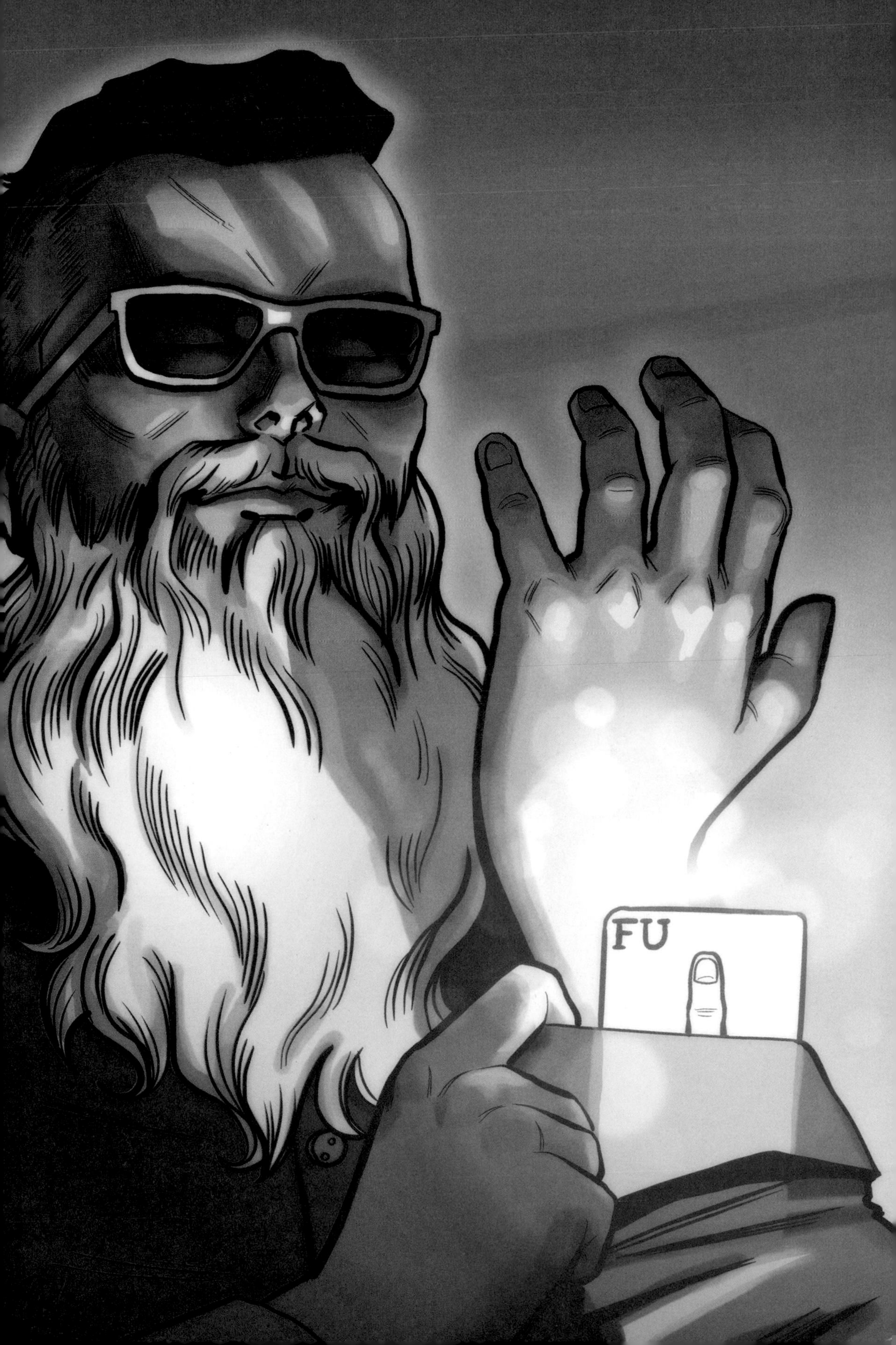
FU

ISSUE THREE VARIANT COVER
BY **PAOLO & JOE RIVERA**

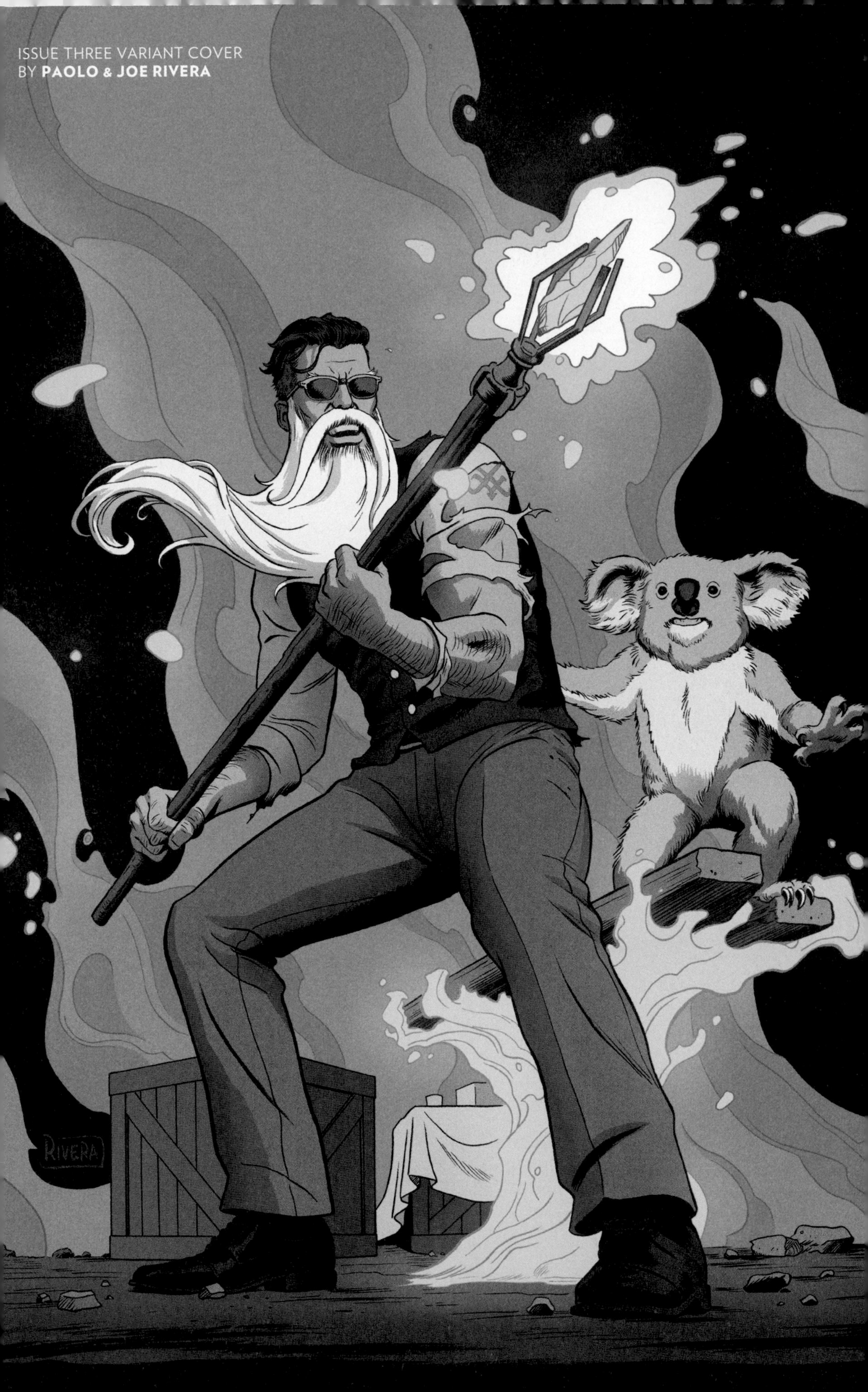

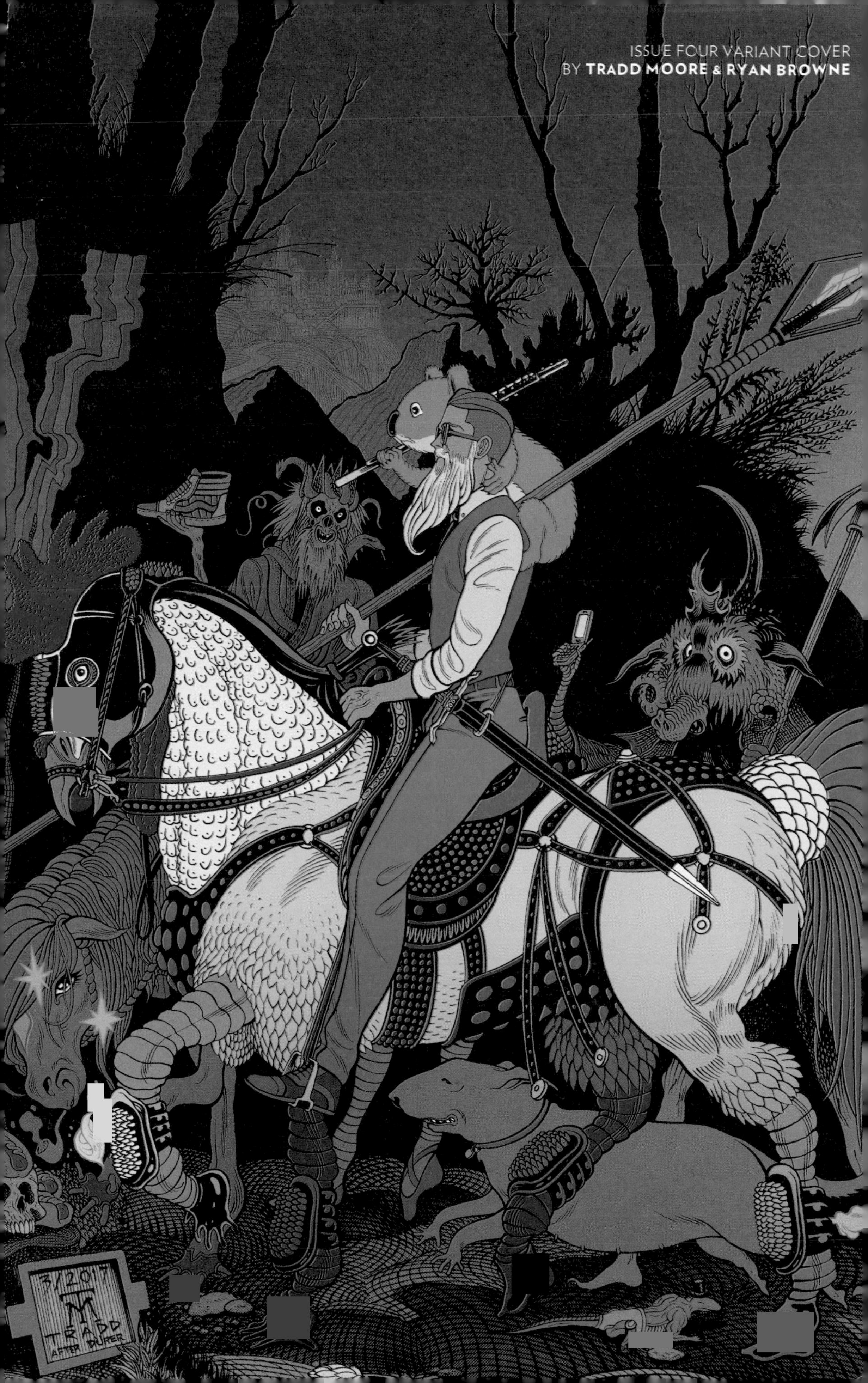
3/2017
TM
TRADD
AFTER DÜRER

ISSUE FOUR VARIANT COVER
BY **TRADD MOORE & RYAN BROWNE**

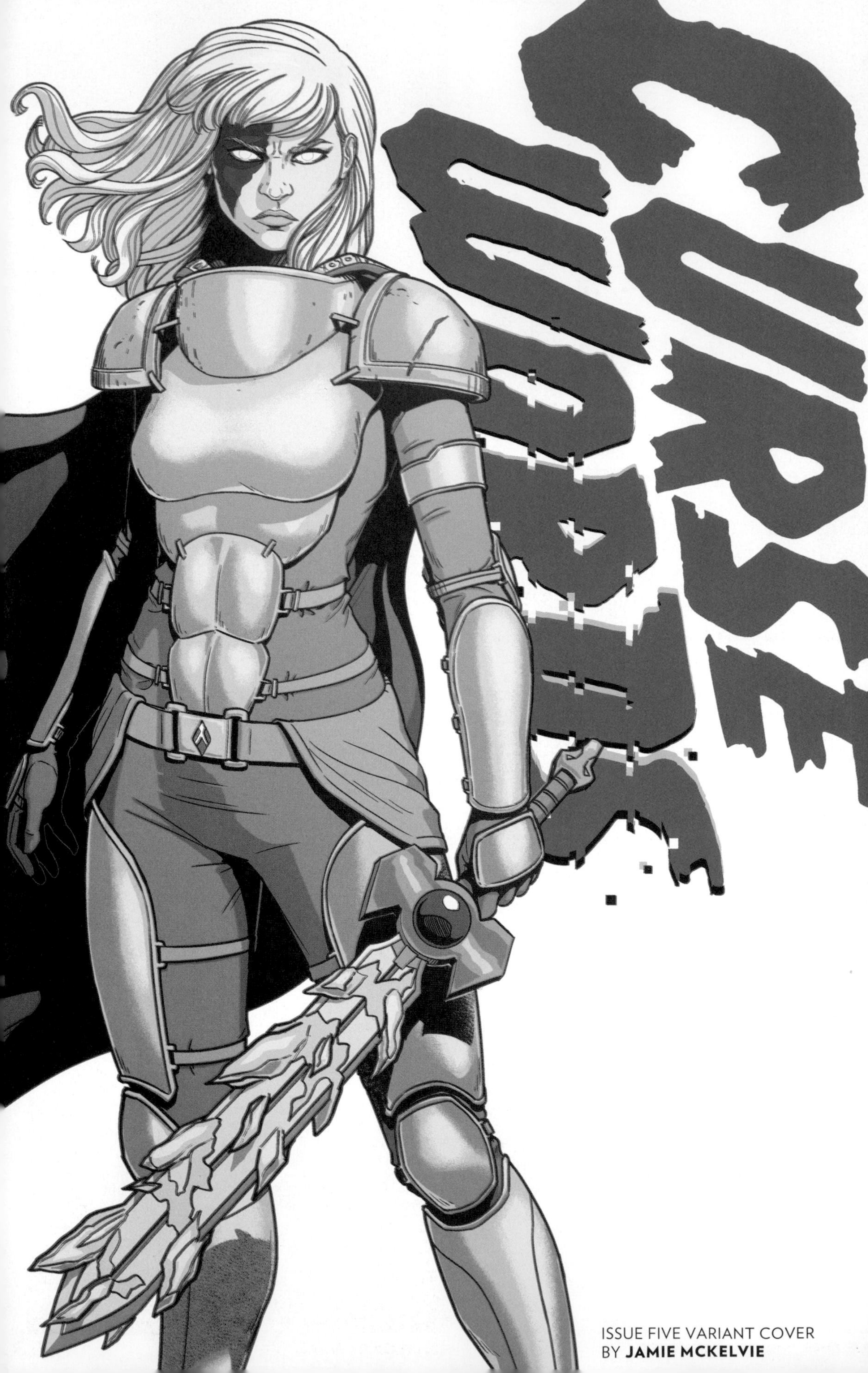
CURSE WORDS

ISSUE FIVE VARIANT COVER
BY **JAMIE MCKELVIE**

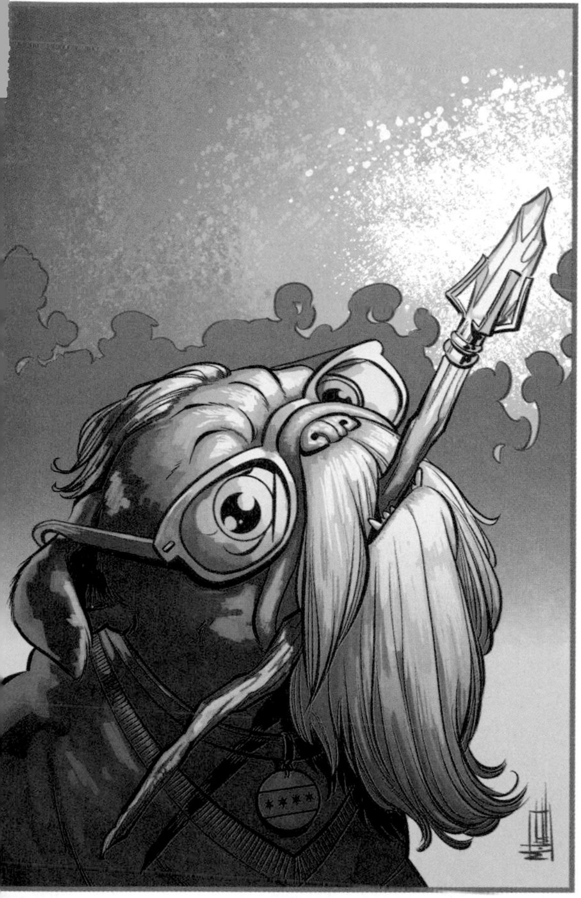

ISSUE ONE *(C2E2 VARIANT BY MIKE NORTON)*

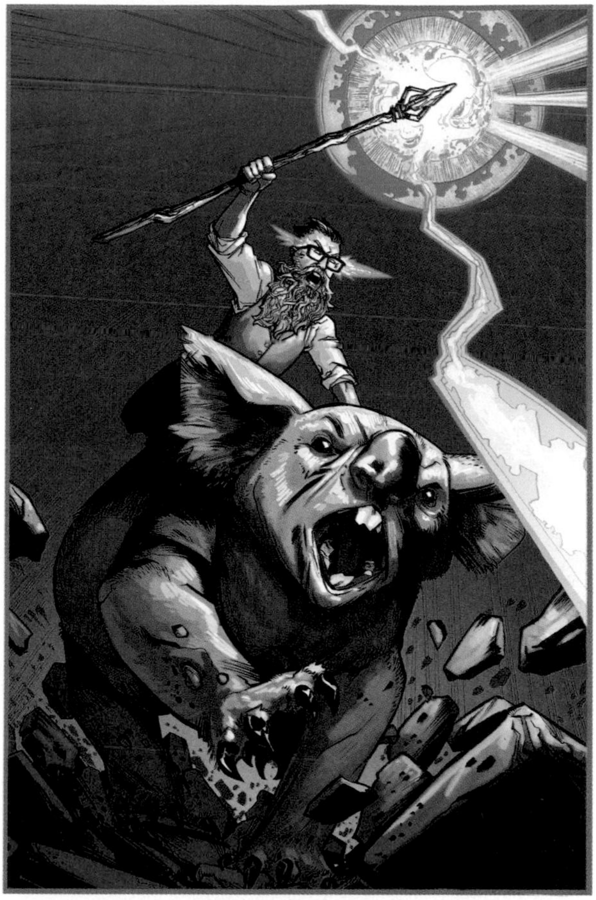

ISSUE TWO *(SECOND PRINTING BY ANDY MACDONALD)*

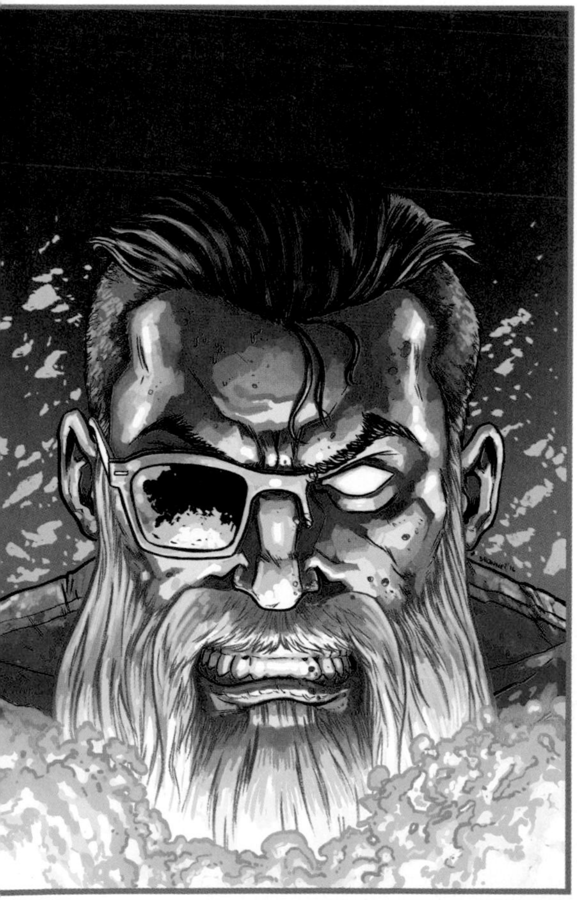

ISSUE ONE *(SECOND PRINTING)*

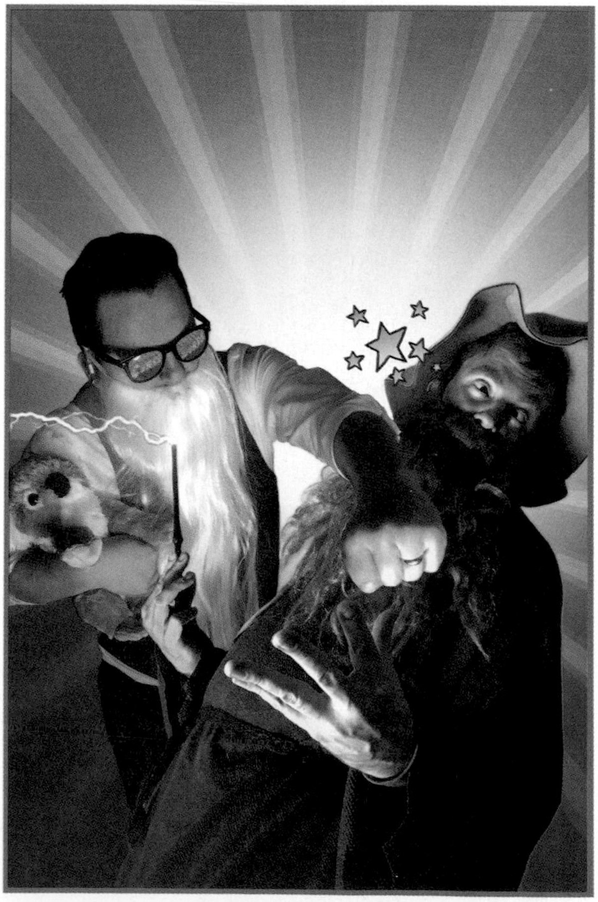

ISSUE ONE *(THIRD PRINTING)*

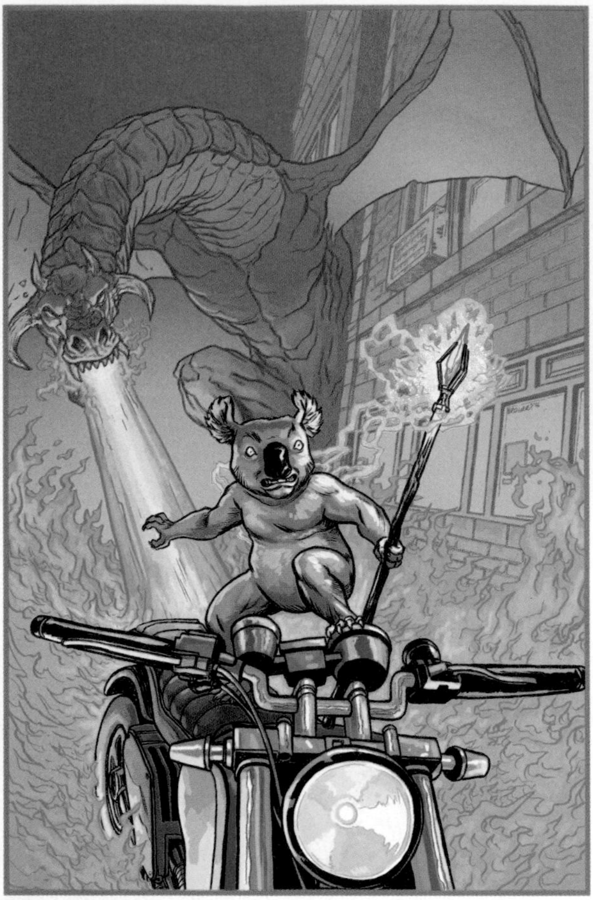

ISSUE ONE *(MARGARET VARIANT)*

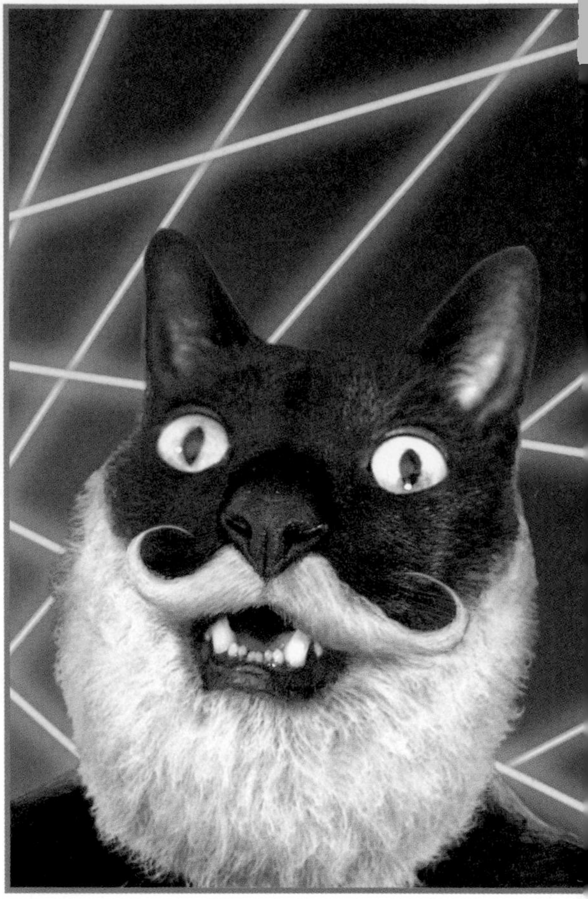

ISSUE ONE *(GLITTER CAT SIMON VARIANT)*

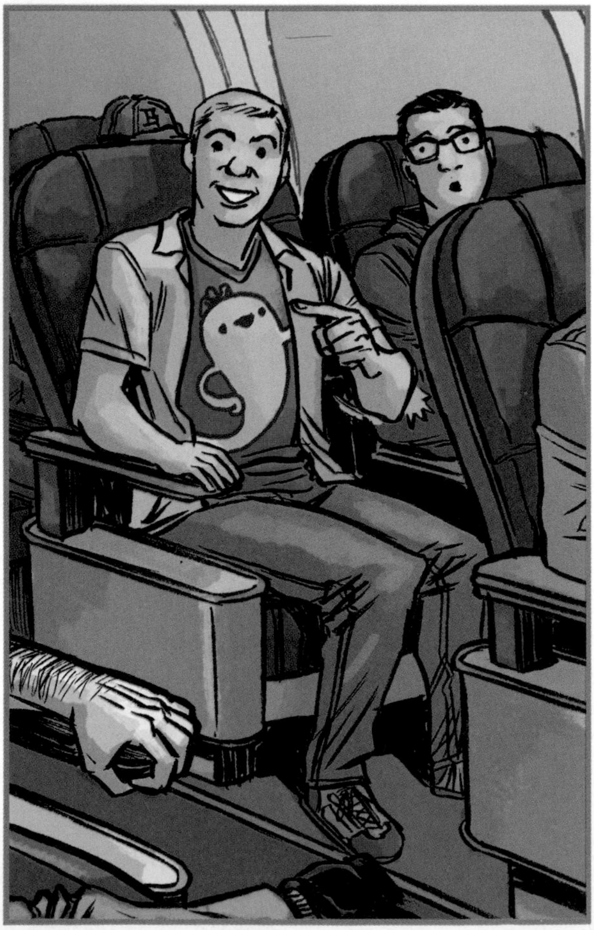

# ABOUT THE AUTHORS:

**CHARLES SOULE** has written many comics for Marvel, DC and others--*DAREDEVIL, STAR WARS, THE DEATH OF WOLVERINE, INHUMANS, SWAMP THING*... all kinds of stuff. He's also the creator of the award-winning epic sci-fi series *LETTER 44* for Oni Press, and his first (hopefully not last?) novel, *THE ORACLE YEAR*. (Don't tell any of those other projects, but *CURSE WORDS* is his favorite.) He lives in Brooklyn, where he also plays music of various kinds and practices law from time to time. Follow him on Twitter @charlessoule.

**RYAN BROWNE** is an American-born comicbookman who is co-responsible for *CURSE WORDS* (which you just read) and wholly responsible for *GOD HATES ASTRONAUTS* (which you should go read if you haven't). He currently lives in Chicago with his amazing wife and considerably less amazing cat. Also, he was once a guest on *The Montel Williams Show*--which is a great story and you should ask him about it. Catch him on Twitter and Instagram @RyanBrowneArt.

Gotta question for the CW letters page? Hit us up at WIZORD@WIZORD.HORSE (yes, a .HORSE url is a real thing and we bought one).